For Kaye —

Lydia

GRAINS
OF
TRUTH

A NOVEL OF SUSPENSE BY

LYDIA CRICHTON

Barringer Publishing, Naples, Florida
www.barringerpublishing.com
Cover, graphics, layout design by Lisa Camp
Editing by Carole Greene

ISBN: 978-0-9882034-9-5

Library of Congress Cataloging-in-Publication Data
Grains of Truth / Lydia Crichton

Printed in U.S.A.

CHAPTER 1

Mallawi, Egypt
Late at night.

Abeer Rashad darted into a dark, abandoned shack. The old wood creaked as she leaned against the wall, jerking away the scarf that covered her mouth, gulping air. Sweat trickled down between her breasts. She knew it came as much from fear as the hot, dry air. Black gloves and robe—making her all but invisible—stifled like a sauna but provided the anonymity urgently required. Without them, she would never have made it this far. The cramped quarters of a shared taxi from Cairo had put her in much too close proximity for maintaining her cover otherwise. For the last several hours she'd said little and tried to breathe out the open window to keep from gagging on the pervasive stench created by too many unwashed bodies packed into the rattling wreck.

Determination, aided by sheer luck, had allowed her to elbow her way through the crowded coffee shop to the counter and insert herself next to the Brother she followed. A strategic reach for the bowl of sugar in front of him brought her ear within inches of his mouth. Even over the din of the gurgling espresso machine, she clearly heard him mention

Mallawi as his destination to the man behind the counter as he released a stream of steamy milk with a practiced hand. Abeer stooped over, feigning frailty, and, with mounting excitement, trailed him to the alley behind the shop. She kept her head down, eyes glued to his back, and watched him climb behind the wheel of a dusty van waiting there.

Now, she peered from the shack's splintered doorway into a narrow, unpaved street. The van sat at the end of it, near a squalid house standing alone beside a ditch. Abeer knew Mallawi as a hellhole of a place, notorious as a perfect example of an Egyptian poverty-stricken nightmare—and the place where President Anwar Sadat had been assassinated.

When the drum of her heart ceased to fill her ears, and she determined no one else prowled nearby, she slipped out to join the shadows, listening warily to the neighborhood settling down for the night. The only sounds audible through the walls of drying laundry hanging from every balcony were the fussy clucking of chickens and the occasional baby's cry.

As she crept toward the parked van, other noises began to emerge, growing louder as she drew near: a scraping and thudding, punctuated by unmistakable human grunts. Intent on interpreting the puzzling sounds, she failed to see the goat tied next to a crumbling mudbrick wall until she stumbled over it. The offended animal bawled in protest and she crouched to clamp its jaw.

Stroking the improbably soft, smooth hair soothed them both. When it calmed, Abeer rose and continued, as quickly as she dared this time, down the road and around a corner of the house. A yellowish light spilled from a lantern hanging from a crude fence of uneven sticks enclosing a small area of dirt yard. Two men raised and lowered shovels alternately in a shallow rectangular hole. One of them grunted each time his foot came down on his tool to penetrate the hard, parched earth.

"Careful. The crates are not buried deep. Trust me—you do not want to damage them." The cool voice came from the darkness, unexpectedly cultured and serene.

Abeer's eyes narrowed as she puzzled at the scene, anxiety making her slow to comprehend. They widened as meaning dawned: These men were recovering something. Something possibly vital for accomplishing whatever despicable—and no doubt deadly—scheme was underway. If she could reach her contact at once, maybe, just maybe, help could get here in time.

She took a cautious step back and turned to retreat. Talons of terror clutched her heart at the sight of the hideous face only inches from her own. Brutish hands shot up to close around her throat before she could make another move.

CHAPTER 2

The scream of a seagull reverberated as it soared up into the Technicolor blue of a late Sunday afternoon sky. Julia Grant closed her eyes and inhaled deeply of the cool, salty sea air. Her lids lifted with the inevitable exhale, and a bittersweet feeling swept over her at the spectacular beauty of San Francisco Bay. People strolled along the Embarcadero, enjoying the picturesque scene flanked majestically by its two famous bridges. Sailboats skipped across white-capped waves beneath a welcome, warming sun; their sails billowed out, filled with the fresh breeze. This was surely as close as one could hope to come to paradise on earth, wasn't it? So why couldn't she find what she was looking for? Why couldn't she decide?

"Just another great day in paradise."

Sitting as she was, alone at the end of the quay, Julia flinched, startled by the proximity of the speaker as well as his apparent ability to read her mind. She turned to find a tall man in a dark suit looming behind her. As he came into clearer focus, she noted the sharp cut of his navy blue jacket and crisp white shirt, open at the collar. Sleek, impenetrable dark glasses added a note of inscrutability. He definitely was not, she knew at a glance, one of the sad, ubiquitous "lost souls" that inhabit San Francisco's public streets and parks.

Her mouth twitched at his cliché. Not wanting to encourage conversation, she murmured, "Yes, always," and turned away. Although his silhouette continued to hover at the edge of her eye, she deliberately refocused on the bay.

The sight never failed to bring a sense of life-giving energy. It beckoned her to dive in and swim across to the quaint town of Sausalito, shimmering up the hillside in the distance. A dozen or so large, rowdy seagulls still bickered and fussed over the remnants of the fish scraps she'd thrown them earlier. Sporadically they would take flight up, up and away into the breathtaking sky. She yearned to spread wings and join them, free to float on the wind.

But Julia could not swim to Sausalito and she did not have wings and she was not free. Oh, sure, it was true enough that she was in the unusual position of being able to start life anew—to re-create herself, in a way. But too much freedom, she had discovered, could be a prison of its own kind. She simply couldn't seem to unshackle the memories and patterns of the past.

"This is a special place, isn't it?" The stranger slid onto the bench. His left arm came up to rest along the back, with curved fingers inches from her shoulder. He casually crossed a long leg, causing his body to lean in toward hers, and looked into her eyes. At least she thought he did. The sunglasses, of an expensive and trendy make, concealed his eyes completely. And as she took a closer look, she couldn't help but notice the stylish Italian leather shoes and smart tan socks adorned with little white whales. No, this was no lost soul—at least not of the street variety.

Julia sighed. "Yes. A great place to think. Alone." Irritated at the intrusion, she considered getting up and walking away but, to be honest, she found him intriguing. And his presence no threat.

This was her first mistake.

Again, he appeared to read her thoughts. "Sorry to disturb you, Ms. Grant," he said, removing the sunglasses to expose eyes of an unusually deep blue, "but I need to speak with you about an important matter."

Her head swung around to face him more fully. "Do we know each other?"

"Well, no," came the slow reply, "not exactly. I know who you are, but no, we've never met."

A puzzled smile wrinkled her brow. "And how, may I ask, do you know who I am?" He was quite nice looking in an over-polished sort of way. His relaxed air suggested lazy days and a life of ease.

Looks can be masters of deception.

He returned the smile, exposing even, white teeth accentuated by the tan skin surrounding it, and reached inside his jacket to produce a card. "Brad Caldwell. U. S. Intelligence. Now, don't get excited," he added quickly as he saw her shoulders stiffen. "People always seem to think the worst when they hear those words. As if everyone had some deep, dark secret to hide." The smile stretched a fraction wider.

Julia's peaceful communion with nature burst like a pin-pricked balloon. The slightest cold shiver flitted up her spine as she looked down at the card in her hand. *Brad E. Caldwell, Special Agent, External Affairs, National Counter Terrorism Center* embossed in stark black type stretched ominously across the heavy white stock. She stared mutely as a cascade of dark thoughts tumbled through her mind.

External Affairs. It wasn't possible that this could have anything to do with her trips to Egypt. Was it? No, of course not. How could they know? And then another obvious and equally chilling thought caused her heart to beat a little faster. How had he found her out here, anonymous in the crowd?

She raised guarded eyes to find him watching her closely. A smile still lifted the corners of his lips, but she suddenly realized that it had never made its way up to those penetrating eyes, as cold and unfathomable as the churning bay.

After an uncomfortably long silence, she swallowed to relieve the dryness in her throat and, in an effort to steady a growing tremor born of anger coupled with a hint of fear, tilted her head to one side. "I can't imagine what you could possibly want to speak with me about, Mr. Caldwell."

"Please call me Brad," he said amiably. "Well, Julia…may I call you Julia?" A slight nod in the affirmative brought another one of those half-smiles. "As you are no doubt aware, the United States is taking strong initiatives in dealing with the critical terrorist situation that's arisen in recent years."

"I'd have to be in a coma not to know that, Mr. Caldwell."

The smile flickered. "Fact is, we're interested in talking with folks who've visited certain countries recently. We're aware that you've spent a considerable amount of time in Egypt in the past couple of years. Now, don't get the wrong idea. We understand that your visits there were of a strictly personal nature. Please don't think for a moment that we have any concerns that you might be involved in activities that could be considered, ah, questionable."

Julia didn't move. She didn't blink. She couldn't breathe. It wasn't possible that he was intimating she was suspected of being involved in terrorist activities. Was it?

"What we would very much appreciate," he continued in a low, reasonable voice, "would be if you could spare some time to answer a few questions and provide us with your impressions of the situation there." He paused, turning to look out across the water. The sun had sunk lower in the sky; a soft breeze lifted a few strands of golden-brown hair from his smooth forehead.

"Surely, *Mr. Caldwell,* our government is thoroughly familiar with 'the situation' in Egypt. We've had a significant presence there, on every conceivable level, for decades. And, as you say, the U.S. is taking strong initiatives in dealing with the terrorist situation by vigorously pursuing *anything* and *anyone, anywhere* in the world that might be remotely involved in activities that could prove harmful to U.S. interests." She drew a necessary breath. "What kind of information could a simple tourist possibly provide that you don't already know?" She failed to keep the sarcasm—as well as the heat—from her voice. But then, she hadn't really tried.

He leaned closer, in a misleadingly comic conspiratorial manner, bringing with him a slightly musky scent, and fixed her with an unnervingly intent look. "You'd be surprised." When he withdrew the look, it was to turn back to the picture-book scene.

"Is it out of line to ask for an hour or two of your time if there's even the most remote possibility that it might prove helpful in protecting all of this?" His mellow voice resonated with genuine emotion as his hand swept across San Francisco Bay in dramatic sunset.

Her eyes following the gesture, Julia had to admit to herself that Mr. Brad E. Caldwell was very, very good at his job. He either knew or had cleverly deduced that one of the strongest of her heartstrings was securely attached to a deep and unbreakable bond with "all of this." Anything that threatened to harm the planet, Mother Earth, was guaranteed to stir her blood. Had he played on any other string—home, hearth, country—she might have resisted. Julia was no fan of the way the "War on Terror" was being waged. But the opportunity to perhaps be of help in some small way in safeguarding this, her beloved environment, proved irresistible.

And, as he said, surely she could spare an hour or two.

"All right, Mr. Caldwell." She smiled. "Brad. What would you like to know?"

An almost imperceptible nod indicated satisfaction in his success. "Okay. Thanks, Julia. Your contribution will be most appreciated. We'd like you to come to the office for a more private conversation. Please be at the address on my card tomorrow morning at nine. You needn't worry about any kind of preparation. Everything will be very relaxed and informal."

Well. What presumption. Did he think she had nothing else to do? No, she understood intuitively before completing the thought; there was no assumption on his part. She found it deeply unnerving to realize that he might know a great deal about her schedule. And yet, she amazed herself by responding, "Yes, I suppose I can manage that. But first tell me something: How did you find me out here?"

Flashing the deepest smile yet, while replacing his dark glasses, he said, "Oh, well, it is, after all, our business to know these things. See you in the morning." With that, he stood to saunter away into the orange glow left by the sun.

Julia sat in a stunned, immobile silence, chewing on her lower lip. The implications of this development were alarming—to say the least. The more she thought about it, the more questions the encounter raised. And they were deeply disturbing.

Who were the "we" he'd spoken of? What kind of information were they looking for? How much did they know about her trips to Egypt? Did they know about Mohamed?

And they had been *following* her. For how long?

Perhaps, on the other hand, it was only as he'd said. They might only be interested in her observations of a country that had become increasingly strategic in the "War on Terror." Damn. She hated that moniker. Anyway, maybe she was over-reacting and being paranoid about "Big Brother" watching her. Maybe. But as a dedicated pacifist, Julia recoiled at the idea of contributing anything—anything at all—that might help perpetuate the tragic violence erupting throughout the Middle East.

From the beginning, she'd fiercely opposed the U.S. invasion of Afghanistan and Iraq. She'd seen firsthand the far-reaching ramifications of those ongoing bloodbaths, for which she believed the government of the United States of America held sole responsibility. In addition to the senseless loss of human life and the thousands of casualties there, the ripple effect continued to be devastating to societies where no cushioning existed to protect innocent, peaceful people from the destruction of their economies and livelihoods.

Julia knew, from personal experience, what dire effects it had had on Mohamed and his family and thousands—no, millions—just like him. It was appalling. It was inexcusable.

A cold wind gusting around her brought Julia back to the present, surprising her at how quickly the night had fallen. Gathering her belongings, she hurried down the walk alongside the now surging black water. Her modest rental car sat alone beside the curb. Shivering, she slipped behind the wheel, uncertain if the chill resulted from the wind or from a premonition of things to come—things that might mirror the dark and treacherous sea.

Dawn had yet to steal into the sky when, after a predictably restless night, Julia left the comfort of a warm bed and automatically pulled on sweats for her morning exercise. She'd learned years ago that, no matter how tired or bad she might feel, a good session of cardio always improved things. Crawling into the gym like a caterpillar, she never failed to emerge a butterfly. And that day she needed to be a perfect butterfly—at ease, with unflappable wings.

On her way out the door she poured some dry cat food into a plastic bowl and grabbed up a couple of anti-war protest flyers from a pile on the kitchen counter. Downstairs, she posted one on the wall by the elevator and crossed the courtyard to the gym. She stopped by the door outside and before she could set the bowl on the ground, a scraggly cat darted out of the bushes. With a scratchy yowl, it rubbed against her ankles. The feline's head dove into the bowl as Julia taped another flyer on the door to the gym.

Once established on the treadmill, she gave herself up to its tempo and allowed her mind to return to the ordeal that lay ahead. Last night, after endless internal debate, she'd decided not to speak with anyone else about this latest extraordinary development. It wasn't that she wouldn't have found sympathetic ears among her good friends or that she didn't value their opinions.

Only one among them knew the complicated history that made this such a potentially thorny situation. And Julia could not quite bring herself to confide in her as yet. So, as had happened with increasing frequency of late, she found herself propelled into unfamiliar and risky territory—uneasy and alone.

After all, she told herself for the hundredth time, she had done no wrong. Well, nothing in a legal sense. Not illegal in this country anyway. Nor did she know of any specific wrongdoing among her friends and acquaintances around the globe. Smiling at the thought, Julia recalled someone once saying that she collected people the way others collected baseball cards or teacups. Those in her collection were remarkably diverse and frequently wholly incompatible, as she'd learned from painful experience. It was inadvisable to attempt to bring too many of them together, as a skirmish of some kind would likely ensue.

"Jesus Christ!"

The exclamation came from a man laboring on the machine a few feet away. People seldom spoke to one another in the gym at this hour, just plugged into their tunes or the TV. Julia looked from his sweaty face to the screen mounted on the opposite wall. A grainy image above a CNN banner showed a terrified man, hands tied behind his back, kneeling in front of a group of hooded men. She clicked off her music so she could hear.

"The Sri Lankan rebel group calling itself the Tamil Tigers confirmed the execution today of one of the hostages taken from a group of French engineers." The announcer's voice faded as Julia switched on her music and averted her eyes, knowing that the sword above the victim's head would fall. It was an all too familiar scenario these days.

She forced herself to refocus on the problem at hand. The rational thing to do would be to learn more about all this before initiating any discussions about what it could possibly mean. After all, there would be only this one meeting; then she would have a fascinating new topic of conversation to share with her liberal friends. Right.

CHAPTER 3

A missile streaked from the rocket, arched high up in the sky then began to descend in relentless pursuit of its target on a distant hill. Within seconds, it exploded into a truck, creating a roaring fireball that could be seen, and heard, for miles.

"Ah. Yes. I see," murmured Mr. Ranakawa to no one in particular, his unfailingly placid voice conveying a subtle note of awe.

"Once programmed, the missiles can't fail," said Alexander Bryant with quiet authority. He cut a commanding figure, with a solid build and close-cropped yet abundant dark hair threaded with silver. His seemingly effortless erect posture suggested a military background; appropriately so, as he'd spent over thirty years in the U.S. Army, retiring as a much-decorated four-star general.

"Well, mate, that's bound to round out your arsenal nicely, ain't it?" asked William Hirschfield, "Billy" as he liked to be called. When people referred to him as "Slippery Billy" he assumed it was due to his uncanny ability to elude the law of pretty much any country on earth, with his shipments of illegal arms, rather than his somewhat reptilian appearance.

A white-gloved servant, gold buttons shining on his spotless white jacket, carefully carried a heavy silver tray toward the three men. Shafts of light from the setting sun danced around crystal flutes brimming with champagne.

"Yes. Thank you, gentlemen." Mr. Ranakawa reached out a hand, the back covered with the brown spots of old age, and raised a glass. "To you, Commander Bryant, for your invaluable expertise. And to Mr. Hirshfield, for such prompt delivery."

Alexander lifted his glass and took a sip, eyeing Billy over the rim. Thus far, he'd held his temper in check at having been coerced into returning to Sri Lanka. Billy had been the one to suggest it and Mr. Ranakawa latched onto the idea like a dog with a bone.

The old man's tortoise-like eyes shone with satisfaction as they slid away. "Ah, here is my wife, come to collect us for dinner."

They turned to watch an SUV speeding recklessly toward them across the field. The young Asian beauty behind the wheel failed to slow as she drew near. Braking at the last possible second, she swerved to a stop less than a foot from Alexander. He hadn't moved a muscle.

Mr. Ranakawa chortled. "Imolee likes to live on the edge."

Imolee Ranakawa smiled coyly through the open window at her husband, almost four times her age, before her luminous black eyes, reminiscent of polished onyx, settled on Alexander. "It's the only way to live, isn't it, Commander? Grab life by the throat and wring it for all it's worth?"

The old man laughed again at his wife's bizarre remark. Slippery Billy looked startled. Commander Bryant showed no expression at all.

French doors opened onto a private terrace off the lavish guestroom. Alexander removed his shirt as he stood watching a peacock, with iridescent jewel-toned tail feathers unfurled, strut across the lush green lawn. A cadre of servants squatted here and there, tending the pristine gardens. He did *not* want to be here. Once the specifications had been finalized, his job was done. Coming back was always a mistake, like returning to the scene of a crime.

As he brooded, he heard the inside door open quietly, then close with a whisper. In the ensuing silence, he said, "You shouldn't have come here. It's asking for trouble."

Alexander turned his head to find Imolee Ranakawa leaning against the door, devouring him with hungry eyes. She really was an exquisite creature. Firm, rounded breasts pushed against the silk brocade of the dress that fitted like a second skin. Black hair, shining like pearls, hung down below her tiny waist. She launched herself across the room to land hard against his solid, bare chest. As she began to stroke him, her long, bright red nails dug painfully into his flesh. He grabbed the deceptively delicate wrists.

"I told you last time: It was the last time. If your husband finds out, he might just kill us both."

Outside, the peacock shrieked, punctuating the grim prediction.

"He won't find out. He's too busy plotting and playing with his toys. There's plenty of time before dinner."

Alexander looked down at her perfect porcelain face as she pressed against the length of him. In spite of his good intentions, his body responded. It always did.

CHAPTER 4

Julia marched into the Federal building on Golden Gate Avenue. Her left-wing tendencies provoked the thought that the imposing structure was meant to either convey confidence in the "system"—or to intimidate those entering, impressing upon them the unyielding power within. Probably both.

Inside the elevator, she fiddled with a blue silk scarf tucked into the collar of her form-fitting suit. With her long auburn hair pulled back in a severe knot at the nape of her neck, she knew she presented a polished, professional appearance. Not that she had any illusions about what difference that might make. At least it gave her confidence a boost.

At precisely nine o'clock, the elevator doors opened on the fourteenth floor. She emerged to find a typical government office: unremarkable, with beige carpet, beige furniture and blank walls. The woman behind the reception desk, dressed in a neat navy suit and off-white blouse, spoke on the phone, eyes downcast with the carefully manicured fingers of one hand pressed to her temple. "Ms. Debra Manning" read the nameplate on the counter. She matched the office perfectly, as if made-to-order along with the furnishings.

"Yes. Yes. Yes, Mr. Bishoff. I understand. Yes. The moment he arrives. Yes, sir." Ms. Manning's thin lips tightened for a telling moment as she returned the phone to its cradle with precision. Well-shaped brows rose slightly over knowing brown eyes as she looked up at Julia. "Good morning; may I help you?"

Julia offered a smile. "Good morning. My name is Julia Grant. I have an appointment with Brad Caldwell."

The eyebrows climbed higher and, with a faint air of condolence, Ms. Manning replied, "Oh, yes, Ms. Grant, they're expecting you." She did not ask Julia to take a seat before picking up the phone and touching one button on the pad. No more than a second passed before she said, "Mr. Caldwell, Ms. Grant is here. Yes, sir." Without further conversation she replaced the phone as she stood.

"This way please, Ms. Grant." Turning with a practiced assurance that Julia would fall in to follow in her wake, she took off at a brisk pace around the corner and sailed down a long hall.

It was the longest hall Julia had ever seen. Quickening her pace to keep up, she passed office after office, all with doors closed. Through the frosted glass panel beside each one she could see the shapes of people behind desks, talking on phones, working on computers or standing in various poses. But absolutely no sound penetrated those walls.

An almost palpable sense of urgency hummed beneath the surface of organized calm. When one of the doors swished open a few feet ahead, a tall man surfaced, holding a computer printout in one hand and a cell phone in the other. He frowned over the top of wire-rim glasses and Julia couldn't help but notice his navy suit, white shirt and expensive leather shoes. Was this some kind of uniform?

Eventually they reached their destination, one of the closed doors indistinguishable from the numerous others behind and before. Debra Manning rapped three times swiftly then opened the door without being bidden to do so. She stepped to one side and indicated that Julia should enter. Brad Caldwell sat behind an impressive desk of dark, rich wood in front of a wide window, blinds open to reveal a sweeping view of the city. He came swiftly to his feet, relinquishing the phone at his ear.

"Good morning," he said, with his lazy grin, as he glided around the desk extending a hand. "Thanks for coming."

As if I really had a choice said a little voice in Julia's head.

Even more nattily turned out today, he sported an expensive navy suit with a narrow pinstripe. A muted red silk tie stood out against his white-on-white shirt. *How patriotic* murmured Julia's sarcastic little voice. He took her hand, placing his other over it, as if they were old friends—or attempting to prevent her from a hasty exit. She noticed the same musky scent from yesterday, stronger in the closer confines of the office. It triggered the image of predatory animals in the wild and kicked up her pulse a notch.

"Please, sit down." He led her to a black leather couch against an arctic-white wall. A multi-hued abstract painting hung above it, competing with the big window to dominate the room. For some reason, Julia found the painting's bright, swirling colors disquieting. "Would you care for something to drink? Coffee, tea, a soda?"

"Water would be nice." She lowered herself into one of two sleek leather chairs in the grouping. It seemed safer, somehow, than the couch—where the enemy could easily encroach. *Oh, yes, he may very well be the enemy.* It was an instinctive reflex, not a conscious designation. In the center of the glass-top coffee table lay a single legal file, with no visible markings. It was at least two inches thick.

Mr. Caldwell, Brad, came to sit on the end of the couch next to her chair. He leaned forward with elbows on spread knees, hands clasped between them and head bent—as if in prayer. When his head came up on an intake of breath, his penetrating blue eyes latched onto Julia's apprehensive ones.

"We're grateful to you for coming, Julia. You can't imagine the difficulty of the task we, as a nation, are facing."

Before she could respond to this innocuous remark, the door opened to readmit the efficient Ms. Manning bearing a tall, clear glass of water. Placing it precisely on a coaster embossed with the seal of the U.S. Government, she departed as silently as she had come.

Julia followed Brad's gaze on her retreating back to see another man enter and close the door quietly behind him. Older, with thinning gray hair, he stooped slightly forward, as if he carried a heavy burden. He'd evidently traded in his uniform for a modest gray suit, with a slight sheen here and there from years of pressing. Otherwise, he presented as neat an appearance as "the others," with not a scuff on his black wingtips.

Removing heavy glasses that left a permanent dent on his nose, he offered a large, time-worn hand and said in a deep, authoritative voice, "Good morning, Ms. Grant. I'm Robert Bronson. Please call me Bob. We appreciate your coming today, especially on such short notice."

Brad had risen in unmistakable deference and remained standing until Bob Bronson sat heavily in the chair facing Julia. A current of anxious energy flowed between the two men beneath their pleasantries. With a slight nod from Bob, Brad cleared his throat and captured Julia's eyes with his own.

"Bob's joined us because the matter we wish to discuss with you is of such great importance." He paused. "We know that you're well-informed regarding the critical global situation. As you're no doubt aware, the government has found it necessary to monitor the movements and activities of our citizens, as well as non-citizens, who travel between the U.S. and certain other countries."

A few heartbeats of silence punctuated the troubling implication. "Through the powers granted us by The Patriot Act, we're much better able to keep our fingers on the pulse of information and activities that might prove helpful in the War on Terror."

This pause stretched on interminably as Bob nodded silently and Julia felt her limbs turn to stone. A shrill alarm clanged wildly in her head. The Patriot Act: The highly controversial power granted by Congress to the government to snoop into the private and personal affairs of every American citizen without their consent—or even their knowledge. Every liberal—including Julia and almost everyone she knew—and liberal organization throughout the country had opposed it and continued to protest it still.

Brad picked up the voluminous file from the coffee table, opened it and continued matter-of-factly. "Your first trip to Egypt, a few months after the attacks on the World Trade Center and the Pentagon, triggered an automatic monitoring of your travels there and elsewhere. Our sources have provided us with details of your movements, contacts and activities since then."

He glanced up from the file and his sharp look said it all. Julia knew what that file contained. It confirmed her worst fears. Heat suffused her entire body. She reached for the glass of water in hopes of dissolving the growing lump lodged in her throat.

Sensing her discomfort, Bob Bronson leaned forward and said reassuringly, "Ms. Grant, please understand that this is all a routine part of government intelligence gathering and in no way do we mean to frighten you. We are simply faced with a daunting challenge and must use all the tools at our disposal to protect the people of this country as well as millions of others around the world."

Julia found the fact that he mentioned not wanting to frighten her incredibly frightening. All she could do for the moment was nod silently. She tucked her chin towards her chest to minimize the shaking of her head, unable to look away from them—mesmerized—as if seeing a pair of cobras hypnotizing her before the fatal strike.

"The urgency of the situation in which we now find ourselves forces us to act much more hastily than we would like. And to make choices that we wouldn't normally consider." Brad spoke with a hint of thinly suppressed frustration. "In fact, we're now forced to make use of resources that would have been heretofore unthinkable."

His eyes bore into hers.

"We've asked you here today not only for the valuable information that you may possess, but also to request that you undertake a relatively simple assignment for your country."

CHAPTER 5

Julia sat paralyzed for an interminable moment. She became aware that, for the past hour, she'd scarcely taken a breath. Exploding back into life, she expelled a sharp laugh. "You must be joking! Surely, if you know so much about me, you know that I have absolutely *no* background for this kind of thing. And surely you must also be aware that I'm a dedicated pacifist—totally opposed to military aggression and violence of any kind."

Bob rose and came to stand beside her chair, placing a heavy hand on her shoulder. Under the circumstances, it shouldn't have felt as reassuring as it did.

"Julia," he said quietly, "please hear us out. You *will* be interested in what we have to say, I promise you. And if, in the end, you choose not to help, we'll respect your decision."

This was beyond belief. A nightmare come true. "All right," she shrugged defensively. "I'll listen. I can't promise more than that."

The two men exchanged another wordless look and, once again opening the file, Brad began to recite in a clipped tone. "Your first trip to Egypt was on a tour. There, you became involved with the tour director, Mohamed Zahar. Returning to the U.S., you remained in contact with him. Your relationship was one of more than friendship but you were not lovers. You returned to Cairo a few months later, making your own travel plans. Mr. Zahar joined you to travel to Luxor, back to Cairo and then to Alexandria. There, instead of staying in separate hotel rooms as you'd done previously, you rented an apartment where you spent three nights together. On this trip, you presented Mr. Zahar with a substantial cash payment, presumably in compensation for his services as your guide."

He paused to allow the insulting implication to hang in the air and then proceeded as her heart sank slowly to the floor. "Again returning to San Francisco, you remained in contact, planning your next rendezvous. You made arrangements to meet in Rome in October of that same year, in order to…"

That did it. Fireworks exploded in Julia's head. She shot to her feet. "Oh my god! You can hold it right there, *Mr.* Caldwell." Her face burned bright with her new-found fury. "It is *not* necessary for you to go on. You've made your point." She clenched her fists and pressed them against her thighs. "You know much, much more about my personal business than you have *any* right to know. Or you *think* you know."

She crossed her arms over her chest, with fingers still in a rigid curl. "Just cut to the chase and tell me why I'm here."

Brad slumped back against the gleaming black leather. The reds and yellows, blues and greens spun in the painting above his head. Silence filled the room like thick smoke, the only sound Julia's shallow breath as she struggled for control. These bastards were sorely mistaken if they thought they were going to intimidate her. Bob stood, shoved his hands in his pockets and went to the window. Her flashing eyes shot daggers at his sloping back. Outside, dark clouds gathered, shrouding the sky all across the bay.

At length Bob spoke in a tired voice, tinged with gloom. "Julia, today we face unprecedented danger. Never, in the history of this country—in the history of the world—have we been up against anything like this. We're fighting on so many fronts and on so many levels that, even with thousands of people working around the clock, we struggle to stay ahead of the game." Returning to his chair, he settled weary eyes on her lovely, outraged face.

"This is the fight of our lives. You must understand that your file and the information it contains is one of many. We asked you here today not to embarrass or to threaten, but because we believe you possess the ability to contribute a real service to your country."

Her breathing had slowed and the hammering in her chest subsided to a steady thud. They definitely had their own version of good-cop, bad-cop down to a science. "Fine. I understand all that. Once again, I ask you: What do you want from me?"

Brad brushed past Julia to step behind the desk and opened a drawer to remove another file, this one much thinner and clearly marked "Confidential - Level 2."

"You're perfectly correct in your assessment of our presence in Egypt. The U.S. has had strong business ties there for many years and we have a long-standing and sound collaborative relationship with the government—particularly in the area of intelligence. But since September 11th," he cleared his throat, "things have changed. And the pressure placed on Mubarak's government by our administration for more democratic reforms has put a strain on diplomatic relations between our two countries."

"A considerable strain," Bob added dryly.

The storm clouds outside the window framed Brad, now seated on the edge of the desk. He flicked a piece of lint off his otherwise immaculate slacks and continued.

"Needless to say, we have agents in place throughout the Middle East. Egypt is of particular importance as Cairo is the main hub for the region and, of course, its proximity to Israel. It's also a hotbed of militants. Since the 1995 attacks on tourists in Luxor, the government has cracked down on them—hard. Their methods, as I'm sure you're aware, are extreme. Outlawing the Muslim Brotherhood did little to diminish its effectiveness. Security appears to be tight around all public places—the airports, hotels, museums and sites of antiquity—but the whole country is essentially wide open. The hard-core militants simply moved their base of operations deeper underground, to the middle region of the country, somewhere along the Nile."

Thus far, he had told Julia nothing she didn't already know. She'd endeavored to learn and to understand as much about contemporary Egyptian society as she could, and the history of the politics in the region played an important role in that. Egypt had been ruled by foreigners for centuries before the 1952 revolution that overthrew the monarchy established by the British several decades before. Once the British gained control of the newly completed Suez Canal in 1869, they had tenaciously clung to their dominance over the government. It was, as usual, a matter of economics, as the canal was vital to their interests in controlling trade in the Mediterranean and, crucially, the sea route to India.

When members of the Egyptian Army finally had enough of Britain's high-handed "protection," they persuaded King Farouk, pawn of the British, to abdicate and then—quite literally—set Cairo ablaze. Since 1954, when Gamal Abdel Nasser became Egypt's President, the same authoritarian group had governed Egypt. Nasser was succeeded by his Vice President, Anwar al-Sadat, who was in turn succeeded by his Vice President, Hosni Mubarak. Mubarak had held the office of President since 1981 and recently had won the election for another six-year term.

Mohamed had schooled her on how the single-party, secular government had steadily caused an increase of resentment among religious leaders and conservative Muslims alike, due to their failure to provide for basic necessities, and the country's staggering economic problems. High unemployment, limited job opportunities, an exploding birth rate, chronic deficits and a huge and cumbersome bureaucracy left the government open to criticism by the fundamentalists.

It was the age-old story of the rich getting richer, the poor getting poorer and the beleaguered middle-class being squeezed down the chain. When the various Islamic fundamentalist groups protested with violence, the government responded with severe repression, turning Egypt into a virtual totalitarian state. This created the perfect environment to foment terrorists bent on Jihad.

Brad broke into Julia's reverie. "As you probably know, four of the terrorists in the September 11th attacks were Egyptian. One of them, Mohammed Atta al Sayad, is believed to have been the leader of the attacks."

His voice dropped an octave. "Recent undercurrents lead us to believe that another major strike may be in the planning stages. Word is that the scope of this one could make September 11th seem like a preview of coming attractions."

The full weight of that prospect vibrated in the air. "Our people are working night and day on this, and I'm sure we don't have to tell you to what lengths we'll go to prevent any such thing from happening."

Brad sighed as he returned to the couch. "The trouble is, with the on-going situation in Iraq, instability in Afghanistan, the issues with Iran and North Korea's nuclear proliferation, the ongoing Israeli-Palestinian conflict and dozens of other hot spots around the globe, our military and intelligence resources are stretched to the max."

Julia lowered herself back into the chair. Again, nothing he'd said was news to her. The media sporadically reported on the failure of several branches of the military to meet recruiting goals. She wasn't aware of any such reports regarding intelligence agencies, but it would be a logical conclusion.

Although she sympathized with the complexities of dealing with these global nightmares, she felt strongly that many of them were of "their" own making. For years, U.S. actions and interventions had led to destabilization throughout the developing world. Julia loved her country but she feared her government and their questionable agenda and choices. And they had yet to shed any light on why they were telling her all this.

"You're probably wondering why we're telling you all this."

Julia's eyes widened in surprise. Was she that transparent?

"Let me emphasize—in the strongest possible terms—that everything you learn within these walls is strictly confidential: Top Secret. Two days ago, one of our operatives in Egypt disappeared. Her assignment was to maintain contact with an undercover agent who has infiltrated the Muslim Brotherhood. We have reason to believe that a radical splinter group, not the Brotherhood itself, may be involved in planning new attacks."

As Brad leaned in closer, Julia caught another whiff of his primal scent.

"She's our only link to the undercover guy and was scheduled to make contact with him this weekend. We have no way of knowing if the information he might pass is of importance. We don't even know for sure that any information *will* be passed. But because of the Egyptian connection in prior terrorist activities, we can't risk missing *any* communication."

Again the two men exchanged a high-voltage glance.

"What we're asking is that you attempt to make the contact and pick up the information."

CHAPTER 6

Bob Bronson, sensing Julia was on the brink of delivering an adamant and unequivocal refusal, once again intervened. "Julia, wait. Hear him out. It isn't what you think. Just listen for a moment longer. Please."

Brad didn't wait for her response. "All we're asking is that you fly to Cairo, spend one day there, then go on to Luxor. You and your friend Mohamed will take a nice Nile cruise to Aswan. As you know, the boat makes several stops along the way at sites of antiquity: Esna, Edfu and Kom Ombo. We'll provide you with a detailed itinerary. At some point during your excursions, the agent will make contact and pass the coded information. When you reach Aswan, arrangements have been made for you to send it on, safely and discreetly.

"As simple as that. The rest of the time you'll merely be on holiday in a country you seem to enjoy—all at government expense."

Julia looked incredulously from Brad to Bob—who watched her with a measuring eye—then back to Brad. Beneath the sudden hush, she could hear the muted sounds of traffic from the street. Forcing her voice past the lump in her throat, she croaked, "You must be joking. Surely, you *are* joking. Why me? Why not one of your own people?"

Bob, the good cop, sighed. "No, Julia, we're not joking. This is a most unusual situation and therefore requires an unusual solution. We know you'll have a number of questions and objections but, be assured, there is a logical response for each of them."

Still holding the slender file, Brad opened it and removed a photograph. He passed her the glossy black and white image.

"This is the agent that disappeared: Abeer Rashad. Her parents are Egyptian but they came to the U.S. in '54 as students after the 'liberation' and she was their last child, born in New York. Her cover is that of a photo-journalist for *Egypt Today*, a popular magazine there. Egyptian Intelligence is aware that she's on our payroll."

He scowled. "We believe that's part of the problem. Up to now we've mostly tried to comply with them in their request that they be apprised of all U.S. Intelligence activities in their country. Unfortunately, we're now certain there's at least one snitch—close to the top. We can't risk sharing this new information with them for fear it might leak to the militants. We need someone who's unknown to them as working for us— above suspicion—and who will remain so."

Julia felt sick. She looked down at the young, vivacious face of Abeer Rashad.

"But *surely*, surely, you have someone more qualified to send? *Anyone* would be," she pleaded, opening sweaty palms in apprehensive appeal.

Bob sat motionless, watching his subordinate answer.

"Unfortunately, we have reason to believe that the Egyptians are either fully aware of, or suspect, the other agents we currently have in place there, as well as several others throughout the Middle East. Fortunately, so far, they're ostensibly unaware of the identity of the undercover man— the mole—although we believe that they may suspect that one exists."

Julia's brain struggled to wrap itself around this.

"We have to send a woman. The mole expects one. And any new face with an American passport or traveling alone will attract attention and be closely monitored. We cannot, under any circumstances, risk a delay in receiving—or even worse, the loss of—this potentially valuable information."

Brad Caldwell once again picked up her file, removed a sheaf of photographs and lined them up across the table, one by one. Julia's mouth fell open as she looked down at images of herself, alone and with Mohamed: in the Valley of the Kings near Luxor, on the corniche in Alexandria, boarding a train in Cairo, in a Bedouin village in Sinai. And on and on.

"You, on the other hand, have the perfect cover. The Egyptians are also aware of your visits there. Since your second trip, you've been closely observed. Your travels alone and with Zahar throughout the country have been monitored, including your excursion to the Western Desert, which is heavily screened by military security. After careful assessment, they've dismissed you as a threat—or of working for us."

The two men's eyes met briefly. The Egyptians might be convinced that Julia Grant was squeaky clean. Neither of them, however, was satisfied that Mohamed Zahar wasn't somehow involved with the militant faction. Using her for this mission had the double advantage of retrieving the communication while learning more about the tour guide's connections. They had agreed it best not to mention this to Julia.

Bob spoke matter-of-factly. "They're convinced your reasons for coming there are of, ah, a strictly personal nature. No actions on your part for this trip would be unprecedented. Or likely to attract undue attention."

Julia's hand, without conscious thought, came up to her chest where, beneath the silk scarf, a golden charm in the shape of an angel lay against her skin—skin that now crawled with the realization that the invasion of her privacy was even more offensive than she'd first thought.

She'd been *followed*. She'd been *photographed*. Clearly, her email had been infiltrated. This, she could live with. But one of the two governments—or both—must have also either tapped her phone or Mohamed's because they'd always been careful in all their emails. Some of those phone conversations had been pretty steamy. Now, it seemed, not only did the U.S. government know intimate aspects of the relationship—so did the Egyptians. This not only put both of them in an unbearably embarrassing situation, it also placed Mohamed in real jeopardy, as a criminal in his country.

"But …," she began, before Bob once again forestalled her.

"Julia, we really need your help on this. The situation developed unexpectedly and if we had someone—anyone—else to send they'd already be on their way." He ran a hand over his thinning hair. "All you have to do is take the trip, receive and pass the information and come home. There's practically no danger involved."

Practically no danger. Easy for him to say.

Brad again became businesslike. "We've made reservations for you on a flight to London tomorrow afternoon, then from there to Cairo. You will, as you've done in the past, obtain your visa at the airport upon arrival. You'll take a taxi to Mena House, again where you've stayed before. Your reason for this trip is to do research for a book that you're writing about your travels in Egypt. This will be validated by the Empire Publishing House in New York, in case anyone should check.

"Arrangements have already been made through Empire directly with Zahar for his services as your personal guide throughout the trip, for which he will be generously compensated. His presence is necessary for continuity and to allow you freedom of movement. He's unaware of the identity of his client, only that he's to check into Mena House by eight on Thursday morning and wait in his room to be contacted. He's already been sent a retainer and an itinerary for the tour. You're to visit several sites in Cairo together that day, then fly to Luxor on Friday morning.

Reservations for two cabins have been made on one of the tour boats."

"Zahar's presence is necessary to deter interest from Egyptian Intelligence," Bob reiterated authoritatively as he saw her again on the verge of protest. "Besides, Julia, you're a very attractive and striking woman. Traveling alone in that environment, you're bound to draw unwelcome attention that could complicate things. Be assured, neither Mohamed, nor anyone else besides the three of us in this room, will know anything of your real purpose."

He pushed himself from his chair with a funereal smile. "Again, thank you for your time today. We certainly can't insist that you take on this assignment. But may we respectfully request that you give it serious consideration before making your decision? If you're unable to agree today, please wait until tomorrow morning at this time to let us know. I sincerely hope that your answer will be yes."

Julia also stood, on unsteady legs, and took his outstretched hand. She felt the current of energy coursing beneath his composed exterior. There was definitely more to calm and convincing Bob than met the eye. He left the room without further comment.

Brad placed a hand under her elbow and steered her to the door. "The flight leaves at four forty-five tomorrow afternoon. You have my card. Call me by nine tomorrow morning with your answer. We need you here by noon for a briefing and then I'll drive you to the airport. It's crucial that you discuss this with no one, Julia, absolutely no one. If you want to speak with me in the meantime, call any time, today or tonight."

He turned to face her with that deceptively lazy half-smile.

"Of course, you'll also be well remunerated for your time and trouble. And," he added as if an afterthought, "we would never have approached you on this unless we had the utmost confidence that you could handle it competently."

The door opened again and there stood the efficient Ms. Manning, who proceeded to lead her back down the endless corridor. Julia heard the faint click of the door as it closed behind them.

CHAPTER 7

Julia found herself out on the sidewalk with no memory of having gotten there. She drifted toward the square in a kind of daze. The great Civic Center Plaza, as always, swarmed with a diverse cast of characters. City Hall, majestic with its impressive black and gold dome, anchored the scene. Massive clouds in shades of gray tumbled across the sky, parting now and then to allow rays of the late morning sun to set the dome's gilded flourishes alight.

Tourists and locals alike entered the spectacular Asian Art Museum to view its world-renowned collection of treasures. Students and academics came and went from the San Francisco main library. Clusters of the homeless loitered in the park, with shopping carts full of the sum of their worldly goods. At that moment, Julia would have gladly given all she possessed to trade places with any one of them.

Still in a state of confusion, she reached the car and sat behind the wheel, trying to focus. The blast of a horn jarred her abruptly from her stupor as another driver nudged her to relinquish the precious parking space. The sound reminded her that San Francisco lore says if you're driving around the city and find a rare vacant space, you should park there and see if you can't find something to do in the neighborhood.

She started the engine and pulled slowly away from the curb, still in a fog, with no idea where she was going. The car seemed to have a mind of its own as it turned onto Van Ness Avenue, moving in the direction of the Marina. As she caught sight of the bay up ahead, her destination became instantly clear.

A left turn on Lombard took her in the direction of the Golden Gate Bridge; soon the celebrated red steel towers appeared over the treetops of the lush forest of the Presidio. Crossing the Golden Gate now, and the Bay Bridge as well, always made her a little nervous. Both landmarks were well-known to be possible terrorist targets. No, Julia thought sadly, we're no longer safe even here in our beautiful "city-by-the-bay."

People weren't safe anywhere as long as fanatics were willing to die in order to destroy the lives and the way of life of those they considered their enemies, all for some twisted version of an otherwise supposedly peaceful religion. It was unimaginable to her that anyone could truly believe that their god—any god—would condone death and destruction in his name. What kind of god would that be?

Reaching the other side of the bridge, she turned onto the road leading up to the Marin Headlands. A few minutes later she stood on the cliff, looking out over the endless magnificence of the Pacific Ocean. White foam frosted surging swells in a palette of icy blues. Great masses of clouds billowed across a big sky. Ships steamed along, coming and going beneath the bridge; on the far horizon, where water merged with sky, they receded into miniature toys.

Julia inhaled deeply as the insistent wind chilled her face and tugged her hair from its neat twist. To perch here—on the edge of the world—always recharged her spirit, as if the fresh sea air swept through her mind, heart and soul, blowing away all the clutter and debris, making it possible for her to think—and to feel—again.

Sometimes she felt she'd been born in the wrong century, though thus far, she'd failed to identify an era that might've been preferable. A student of history, she'd only found that not much had changed over the millennia. Human beings were basically the same as they'd always been, with the same qualities and characteristics, the same hopes and dreams, the same attributes and shortcomings. And, lord knew, there was no shortage of shortcomings.

Julia's thoughts wandered to her own personal dilemma. She was now without any close family ties. As a young adult and only child, she suffered the untimely death of her mother in a car accident and, more recently, watched helplessly while her father swiftly descended into the vagueness of Alzheimer's. He now lived completely in the past with his hazy memories, no longer recognizing Julia or anyone else other than the caring attendants in his new, diligently controlled home.

Over time, in an almost imperceptible yet remorseless advance, she'd drifted into a kind of emotional wasteland. Although she'd once been well-known for her good humor, laughter was an infrequent visitor now. And yet she'd moved beyond tears. A mantle of dull, mind-numbing apathy had settled over her, threatening to harden into a permanent shell of impenetrable indifference.

Her mind inevitably swung back to this new, this daunting, situation. If she obeyed the instructions of confidentiality, it meant she couldn't discuss the extraordinary development with anyone. How could she possibly make a decision of this magnitude without input from those whose opinions she respected? From those who cared for her well-being? Sarah would have an absolute seizure if she found out that she'd gone off on an escapade like this without consulting her. The thought of her friend's predictable, and no doubt vigorous, indignation tugged the corners of her mouth into a grin.

❖

Sarah Littlefield was Julia's oldest and closest friend. Daughter of a prominent "establishment" San Francisco family, she looked every inch the patrician. Barely five-foot-two with the physique of an athlete, raucously curly natural blonde hair, green eyes that flashed like brilliant-cut emeralds, and an infectious smile, she traversed life with a supreme, unshakable confidence.

People regularly underestimated Sarah's uncompromising core of obstinate determination. Her parents, pillars of the community, had been delighted when she was awarded a scholarship to Stanford University to study art history. They were less than thrilled when, after the first year, she switched majors to political science and relocated her academic endeavors to U.C. Berkeley.

It hadn't taken long for Sarah to channel all her brilliance, energy and resources into becoming a major force in the Berkeley peace movement—and she never looked back. If there was a peace rally in the Bay Area, Sarah Littlefield was involved, if not the instigator. As a political activist, she effectively—and tenaciously—led the pack.

Some twenty years later, she'd evolved into a staunch feminist, pacifist and environmentalist. Her single-mindedness was amazing, unyielding and often exasperating. She worked tirelessly for her causes, many of which were in direct opposition to the views held by her conservative family. That never stopped her from making the most of her media-worthy name and substantial inheritance.

The two women had met during the late '70s when they were both young and idealistic. Shortly after Sarah had been released from jail after handcuffing herself to the iron fence outside City Hall in a peace protest, they sat cross-legged next to one another in a sit-in for women's rights. Over the years, their instant friendship had matured into an enduring and committed one, where it didn't matter if they hadn't seen each other or even spoken for weeks; they could always pick right back up where they'd left off.

Visually they couldn't have been more different. Julia's tall, lanky frame, pale complexion and long auburn hair made a striking contrast to Sarah's petite, perpetually-tanned golden exterior. Ideologically they were in perfect sync. Frequently, they simultaneously spoke the same words, which always resulted in a good laugh.

Sarah was the one person who knew most of the details regarding Julia's mad and maddening relationship with Mohamed. Most of the details, not all. And she was practically the only one who'd supported her and her compulsive behavior throughout the entire saga.

Julia quivered with the urge to jump in the car, drive to Sarah's bungalow in the Berkeley hills and spill this latest, unbelievable story, to hear her friend's adroit and, no doubt cynical, assessment. Sarah could be trusted to keep a secret. But something held Julia back: the realization that "they" would know and would not approve. They hadn't gone to all the trouble of keeping her under surveillance for over two years to let her run off and expose their shocking, reprehensible activities at the first opportunity. Oh, no, they were still keeping tabs on her. That was a given.

Besides, she couldn't bear the thought of involving Sarah, or anyone else, for that matter. There might be "practically no danger," but she wouldn't dream of putting any of her friends in harm's way, even if there was the slightest chance. Her impulsive actions had gotten her into this mess and it was up to her to find a way out.

But was getting out what she really wanted? That nagging question had been worming its way up through her sub-conscious for the past hour. A part of her was appalled at the proposal. It clashed against her every conviction. And, if she was to be strictly honest with herself, another part of her—the emotional, impulsive, adventure-seeking part— was intrigued. No, not intrigued. She was excited by the idea.

And, of course, the prospect of seeing Mohamed again sent sparks of anticipation surging through her veins. It had been long enough since her last trip to Egypt for her to remember only the good things that drew her there, and forget the many things she found repellant and infuriating, including, at times, Mohamed. She was, as always, the proverbial moth to the Egyptian flame.

Had she completely lost her mind? Well, yes, probably some time ago. She often took solace in the thought that persons far greater and wiser than she had made much bigger and more public fools of themselves. At least so far, anyway.

As presented, it was an easy, simple, one-week trip. She could tell Sarah a fabricated tale of a sudden unplanned hiking outing—to keep her from worrying. No one else even needed to know she was gone. There was nothing pressing on her calendar that couldn't be rearranged. The trip might allow her to finally put things in perspective. Then maybe she could make some kind of damn decisions about her future. And she would even possibly be making a small contribution to the prevention of more violence.

Julia grimly acknowledged she was slipping towards a decision in favor of the astonishing assignment. Her heart, she realized, had taken control and was urging her head ever closer to a decision she might come to regret. With a deep sigh, she turned back to the car, aware that hours of tortuous internal debate lay ahead. It was going to be a long day, and an even longer night.

As she swung along the sidewalk on Haight Street, Julia caught sight of the old woman who'd staked out her regular spot. Covered in layers of tattered clothes, she sat cross-legged on a worn blanket amidst piles of junk. The young dog stretched out beside her thumped its tail when Julia bent to pat his head. With her free hand, she reached in her suit pocket, took out a folded ten-dollar bill and held it out.

She was rewarded with a snaggle-toothed grin. "Thanks, Julia."

Julia kept a firm grip on the bill as a gnarled hand tried to take it. "For food. Not Starbucks."

The old woman cackled as she palmed the bill; the dog licked Julia's hand. Shaking her head, Julia moved past them to push open the door of a rundown store front. Above the handle, a bumper sticker proclaimed *There is no way to peace. Peace is the way.* Posters in every window called for peace in Iraq, Afghanistan. Inside, more posters covered the walls, and stacks of flyers overflowed tables around the perimeter of the room. The churning of a copy machine drew her to the rear, where the figure of a gray-haired woman, a long braid hanging down the center of her back, stooped over the machine. At sight of Julia, she switched it off.

"Wow. Look at you. All dolled up. How'd it go at the lab?"

Julia gave her a quick hug. "Good. My hemoglobin is normal." She rubbed the band-aid on the inside of her wrist where the demonic needle had extracted her blood.

"And has that jackass doctor ever admitted that you had parasites?"

Julia shook her head. "Oh, no. If they can't define it, it doesn't exist."

"Jackass. I wish I'd known you then. I could've told you . . ."

"Never mind. At least I lived to tell the tale." Julia nodded at the stack of freshly printed flyers. "I'm finished with my pile. Want me to take more?"

Her friend Passion poked her shoulder with a stubby, be-ringed finger. "What I want is for you to take a break. You've done enough, more than enough."

"But we have to…"

"Listen, you runnin' yourself ragged won't change the world, darlin'. What you need to do now is concentrate on gettin' your own life back."

❖

By the time Julia left "Peace Headquarters," the morning clouds had all

42

blown out to sea. She ambled back in the direction of her car, enjoying the warm fingers of sunlight dancing through the leafy trees to caress her face. Sweet birdsong filled the soft, cool air. She slowed as she passed beside a row of polished limousines parked at the curb in front of a small chapel tucked in between a row of brightly painted Victorian houses— the "painted ladies."

The church bells suddenly rang out, joyous and strong. Julia looked up at the vine-covered building as people began to spill from it doors. A bride and groom came bouncing down the steps. At the bottom, he caught her up in his arms and she welcomed his ardent kiss. The crowd cheered approval and pelted them with birdseed. Tears welled up in Julia's eyes, even as she smiled.

Back in her utilitarian studio apartment, Julia opened the refrigerator and stared vacantly at its contents. After assembling an odd assortment of leftovers on a plate, she sat down in the one comfortable chair with the plate on a tray in her lap and surveyed her surroundings with a judicious eye. The ceaseless white noise of traffic on the Bay Bridge hummed away in the background, with an occasional siren punctuating what would have otherwise been a deafening silence.

Before her last trip to Egypt, she'd sold her home, her car and put all her belongings in storage. The plan had been to remain there indefinitely. When things hadn't gone exactly according to plan, she'd returned to San Francisco, taking what was meant to have been a temporary apartment until she could decide what to do with the rest of her life.

Right away she began to feel seriously unwell. The first diagnosis had been depression. They always wanted you to be depressed. Overnight it changed to profound anemia and she was rushed to the emergency room for a massive blood transfusion. It seemed she had very few red blood cells.

"I've recently been traveling in Egypt," she explained. "Could this be related in some way? Some kind of parasites, perhaps?"

"Oh, no, it's not parasites," a parade of self-assured medical professionals insisted. Six months later, after every test imaginable (and some unimaginable), she continued to suffer the debilitating effects of whatever unknown malady was causing the exhausting, brain-draining anemia. The doctors remained baffled.

"Parasites?" she asked for the umpteenth time.

"No," the hematologist said in his patronizing way. "It is not parasites."

One day, in a chance encounter, a stranger encouraged her to consult an alternative medicine professional—a naturopathic doctor. Well, she thought, what have I got to lose? She felt as though she'd aged twenty years. The future at that point looked pretty bleak, with having to make weekly hospital visits for the rest of her life only to cling to a dreary existence of fatigue and despair.

"Parasites," pronounced the herbalist after a simple and splendidly non-invasive saliva diagnostic. "You have numerous, nasty little parasites."

From the day the herbal cleansing commenced, Julia began to improve. Four months later her blood count was almost normal. It would take some time to repair the damage done, but she felt better every day. The next time she traveled to a developing country she would be a damn sight more careful.

The diminished delivery of oxygen to her brain had made it impossible for her to think clearly or to make any major decisions. Apart from her new-found friend Passion and helping her with the peace rallies, she'd done little about getting her life back on track. Now here she sat, almost a year later, in her "temporary" room, contemplating a course of action that would never, in her wildest dreams, have occurred to her. It was only for a week, she told herself, not a career move. What's wrong with that?

A strange phenomenon had also occurred during her illness. Her mind, now free from a lifetime of left-brain domination, frequently took off on elaborate and lengthy flights of fancy. Returning from these trips usually left her confused as to what she'd been doing before take-off.

Looking down in mild surprise at the untouched food in her lap, she set it aside and went to open the closet door. The decision was not firm in her mind, but at least the act of packing was something to do. Julia had always been a woman of action. Physical motion now provided a degree of comfort, along with some relief for her conflicted emotions.

Sleep came at long last, and when Julia awoke in the early dawn it was with a clear resolve to undertake this next journey. It must be, she concluded, one of life's never-ending tests.

CHAPTER 8

Alexander Bryant stepped from the black London cab in front of the Connaught Hotel and walked briskly to the entrance. The doorman, splendid in a silky black top hat and immaculate white gloves, greeted him by name as he ceremoniously opened the door. Alexander in turn thanked him by name and strode purposefully through the lobby, which had more the air of an ambassadorial residence than an exclusive hotel.

He paused at the entrance of the main dining room to scan its occupants for his luncheon appointment. One of the city's most respected and time-honored eateries, paneled in old mahogany and comfortable in understated elegance, the room perfectly reflected the grandeur of its one-hundred-and-fifty-year history. According to tradition, the tables were set with seasonal flowers, polished antique silver and sparkling crystal. Today, brilliant deep purple and pale yellow tulips stood out against crisp white linen cloths. One could easily imagine royalty seated among the distinguished guests, as they frequently were.

Zeroing in on the man he sought, Alexander worked his way through the tables to one by the window. Leave it to James to commandeer the best spot in the room.

"Good day to you, Mr. Marshall," he said as the rotund, rosy-cheeked Englishman rose to grasp his hand.

"Alex, my boy! Very good of you to come, and on such short notice, very good indeed." Collapsing back in his chair, James added, "I say, you're looking quite fit, and about time, too."

Alexander inwardly winced at the abbreviation of his name but, after all these years, he'd become resigned to it, more or less. He strategically chose a chair backed to the wall, which provided a full view of the other diners as well as the entrance. A force of habit, this placed him next to his companion rather than across, as he felt more at ease in having complete awareness of all that transpired around him.

"Well, I've somehow managed to stay at home for more than a few hours at a time. It's a distinct pleasure to wake up in my own bed for a change. And how do the Marshalls fare these days?"

"Excellent, excellent," replied James as he signaled the waiter for menus. "Went abroad for all of August. Rented a lovely cottage in the south of France and had a proper holiday. First one in several years. Liz was over the moon. Had the damnedest time getting her to come back to what she calls 'the daily grind.' Doesn't seem to realize she's living the Life of Riley."

Alexander had to agree. The Marshalls resided on an ancestral estate: a grand thirty-room Georgian manor on over a hundred acres of magnificent country gardens in the heart of Gloucestershire, the entirety tended, as expected, by an army of staff. Picturing life there "a daily grind" certainly did challenge the imagination.

"Let's order straight away, shall we? Then we can talk." James took the red leather folder embossed in gold bearing the tempting offers of the day.

Angela Hartnett's Menu, as the dining salon was now called after its illustrious chef, was known far and wide as one of London's finest eating establishments. James took his culinary experiences seriously, as his ever-expanding waistline testified, and was always more than happy to play host in their pursuit—especially when he sought something in return.

Alexander watched with amusement as the gourmand queried the waiter on several points and then, after the food had been meticulously selected, spent a considerable amount of time in choosing the proper libations to complement it. He faithfully adhered to the custom of his countrymen in enjoying abundant spirits with the midday repast.

This presented a challenge for Alexander. Of course he wanted to appear an appreciative guest but found that downing large quantities of alcohol in the middle of the day could be problematic. Once, after an especially overindulgent episode, he had "fallen asleep" on the train home and awakened several stops past his own. He now practiced strict control over his consumption during daylight hours.

"Fine, now then," said James with satisfaction while rubbing well-padded hands in anticipation, "how's business these days?"

One of James's more likeable qualities, as far as Alexander was concerned, was his habit of getting right down to the issue at hand. Here in "jolly olde" England, it usually took several meetings for the crux of the matter to even be introduced. He still occasionally found himself grinding his teeth as the latest cricket match was dissected ad infinitum.

"My business, as you might imagine, has never been better," he replied with the slightest hint of regret. "Thanks to your lead in Somalia, I bought that Italian villa I've had my eye on. And circled the globe at least three times since then."

Alexander Bryant preferred to think of himself as more of a military advisor than an arms dealer. Strictly speaking, he didn't sell weapons. He developed strategic defense plans for struggling countries, wealthy families and individuals and then put them in contact with those, like Slippery Billy Hirschfield, who could provide his recommendations.

After all, he rationalized, if every illiterate red-neck in the U.S. could brandish a shotgun at the slightest provocation or "hunt" game with an AK-47, why shouldn't people living in violent communities rife with civil unrest have the means to protect their property and loved ones?

Most of his clients were wealthy beyond imagining, to be sure, but the rich were no different than anyone else. It was just that their wealth allowed them to further develop their desires, as well as their eccentricities and failings. But that was not Alexander's concern. He provided a service—no more, no less. It was, in his precise military-trained way of thinking, a black and white situation.

James harrumphed as he shook his head. "Oh, yes, I can well imagine. These are turbulent times, my boy, turbulent times. Violence is a frightening reality these days and each of us must do what we must."

He was presumably quite current on his country's activities in "doing what they must" in this area, due to his long-standing position as a member of the House of Lords. And his years spent in military service had left extensive connections throughout the intelligence community. James had also been discreetly involved in a number of Alexander's transactions, to their mutual financial benefit. The extra income went a long way in subsidizing the upkeep of his princely country estate, and made possible holidays in "cottages" like the one in France. The fact of these exceedingly lucrative collaborations was not widely known.

They sat back in their comfortably upholstered chairs as chilled plates of Scottish sea scallops in lime and cucumber marinade were placed before them. Lord Marshall examined the dish with a critical eye before reaching for his fork. Alexander sipped the splendid Semillon Blanc from the Loire Valley and waited. The man definitely had an agenda. Best to let him proceed at his own pace.

After reveling in a succulent bite, the Englishman sighed with satisfaction. "Alex, we're of the same mind on these matters, as we've discussed before. In the past, we've collaborated and been more than satisfied with the results."

He reached for his wine, taking an appreciative sip. "Things change now from day to day, sometimes moment to moment, or so it seems. Even the rules are changing and it's damned difficult to know who is on whose side. When things go wrong, fingers point in every direction. Our right is someone else's wrong—our truth, someone else's lie."

Murmurs from diners at nearby tables filled the momentary lapse in James's philosophical observations. Then he cut straight to it.

"A dodgy situation's popped up down in Egypt and you naturally came to mind. Needless to say, this is all very hush-hush. Seems that a group within the Muslim Brotherhood is planning a show, perhaps a rather big show. Don't have the full picture yet, but they are definitely in the market for some merchandise and appear to be particularly well-funded."

Had it been possible, Alexander would have sat up straighter in his chair. "I was under the impression that Mubarak's boys had driven the militant arm of the Brotherhood underground and were having a hard time following their activities these days."

"Yes, yes, that's true enough. Even so, seems you Yanks managed to get a few well-placed moles in line before they went to ground." He waved his fork to punctuate. "One of the regulars, working for your boys but known to the Egyptians, has disappeared. In the meantime, the buyers are getting anxious. They need the merchandise soon to keep the show on schedule."

He paused as Alexander's guarded eyes warned of the waiters' approach. After whisking away the empty plates, they presented a tantalizing caramelized moulard of duck breast with a flourish, and a jewel-like '83 Chateau Ausone Saint Emilion cascaded into his host's fresh glass. Alexander knew the price of this particular vintage to be well over three-hundred dollars a bottle. This was superb salesmanship indeed. James closed his eyes and inhaled the fruity aroma, indicated approval and waited for the servers to retreat.

"It might be a good idea for you to nip down and have a look 'round. I know I don't have to tell you the edge you have over the other boys. And one never knows what possibilities might develop."

The two men sat in silence for several long moments, thoughtfully chewing the tasty fowl and savoring the fine wine. Although little had actually been said, they both fully understood the implications—as well as the ramifications—any number of actions might bring. Alexander was the first to speak.

"Of course, this would be a solo operation." His eyes narrowed as he added, "with the utmost discretion." These were statements, not questions.

Raised bushy eyebrows and a slight nod constituted his only answer.

"James, my friend, you possess, as always, a great deal of information that would send any number of governments, especially Washington, into a state of pandemonium."

The other man shrugged at what he clearly considered a compliment and sipped the silvery-red liquid.

Once the outstanding meal had reached its conclusion and the proper accolades bestowed, Alexander said circumspectly, "Give me some time to think about it, all right?"

"Bloody little time is what you'll have. In order to make the connection, you'll have to be on your way to Cairo by tomorrow afternoon."

CHAPTER 9

Julia sat on the edge of the sleek leather sofa next to Brad Caldwell. His jacket hung squarely on a hanger on the back of the office door, leaving him looking disarmingly harmless in a perfectly pressed shirt of light blue that softened that of his eyes. He opened and turned on a laptop computer on the coffee table as he spoke in a brisk, business-as-usual tone.

"Okay. You'll carry this with you. It contains files for the book you're supposedly writing, in case anyone should check. "It has special software here," he pointed to an icon, *Vocabulary*, on the screen. "It appears to be a simple writer's tool. In fact, it's a program that codes and decodes messages for safe transmission over the net. The message you're to collect will also be in another cipher, for double security."

"But why can't your agent just send you his message?"

"Good question, Julia. You have good instincts. Trust me, he can't. It's too risky."

Without elaborating, Caldwell returned to the briefing. "It's also programmed for wireless internet, but service there can be irregular. Every afternoon, you're to send an email to the publishing house, with an attachment of your writing for that day. The manuscript files are set up in sequence; all you have to do is add the current day's date. This will establish a normal routine and let us know that things are going according to plan—again, just in case. There may be times on the boat when you'll be unable to find a wireless connection. He handed her a flash drive that fit easily in the palm of her hand. "If you can't, copy the text onto this and go ahead and send it from another computer. But this should be the exception rather than the rule."

Julia nodded comprehension. The whole thing felt increasingly surreal.

"When you make contact with the undercover agent, code name Zed, he'll pass you a devise of some kind. Download it and use Vocabulary to convert the data. Date the file and save it in the manuscript folder. Destroy the devise—thoroughly—and dispose of it. Discreetly. When you reach Aswan, attach the file to your daily email. This transmission must be sent on the laptop. Under no circumstances send it any other way. After that, continue with the daily emails until you leave Egypt."

"I know," she said, one end of her mouth pulling to the side, "just in case."

Brad shut down the computer and zipped it back into its carrying case. "Go to an internet café or a place that has Wi-Fi every afternoon. Establish a routine. Zahar is always to escort you. Don't go alone."

He sat back, throwing an arm up along the back of the couch. His cloudless blue eyes focused on her tense, chiseled features. "In the unlikely event we should need to communicate with you, it'll be through the publishing house. Every day, visit the website and click on *Special Events*. If that day's date is posted, click on it, copy the text into a Word file and save it. Once you're safely back in your room or cabin, copy the data into *Vocabulary*. Once it decodes, read it, then delete it and clean out the trash."

He pulled a card from his shirt pocket and held it out. It bore his name, with the title of "Editor," along with a website address for Empire

Publishing. "If you need to contact us, send an email to this address with an attached message pre-coded in *Vocabulary*. You won't have access to the preliminary cipher, which means these messages aren't fully secure. Ditto for whatever we might post for you. They could be intercepted and decoded, so be cautious with anything you send. In an extreme circumstance, you can email that you want to call and we'll make arrangements, or you can call my cell phone—but only in a dire emergency—like life or death." His boyish grin failed to lend the humor he'd obviously intended. "The call might be monitored by the Egyptians and could blow your cover."

External Affairs Special Agent Brad Caldwell hesitated for a moment before turning serious again to add a warning. "Julia, you must never allow anyone else to have access to this computer. Never. Carry it with you at all times; as a writer, it's perfectly natural. Use it several times a day in full public view. Make journal entries, whatever."

With something between a grimace and a grin he added, "Just in case."

"Ms. Manning will take you now to provide your itinerary, tickets, documents and cash for expenses. Ten thousand dollars has already been transferred to your bank account from the publisher as 'an advance' for your travel book. You'll return here to go over a few more points before we leave for the airport."

His eyelids slid down halfway. "You're too quiet. Are you all right with this?"

Julia lifted a steady gaze from her hands, resting on top of the computer case. "Yes, Brad, as a matter of fact I am. This will probably come as no big shock to you, as you're so familiar with my intimate affairs." She felt a ripple of satisfaction as he winced. "But the actual assignment isn't the most difficult aspect of this trip for me."

He bowed his head in mock defeat at the barbed rebuke.

Without warning, Julia sprang to her feet to stand over him, hands on hips. "There is one thing that I still don't understand about all of this." Her eyes narrowed to complete the picture of a woman who wanted answers. *"Why me?* I mean it would be pretty damn difficult to find someone less suited to the job."

Brad regained his composure and stood to meet her eye-to-eye. "That's *exactly* why, Julia. No one would believe it." He gave her his boyish smile. "Besides, it really is just a simple communication pick up. Completely routine. No cloak and dagger stuff, no big deal."

A few seconds of silence stretched out across the less than two feet that separated them before Ms. Manning reappeared noiselessly at the door.

When the two women returned to Brad's office half an hour later, they found him with Bob Bronson in quiet conversation. The men stood politely as they entered; Julia noted a tray of sandwiches on the coffee table next to several bottles of Evian. After shaking her hand, Bob took Julia's elbow and steered her to a chair.

"We thought you might enjoy a light lunch before the flight."

They ate the somehow incongruously dainty sandwiches of smoked salmon and thinly sliced roast beef, and chatted about inconsequential things. Julia sensed an air of uneasiness about something as yet unsaid. When Bob cleared his throat, she braced for bad news.

"We've received a disturbing communication." The furrows across his broad brow deepened. "Abeer Rashad's body was discovered late yesterday. In Mallawi, a town halfway between Luxor and Cairo. We have no idea what she was doing there."

Julia knew about Mallawi. Mohamed had told her it was a center of conflict and armed rebellion in the 1990s and remained today a very tense place. The populace, among the poorest in the country, were trapped by the stagnant economy, restless and resentful. Travel there was strictly controlled by the police, and the only way to get in or out was by private taxi or in your own vehicle, with a police escort.

What in the world *had* Abeer Rashad been doing there?

Brad saw the color drain from her face and leaned forward. "Julia, you can still change your mind if you like, but we sincerely hope you won't. As long as you stick to the plan, it'll be okay."

Sure. Who did they think they were kidding?

Julia saw in her mind's eye the vibrant young woman in the photograph. She swallowed with difficulty and asked, almost a whisper, "How...how did she die?"

Bob scowled down at his clasped hands while Brad said, "We don't have all the details, but she appears to have been strangled. It was reported to the press that the chief suspect is a distant male relative who took offense at her 'decadent' Western lifestyle."

In the strained silence that followed, Julia heard the wail of a siren off in some distant part of the city.

Bob's calm, reassuring voice filled the void. "Because of this latest development we're making arrangements for you to be observed on the boat. We haven't confirmed who it will be but that's irrelevant to your purpose. Whoever we send won't identify himself unless absolutely necessary."

Brad held up a forestalling hand to the obvious question. "We still need you to make the connection, Julia. Zed expects a woman. And anyone else traveling at the last minute might be followed. We simply can't risk that."

Bob heaved himself from his chair. "You have our most sincere gratitude. Please don't hesitate to ask any further questions of Brad before you go." His big, bear-like hand enveloped her slender one as he looked her straight in the eye. "All you have to do is stick with the plan, receive the information and come home safely. And remember," he added with a warm, almost melancholy smile, "we are all on the same side."

The lights dimmed and the other passengers settled down for the movie, to read or sleep. Julia had, in the end, taken the coward's way out and left a message for Sarah when she knew she would be out for her morning jog. In truth, it was fear that kept her from speaking with her sympathetic friend: fear of spilling everything to the only person alive who could possibly understand the anomaly of Julia's apparent abandonment of the values she held so dear.

Only Sarah knew of the one thing—the only thing—that could induce her to become involved with a faction she'd always found reprehensible. She would, no doubt, be furious when—if—she ever learned the truth. But the choice wasn't Julia's to make.

She closed her eyes and, accepting that sleep would be elusive at best, surrendered to the urge to wander back through time to that first trip to Egypt, Land of the Pharaohs. It was an indulgence she seldom allowed herself now: to relive, to relish every moment, every nuance, of her strange and powerful connection to Mohamed Zahar. It was only when she looked at it from beginning to end that even she could believe it had all come about. Especially the way that it had.

CHAPTER 10

Mohamed had loved her. Julia believed that. As far as she knew, he loved her still. To say that she loved him seemed pitifully inadequate. From the beginning, from that first moment when he'd stepped aboard the bus and said, "I am Mohamed Zahar," in his meticulous English, "I will direct your tour and share with you the many treasures of Egypt," she began to fall under his spell.

Years of working endless hours counseling the families of disabled children had left Julia limp with fatigue. An ever-increasing disenfranchisement with Western culture and the manic mass-consumption that it insists paves the path to happiness added weight to the burden dragging her down, down. In the constant struggle to find funding for her work, she'd become disillusioned by corporate chaos and corruption. She suffered from a life-threatening ebbing of spirit that would surely destroy her if she failed to find a kinder, gentler way of life.

The long-awaited trip to Egypt was a sabbatical—an escape, really. Mohamed's engaging smile, framed by a neatly trimmed black beard and mustache on a rugged, bronzed face, had undeniable appeal; it was, however, the warm, passionate quality of his voice and clear feeling for his subject that had instantly captivated her. For the first few days they kept a respectable distance. He lectured. She, along with the others, listened. Yet they drew inexorably closer—like a river gaining momentum as it approaches the falls.

As they toured the awe-inspiring sites of the ancient civilization, Julia came to know and respect her guide. They joked and laughed, enjoying the unacknowledged attraction. But she had no intention of anything more. Apart from the fact that a holiday fling held no interest, he was much younger—and married. He was also a Muslim, with all the strict codes of conduct that implied. No, she would allow herself to enjoy the fantasy, but nothing more. Surely there could be no harm in that.

"Come, Julia, the more you give, the more they will want."

Mohamed looked on with a mixture of amusement and exasperation as Julia, surrounded by shouting children, passed out ballpoint pens. She'd read somewhere that this was a good thing to do. Education was a much-valued opportunity there, and most of them couldn't afford school supplies, so she'd stuffed her bag with them and shared her bounty whenever she had the chance. She also couldn't resist distributing *baksheesh*, the handout expected from anyone who had a little extra to give, to every beggar woman and unfortunate handicapped person that crossed her path.

Julia moved through Karnak Temple in Luxor, with its monumental Hypostyle Hall, and on to the Valley of the Kings, as if in a dream. Mohamed lectured his group on how the burial place of Egyptian royalty for five centuries, the Valleys of the Kings and Queens, lay on the west bank of the Nile, across the river from modern day Luxor. He pointed out the stark line that marked the jarring reality between the lush crops—farmed on land enriched by the life-giving silt from the river—and the sterile desert of the Theban Mountains.

At each remarkable site, the Egyptologist retold stories from down the millennia of legendary figures, bringing them richly to life. Charming and erudite, Mohamed was the quintessential guide through a bygone world of miraculous splendor. By the time they set out for the journey upriver to Aswan, Julia found herself completely possessed. Sleep was impossible and food held little interest. She spent every waking moment when not ashore on the upper deck, with every new sight, sound and scent stirring her senses into a state of delicious anticipation.

The boat steamed up the longest river on earth in the steady north wind. Migrating birds from other continents sailed above stoic oxen toiling in the bright green fields. It could have been two thousand B.C.E., the pastoral scene exactly the same as it had been since that time. That first night on the deck, Julia heard the faint call of the *Maghrib*, the sunset call to prayer, in the far distance. As each *muazzin* from mosques along the river joined the call, the enchantment of it all washed over and through her, filling her with a serene calm. Something tight in the depth of her soul began to release, like a flower opening its petals to the sun. She was lost and she was found—spellbound—and utterly vulnerable for what was to come.

The boat docked in Aswan late one night, and Julia awoke next morning to a glorious scene. The wind-filled sails of *feluccas*, the same sailing boats that had plied the Nile for thousands of years, flitted like swallows across the swift current. Palm fronds whispered gently in the breeze. The sun god, Re, appeared dramatically over the eastern desert, washing the land with dazzling rays while the river reflected its golden light. Islands scattered in the swiftly flowing waters teemed with exotic birds. For a woman who'd always preferred nature to urban environments, this was nirvana.

That night the crew gave a fantasia. Local musicians and low lights transformed the boat's lounge into an enchanting Nubian village. The passengers and crew wore native costumes for the after-dinner games and dancing. Julia had bought a sapphire-blue galabeeya, the traditional caftan, with a vest, all lavishly trimmed in gold braid. A matching scarf edged with gold coins covered her auburn hair and caught the light, mirroring the sparkle in her eyes.

She was the only one among his group traveling alone, and Mohamed made sure that she participated in the boisterous festivities. At the end of the fête, when almost everyone else had gone, a DJ spun a slow tune and one or two couples took to the floor. Mohamed came to stand before her. Her eyes found his. "Come, Julia. Dance with me." He turned and walked away without waiting for a reply.

She rose to follow. There seemed to be no question that she would. When he turned back to face her, holding out his hand, Julia looked at the upturned palm and, in a dreamy slow motion, met it with her own. In an instant their bodies melted together, as if joined by an invisible and unrelenting force. It took her breath away. The world and time itself stopped. Everything else faded away, leaving only his body pressed to hers. His beard brushed her ear, sending ripples of pleasure down her neck. They moved, as one, to the sound of a distant cadence, heard by no other.

They'd tried to fight it. They both had tried. Julia hated the idea of being "the other woman." And it was risky. This was not California. It was Islam.

But they continued the erotic, irrevocable dance, moving ever closer into the sweetly aching need of each other's arms. He rubbed his trim beard against the side of her neck, forcing a low moan from deep within. When the music stopped, they turned wordlessly to the door. In the foyer, he raised a hand and motioned to the stairs. "Come, Julia, let us go up onto the deck."

Again, he led the way and she followed. Climbing the two flights of stairs gave her mind a chance to harness her run-away heart. They emerged into the balmy Egyptian night, and he strolled to a far corner, to lean against the rail. Every star in the universe shimmered above in an indigo velvet sky. They stood looking out over the eternal flow of the river, as moonlight betrayed their conflicting emotions.

Julia's eyes remained fixed on the dark water. "You took me by surprise."

"Did you enjoy it?" The quiet question sounded both like a tease and a challenge.

"Yes. It was a wonderful dance. I was only surprised because I thought your faith didn't allow you to dance with women other than your wife." She summoned the courage to tilt her head to study his somber profile.

"Julia, you are the first and only woman I have danced with since my marriage, seven years ago."

She had to swallow and wet her lips before she could speak. "Well, you must think of me as an 'immoral infidel,' but you're wrong about that."

"Oh, no, Julia, no, no. I would never think of you in this way." Finally, he turned to face her. "You are a fine and gracious lady, like a goddess. Tonight you are so beautiful, I simply could not resist."

What does one say to something like that? She breathed deeply of the mystical night as she turned away. "And you, Mohamed, are a charming and handsome man. But you realize, of course, that we can be no more than friends. I admit that I'm attracted to you—very attracted. But surely this kind of thing happens to you all the time. Women must fall in love with you on every tour."

She shook her head. "Even if we wanted to go further it would be a mistake. What good could come of it? You're married and we're here together for a short time; then we go back to our different lives on opposite sides of the world. I'm not interested in a casual romance. I like and respect you too much to allow the physical attraction between us to spoil our friendship. And we are friends, Mohamed. I hope we always will be. I know you feel that, too." Again, she shook her head. "No, it would only make us unhappy. Let's leave it with a dance."

The words came spilling out. She had no control over them and was taken aback at her own bluntness. Poor man, she thought. He probably thinks I'm insane.

"I don't know what to say, Julia." He looked down at his hands, wrapped around the rail. "You're right, of course. I cannot go further. It is *haram*: forbidden." He raised earnest eyes to hers, declaring fiercely, "But I, too, hope that we will always be friends."

"I know we will," she said, her relief tinged with more than a little disappointment.

They then spoke of other things. She asked about his work and about his family. He confided how he lived in two completely different worlds, moving from his job where he spent much time with people from Western cultures to his other life, deeply rooted in Islam. Sometimes it troubled him that he managed this with such apparent ease. But it was not easy. After touring with a group, enjoying the freedoms and luxuries, he often experienced conflict in returning to the strict structure of his religion and the financial constraints of his everyday life. And life had changed dramatically for the worse since the terrorists had begun their global Jihad, with many tours cancelled.

This Julia understood. She saw how hard life was for the people here. Societal norms dictated that the man worked, usually either for the government in the monstrous bureaucracy that shackled progress, or in the massive field of tourism, which comprised the largest sector of the economy. The wife stayed home, raised the children and cooked the labor-intensive meals expected each day.

There were, of course, exceptions to these norms, but mainly within the minute minority of the wealthy class. They generally took their religion less seriously and lived much more lavishly, embracing Western ways. The *fellahin*, Egypt's poorest class, made up the vast majority of the population and lived the most basic, primitive existence, much like their ancient ancestors.

Mohamed, coming from an educated, hard-working family, but not one of marked privilege, fell within the middle-class. His intelligence and charm, along with fluency in several languages, should have opened many professional doors. His degree in Egyptology would entitle him to a high-level position in academia in most other countries. After graduation from university in Egypt, he'd spent a year in England and a semester in America. In Egypt, university positions were rare and difficult to attain.

As the unlikely friends spoke quietly in the peaceful, dark night, Julia caught a glimpse of the depth of his character, and the conflicts he faced daily. The insight only drew her even more fully under his spell, going far beyond the physical or the obvious.

This is all very nice, she admonished herself sternly, but completely irrelevant. He's not the man for you. Besides, she knew that Egyptian society frowned upon promiscuity and infidelity. "Frowned upon" was putting it mildly. Islam decreed sex outside marriage as a sin—a crime. And, although this country was supposedly a secular state, the Egyptian government was strongly rooted in Islamic law. The authorities had been known to take action when they found evidence of improprieties, even to the point of jailing or deporting unmarried offenders who flouted the customs.

In due course, they became aware of being alone on the deck. Looking at her watch, Julia was shocked to see the time. "Oh. It's late. We'll be dead on our feet tomorrow."

"Tomorrow, Julia? It is already tomorrow."

She felt completely at ease as they headed for the stairs. Then, in the stairwell where no one could see—like a bolt of lightning—his arms enveloped her and his lips were crushing hers. She had no time to even think of resisting. Releasing her even more abruptly, he wordlessly retreated down the stairs, leaving her astounded and alone.

Damn! Everything had been under control. And now this. Julia wanted this man. She wanted him more than she could remember ever wanting anything—to feel his arms around her, his body pressed to hers. It was impossible. They could not. She would not.

The next, and final, night on the boat found them once more up late on the deck. One last time, in the seclusion of the stairwell, he impulsively pulled her into his arms. This time she returned his kiss, with a passion she'd never known. His hands ran hungrily over her body, leaving impressions that would ache for years.

On her last day in Cairo, they met in the garden of the Egyptian Museum. He extended a hand, taking hers in a firm grasp—the only proper public gesture of greeting his society would allow. Those two brief hours burned like a torch in Julia's memory. They wandered through the less popular areas of the hot, dusty, noisy building, murmuring now forgotten words and touching whenever they dared.

The next morning Julia left Cairo. Left Egypt. Left Mohamed.

CHAPTER 11

"It's impossible," Julia confided to Sarah. "You have to help me find the antidote."

Back in San Francisco, each day she told herself resolutely that the overwhelming feelings she'd experienced in Egypt were more about self-discovery and long dormant passion than about the object of that passion. It was the sensible thing to do. Oh, but the nights. The nights plagued her with longing and devastating desire. She tossed and turned while reliving—over and over and over—that haunting dance, often waking with the tantalizingly memory of the heat from their entwined bodies, crushed to discover it only a dream. It was obsession. Torture. Sweet, delicious torture.

Sarah, and everyone else Julia could draft, embarked upon a campaign to "fix her up" with eligible men. She even joined one of those social clubs for singles in a desperate attempt to ease the longing she felt for her Egyptian "friend."

After three weeks, there'd been no word from him. He hadn't answered her studiously breezy email, sent as soon as she got back. Julia had an illogical feeling that something was wrong. Maybe he'd simply chosen to forget her. Just when she thought she'd explode with frustration, a response finally came. Sight of it brought a dizzying lightheadedness. Reading it caused her heart to plummet: something *had* been wrong. The day after she left, Mohamed was hospitalized for almost three weeks. In addition to the pain and discomfort of his infirmity, she instinctively knew what a hardship it was for him to have been unable to work all this time. Abandoning all caution, she called.

"I knew something was wrong."

"We are connected, Julia, you and I. From the moment we met, an unbreakable bond formed between us that will last our lifetime. You are my angel."

She couldn't speak. She'd never been anyone's angel before.

Later, as Julia learned more about life in Egypt and about Islam, she discovered something that gave her pause. What she'd thought a mere term of endearment actually carried a much deeper meaning. Belief in the existence of angels was one of the fundamental articles of faith in Islam, where angels carry out God's commandments in nature and the universe. They were often fierce, and avenging. One of their jobs was to watch over people. This made her feel both good and bad—thrilled to be so important to him but frustrated to distraction by her inability to help solve his problems.

Sarah became aggravated as Julia failed to find a suitable male to transfer what she called her "sexual fixation." After a while, aggravation gave way to serious concern.

One day as they hiked in the East Bay hills, Sarah rounded on her. "Talk to me, Julia. In all the years we've been friends, I've never seen you like this. You have the strictest standards for date-material of anyone I've ever known. Compromise just isn't in your vocabulary. This guy doesn't even come close to your famous litmus test. Are you actually in love with him?"

In addition to their many differences, in the whole of her life, Julia never remotely considered becoming involved with a married man. Apart from anything else, she hated the idea that there might be even the slightest possibility of her causing the break-up of a family. In Egyptian society the family was everything, coming first over all else. She could never be a part of that. What did that leave for her?

"You are my angel," Mohamed would say. "Somehow, Julia, I feel that I can speak to you of anything. Never before have I felt this closeness with anyone."

Later, when they returned to Sarah's house, Julia followed her wordlessly across the split-level back deck and in through open French doors. A wall of windows and a skylight flooded the state-of-the-art kitchen with sunshine. She sat on a stool at the center island to rest her forearms on its cool granite surface as Sarah pulled two bottles of water from the fridge. With cheeks a rosy glow, partly from the climb, Julia made her quiet announcement. "I'm going back."

Sarah's jaw dropped. "Have you completely lost your mind? What if you go all the way back there and find out that you really *do* love him? What will you do then? Where can this relationship possibly go?"

"I don't know. I honestly don't know. All I know is that I have to try and find out. Find out the truth about my own feelings. I have never felt this way about anyone, Sarah, never. It may be, as you say, infatuation and…and lust. Maybe. But I need to know, to try and understand." She straightened her shoulders. "And he needs me. By going there I can help him, help his family. I know you care about me," she said as she hugged her friend fiercely, "but this is something I have to do, something I need to discover about myself."

❖

Julia planned everything, for their "vacation together from life."

68

Mohamed met her at the airport at midnight. Seeing him waiting, dignified and patient, near the end of the agitated crowd, should have brought relief. Instead, she tensed with alarm, asking herself for the thousandth time what the hell she was doing here.

He held out a hand. "Welcome back to Egypt, Madame Julia."

They drove to a hotel not far from the airport and, after checking in and frowning over her tired, travel-worn reflection, she joined him in the coffee shop. Her nerves stretched like violin strings wound to the verge of snapping. After going through the ritual of prescribed greetings— inquiring about her journey, one another's health and family—they moved on to the more practical matter of the schedule. As they sipped strong, sweet, mint-flavored tea, he delivered the first bombshell.

"There has been a change of plans. I have been given work in the morning." He looked away, clearly uncomfortable. "We must meet at the train station."

In her overwrought state, this was bad news. She'd forgotten how the best laid plans changed here, like the shifting desert sands. "All right," she heard herself say. "I can do that."

"I'm sorry, Julia. I could not refuse the work."

She nodded, dreading the thought of making her own way to the famously chaotic Cairo train station. When he started to say goodnight, she remembered to take the thick envelope from her purse. Thoughts of this moment gave her considerable trepidation. Mohamed was a proud man. She worried endlessly on how best to handle the subject of the money. In the end, she decided on the direct approach.

"This is for you, for our tour." She went on hurriedly as he sat back, away from her, in his chair. "And please listen to me for a moment. You're taking these two weeks to spend with me and won't be able to accept other work. It's fair and right that you should be compensated for your time. This is not debatable."

With lowered eyes, he shook his head before reaching for the envelope. "Thank you, Julia. Thank you for being you."

After a ten-hour train ride, finally at the hotel in Luxor, she pulled a white cotton *galabeeya* over her head and glided down the hall. Answering her knock at once, he reached for her hand and drew her into his room. A breath of blissful release escaped her lips as his arms wrapped around her, as they did time after time in her dreams. His mouth came down on hers and they kissed like two lost souls, at long last reunited after centuries apart.

Thus they stood for the longest time in the dark room, with the night breeze ruffling sheer curtains through an open glass door to the balcony. He lifted the robe to reveal her naked body and his hands began to explore the smoothness of her skin as he left a trail of smoldering kisses along the way. This was what they'd waited for, longed for. It was a perfect moment.

Well, Julia thought later with a sigh, not entirely perfect. Their union was certainly passionate and loving. In spite of all this, they did not make love. Not really.

"I cannot," he said with guilty remorse. "It is forbidden by the Koran. Only with my lawful wife can I complete the act of making love. In all my life, I have obeyed this, Julia. I cannot."

The days drifted by in discovery and, to some extent, contentment. In the cool of the mornings they revisited the sites where their ardor had blossomed. They discovered a shared interest in two of Egypt's most notorious pharaohs: Hatshepsut, the ambitious queen who declared herself pharaoh; and Akhenaton, the controversial ruler who plunged Egypt into turmoil by abolishing worship of all gods save one: Amun-Re. By glorifying the sun god, he created the world's first monotheism. When Mohamed spoke of Akhenaton, Julia asked if they could visit Amarna, the ruined capital city built by the "heretic" pharaoh along the Nile between Cairo and Luxor, near Mallawi.

He shook his head. "This is not a good idea. The villages in that area are not safe, even for Egyptians. The Muslim Brotherhood is strong there and militants cause much trouble. Even I, the bravest of men," he said with a droll smile, straightening and touching his proud chest, "would not feel safe to go there."

Four days later, Julia watched him approach from where she waited on a plush sofa in a deserted upstairs lobby of her stylish Cairo hotel. At her suggestion, he'd spent the previous day and night with his family. It was important to her that he understood how much she respected his commitment and devotion to his family. Today she knew instantly by the look on his face, like that of a stone statue of a long-dead pharaoh, something was wrong.

"What is it?" she murmured as he sat in the gilded chair next to her.

"Nothing. It is nothing." His voice sounded like grinding gravel. "Are you ready to go?"

"Mohamed, don't lie to me. Something is very wrong. Please tell me what it is."

He shook his head with a sad smile. "I cannot fool you, can I? How is it that you know me so well?"

"Tell me," she said softly.

"It is a friend. A good, close friend. He is," he took a deep, ragged breath, "he has committed suicide." The words now poured like molten lead from the depth of his pain. "We were at school together. He was best man at my wedding. He was an engineer, a fine, good man. He had no work in almost two years and could not provide for his wife and child."

Tears gathered in Mohamed's dark, fathomless eyes as he forced out each word. "He set himself on fire. In shame. This is how he died."

Paralyzed with horror, Julia felt cold to the bone. She wanted to put her arms around him and hold him close. To comfort him and let him weep on her shoulder for this tragic loss, this unthinkable atrocity. But she could not. They could not touch in public, for propriety's sake. She couldn't even hold his hand.

She felt like screaming, from the feelings of helplessness and despair, for the ghastly realities of the economic stagnation that caused good men to set their bodies on fire in final, desperate, tormented defeat. Guilt and shame flooded over her for her shallow and selfish carnal desires and her stupidity in thinking it possible to take a "vacation" from the heavy burdens these men carried every day of their lives. While she daydreamed of love and romance, he lived a daily nightmare of struggle for survival. His friends set themselves on fire.

There they sat, separately and in silence, making a heartbreaking effort to keep their sorrow from spilling out into the elegant lobby. This marked the dawning of Julia's awareness, and abhorrence, of the dark side of modern Egyptian society.

Love is a gift. Julia now knew she'd been given the gift of loving this man. This unattainable man, shackled with commitments and full of contradictions. He made her heart remember how to sing.

She loved him as she'd never loved before.

Despite the differences of age, culture, and religion, they communicated on a visceral level. The connection between them resonated like a live wire, an astonishing bond. The inescapable intensity of it provoked her imagination to seriously consider the concept of reincarnation. Nothing else came close to explaining it. The complexities and difficulties that lay ahead made her afraid. But she'd waited her entire life to love this way—to the core of her being—and, somehow, someway, love him she would.

An armed guard dozed in his chair at the end of the hotel corridor. Julia gently closed the door to her room so as not to wake him. These guards were everywhere in Egypt, at least everywhere the "wealthy" tourists were expected to go. And the island of Zamalek was definitely one of those places. Her research in preparation for her return drew her here.

In 1869, Khedive Ismail, Egypt's viceroy, planned elaborate celebrations to mark the inauguration of the Suez Canal. Empress Eugenie of France was persuaded to open the ceremonies and, in her honor, a lavish palace was built on the island in the Nile, in the heart of Cairo. A French landscape architect transformed the entire island into a magnificent formal park.

For decades, the palace served as one of the Middle East's largest and most frequented hotels. Julia chose it not only for its central location but also for the sheer spectacle. Tables shaded by large umbrellas lined the terrace overlooking lush gardens. Water splashing in ornate stone fountains provided the perfect backdrop for an endless parade of international visitors along the garden promenade, like a film set.

Men in white robes with red-checked head cloths were trailed by their women veiled from head to toe. The female feet contradicted their show of modesty, with painted nails in golden sandals glittering with jewels. Men and women in western business attire negotiated at tables strewn with various types of state-of-the-art technology. Young men, casually and expensively dressed in the latest fashions from Milan, strolled by, speaking with animation into mobile phones in various Arabic dialects.

As Julia came down the walk and spotted Mohamed waiting patiently at one of the tables, her heart, as always, skipped a beat. He rose at her approach, with the inevitably extended hand. They sat for a while, not saying all the things in their hearts, as their untouched ice cream melted in the desert sun. At length, he folded his napkin, placing it carefully on the table, and pushed back his chair.

"I must go."

She nodded mutely and followed him through the sliding glass doors that led to the lower level of the lobby. Two waiters loitered at the entrance to the indoor café and bowed in greeting as they passed. They watched the handsome couple ascend the wide mahogany staircase, side by side. Halfway up, Mohamed stopped a step above, uncharacteristically placing a hand on her arm.

"Don't come any further, Julia. It's time to say goodbye."

She looked up into his dark, expressive eyes. He bent to kiss her, first on one cheek, then the other. Without the slightest falter, his lips brushed hers, their coolness belied by the strength of his grip on her arm. The unprecedented public familiarity dazed her into immobility. At the top of the stairs, he turned for one last look and found her as he'd left her, motionless—eyes only for him—with a hand on the rail.

And then he was gone.

Chapter 12

James Marshall's silver Bentley wove through heavy traffic toward the terminal. The perpetual state of reconstruction of London's Heathrow, one of the world's busiest airports, made the going slow. An understandable need for improvements failed to negate the resulting constant confusion—or the fact that it presented a security nightmare. It was one of the many places where people had once felt secure, and were all now too aware of an incipient vulnerability. International throngs trailed in and out of buildings, up and down escalators, on and off shuttle buses and stood in endless lines to move from point to point.

Alexander Bryant checked his single suitcase and worked his way to the VIP lounge. Within its tranquil comfort, a cold beer on the table before him, he popped opened his briefcase. On top lay the manila envelope James handed him as he dropped him off at the curb. He broke the seal and quickly scanned the contents: a few photographs and two sheets of closely printed type, along with a handwritten note directing that he destroy everything before disembarking in Cairo. Good old James. He never failed in his thoroughness, or attention to detail.

❖

Alexander leaned back to sip his beer, its temperature a clear indication that he'd been pegged as an American: unlike the Europeans, Americans always wanted their beer cold. An unconscious frown creased his brow as his thoughts jumped unbidden to another time when he was automatically served the same in this very lounge.

Anne had returned from the duty-free shops and laughed at his chagrin over being so easily categorized. Anne. How he missed that laugh. How he missed her—her everything. He missed the straw-pale, straight blonde hair framing her sweet, shy smile. She was the antithesis of his first wife, his college sweetheart. Guilt rippled up from his subconscious at the thought of Debbie, who personified the outgoing, take-charge sportswoman but never felt at ease as a military wife. Only after it was too late had he realized the depth of her resentment of the constant relocations. After the first few years, they'd spent more time apart than together. He unintentionally let that marriage just fade away, like a silent film in slow motion.

Alexander took a long pull at his beer, allowing himself the rare indulgence of his memories. After he somehow managed several lonely years as a single soldier, Anne came into his life like a cool, refreshing breeze. They stopped in this lounge on their way to France, after a year of marriage, at last taking the much-delayed honeymoon, a month of idyllic bliss. Wandering down narrow, cobble-stoned Paris streets, hand-in-hand, peering in shop windows. Dining in the moonlight overlooking the Seine. They shared stories and secrets from their pasts. She taught him how to laugh again, at life as well as himself. They drifted through the charming villages of the Loire Valley—the Garden of France—delighting in its world-renowned cuisine and old historic chateaux.

One night in a famous hotel where kings and queens once lived and loved, he and Anne made love with the doors of the balcony flung open in welcome to the incandescent light of a colossal moon. It was the first time in his entire life that he felt pure, all-consuming joy. The first time he opened himself to another, holding nothing back, exposing his very soul. It marked the beginning of a whole new world for him, and he found himself ecstatic in the wonder of it.

A week after their return home to the quaint, thatch-roofed house in fashionable Chiswick-by-the-Thames, Anne was diagnosed with breast cancer. She suffered stoically through an agonizing year of treatments, hope and uncertainty, only to surrender in the end. Her death left Alexander an empty shell. He managed to function—to walk and talk, to breathe. But he lost all feeling for life.

After a while, he resumed his professional activities as a "military advisor," pursuing them with a vengeance. Completely gone was any weight on his conscience or trace of remorse he may once have felt for the consequences of how he now made his extremely lucrative living. He took up a grueling schedule, with exhausting trips to far-flung places, often to war-torn countries where the constant presence of danger lay like a heavy, wet cloak. It put him in close contact with the "upper echelon" of societies in developing countries where the general populace, inevitably depressingly poor, was perpetually restless—if not in open revolt.

Women were attracted to Alexander Bryant, always had been. His overt masculinity and polite indifference drew them to him like freezing fingers to a flame. Frequently the daughters, sisters and sometimes wives of his clients made subtle—or not so subtle—advances that placed him in awkward situations. Like Imolee Ranakawa in Sri Lanka. A lifetime of military discipline enabled him to resist their charms, for the most part. When he did succumb, it was never more than a brief meeting of the flesh.

The loss of his beloved Anne had left a scar that repelled all feeling other than the occasional primal urge.

As a leggy flight attendant bent across Alexander to set a glass of neat scotch on the tray beside him, her ample breast brushed his arm. Mischief lifted the corners of her mouth, assuring him it was no mistake. Other passengers began to board and she grudgingly stepped aside.

Alexander looked up as a slender, auburn-haired woman came down the aisle. Their eyes met for one brief moment before she passed and made her way to her seat.

Julia stared at her reflection in the window as the plane pulled away from the gate and taxied to the queue for take-off. As soon as they were air-borne, she reclined her seat and closed her eyes.

CHAPTER 13

"We are meant to be together, Julia. It is fate, out of our hands. *Inshallah.*"

We create our own reality. As Milton wrote in *Paradise Lost*, *The mind can make a hell of heaven, a heaven of hell.* Somewhere along the way, Julia realized she'd lost the ability to comprehend her reality, to separate fact from fiction. Back in San Francisco, life loomed dull and flat. Without Mohamed, what would she do? When his proposal came, light came flashing brilliantly back into her world.

"Marry me, Julia. Be my wife."

Not one second of doubt crossed her mind. No thought of what it would mean to be the number-two wife of a devout Muslim, for there was no question that he would end his marriage to Shahida. Nor did she want him to. They'd been through all that and the subject need not even be mentioned. But how would it all work out? That they would resolve in Rome.

Rome. He always dreamed of going there, to see the great capital built by a civilization "almost" as great as that of his ancient ancestors. The would-be lovers made plans to meet there, to marry.

If anyone ever, in her wildest dreams, suggested to Julia that she would consent to—even consider the *thought* of—becoming the "second" wife of any man alive, she would have collapsed in hysterical laughter. Julia Grant: dedicated feminist and proponent of equal rights. But there it was. Mohamed was unquestionably the man with whom she wanted—needed—to spend the rest of her life, and this was the only way.

So be it.

The day drew near for departure and he hadn't told Shahida. Although Islam technically allowed him four wives, the practice was rare. He was obliged to inform her before he took a second wife and, of course, dreaded the thought of the unhappiness it would bring her. It was unthinkable to him that she might choose divorce, as their religion entitled her to do. She would do what was best for the children and, eventually, come to accept the arrangement. Once he had his visa and plane ticket, he told Julia, he would take Shahida away for a couple of days and they would talk it out. She must be told before he left for Rome.

Julia shared his anguish at the thought of this difficult responsibility but couldn't begin to contemplate the alternative: the alternative of giving him up.

Calls between the two countries were often problematic. When Julia phoned at the appointed time to finalize their plans, Mohamed's mobile phone rang endlessly without answer. Suppressing her irritation, she waited a few minutes and called again. And again. Finally he answered. In that one word of greeting, she heard his pain.

"I'm sorry, Julia, that I did not answer before. I could not bear the thought of telling you this bad news."

A long silence ensued as she heard him take a ragged breath.

"My visa has been denied."

Neither ever acknowledged the glaring unlikelihood of a thirty-something Arab male obtaining a visa to travel in the West. The Islamic

Jihad saw to that.

❖

Julia's head cracked against the window as the plane jolted and shuddered through the air.

"Sorry, ladies and gentlemen. We've hit a patch of unexpected turbulence. It may be a bit bumpy for a while. Please return to your seats and fasten your seatbelts," instructed the captain.

Julia gingerly massaged the sore spot on her temple as she shifted in her seat and resolutely returned to her painful memories. She remembered all too well how, following the failure of their marriage plans, she drifted into a kind of paralytic limbo. Mohamed said they should wait and take some time before making any more plans. She reluctantly agreed. What else could she do? She sensed something was happening, an almost imperceptible, indefinable shift in his devotion.

Tourism was down again and work slowed to barely a trickle. He spent more time at his prayers and at the mosque. Without his saying so, Julia thought she understood this subtle change of attitude. Oh, he still wanted her, desired her, needed her. That was plain enough. His ardor came loud and clear across the six-thousand miles that separated them. But his burgeoning religious fervor brought with it increase of another emotion: guilt. And she knew that the guilt, for him, was another torment.

Julia tried to go back to work but found herself unable to bear the thought of having to deal with other people's painful problems. After several months of endless soul-searching, she reached a decision: She would return to Egypt. Maybe they could start some kind of business together. Whatever happened would happen.

Mohamed was wary. "Things will not be easy for you here," he cautioned. His prophecy quickly came true. From the time of her arrival, circumstances contrived to keep them apart. Inexplicably, he was suddenly in great demand at work.

Julia did her best to fill the days. She visited and revisited the many museums of Cairo. She made a few friends among other English-speaking expatriates, like her, drawn to the island oasis of Zamalek. She volunteered at a shelter for Sudanese refugees. But after a few months of this, she descended into a valley of loneliness and discouragement. In the beginning, the days were not long enough to revel in the wonder of her new-found love. As reality crept across her heart, time stretched monotonously ahead.

And life in a patriarchal society quickly became an unanticipated irritant, like grains of desert sand trapped in a favorite shoe. Almost every encounter with an Arab male left her feeling uneasy, sometimes even sullied in a frustrating way. The endless demands from vendors selling unwanted wares and beggars with hands outstretched depressed and exhausted her compassion. With Mohamed by her side, she could've endured these ordeals.

But he was seldom by her side.

Darkness obscured the view from the airplane window as Julia absent-mindedly rubbed the sore spot on her forehead. Mohamed did, she forced herself to recall, hold himself just beyond reach. His religious beliefs made it impossible for him to be with her without terrible guilt. They both knew if they were alone together again he might succumb to the temptation. She suspected he might be hoping, in his passive way, that she would seduce him, thereby fulfilling his ardent desire while relieving him of the decision to sin. And she couldn't deny that she'd thought about it. That fantasy kept her company many a lonely night. But she fought against her own powerful desire. She refused to take that responsibility, knowing that he might come to resent her for it. Maybe even despise her.

Mohamed's conflict was palpable. He didn't know what to do. The truth was, even with his busy schedule, he could have found more time to spend with her. He admitted that he wanted to be with her—desperately so. He admitted that he lay awake at night beside his sleeping, faithful wife and imagined being with his angel.

Even after all these many months, Julia's body tensed at the memory of his tormented confessions. They sat, side-by-side, close enough to touch but holding back, on a bench in the garden of the Egyptian Museum. He told her how the thought of her soft, sweet-smelling skin, her exquisite firm breasts and moist inviting lips made him ache with need. How he found it impossible to even be near her without wanting to enter her inviting, loving, beautiful body…making her finally, utterly, forever his.

But he could not.

The miserable realization of the impracticality of having two wives only brought more guilt, and more pain. He could not have her—but he could not let her go.

One day, when he carved out some time for her, they sat on stools in their favorite coffee shop, crowded with local businessmen, sipping cappuccinos.

"My Mohamed, you know how much I love you, but I'm going back to California."

He stiffened as he turned to her. "Why, Julia? Why now? I know I haven't spent much time with you, but when things slow down we can be together. Then we will make our plans."

She steeled herself against her heart. "Well, my friend, I think the time has come for us to be honest, with ourselves and with each other. And to face the truth." Inhaling deeply, she delivered the carefully rehearsed words. "The truth is, there's no place in your life for me. Another truth is that I can't bear to be here without seeing you, without being with you." Not wanting to add more pressure to his already stressed state of mind, she reached down to touch his arm under the counter.

"We will always be friends. Always. And this doesn't mean that I won't come back. It doesn't even mean that we won't somehow find an answer. But I need to go home for a while, take care of some business and personal matters, and think things through." She couldn't keep from adding, "If you still want me, you know that I'm yours."

She smiled in spite of the tremendous effort it cost her to keep the tremor from her voice, and the tears from her eyes. "The decision is, as it has always been, yours. Tell me you still want me, as your wife, and I'll come back, in a heartbeat."

His dark eyes spoke eloquently of the deep and conflicting emotions tearing him apart. The clatter of the coffee shop faded from their collective consciousness, as they communicated wordlessly through their intoxicating bond.

A few days later they met in a small garden in Zamalek, along the river Nile. Courting couples sat, crooning softly, on benches facing the ever-flowing water. Julia looked down at her palm, at his parting gift: a golden charm, in the shape of an angel. Tears threatened to spoil her determined calm at the sight of the exquisite object that he could so ill-afford. It meant all the more for that.

They strolled toward the arched wrought-iron gate, both sensing that passing through the portal represented an inevitable change in their extraordinary, their unlikely, their bafflingly complex relationship.

When they parted, neither allowed a look back.

CHAPTER 14

"Good morning, ladies and gentlemen. We've begun our descent into Cairo. Estimated time of arrival is on schedule, at twelve-fifteen."

The captain's voice filtered through Julia's semi-consciousness. Even at this late hour, lights glittered on the land below as far as the eye could see. Once on the ground, after the tedious process of obtaining her visa, clearing customs and the passing of much *baksheesh*, she looked out over the throng for the driver sent to meet her. In the midst of the agitated crowd, she spied a man in a much-worn suit and tie holding up a sign with her name. At her approach, he lowered it to eagerly grab her hand.

"Welcome to Egypt, Madame Grant! Welcome! I am Hassan. Did you have a comfortable journey?" His every word, spoken in scrupulously precise English, reverberated with excitement, as if he'd waited his entire life for this moment.

"Yes, thank you, Hassan, but I'm very tired," she said, stifling a yawn.

"Of course, Madame. I shall take you promptly to the hotel." He commandeered both her bags and reached for the laptop case hanging on her shoulder.

"Thank you. I'll carry this one." She kept one hand firmly on the strap.

"You lead the way."

Sixteen million people lived in the chaos that comprised Cairo. Another four or five million converged on the city each day, culminating in a thriving, colorful, heaving, congested mass of humanity. It never ceased to amaze Julia what nocturnal people these were. Of course, activities were more pleasurable after the unrelenting sun went down. The populace certainly made the most of the cool evening and early morning hours.

Once in the back seat of the van, she opened her window to better absorb the endless layers of exotic Egyptian life. Driving through Cairo at midnight was always like rush hour in Manhattan. In that metropolis, however, people did generally observe the traffic lights. Here, they were completely ignored, with shouts, gestures and honking horns taking their place. Manhattan also tended to be relatively free of livestock, such as the abused little donkeys pulling carts overloaded with fresh corn or other produce, or the occasional surly camel being urged through the din.

The van crawled through the traffic and turned onto a street that ran alongside the edge of a market, or *suk*, pulsing with life. Next to the vendor in a ragged *galabeeya* selling oranges from his donkey cart stood a businessman in a Western suit, jabbering into his mobile phone. Short, wide women in voluminous black robes, their faces covered by the *burqa*, elbowed their way through the crowd. Young girls, arm in arm, heads modestly covered with the *hijab* while bodies appeared to be poured into skin-tight jeans, giggled at the boys looking their way. Two young men wielded razor-sharp knives, slicing away with practiced hands at a cone of *shawarma* as the spiral of sizzling meat sent a tantalizing aroma wafting through the air. Barefoot children darted in and out of it all, shouting and laughing.

Julia leaned her cheek against the window, allowing the sights, the sounds and the smells to infiltrate her every pore. *She was back.* For better or for worse, she was back.

❖

The child wailed, tears staining his smooth brown cheeks. Exasperated, Mohamed picked him up gently and held his face inches from his own.

"No, Yahiya. You cannot have my mobile phone. It is not a toy. And Papa has to go to work now." He carried the boy to the next room and sat him on the rug amongst a scattering of games. A fan in front of an open window stirred the hot, dry air. "Play with your own things and stop crying."

The front door slammed and a moment later a small woman, head and arms modestly covered, hurried into the room. "What's the matter now?" Shahida asked anxiously as she picked up the boy and cradled him in her arms.

"The matter is that he has turned into a little devil," Mohamed said evenly as he turned away. "He is spoiled and cries whenever he does not have his way."

Returning to the room he shared with his wife, he zipped up the suitcase lying open on the bed. She followed, still holding the now-silent child. "You are leaving?"

"Yes, it is time for me to go. I have left money for you on the dresser." He sighed as he turned to face her, placing a hand on the back of his son. "I know it is not enough. But it will have to do. For now."

She nodded wordlessly and watched him collect the rest of his things.

"I am to be well paid for this tour. It will hopefully bring what we need for the mortgage payment. *Inshallah,*" he added reverently.

"*Inshallah,*" echoed his wife.

He carried the worn suitcase down four flights of stairs and tossed it into the trunk of his car. As he drove away from the drab beige building, clustered together with countless similarly drab beige buildings in the beige desert, he thanked Allah for his many blessings. He had married a good woman, a good mother to their two young sons. The twenty-year-old car he drove had seen better days for sure, but he was among a small minority who were lucky enough to have a car at all. Three years ago they'd been most fortunate to have won the opportunity, by lottery, to purchase the flat.

The massive apartment complex, several miles to the east of Cairo, was originally built as part of a military compound. Its cheerless dwellings were not luxurious by any standards but provided the basic necessities. Mohamed hoped one day to be able to afford an air conditioner for their fifth-floor flat. With no elevator, lugging up groceries and young Yahiya was hard labor. Hardest on Shahida, who cooked and cleaned daily in the oppressive heat. She seldom complained, he thought gratefully, unlike many of the other wives who constantly wished and whined for new furniture, clothes and jewelry.

The same thoughts trudged through Mohamed's mind for the thousandth time: Good jobs were few. Leading tour groups was certainly beneath a man of his qualifications, but he should be thankful for work of any kind. The horrendous attacks around the world by the Islamic Jihad left a permanent blot on travel in the Middle East. Egyptian tourism never fully recovered, resulting in millions of people finding themselves out of work. He knew all this by heart, but it didn't make any of it any easier.

Mohamed now worried continuously about being able to make the mortgage payments. The tour companies used the drop in business as an excuse to cut the pay of all employees below the mandatory minimum wage. Permanently. The few tours he conducted dwindled considerably from the groups of thirty to forty or more of the past. This resulted in a drastic reduction in the gratuities that made up a large part of his income.

Some of the tour guides yielded to the temptation of selling jewelry and other trinkets to their groups to supplement their diminished income, but not Mohamed. He was a professional—an educated man, an accomplished Egyptologist. He would not demean himself in this way. Still, it was hard to spend so much time in the company of tourists who paid more for a gold chain than he needed to feed his family for a month.

Without Julia's help, he would've lost the flat. He tried not to think of what might have been if they'd managed to be together, to start some business together. He tried not to think of her at all. His thoughts transcended into a reminiscence of something unearthly—a goddess—far removed from his all too mortal reach.

CHAPTER 15

After surely what could have been no more than a few hours of restless sleep, Julia swung her legs to the floor to squint at the clock. Doubting the numbers there, she padded to the window and pushed open heavy drapes. Over the tops of dusty palm trees, the Pyramids of Giza stood out against a cloudless sky, drenched in sunlight. Damn. She'd overslept. Heart now pounding, she dialed the operator and asked to be connected with Mohamed's room.

What would he say? Would he be angry when he learned that she was his client from the New York publishing house and hadn't let him know? Although he did his best to be supportive during her long illness, they hadn't been in touch for almost two months now.

The phone rang and rang. She sighed, thinking how typical for him to not be there as planned. Nothing ever went as planned in Egypt. Finally, the operator came back on the line.

"Please leave a message for Mr. Zahar to meet his client in the lobby. He will know her when he sees her." Let him wonder about that.

Julia took her time in the shower, letting the powerful jets of water poke and prod her back to life. Then she dressed carefully in a white, long-sleeved, loose-fitting linen blouse and slacks. From past experience, she felt comfortable in this kind of attire as it covered her modestly, while allowing her to keep cool, more or less. Gathering purse, scarf and laptop case, she made her way to the opulent lobby.

Mena House, originally built as a hunting lodge on the very edge of the Great Pyramids, offered dramatic views of the last of the Ancient Wonders of the World. Julia stayed here on one of her previous trips, where she and Mohamed had spent long hours talking in the gardens, with the Sphinx raising its enigmatic head above mimosa trees in riotous red bloom.

Nostalgia enveloped her as she came down wide, thickly carpeted stairs to reach the marble floor and find him sitting in a corner chair. His dark, captivating eyes drew hers as she clung to the rail. Everyone and everything between them faded away.

She somehow managed to cross the room without bumping into anything. He stood, never taking his eyes from hers. "It is lovely to see you again, Madame Julia." He offered a hand. "I hope that you are well."

A rush of warmth surged through her limbs at the contact. Her other hand pleaded in vain to reach up to touch his cheek. "Thank you, Mohamed, I'm very well. I hope that you and your family are in good health."

He gestured to the opposite chair, and as they lowered themselves she said, "You don't seem surprised to see me." Her pulse raced. This was going to be more difficult than she thought.

"No, Julia, I am not surprised." He smiled. "You could say that I knew you would return. It was only a matter of time."

She let that sink in. Then they began to converse in the prescribed formality—for once, a welcome defense against emotion—and caught each other up on what was happening in their lives. Julia felt awkward as she spoke of her "book." She'd never lied to him before. This deception made her distinctly uncomfortable. At last they came to the issue around which their words had danced.

"It is wonderful to see you again," he said solemnly. "But, honestly Julia, we can be no more than friends."

This came as no big shock. Julia said it herself any number of times. It was for the best that he appeared to accept it. Finally. They both knew it was for the best. Even so, the words stung.

Attempting to lighten the moment, she produced a smile. "Of course, Mohamed, but you would never forgive me if I hired another guide. Besides, I must have the very best and there is no finer Egyptologist in all the land."

"Of course," he echoed, sitting up straight and thrusting out his chest in a parody of manful pride, causing them both to laugh.

Thank goodness. It would be all right after all. They would be able to keep things on a professional basis and still be friends—just good friends. Relief washed over her, at least on that score. Not far behind, apprehension crowded in to supersede all else: apprehension about her real purpose here.

Try as she might, Julia couldn't erase the image of Abeer Rashad from her mind. It haunted her, this image of a young woman, full of life, strangled in a poverty-stricken village, her body abandoned among the garbage and starving stray dogs.

And the morning papers were full of news of militant unrest throughout the region. Two days before, another explosion had ripped apart the lobby of a hotel in Sharm el-Sheikh, the Red Sea resort on the tip of the Sinai Peninsula. Western tourists no doubt were the targets in this luxury destination, but, as usual, it was mostly local workers who died in the blast. The entire region was like a ticking time-bomb. It made her want to scoop up Mohamed with his entire family and whisk them away to a safe place.

Sadly, she couldn't think of one.

❖

Revisiting the Giza Plateau took up several hours, after which Mohamed suggested lunch at one of the nearby restaurants they'd been to in the past. Julia's purse was typically stuffed with pens for the children and *baksheesh* for the peasant women. Weary from the exhausting process of distribution, but pleased to make the effort, she gladly agreed to a break.

They were shown to the rear of the large, open-air room, where Julia removed the laptop case from her aching shoulder. It grew heavier as the day progressed. Mohamed ordered a typical Egyptian meal, always a favorite of hers. Tender roast chicken, hummus, couscous, stuffed grape leaves and olives were spread before them along with a platter of flatbread fresh from the stone oven, visible in the adjacent courtyard. She eyed the offerings warily.

"You're not eating, Julia? Is something wrong, with you or with the food? You're not hungry?"

Her gaze remained fixed on the mouth-watering feast while she slowly shook her head. She'd skipped breakfast and her stomach complained audibly.

"No, no, nothing's wrong. Everything looks delicious. And I'm very hungry. It's only that," she hesitated, "well, to be honest, I'm thinking of how sick I was after my last trip. I almost died, Mohamed. Feeling awful for months on end, and not knowing the cause was the worst thing I've ever been through. The possibility of that happening again is a very scary thought."

He rolled his eyes. "Does this mean that you don't plan to eat at all on this trip? You're already much too thin, Julia. This is a respectable restaurant with a proper kitchen. Tourists eat here all the time. I know of no one who has died. As long as you stay away from the street food and drink only bottled water, everything will be fine. I will ensure that you always have a bottle of clean water." He tapped the one standing between them on the table.

Unable to resist any longer, she reached for a piece of the still-warm bread and dipped it into a bowl of spiced hummus. He smiled approvingly as she ate with something approaching her old gusto.

They visited the Citadel and the magnificent Muhammad Ali Mosque. Regarded as the "founder of modern Egypt," Muhammad Ali established in the nineteenth century a dynasty that would rule Egypt and Sudan for almost one hundred and fifty years. The impressive shrine, Julia thought, paid a fitting tribute.

Later in the day, they descended into the hub of central Cairo and went, as per her instructions, to a café she knew to have wireless internet. Julia chose one in Zamalek where she was a regular while staying previously on the island and was greeted like an old friend. The upscale neighborhood was home to a number of embassies and restaurants frequented by the international crowd. They drank cappuccinos while she sent the transmission and checked her email before crossing the river to the Egyptian Museum.

From the beginning, on that first fateful trip, this famous treasure trove had captivated Julia. The bulging collection of extraordinary ancient artifacts could fill ten museums. She never tired of visiting the lavish funerary gear of Tutankhamun, where the chariots, coffins and jewelry gleaming in gold opened a door to the past. Voices echoed from the flocks of tourists being herded through the cavernous building by guides reciting their lectures in too many languages to count. The richness of the collection almost made up for the lack of air conditioning, with windows open to the city's perpetual pollution and grime.

Julia felt the same thrill she did each time she beheld three-thousand-year-old wigs worn by priests to the gods of the ancients, tucked into unheralded corners and forgotten by the crowds. She tried not to dwell on the poor display cases bearing few labels to illuminate the past for the visitor. And, as her personal guide led her through the endless treasures, it was difficult to not be saddened by the sight of a deteriorating ostrich feather fan from the tomb of Tutankhamun; or the linen robes of a glorious ancient queen, with particles drifting away before her very eyes, simply turning into dust.

The orderly world of ancient Egypt departed long ago, thought Julia as she followed Mohamed out into the sunlight and down the museum steps. He left her sitting on a low, shaded stone wall in a familiar corner of the garden, away from the hustle and bustle of the crowd, while he went to get bottles of cold water.

She gazed up at the palm trees, standing regally like stoic sentinels, fronds rustling gently in the faint late-afternoon breeze. Beauty, she reflected as she often did, lies not in the eye of the beholder, but in the heart. One must open one's heart to beauty before the eyes can acknowledge it. Plenty of unfortunate people saw only the dark, ugly side of things. Without question, there was plenty of ugliness in the world to see. Sometimes it took immense effort to seek out beauty, in all its forms. These philosophical thoughts produced a deep sigh.

She turned her head to look around. This garden was always a favorite spot for her. Massive stone statuary from ancient Egypt's glory days surrounded a central pond of water lilies and blooming lotus. Peopled by tourists from countries around the globe and overseen by armed guards, it also provided a constant spectacle of human diversity.

Often, Julia felt irritation at the provocative way some of the tourists dressed and at their occasionally offensive behavior. When traveling in the Middle East, she always modified her dress, especially in public, to fit within the Islamic code of modesty and, quite frankly, to keep from drawing unwanted attention to herself.

The day was typically warm, and some of the women wore only skimpy bathing suit tops over short-shorts and men removed their shirts, leaving them bare-chested. They would undoubtedly take great offense if any of the "natives" made derogatory comments about their attire, or lack thereof. Small wonder the fundamentalists wanted these disrespectful "infidels" out of their lands. Not that there was any excuse for the excessive violent response.

What a mess people made of things.

The evidence before her of these endless societal contradictions sent Julia's thoughts down a familiar path. A region-wide revival of Islamic conservatism was currently taking place. Here in Egypt, women, more and more these days, covered their heads in the traditional *hijab*, appearing to move backwards in time. The women's rights movement, however, was still strong despite the deeply held belief that their lives could only be successful within the context of marriage and family. Again, Julia sighed. For a woman in business, it was always an uphill struggle.

A university professor of Middle Eastern history, a friend made during her long stay in Cairo the previous year, had illustrated the irony. One night, over endless glasses of minted tea in her home, she expounded on the subject as Julia sat fascinated.

"You see how we struggle for equality now. How we must be fierce in our demands for respect." The professor, black hair shining like jet to match the sparkle in her eye, held up a rigid finger to emphasize her point.

"And yet, Khadija, first wife of Mohammed the Prophet, was a successful business woman, a wealthy widow fifteen years his senior. He, an illiterate camel herder, entered her service at the age of twenty-five and she, as the story goes, became impressed by his prudence and integrity. Their relationship deepened into affection, then love. When no one believed in him, not even he himself, Khadija remained steadfast and consoling. Even through the long, bleak period of preparation before his ministry began."

With a knowing smile, the professor gave a philosophical shrug. "Without her love and support, who knows what might have been?

"Now, here are the fundamentalists extolling the ideology of their narrowed vision of our faith as 'the only true path,' attempting to banish women back into obscurity." Again she shrugged. "Go figure."

Julia shook her head, making a conscious effort to rein in her wandering thoughts and return to the garden scene. She felt tired and drained, having taken copious notes that day for her imaginary book. She glanced at her watch. *Where the hell was Mohamed?*

As she searched the milling crowd for sight of him, her attention was drawn to a tall, attractive man with close-cropped, silvered hair, standing only a few yards away. With an odd jolt of recognition, she remembered him from the plane. He was engaged in subdued conversation with another, younger man, probably Egyptian, dressed in casual Western clothes and carrying a worn leather bag over his shoulder. These days, Julia always nervously noted anyone here carrying a bag of any kind. At least inside the museum gates, she could feel sure it would've been cleared through security.

As she continued to watch, the two men shook hands, and the younger one walked away toward the exit. The tall one's gaze followed him until he reached the gate. Then the man from the plane glanced pointedly at Julia before turning to enter the museum. The quick tableau left an uneasy feeling in the pit of her stomach. It was near closing time, and she couldn't help but wonder why he would've left it this late.

Early next morning, Julia and Mohamed checked out of Mena House and headed for the airport. Once there, they plunged into the clamorous confusion to push their way through to security control. As she waited to place her bags on the ramp, Julia noticed a distinctive head above the crowd. Then her full attention was required for the tedious process of getting through clearance. After a long exchange, of which she understood little, and the passing of *baksheesh*, they proceeded to the departure gate.

There again was that familiar figure. The man from the plane sat reading a newspaper but looked up to nod as she passed.

"Is this some friend of yours, Julia?" Mohamed impulsively laid claim to her elbow and steered her firmly to a far corner.

"No. Just someone I've seen around." She found a seat and began to leaf through the latest issue of *Egypt Today*.

The plane arrived in Luxor, amazingly without delay, and they took a quick and relatively direct taxi ride to the boat. As usual, Mohamed greeted numerous friends and acquaintances along the way. They all, to a man, darted sly glances at Julia from the corners of their eyes, no doubt assuming the worst of her character and moral virtue. With head held high, refusing to acknowledge the affront, she nonetheless could not control the grinding of her teeth before she was at length shown to her cabin.

The *Isis* was a fine tourist craft, considerably more luxurious than many, certainly several steps up from the one of Julia's previous cruise. In addition to the tasteful decor, it boasted a hot tub by the swimming pool on the upper deck, an exercise room, and even a small token library.

"Nice to see taxpayer dollars at work," Julia said to herself as she surveyed the well-appointed cabin. On the other side of the king-sized bed, a comfortable seating area filled the space beneath a large picture window that framed the river and opposite bank. She collapsed in a plush chair and looked out at the ageless scene.

This was where the magic began. The mighty Nile—the heart and soul of Egypt. Some memorable prose from an old forgotten tome flowed through her mind.

"The same rhythms of rising sun and dispersing mist, of village and fields, the long shadows and rosy light of sunset were as old as ancient Egypt itself."

The Nile had always been an important travel corridor for Northern Africa. While the river itself flowed north, into the Mediterranean Sea, the prevailing winds blew to the south. For at least five thousand years, it was a perfect natural route, with boats drifting north on the strong, unfailing current and raising their sails for the return trip upriver. Historically, the Nile cruise was the only way to visit the temples and tombs located along its banks.

Julia rose to stand at the window, allowing herself the idle diversion of remembering lessons learned. It had also been said that Egypt was the gift of the Nile. The rich silt deposited along its banks over the centuries made possible a diverse and bountiful agriculture. Once the "breadbasket" of the Middle East, Egypt produced grain, corn and dates that fed the peoples of many lands. Today, the *fellahin* lived along the banks, much the same way they did thousands of years ago: in mudbrick houses, moving their crops on over-burdened little donkeys, and tending their fields with wooden plows pulled by water buffalo.

Across the river, on the opposite bank, Julia watched a young man, shirtless and knee-deep in mud, prodding one of the stoic water buffalo with a stick.

Julia took a brief rest and then joined Mohamed for a light lunch. They left the boat shortly thereafter and, according to her detailed schedule, took a taxi to Karnak Temple. Entering the site was an acute kind of anguish for them both. An ever-bright sun heated the massive stones around them, adding to the warmth of the day. They walked silently, side-by-side, through the delicately painted ancient columns in the Hypostyle Hall, flushed with the remembrance of their first time there together.

The strident voice of a German woman calling her husband's name mercifully relieved the bittersweet moment. This jarring note brought Julia back to the job at hand. She glanced around for sight of a man who might be Zed. Nothing. She shifted the copy of *Egypt Today* that she carried in one hand in order to remove a notebook from her purse. "Mohamed, tell me something about these hieroglyphs."

He also appeared grateful to be rescued from his memories and began to lecture. "You of course recall that Thebes was the city of Amun-Re, the sun god, one of the most ancient deities of Egypt."

The richness of his mellow voice inevitably began to weave its old spell. She bent her head and concentrated on note-taking. The task provided a much-needed shelter from her disquieting feelings as they moved through the temple. When they came to the sacred lake, he reminded her of how the temple priests had monitored the rise of the water in the spring of each year. It was connected underground with the nearby Nile, which brought the annual deposits of rich silt along its banks. The higher the water level, the better would be the crops, thus the heavier the taxes on the farmers.

"Very clever, those priests, as priests tended to be, certainly in matters of finance," added Mohamed with a touch of characteristic sarcasm.

Julia touched the back of a hand to her damp brow. "Let's go sit in the shade for a rest and have a cool drink."

He nodded and they strolled to the nearby café. Seated under the protection of the palm-frond awning, with fans turning lazily overhead, Julia removed the laptop and began to tap in the notes just taken.

Mohamed relaxed back in his chair, gazing out over the artificial lake. "Tell me, Julia, about this book of yours." He raised an eyebrow. "Am I in it?"

She smiled in spite of her anxiety. "Naturally. How could I write about Egypt and not include you? You're the star of the show—the Egyptologist Extraordinaire."

"Ha. I think you may be lying. Let me see." He reached for the computer.

"Later," she pronounced, quickly closing it. "You may read it after I've finished this chapter."

Their last stop before returning to the boat was the local internet café. Mohamed greeted the proprietor and carried on a lengthy and animated conversation while Julia completed her business. She also checked her own email while she was at it. At the top were two messages from Sarah. The first wished her a good time on her hiking trip. The next inquired where the heck she was.

If only she knew, thought Julia with no small amount of guilt. If only she knew.

A cadaverously thin man on crutches collapsed against the wall, releasing one hand to clutch at his throat. Unable to balance on his one remaining leg, he fell to the floor of the dirty, crowded ward. Throughout the room, other patients and hospital staff choked, retching as their eyes burned into blindness. Two figures in *galabeeyas*, their faces eerily covered with alien-like gas masks, watched from the doorway as everyone around them writhed in agony.

At length, they turned to weave their way down a hall littered with overturned trays and carts and more victims suffering the effects of the gas. Outside, they ducked into an alley near the seedy hospital in the slums of Mallawi and removed the masks.

"Excellent. They are completely incapacitated, as promised." Ahmed spoke in his customary cool, dispassionate voice, as if he were describing a scene in a play.

"But for how long?" The hideous features of his companion twisted with doubt.

"Supposedly at least two days. You will remain here. Report to me when they begin to recover."

"But what if..."

"Do not concern yourself. No one will suspect you. Why would a good Muslim intentionally poison his brothers?

CHAPTER 16

"Is this strictly necessary?" Alexander Bryant firmly suppressed his annoyance.

They sat on the terrace of The Old Winter Palace Hotel in Luxor, looking out over the throng on the street to the river and the Theban Mountains beyond. The famous old establishment would not have been his first choice, being overly grand for his taste. Built in 1886 to attract the nobility of Europe, the hotel had less the air of Egypt than that of a refuge of European flavor and Victorian charm. Howard Carter had been in residence when he made his world-awakening discovery of the tomb of Tutankhamun. The ultimate privilege of days gone by was to have one's private *dahabeeya*, or yacht, moored along the quayside, opposite the grand hotel.

But Jalal insisted when they met in Cairo that he stay here—probably because they had "connections" in place who could keep an eye on him. Alexander found himself situated in a spacious room in the original building, overlooking a newer addition, which boasted a colossal pool and health club. At least he'd be able to work out and do his laps. In any case, with this latest irritating development, he'd be here for only one night.

"I assure you, Commander Bryant," came the unruffled reply, "it is necessary. Your entry into the country will definitely have been noted by the authorities. They most probably will still be monitoring your movements. We cannot risk your being followed. This diversion may allay their fears." He shrugged with the hint of a smile. "It will also make it more difficult for them to keep you under surveillance."

Alexander doubted that, but he had no choice in the matter. If he hoped to make contact with the buyers, he had to play their game. As much as he wanted to expedite the process, he knew from past experience that these things couldn't be rushed.

"Understood. Give me the details."

After the man calling himself Jalal departed, Alexander strode in his purposeful way to the reception desk to inquire after his messages.

The eager face of the uniformed young man behind the desk broke into a euphoric smile. "Ah, yes, Mr. Bryant! A package came for you only moments ago!" This may well have been the highlight of his day. He addressed an even younger attendant, only a boy really, in rapid Arabic, and a heated debate ensued.

"*La! La!*" protested the boy, over and over, evidently denying any culpability in the disappearance of the alleged package. After a considerable amount of shuffling around under the desk, in the cabinets behind it and the office behind that, the package miraculously appeared.

Alexander couldn't help but grin as he handed over the expected gratuity for such a performance. With the heavy parcel tucked under his arm, he climbed the stairs to his room. Inside, he locked the door and slid the bolt firmly in place before laying the well-wrapped box on the bed. It was, as instructed, hand-delivered, with only his name and the hotel's address printed in large block letters. No return address.

He retrieved a pocket knife from inside his jacket and sliced open the wrappings to remove the contents, positioning them in a neat row on a table by the window.

Sunlight streamed through the glass onto the arsenal.

The weapons represented what he considered to be the best of what was available on the market today in small firearms. The .44 Remington Magnum provided maximum power at a level of recoil that could be handled by any shooter determined to cope with it—an extremely powerful gun. The M2 Mauser, the safest of the semi-automatic pistols, could be easily concealed. As requested, a shoulder holster for it was included. Lastly, the Beretta Px4 Storm offered excellent flexibility and versatility. It could be adapted to different hand-sizes, shooting styles and levels of concealment.

After methodically inspecting each weapon, he loaded the Mauser and slid it into the shoulder holster. His mouth stretched into a hard line as he put the other two revolvers in the safe inside the closet. Jalal was quite specific in Cairo about wanting only handguns. If James Marshall's information was accurate—and Alexander had no reason to believe otherwise—it didn't make sense: Why wouldn't they be interested in larger, more effective pieces and heavier artillery?

The only logical answer he could think of made him distinctly uneasy.

Dinner on these cruises customarily provided an agreeable occasion, presenting an interesting social dynamic. The various tour groups usually sat together, mixing and mingling among themselves, but maintaining their distance from others. These factions were much smaller than in the past, when they could number as many as sixty. On the *Isis*, Julia quickly identified three different groups. One, numbering about fifteen, all English-speaking, appeared to come from several different countries. Eight Italians made up another. The largest, and by far the most boisterous, were the Germans. Then there was the odd scattering of couples and individuals.

Julia speculated on who the other agent might be, ostensibly sent to keep an eye on her. That diverting thought brought a welcome crumb of comfort. She looked forward to spending the first evening on the boat with Mohamed, but he announced right before they went to their cabins to change that he'd made arrangements to go ashore to see a friend. She mocked herself for failing to remember not to count on things going as planned.

After pausing briefly in the doorway, she headed to an empty table at the back of the dining room. As she neared another table, occupied by an elderly couple, the slightly-built man rose, looking vaguely expectant.

"Good evening, my dear," chirped the woman, with a pleasant smile. "Are you dining alone? We'd be so pleased if you would care to join us."

Her male companion had already pulled out a third chair, so Julia returned the friendly greeting and slipped into it. Lord only knew when Mohamed would resurface, and their company might prove a pleasant diversion.

"I'm Henrietta Langley and this is my devoted spouse, Henry. We're from Indianapolis and tickled pink to be in this fascinating land." Her voice held a musical quality that soothed Julia's ear. And it was always nice to meet people who appreciated the finer aspects of Egypt instead of dwelling on the negatives—such as the rampant poverty and poor hygiene, as did many Western tourists, especially Americans.

"Julia Grant from San Francisco." She took Henrietta's frail hand. "Thanks for the invitation. My guide may join us later, if that's all right."

"If he's the charming young man we saw you with earlier today, we'd be delighted. Wouldn't we, Henry?" Henry bobbed a good-natured assent. "Everyone in our group has already been gossiping about you two." Henrietta frowned severely. "That's one of the reasons we chose to dine apart."

Julia decided on the spot that she liked Henrietta Langley. No beating around the bush for this old girl. She chuckled. "Don't worry, we're used to that. In this country, any man and woman who aren't married and traveling alone together are regarded as sinners—especially when it's an Egyptian man and a Western woman." She leaned closer with a stage-whisper of conspiracy, "We're all brazen and decadent infidels, you know."

The Langleys laughed and the next hour flew by, with Julia answering questions about her mythical book. As she elaborated on "her work," she became aware of, with some amazement, not only the genuine depth of her knowledge on the subject, but also their seemingly genuine appreciation of her personal point of view. She glanced down at the laptop. *Maybe I should write a book.*

As they lingered over dessert, Mohamed strolled in and Julia made polite introductions.

Henrietta batted eyelashes up at him. "Won't you join us, Mr. Zahar?"

"You are most kind, Madame Langley." He rewarded her with a captivating smile. "I've already eaten with friends, but perhaps you would all care to join me in the lounge for coffee or after-dinner drinks?"

They adjourned to the lounge, where Mohamed further entranced Henrietta with tales of Egyptian folklore and humorous incidents from past tours. He was at his very best in this kind of situation, and Julia enjoyed the entertaining performance along with her new-found friends. But she did wonder what could've happened to put him in such a good mood.

In the cool of the morning, Julia and Mohamed crossed the river to the west bank. Again, at first, it was hard on them both, but Julia steeled her nerve and fired question after question until he found his natural cadence and lectured with detached professionalism.

They returned to the Valley of the Kings, where he managed to gain entry to one of the rarely visited tombs: Tomb No.35. The wall paintings there were completely different from any others Julia had seen, with reliefs in stark black on white enhanced by no other color. The profound silence of the three-thousand-year-old burial chamber surrounded them like a time warp, as if they were the last people on earth.

Outside, the temperature had climbed quickly, and they stopped to sit on a bench beneath the shade of one of the open-air buildings roofed by palm fronds. Julia pulled out the laptop and tapped away at the keyboard. She made an emphatic point of needing to stick as closely as possible to the itinerary. This was not the way things normally worked here. Her feeble explanation of the fictional publisher's expectation of receiving her daily notes in a specific sequence sounded ridiculous, even to her ears.

Mohamed shook his head. "You Americans. Always so organized."

At the end of the day, they went back to the internet café. Julia checked her email and the *Events* page on the publisher's website, finding nothing unusual there.

So far, so good. But still no sign of Zed.

They returned to the boat near dusk. Mohamed stopped to *fhaddle* with one of the crew and Julia climbed the stairs alone to the upper deck. She leaned against the rail at the stern as the *Isis* smoothly left the bank and began to move against the current up the mighty river. This was always her favorite time of day here—the passing of light into dark, from warm sunshine to cool evening breeze. Lights began to twinkle in the distance and a symphony of crickets softly chirping along the bank lilted through the air. Magic.

Lost in the cocoon of the moment, Julia failed to hear the approach of the man who noiselessly appeared nearby. Mildly surprised to recognize him, she wondered when he'd come aboard.

"A lovely evening," murmured the man from the plane, from a few feet away along the rail.

They exchanged tentative smiles. "Yes. Beautiful," she replied, returning her gaze to the dreamlike scene sliding past.

He stood quietly for a few minutes more and then, without another word, turned and walked slowly away. *Definitely an American.* Curious, she thought after he left. Odd that a man like that would be on such a cruise alone. A new idea presented itself: Could he be the agent Bob Bronson mentioned at the last minute? Well, perhaps he isn't alone at all. He may have a companion tucked away somewhere.

It was interesting to conjecture all the same. And, for an indefinable reason, strangely unsettling.

Later that evening, Julia observed the tall American enter the dining room sans companionship. It *did* seem strange that such an attractive man would be traveling alone. His manner was cordial enough as he interacted with several people near the door, but a conspicuous air of reserve hovered over him—an intriguing aloofness.

"Ah, I see you are watching your friend," said Mohamed in a tone ripe with reproof. "When did he come aboard?"

"I have no idea. And he's not my friend." She replied more sharply than she'd intended, embarrassed that she'd evidently been staring. "I find him interesting, that's all. Interesting that he's traveling alone, I mean," she attempted to explain without offense.

She then asked herself why he should take offense. They were, after all, just friends. Her eyes narrowed as she added, "Not that there would be anything wrong with my finding him attractive—as a woman is attracted to a man, that is."

"Certainly not, Madame Grant, you and every other unattached female on this boat."

Of course. All her attention had been focused on the object of intrigue, so she'd failed to take note of the behavior of those around him. Even as they spoke, a gaunt looking woman sidled up next to him and, with lowered lashes, began to speak in dulcet tones. Unfortunately, Julia couldn't hear what was said, but his response must've been enough to embolden the woman to slide her arm in his and lead him proprietarily to a nearby table.

The Langleys, it seemed, were reclaimed by their group, and sat at a large table in the center of the room. Henrietta wiggled fingers as she caught Julia's eye, sending an unmistakable message of mischief.

"What about the other unattached man?"

"What? What other man?" Julia followed Mohamed's nod to a table in the opposite corner, where a bespectacled and tousled brown head bent over a book. The fork somehow made its way to the mouth without the aid of sight. Surely, she thought disparagingly, he wasn't her guardian agent. Julia rolled her eyes and shook her head, disdaining comment.

After dinner they wandered up to the deck and discovered the "odd couple" had preceded them. "Mutt and Jeff," Julia muttered to herself uncharitably.

The American gentleman gave every appearance of listening patiently to the monologue being delivered by the bird-like woman in a shrill English accent. A caricature of a woman of a certain age—a woman on the hunt—she plainly determined the man to be her prey and seemed to think that the best way to entice him was to inflict a never-ending litany of trivia. He nodded occasionally while no doubt wondering if there were any crocodiles left in the Nile.

"You've missed your chance, I'm afraid," Mohamed teased.

They turned away to stand with hands on the rail, looking down at the eternal flow of the river in the darkness.

Julia tossed her head, unable to keep the laughter from her voice. "Well, there's no accounting for taste. He's not my type anyway."

"I know, Julia. I know what your type is." His voice was low, seductive, as he slipped a surreptitious hand over hers.

A thrill ran through her veins as she looked down at his bronzed fingers covering hers on the rail.

"No. Don't start." She snatched her hand away, suddenly furious. "We've been through all this. We both know there's no future for us. Nothing. It would only bring more pain. Friends, remember? Just friends."

Eyes locked in combat, they struggled against all that lay behind them for an endless moment before she whispered a good night and retreated to the safety of her cabin.

She was sitting up in bed staring sightlessly at an open book when the phone rang.

"You are right, Julia, as always, you are right. We are friends and can be no more. I'm sorry. Please forgive me. It won't happen again."

"Thank you, Mohamed. Let's please, please be careful. We mustn't hurt each other any more than we already have." She spoke with more conviction than she felt. "Thank you for calling. Good night."

"Good night, Julia."

Several seconds of heavy silence passed before she heard the phone click.

The flame of anger flared in Julia's chest. She leapt to her feet and began to pace the cabin. A brush on the dresser caught her eye and she grabbed it up to assault her hair. Honestly, the man was impossible. This passive-aggressive crap was getting old. First he wanted her—then he didn't. He brought her to the brink of all-consuming passion—then backed away. He wanted to marry her—then he didn't. He wanted to be with her—then had no time.

It was always *Inshallah* this and *Inshallah* that. It was becoming seriously annoying. Oh, she'd been annoyed before, for sure, but always came around to be understanding and forgiving and supportive. Blah, blah, blah.

Honestly, things could *not* go on this way. He needed to make up his mind, one way or the other, once and for all and let her get on with her life. He really did.

CHAPTER 17

The boat stopped early next morning at Esna, one of the temples where the ancients had celebrated the goddess Isis. On her first visit, Julia found this site fascinating. This time around, her preoccupation made it impossible to take much notice of her surroundings. Surely Zed would make contact here. With her nerves tingling in anticipation, she felt a sense of hyper-awareness overshadowing everything else as they disembarked.

It was, for some inexplicable reason, unsettling to see the man now known as Alexander Bryant—Mohamed had done his homework during the night—heading away from the tour groups on his own. His erect figure exuded an unmistakable masculinity, even though in beige slacks and a tan jacket he looked more like a businessman than a tourist.

An American tourist who booked a one-way ticket to Aswan at the last minute, Mr. Bryant traveled alone. That was the extent of the report for now. But, Mohamed assured her, he intended to learn more.

Whatever, thought Julia with irritation, dismissing him from her thoughts. She had more important things to worry about.

Mohamed led the way through the horde of peddlers, beggars and barefoot children to a waiting taxi. Once inside, they drove straight to the Temple of Khnum and disembarked. As instructed, Julia carried the current copy of the magazine, *Egypt Today*, prominently in her right hand while steadying the laptop case on her left shoulder.

They progressed through the site with Mohamed delivering what would've no doubt been, under other circumstances, a fascinating lecture. Julia scratched erratic notes and tried not to be too obvious about searching the crowd for anyone who resembled an undercover agent. Not that she had the faintest idea what to look for. All she knew was that he was a "he," but no photograph was available.

As they came around a corner at the back of the temple, she caught a glimpse of Alexander Bryant, absorbed in conversation with two men who looked to be locals. Slowing her pace, she feigned attentiveness to whatever Mohamed was saying, while watching the unlikely trio from the corner of her eye.

Julia had no idea what prompted her suspicion, but after a few minutes she felt an unpleasant jolt, realizing that one of them was the same man she saw with Bryant in the museum garden in Cairo. Although he wore a *galabeeya* and sandals this time, it was definitely the same man. They remained intent on their discussion until a tour group came through a doorway right next to them. Startled, they looked up with what she could only call furtive glances, and moved to the end of the corridor to disappear.

"Julia, what's going on? You're not listening to me at all. I'm talking to the wall."

"Sorry. I'm sorry," she shrugged. "I have a headache." She hoped Mohamed hadn't noticed her scrutiny of Bryant. This was very odd.

They continued the tour through the temple, without any unusual encounters. Back at the main entrance, she asked Mohamed to get some cold drinks from the vendor in the outside courtyard. As he walked away, she leaned dispiritedly against a towering stone wall, glad for its shade. The temperature climbed as the day reached its height, spawning the threat of a real headache.

A barefoot beggar in a dirty robe sidled toward her with an outstretched grubby hand. *"Baksheesh?"* he croaked.

Julia gave him a distracted glance then looked down to reach into her purse for change as he came closer.

"You are not the one I expected. Where is Abeer?"

Her head jerked up, widened eyes on the grimy turban of the decrepit man's bent head. "She," Julia swallowed over the lump that sprang up in her throat, "she couldn't come. I'm her replacement. I'm to take the message."

The beggar darted a look around to ensure no one could overhear before snapping out, "I cannot give it here. We have a problem. That man, the tall one in the tan jacket, do you know who he is?"

Julia shook her head, knowing with a sinking feeling in the pit of her stomach exactly who he meant. She followed his glare to Alexander Bryant, standing alone near the high arch of the stone entryway. "No. I mean yes. Just someone from the boat. He came on board at the last minute."

"He is Alexander Bryant, an international arms dealer. He met here with the Brothers. It is a very bad situation. If they recognize me, I will die." He kept his head lowered at an angle, shielding his face, evidently well-disguised. "Who is the man with you? Another agent?"

In the outer courtyard, she saw Mohamed pay the vendor and start back with two bottles of water. "No, he's my guide. He knows nothing of this. What...what am I to do?"

"Return to the boat. I will try to meet you again in Edfu. Or send a message. It will come from Zed." He hissed as Mohamed closed the distance between them. "Quickly, give me *baksheesh.*"

"*Shukran,*" he gasped, thanking her like a tired old man, "*shukran,*" and scuttled away, bent from the waist.

Julia's heart thundered in her chest. As she turned back toward Mohamed, only a few feet away now, she froze at the sight of the brown-headed bookworm leaning against the temple wall nearby. He was not there before—she was certain of that. What if he was listening? How much might he have heard? Perhaps he was the other agent, after all. If what this man called Zed just told her about Alexander Bryant was true, it sure as hell wasn't him.

There was no convenient internet café at Esna, wireless or otherwise, Mohamed assured her, so they went directly back to the boat. Lunch would be served as the *Isis* slid back into the current, heading to Edfu. The dining room overflowed with people chattering about all they saw that morning.

Julia paused at the entrance to scan the crowd. A tall figure came up beside her and said, "Good afternoon, Ms. Grant. If you've not arranged to lunch with anyone, perhaps you'd care to join me?"

A rush of heat suffused her face; she clenched her hands to keep them from shaking. While wondering why this bothered her so much she said, "No, thank you, Mr. Bryant. I'd rather dine alone." The words chilled the air as she turned her back and stalked away. It didn't dawn on her until later that, although they hadn't been introduced, they'd addressed one another by name.

When she had more time to think about it, Julia's head spun with dire thoughts. This could be a decidedly nasty turn of events. "Almost no danger" suddenly could turn into what might be a well-camouflaged patch of deadly quicksand. What in the world was she supposed to do now? She had no ready means of communication with Brad, to ask for guidance. The other agent, whoever it might be, hadn't revealed his—or her—identity. What was the significance of an arms dealer in all this? What should she do about it, if anything?

Stick to the plan, Bob had instructed her.

Okay, she would stick to the plan. But she didn't like this, not one bit. And she felt an illogically sour indignation at the odious occupation of the misleadingly attractive Mr. Bryant. Anger welled up inside at the thought of his earning a living, no doubt a princely one, trading on the oppression and destruction of his fellow human beings. Unreasonably, she felt betrayed. This made her angrier still.

Mohamed failed to show for lunch. It was a solitary and unsatisfactory meal, every bite sticking in her throat. After only a token attempt at getting anything down, she left the noisy room. She found him on the upper deck and slumped into a chair next to his. Mohamed regarded her thoughtfully.

"Julia, what's going on? What's wrong? I know you and something is not right."

"I told you," she said with a long, tired sigh, "I have a headache, that's all." With lowered eyes, afraid he might read the muddled emotions swirling behind them, she said, "I think I'll go to my cabin and rest for a while." She fled the deck and his keen scrutiny.

Much too agitated for the confines of her cabin, Julia instead sought refuge in the library. The limited offerings there would be predictably eclectic, but she always found it soothing to touch book bindings as she read the titles. Entering the minuscule space, she executed several deep breaths and began to feel slightly more relaxed. When the door swung open a few minutes later, it was to admit the bookworm, heavy glasses sliding down his nose.

A self-conscious smile turned up the corners of his mouth as he said, "Hullo. I'm Peter Werner." He held out a hesitant hand.

In such close proximity, Julia found him much more imposing than she'd realized. The rolled up sleeves of his wrinkled cotton shirt exposed muscular forearms. She shook his hand, introducing herself, as her eyes traveled up to his well-tanned face. An expression of unmistakable speculation smoldered behind the heavy lenses. She waited with bated breath for him to reveal himself.

The question hovered on her lips. She almost blurted out the disclosure of the presence of an arms dealer on the cruise, but a thread of belated caution held her back. What if he wasn't who she thought he was? Reeling into further confusion, she mumbled a lame excuse of fatigue and retreated once again, this time heading straight for the sanctity of her cabin.

As she fled down the passageway, she glanced through the glass door to the exercise room. Henrietta Langley marched along on the treadmill while Henry pumped impressive iron. Those two, she thought, smiling in spite of her troubled mind. No wonder they gave the impression of having discovered the fountain of youth.

Alexander closed the door to his cabin and shrugged off his jacket, tossing it across a chair by the open window. First unstrapping the shoulder holster with the small but deadly-accurate Mauser, he placed it in the safe and reset the combination. Not that he had any false sense of security that a child couldn't open it if so inclined. It would at least be out of sight should the steward or anyone else wander in while he was there. At all other times, he wore it snugly under his arm.

In the bathroom, he turned on the faucet and methodically washed his hands. While drying them, he studied his reflection in the mirror. What was it? He asked himself. What did Julia Grant see there now that she found so repugnant? He overheard one of the other passengers mention her name. At first she thought him interesting; he could tell. Most women did. But her attitude at lunch was cold and aloof—downright rude, as a matter of fact. It was strange. When had the change taken place? They exchanged brief pleasantries in passing at breakfast only that morning. Then the icy brush off.

Not that it mattered. She was beautiful, of course, and intelligent, he could tell. But there was definitely something between her and her Egyptian companion, her "guide." They did have separate cabins and their behavior in public was proper enough, but Alexander sensed that something—something deep and personal—lay between them. This bothered him. Like a burr under the saddle. And it bothered him that it bothered him.

He shook his head as if to clear it as he opened the closet to remove a clean shirt. Ms. Grant was not his concern, other than that everything concerned him when on this kind of operation. He missed very little of what transpired around him. The most seemingly insignificant factor might mean the difference between success and failure, even life and death.

The situation here was definitely tense. Tense and treacherous. Jalal assured him he would be able to make the introduction to the customer. The clever idea for Alexander to travel by boat to Aswan theoretically made it more difficult for the Egyptian security forces to monitor the necessary preliminary meetings at stops along the way. If Alexander passed muster, the important meeting would take place in Aswan.

He met with Jalal twice and was introduced to another of the Brothers at Esna. This was all well and fine, but patience did not number among Alexander Bryant's virtues. Slowly cruising up the Nile, however pleasing it might be under other circumstances, was decidedly irritating.

And now this annoying distraction of Julia Grant. The nature of the relationship between her and her guide was none of his concern. But he couldn't seem to banish her from his thoughts.

CHAPTER 18

After-dinner festivities were planned in the lounge that evening. Julia put the finishing touches on her makeup, inspecting her reflection closely in the mirror. For some curious reason, the sleeplessness and stress didn't show in her face. This was difficult to understand. By this time, she expected to see the portrait of a deteriorating Dorian Gray.

"Ah well, *gather ye rosebuds while ye may,*" she whispered, laying a gold silk chiffon scarf over her neatly piled auburn hair. There was to be dancing after dinner and, to be a good sport, she dressed up for the occasion. Certainly not because she wanted to impress anyone. Certainly not.

The dining room, near full, hummed with animated conversation as she entered, pausing as she'd become accustomed, to survey the scene. Henrietta, seated with Henry at a table of their own, waved her over to join them. As Mohamed had told her earlier he planned to dine with the other guides on the boat that night, she gratefully sank into the chair offered by the always gallant Henry. Evidently they'd once again escaped their group and she was glad of it. Julia thoroughly enjoyed their spirited company, even more so when they discovered a mutual passion for bird watching.

"Did you see the white storks along the bank as we left Esna?" Henry asked with contagious enthusiasm.

"Oh, yes, they were beautiful, weren't they? And such a large flock, a spectacular sight."

"Ooooo, there's that divine man," cut in Henrietta with more than a hint of awe. "You two would make such a lovely couple," she added as she waved to Alexander. "If you could pry him away from the fading English rose, that is. Did you see the ridiculous way she behaved over the stuffed T-shirts?"

Members of the crew had entered several passengers' cabins the previous evening and stuffed T-shirts with pillows, accessorizing them with hats and sunglasses of the occupants. Fiona MacDonald, it seemed, took a harmless prank, meant as an innocent joke in the spirit of fun, and turned it into the crime of the century, filing a formal complaint with the manager. Disapproval and disdain clouded Henrietta's normally sweet features.

Julia stiffened at the sight of the man she now knew to be nothing more than a mercenary dealer in weapons of destruction, while suppressing the sarcastic comment on the tip of her tongue. He reached the table and sat with irksome self-confidence in a chair next to hers. At such close quarters she was uncomfortably aware of his solid physique and calculating eyes. Were they green or gray? In this light they looked dark gray—gun-metal gray, she thought dismally. Aware that, under the circumstances, her stare was overly severe, she turned away without a word.

"Hello, Alex. How did you enjoy the sites today?" asked Henry, seemingly unaware of the sudden chill in the air.

"Fascinating." Leaning forward, Alex added, "Did you see the magnificent white storks as we left Esna? I thought of you at once,

Henrietta."

Startled by this, Julia's head swiveled back in his direction. The remark seemed genuine enough. Well, what of it? Lots of despots and barbarians appreciated the beauty of nature.

"Oh, Alex," Henrietta simpered. "Quite a marvel, weren't they?"

"So, Alex, what brings you on a Nile cruise all on your own?"

He focused a clear, disconcerting look on Julia as he politely answered her unaccountably sharp question. "It was a last minute thing. A gift from a friend who booked the trip a while ago and was called away on business." The lines at the corners of his eyes crinkled pleasingly. "Something I'd always wanted to do, actually. Egyptology is a long-time hobby of mine."

Julia's brows shot up. That didn't square with what Mohamed told her. So he was a liar, too. She stewed in silence, listening with reluctant curiosity as the others discussed the temples in Luxor and Esna. His knowledge on the subject proved annoyingly correct.

"Julia's writing a book on Egypt," announced Henrietta, with a touching pride.

"Ah," said Alexander as he glanced down at the computer case that was Julia's constant companion.

The conversation flowed along on subjects of mutual interest. In spite of her prejudice, Julia increasingly found this new adversary to be an informed, engrossing conversationalist. He was impressively well-versed on the sites they'd visited thus far, but neither boastful nor offensive, as many tourists tended to be. He demonstrated respect for the local people and an appreciation of the hardships they faced. When talk naturally turned to politics and world affairs, Julia felt considerable surprise at his views along those lines.

"The Middle East is what it is today both because, after World War I, the European powers deliberately undertook to re-shape it for their own purposes, and because Britain and France failed to ensure that the states and political systems they established achieved any kind of stability."

Julia fiddled with her fork as the Langleys looked grave.

"Britain's politics were particularly incoherent and devious, flagrantly contradicting their supposed principle of self-determination with the politics they practiced. They simultaneously and incomprehensibly promised Palestine to both the Zionists and the Arabs. Today the world is paying for that inconsistency."

If he meant what he said, this was another unsettling aspect of Mr. Bryant. Julia's resentment for the way he earned his living was temporarily forgotten as she became immersed in the discussion of issues so close to her heart. She found herself genuinely enjoying his unexpectedly cultured company.

The hawk and the dove regarded one another with a tentative esteem.

The thought of Mohamed's absence, after those first few tense moments, did not enter her mind. In fact, it was a distinct relief to be free for a time of the emotional conflict his presence created. Thus far, the evening was most unpredictably pleasant. Until, as they lingered over coffee and dessert, an ominous sound burst across the now near-empty dining room.

"Oh, dear," murmured Henrietta, "it's the faded rose."

Alex tore his eyes from Julia's face, where they spent a great deal of time, and raised them to find Fiona McDonald bearing down on the group.

"Hello, darling people," she sang out. Alex automatically rose to pull out the chair on his other side, into which she fluttered. "The gala is well under way. Aren't you coming up?" Although presumably addressing the table at large, her beady black eyes affixed hungrily on her prey. Julia's fleeting thought that at least she could dismiss this creature as the other agent was displaced when she noted for the first time that her teeth were rather large, vaguely reminiscent of those of a horse.

"We were having an exceedingly serious conversation on the subject regarding the latest revelations on the mistreatment of detainees in the War on Terror," said Henry in his mild-mannered way.

Before anyone else could add to that, Fiona scoffed, "Well, as far as I'm concerned the authorities can do whatever they like. Torture and death are too good for them. After all, they're criminals of the highest order."

Julia broke the awkward silence with an obvious attempt at self-control. "Actually, Fiona, no one knows whether those being held are guilty or not. None of them have been charged with anything or been given the benefit of legal council or a fair trial in a court of law."

"Oh, *of course*, Julia," snorted Fiona. "I've heard that you come from San Francisco. You must be one of those left-wing liberals we hear about. Do you march along in protest at the peace rallies we see on the news?" She tittered derisively, as if she found the idea utterly ridiculous, which she clearly did.

A steadily rising heat colored Julia's expressive face, distaste clearly written across it. She carefully placed both hands on the edge of the table to steady her temper.

"As a matter of fact, I *have* marched in peace protests—many times for many years. Peace has always seemed to me a worthwhile goal." Although her voice remained steady, her eyes bore into those of the other woman with intense dislike.

"And as for the mistreatment of detainees: I believe in the Rule of Law. Without rules and laws, we're no better than savages living in anarchy. It's counterproductive for our governments to flout the rules of the Geneva Convention. 'Do as I say, not as I do' has never proved an effective tactic in establishing cooperation or respect. By lowering ourselves to the abusive practices of our enemies, we compromise our integrity and the very values we strive to protect. Ignoble means are seldom justified by a noble end.'"

All eyes riveted on Julia's flushed face in the ringing silence that followed her passionate words.

The dark, predatory beads shifted to Alexander, and Fiona sniffed with contempt. "Yes, well, think what you will, but pacifism had no place in two World Wars and it has no place in this one."

It would have been difficult for the thickest skin not to feel the barbs of animosity projected towards her from all sides, but Fiona appeared totally oblivious as she stood. "Now, come along, everyone, let's not be depressing. It's time to dance!" With that pronouncement, she gave Alex's bicep a squeeze and trotted from the room.

Henrietta broke the stunned silence as she pushed back her chair. "Thank you, Julia, dear. I thought you put that rather well." She tucked her arm into that of the dove and led her to the door.

Revelry in the lounge was in full swing. A fresh air of solidarity surrounded the foursome as they found an unoccupied table near a window. Alexander pointed Julia to an armchair before lowering himself next to it. He unfastened the button of his dinner jacket and stretched out powerful legs. Julia knew they were powerful because she'd watched him effortlessly run up three flights of stairs that morning after breakfast.

The Arabic musicians vigorously performed an improvisation. Drums and guitars undulated, rising and falling hypnotically while, according to tradition, the audience clapped and sang along. When the live music ended to thunderous applause, a DJ took over, and the air reverberated with western sounds of the Big Band era.

"Hey, honey," Henry exclaimed, "listen, they're playing our song."

"Oh, let's all dance!" enthused his sprightly bride.

The couple bounced to their feet, looking expectantly at their companions, who evidently had no choice but to join them. Julia glanced nervously over Alex's shoulder at the laptop beside her chair as he took her into his arms. She felt stiff and ill at ease at first, but in no time his skill and innate command had her spinning and whirling. When a slow tune followed the energetic one, without asking permission, he pulled her closer and continued to guide her smoothly around the floor. The heat from his rock-hard body and clean, masculine scent produced a decidedly disconcerting effect.

"How's the book coming along?"

Julia went blank. Book? What book? Then she remembered. "Oh, fine, fine," she said lamely, flustered by how good it felt to have his arms wrapped around her. "I sincerely doubt that it will ever make the best-seller list, though."

"Is that bad? As long as you're enjoying the process, that's the main thing."

She was definitely beginning to enjoy this process, she thought with a shadow of guilt. Until, as he adeptly turned to avoid another couple, she caught sight of a familiar figure leaning against a far wall.

With arms folded across his chest, Mohamed followed the dancing couple's every move, his dark eyes glinting in an inscrutable sphinx-like mask.

CHAPTER 19

While the boat prepared to dock at Edfu, a cluster of passengers watched from the upper deck the jumble of activity pulsing along the river bank. Julia, leaning against the rail, was very much aware of Alexander a few yards away. Conflicting emotions from the previous evening were supplanted by sobering thoughts of her impending rendezvous with the undercover agent, Zed.

Mohamed joined her as the boat bumped into place. "Let's wait for the others to disembark before going ashore." He made no reference to last night's activities in the lounge. After all, what could he say?

"You're still looking rather pale, Julia. Do you feel all right?

She produced a brilliant smile. "Yes, thank you, my friend. I'm tired, that's all. You know how I sometimes find it difficult to sleep on these trips."

Yes, she fretted—difficult when images of young, strangled women and men toting weapons bent on Jihad invade my dreams. Looking out over the rail, she observed Alexander, in his tan jacket, moving down the gangway and stepping lightly onto shore. He advanced upon a row of shabby horse-drawn carriages lined up along the street and decisively chose one in the center of the line, swinging himself up into the seat. The driver flicked his whip and the horse plodded away from the curb. Off to do his part for the destruction of the world, no doubt, thought Julia dismally.

"He is not what he seems." Mohamed spoke in a low, dispassionate voice; yet his carefully arranged features failed to cover his dislike.

Taken aback by this astute observation, she turned to face his rigid profile. "What do you mean?"

"Think, Julia: A man like him, traveling alone on a cruise. Booked at the last minute. And he carries a gun."

"*What?* How do you know that?"

Looking particularly enigmatic, he slowly shook his head. "There are no secrets on a boat, Julia. You should know this. Come, we must go if we are to maintain your precious itinerary."

She followed him to the stairs as a ferocious premonition gnawed away at her insides. Being an arms dealer was one thing. Carrying a gun, strictly illegal and incredibly dangerous in this country, was something else altogether. Why? Why would he risk it?

They worked their way through the Temple of Horus, adhering to her "precious itinerary." Julia made a brave attempt at normalcy, but the monumental effort took its toll. Her renewed indignation towards Alexander Bryant at least provided ammunition to write off the disquieting and unwelcome attraction of the night before. It also helped to keep romantic thoughts of Mohamed at bay. She would now find it difficult to even look at the one man without revealing her contempt, while concern for the safety of the other had suddenly eclipsed all else. Whatever happened, she could not—under any circumstances—allow any harm to come to Mohamed.

Throughout the excursion around the site, she saw no sign of Alexander—or of Zed. Instead, everywhere she turned, Julia irrationally felt the eyes of the statues of the falcon god Horus watching, always watching. As they wandered back through the street market she caught a glimpse of the unmistakable tan jacket at the end of a crowded alley. Oh, no, he's definitely not what he seems. And he's up to no damn good, she thought bitterly.

Failure to make contact with Zed in Edfu left Julia depressed and drooping with fatigue. Where was he? Had something happened to him? She wanted this to be over. To get the damn message, pass it on and sleep for a week. If she failed in this, she knew, it would always haunt her. She hated to fail—at anything—especially something where the stakes might be so awfully high.

Back on the boat, she trudged alone to the upper deck and sank into a lounge chair facing downstream. The slow churning of the engine and the tranquility of the river lulled her into a state of peaceful drowsiness. She noticed a brown head bent over a book a few chairs away. The bookworm's presence provided an additional sense of security and, covering her face with her wide-brimmed hat, Julia drifted into exhausted sleep.

An hour later she gradually regained consciousness, with a pleasant sense of calm. A luxurious stretch brought her to her feet to stretch again. The clock over the bar told her there was time enough to bathe and change before lunch. A cool shower completed the restoration. In a much more positive frame of mind, she pulled on a clean pair of slacks, a big, white cotton shirt and headed for the dining room feeling better than she'd felt in days.

After a leisurely lunch the boat stopped at Kom Ombo. Zed had to make contact here. It was the last stop before Aswan. She adjusted the laptop case on her shoulder and clutched the now-worn copy of her magazine as they moved through the ancient ruins. With renewed anxiety, she approached every beggar, handing out *baksheesh* generously, expecting a repeat of the past performance.

No contact came. Back at the entrance to the site, she slumped down on a stone wall at the edge of the suk, fanning herself with the ragged magazine. The laptop weighed a ton and the strap dug into the groove it had carved into her tired shoulder. Mohamed had stopped several yards back to speak with a couple of the guides. As usual, she found herself promptly surrounded by barefoot, dark-eyed children, and she smiled while distributing pens. When the supply ran out, she waved them away and morosely contemplated her failure.

"Blankets, madame, I have good blankets," whined a vendor from the stall next to the wall where she sat.

"*La shukran,*" she thanked him, declining indifferently, and pointedly turned to look the other away.

The heavily bearded man in robe and turban edged closer, holding up a lovely green wool blanket that shaded his face from the crowd.

"Come," he said in a low urgent voice. "We haven't much time."

Adrenaline flooded her bloodstream like a raging torrent as she rose and followed him to the stall.

"Look at the blankets as I hold them up. Choose one. I'll wrap the information in it," Zed instructed, smiling through falsely blackened teeth as he offered a blanket of royal blue.

"Since preparing the message, I have learned more. It is very bad. And I think I may be suspected. You must get word to the agency right away."

His rapid speech raised the hair on Julia's arms in alarm.

"The new information is written by hand. I did not have time to put it in the final code. I will pass it to you with your change."

She nodded mutely as he held up another blanket, this one a bright scarlet. She pointed to it and watched him adeptly fold it around a small, square envelope. Digging in her purse, Julia removed two one-hundred-pound Egyptian notes and held them out to him. When he gave her the change, a white piece of paper, folded several times, lay between the bills. She stuffed the money in her purse and jerked the zipper closed. When he passed her the blanket, she saw that his hands were shaking.

"What can I do to help you?"

"Nothing. Just go." He turned, grabbing up a worn, brown cloth bag in one fluid movement and raised a flap at the back of the stall. He paused only to look from one side to the other and, without so much as a backwards glance, he disappeared. The flap fell behind him, leaving a startling void.

Stunned, Julia stood perfectly still as several seconds ticked by. When she turned, the surrounding scene seemed surreal. Unchanged, tourists continued to haggle with vendors. Mohamed still *fhaddled* with the guides. The entire transaction took no more than a minute or two.

She stumbled back to the wall and sat holding the blanket in her lap, stroking it with a sweaty palm. The pounding in her ears intensified the elation. Thank goodness! She had the message, and the ordeal would soon be over. All she had to do now was transmit it tomorrow in Aswan and the mission would be complete. Relief washed over her like a cool tropical wave.

Ahmed squatted on his heels near the top of the steps leading up to the small temple to Sobek, the crocodile god. Tourists never seemed to tire of viewing the pathetic reptile mummies within the temple. He looked away, careful not to make eye contact with anyone, lest his contempt be observed.

It was risky for him to be here. But he felt it necessary to familiarize himself with Alexander Bryant's appearance, as well as observe his movements. Thus far he'd seen nothing to cause alarm. At least not as far as Bryant was concerned. Something else caught his attention when he first arrived on the site. It nagged at the back of his mind the whole time he followed Bryant, until the truth finally dawned.

His present location provided a clear view of both Bryant, who had stopped near the edge of the ruins, and the last stall of the *suk*. His eyes narrowed with a cold suspicion, focusing on the merchant. What was Gamal doing here, in disguise, selling blankets to tourists? For he was certain that it was Gamal, or the man he knew as such—one of the Brothers. Supposedly, he'd gone ahead to Aswan to assist in making arrangements for the meeting with the arms dealer. Now, here he was, posing as a peddler. What could he be up to?

Whatever it was, it spelled trouble—not only for the operation—but for Gamal.

Ahmed could not help but notice the tall, striking woman seated near the stall as she gave handouts to the children. At least she was giving and not taking, or trying to bargain down to the bone, he thought scornfully.

He continued to watch surreptitiously and was intrigued to see Gamal approach her, invite her into the stall. The encounter appeared innocent enough. It could be a legitimate transaction. But Ahmed learned long ago that if something seemed too coincidental, it probably was not coincidence at all. Gamal approached the woman. She did not wander into the stall. He seemed jittery and after selling her the blanket, quickly disappeared. With a last hard look at the woman, committing her distinctive features to memory, Ahmed rose with ease and moved back in the direction of the main temple.

Once breath returned and her pulse slowed, Julia came to her feet and started toward Mohamed and his friends. Before she got halfway there, a loud noise exploded from the back of the ruins. It sounded like a gunshot. The men with Mohamed spoke sharply in Arabic and they all ran in the direction of the disturbance. A sick, new panic engulfed her and Julia ran after them with mounting fear crawling up her spine.

A small crowd clustered in an open space behind the temple columns, their voices raised in agitation as they gesticulated at something on the ground. She pushed her way through the men and froze.

Zed lay in the dirt, in a pool of spreading blood, eyes open, staring sightlessly into the cloudless blue sky. Julia stood motionless while the crowd around her grew, even as the guides attempted to wave them away. A vise-like grip encircled her arm and roughly pulled her back.

"We must leave. *Now*," said Mohamed.

Tearing her stupefied gaze from the grisly scene, Julia turned into the menacing stare of Alexander Bryant. Their eyes locked for an electrifying second before Mohamed yanked her down the hill.

CHAPTER 20

Ahmed Abdel Latif rose from *Asr*, the afternoon prayer, and wordlessly left the mudbrick shack in the center of the field of corn. He moved gracefully through the high stalks, their golden silk glistening in the sun. His long legs took him down to the river, where he climbed into a waiting boat, no more than ten feet long. Ahmed signaled his command with a single nod to the young man at the stern. The purring outboard motor revved into a roar and the boat pulled away from the muddy bank to head upstream.

Ahmed sat up straight, proud and tall, on the cracked wooden bench, with the wind at his broad-shouldered back. He half-closed his eyes against the bright light—those lushly fringed, dark, unreadable eyes of the Middle East. A hawk-like nose dominated sharply-cut features artfully arranged on his bronzed skin. Generally, his demeanor was measured and resolute, his speech marked with an unruffled deliberation so that one could not doubt the deeply-held conviction of his words—whatever they might be. The expression on the face of the younger man steering the boat left no doubt that he held his Brother in considerable awe.

From an affluent Jordanian family, his early life one of privilege, Ahmed had benefited from an expensive education that included four years at university in London. The journey from that advantaged upbringing to his present position of leadership in the Mujahideen took place over a period of several years. His commitment was now absolute to the cause of putting a stop to the encroachment of Zionism and to the crusade of the Western Imperialists.

The small boat advanced steadily against the current, passing other larger crafts chugging along at a more leisurely pace. It was imperative that they arrive in Aswan before the *Isis*. Plans must be changed. And arrangements must be made for dealing with the woman. His Brothers had been unable to tell him what her role might be, but he knew— without doubt—that she was somehow involved. They would take advantage of this opportunity, rather than let her disrupt their carefully laid plans.

His full lips stretched in a smile as his computer-like mind reviewed the intricate details of the scheme, with its innumerable contingencies and deceptions. No, no one could spoil this foolproof plan. In less than two weeks time, the world would cower and bow to the will of almighty Allah.

It took quite a while before the local police allowed the *Isis* to continue on her journey. They questioned the guides endlessly, who had first appeared at the scene of the crime. Praise Allah, they all had alibis. The passengers still ashore were all shepherded into the lounge and told to remain there until further notice.

Julia sat alone in a corner, looking down at the red blanket in her lap and seeing the pool of blood. An unpleasant taste emerged on her tongue and would not go away. This was inconceivable—beyond belief. Zed was dead. Murdered. Only moments after passing the message. What consequences would this have for the mission? What peril did it mean for her? Because, of course, she thought miserably, anyone could've seen her with him.

Would the killer—or killers—find anything suspicious in the purchasing of a blanket?

She shivered in spite of the heat and tried to suppress the fear clawing at her throat as she waited to be released to go to her cabin, where she could examine the messages. She fought an almost overwhelming urge to look at the handwritten note stuffed in her purse. As much as she craved to do it, it was out of the question here in the lounge. What did they contain—these messages that may have cost the lives of two people?

Two that she knew of: Abeer and Zed. There might be more.

Alexander looked restlessly out one of the portholes, too agitated to sit. What a damned unfortunate turn of events. Thank god, he'd managed to slip back to his cabin and stash away what the police would no doubt regard as highly incriminating evidence. As an American tourist, it was unlikely he would be suspected, and even more unlikely that he would be searched. But still, having them find the gun was a chance he couldn't take.

The scene he observed shortly before the assassination made him edgier still: Julia Grant in direct contact with the victim literally moments before the shooting. How was she involved in this business? It was glaringly evident to him that she must be involved in some way. That surely meant that her guide, Mohamed, was in it too. Was he a member of the Brotherhood? Or could he be working for the Egyptian Secret Service?

Damn. Damn. Damn! This definitely complicated things. He would have to learn as much as possible about the pair before his next contact with Jalal. That was another thing. He spotted Jalal in the excited group gathered around the lifeless body. Their eyes met for a split second before he faded into the crowd.

❖

Mohamed had never—in his entire life—felt such fury. How could she *do* this? How could she deceive him? For he was certain that she had. He seethed with righteous anger as he turned from the dining room where he and the other guides were questioned interminably by the police. Praise Allah, they were all together, in plain view of several dozen witnesses, when the murder took place. He climbed the stairs two at time and entered the lounge, scanning the room for the object of his wrath.

His stormy eyes descended on hers, sending fresh waves of cold fear through Julia's body. What was wrong now? He stalked toward her as one of the policemen, shouldering a rifle, followed close on his heels and spoke from the doorway.

"We have completed our investigation. For the time being. Everyone is free to leave the lounge." He amended the announcement in a surly tone. "But no one is to leave the boat."

Mohamed reached her chair and stood before her, glaring down. "Come with me. Now."

When he reached a far corner of the upper deck he rounded on her, his voice uneven with the effort to remain in control. "All right, Julia. Tell me what is going on. And don't insult my intelligence further with tales of headaches and insomnia. I know you are hiding something from me. This precise schedule. Dragging that ratty magazine around like some kind of beacon. Now a man is dead. A man that you spoke with minutes before he was shot. Talk to me, Julia. I want the truth." His eyes bore into hers like a burning infrared beam.

Julia looked away, speechless. This possibility had not occurred to her. How could she have been so stupid as to have underestimated Mohamed's keen perception? But how could she tell him the truth? She reminded herself of the need for discretion—for his safety as well as her own. She must tread very, very carefully here.

"Yes, Mohamed, it's true. I haven't been entirely honest with you. But please believe me, I haven't done anything wrong." She swallowed with difficulty, forcing herself to speak slowly. "The man that was killed was an undercover agent for the American government. They asked me to make contact with him, to collect some information. That's all."

Mohamed threw up his hands and rolled his eyes in disbelief. "That's *all?* To what *purpose,* Julia? To what purpose?"

"He was to, ah, pass some information about the Muslim Brotherhood. Something of great interest to the U.S." She mumbled the words, fear fading into confusion and embarrassment at having believed for a single second that this would be a simple job. Guilt also began to overshadow all else at having allowed *him* to be used. But what choice did she have?

"Oh, my god! What could you have been *thinking?* Do you not understand the danger you place yourself in? The danger you create for *me?*"

"I'm sorry, Mohamed, really sorry, but honestly I had no choice. I *will* tell you how it all happened, but first let me tell you that it's over. I have the message." She attempted to swallow the bitter taste in her mouth. "I'm sorry that the man is dead. But my assignment is over. And we're safe. Nothing more can happen. Please, just let me go to my cabin," she pleaded. "I'm a complete wreck. I promise I'll tell you the whole story later, when we've rested and have more privacy." Her eyes shifted in the direction of other passengers nearby.

She drew a deep, ragged breath and reached out a tentative hand to touch his arm. His icy glare caused her to pull it back. "Everything will be all right."

Far from pacified and unquestionably displeased, he gestured impatiently and she took advantage of the lull in the tirade to flee. Before reaching the stairs, she glimpsed Alexander Bryant's profile in the near distance at the rail. She wondered how much of the heated conversation he might have overheard.

The thought of a hot bath was tempting—to try and wash away the memory of those staring eyes. But more than that, she needed time to think about what happened. And how much she should confess. Most of all, she needed to find out what those messages contained. The messages that may have caused a cold-blooded murder.

CHAPTER 21

Brad Caldwell strode down the long hall to the corner office. Bob Bronson rarely summoned him and almost never using the word "immediately." He rapped on the door and waited until he heard a faint buzzing sound before turning the knob. It reminded him that the high level of Bob's position made tight security more of an imperative these days.

His boss stood behind a littered desk, glasses balanced on the end of his nose, scanning a document in one hand while the other absentmindedly rubbed a bristly chin. The wall of windows behind him usually provided a panoramic view of the bay and Golden Gate Bridge. The present view was a gray blank, dense with the fog that had cloaked the city all day. Through its thick, damp blanket could be heard the steady moan of fog horns, warning ships entering the ports to proceed with caution. Good advice, thought Brad morosely.

"Sit down, Caldwell."

Brad lowered himself guardedly into one of the chairs facing the desk, keeping his eyes focused on the weary, down-turned face. Whatever it was, the news was bad enough to rattle the normally unshakeable senior agent.

"Another man down." Bob looked up with a scowl. "In Egypt. Zed was shot in broad daylight earlier today. Word came "unofficially" to our Cairo office from the Egyptian Security Service two hours after the incident."

Brad didn't need for it to be spelled out. If they received notification, that meant the Egyptians were onto Zed. They knew he worked for the U.S. It also meant that the leak in the Egyptian forces may have blown his cover, resulting in his death.

"Where?"

"Kom Ombo. At the site. Most of the groups from the boats were still there."

This meant that Julia Grant, who Brad knew to be in Kom Ombo that day, might know that Zed had been eliminated. Or she might not. They might not have made contact. Both men were painfully aware they had not heard from her in almost two days. And they knew that there was probably no place for her to transmit anything now until the boat reached Aswan.

If she had the message. If she reached Aswan.

Brad kept an impassive face as he asked, "Was there any mention of Julia from the Egyptians?"

"No. Not yet."

"Well, that's something, anyway."

"No further word from her backup on the boat?" Bob asked in turn, already knowing the probable answer. "Anything on Zahar?"

"Nothing since Luxor. And he's a hard one to track, but we already knew that. I'll put a message on the web for her to keep calm and stick strictly to the plan. Anything else?"

Bob jerked the glasses from his nose and rubbed tired, burning eyes as he flopped down in his chair. "Yes, damn-it-all-to-hell, there is something else!" he blurted out uncharacteristically. "Could you please tell me who for Christ's sake we think we are, sending an untrained, innocent civilian into what amounts to a combat zone?"

Brad looked down at his neatly trimmed nails, unable—and unwilling—to answer his boss's rhetorical question. America's spying operations were in a big mess and everyone involved knew it. After September 11th, all fifteen of the unwieldy agencies, including the C.I.A and F.B.I., had been reorganized under the leadership of one man: the Director of National Intelligence. But the secret world of the U.S. was, and had been for a long time, in a ludicrous state of inefficiency and disorganization.

The arcane agencies failed—time and time again—to predict impending disasters both at home and abroad. It was widely recognized that the agencies were guilty of not sharing information, poor management and shockingly inadequate intelligence collection.

Although this new director ostensibly possessed the authority to bring about some kind of cohesion, it was unclear who, in fact, controlled the budget. The buck, as always, was the bottom line. It would be some time, perhaps a very long time, before the agencies could function comprehensively and efficiently. Add to that the difficulties of dealing with the constant threat of terrorism, now being conducted in a global grass-roots-style Jihad, and their jobs had become excruciatingly difficult—if not downright impossible.

"My responsibility," Brad said, "my bright idea."

"No, you know damn well where the buck stops. Now all we can do is wait." Bob made a sour expression and shook his head in disgust. "Keep me informed of anything relevant. Day or night. That's all."

At the curt dismissal, Brad made a grateful—and hasty—exit.

Julia locked the cabin door with shaking hands and leaned against it with eyes closed, crushing the red blanket to her chest. "Oh, please," she whispered, "please, dear Lord, Allah, Buddha and anyone else listening, please don't let anything happen to Mohamed."

She laid the blanket, laptop case and her purse on the bed. On unsteady legs, she crossed the cabin to close the curtains, noticing as she did that the boat was again moving up the river. Her hand shook only a little as she poured a glass of bottled water and drank it thirstily, in a vain attempt to relieve her painfully dry throat.

Finally sinking onto the bed, she unzipped her purse and removed the wad of bills Zed handed her. She shivered at the thought of the man's hand touching them in his final moments. The money spilled out on the bedcover to reveal the single piece of paper, folded several times. After she carefully unfolded it, surprise raised her brows to see words written clearly in English. On closer inspection they didn't make sense: something about the scent of the flowers of the prophet. Hmmmm. Curiosity began to supersede fear.

Her forehead wrinkled as she remembered him saying he hadn't had time to put it in the final code. She turned to the case, removed the computer and switched it on. While it started up she picked up the blanket. Cleverly tucked into the last fold was the square envelope. It contained another, well-padded envelope, which in turn contained a Data Traveler—the same kind of flash drive Brad Caldwell had given her in what seemed like a lifetime ago. Huh, she thought, must be government issue.

With an almost steady hand, she inserted it. Following her instructions, she double-clicked on the *Vocabulary* icon then opened the flash drive. Only one file appeared on the screen. She opened it. Gibberish. Copying the text, she pasted it to a new document then saved it in Vocabulary. To be safe, she closed the flash drive file and removed it. In such an agitated state, it would be just her luck to accidentally erase the whole damn thing.

Her throat was still so tight and dry she could barely swallow. She gulped water straight from the bottle this time. It took, once she clicked to open the saved file, an agonizingly long time before anything came up on the screen. This time the text was intelligible but was merely several pages of flowery descriptions of ancient Egyptian ceremonial rites. Certainly nothing that remotely pertained to terrorists or their activities.

Well, she thought with mixed feelings of disappointment and relief, she'd followed the instructions exactly. This must be right. The coding of the *Vocabulary* program was a total mystery but, as Brad said, the message would first be coded, then further encrypted by the program. Or something like that. This was definitely beyond her area of expertise, and Julia was not, as she considered it, devastated by not knowing the content of the real message within the message.

The handwritten note lay next to her leg on the bed. She picked it up and typed the words slowly, painstakingly inputting every letter exactly as written. First saving it as a new document in *Vocabulary*, she waited, expecting it to morph into more of the same coded prose on Egyptian culture. When the short paragraph popped onto the screen, it made her blink. And blink again.

WEAPONS SMUGGLING INTO ISRAEL FROM ALL SURROUNDING BORDERS CONFIRMED. JIHAD INVASION AND TAKING OF DIMONA NUCLEAR FACILITY TO BE AIDED BY DIVERSION OF DEADLY BIOCHEMICAL ATTACK ON JERUSALEM. CHEMICALS TO BE SMUGGLED FROM EGYPT WITHIN NEXT WEEK.

"Oh, no," she moaned, "no, no, it can't be." But of course it could. The room spun around—ceiling, walls and windows colliding without sound in the suddenly airless vacuum.

When she was able to refocus, one thing became excruciatingly clear: Julia's entire adult life had been spent searching for and supporting rational, peaceful solutions to difficult problems. Everything she believed in before this moment and the harrowing realities of the past week crashed together and crystallized, in a blinding clarity.

Absolutely nothing and no one, including concern for her own safety, must prevent her from doing whatever she could to circumvent this horrifying conspiracy—this conspiracy to commit genocide.

CHAPTER 22

Passengers strolled the deck, taking advantage of the cool evening air, or sat in lounge chairs enjoying the scenery along the river banks as the boat glided steadily toward Aswan. Alexander rested his forearms on the rail, brooding over the day's events.

The assassination in Kom Ombo was most unfortunate. The resulting unrest and police activity had prevented him from making his scheduled contact. He hoped this wouldn't deter the customers from keeping the appointment in Aswan. Thus far, he'd learned bloody damn little of what was planned or needed. Once they reached shore, he fully intended to communicate with James to ascertain what, if any, knowledge he might possess about the possible role Julia Grant could be playing in all of this.

For, after considerable deliberation, he was convinced that she was somehow involved. Her behavior before and after the killing, as well as that of her friend Mohamed, had been peculiar—and highly suspicious. At present, the only course of action open to him was to get closer to the pair and see if he could find out what they were up to. Julia had made a point of ignoring him completely while they were confined in the lounge earlier. He hesitated to approach her directly. He would have to make an attempt to befriend the Egyptian. As he moodily mulled all this over, a strident voice trilled out his name, jarring him from his sober thoughts.

"Oh, Alexander, my darling man! How lovely to find you here in this delicious twilight." Fiona MacDonald's bright eyes shone with determination, as if zeroing in on a long-awaited meal. She flitted to his side, tucking her bony arm into his as she looked possessively into his eyes. "Would you mind awfully accompanying me on a promenade around the deck before dinner?"

He looked down at the eager upturned face and experienced an unexpected pang of sympathy. Beneath her irritating aggression must lie a real and aching loneliness. He knew a great deal about loneliness and how it chipped away at your soul. The persistent pain of it manifested itself in many ways.

"Of course, Fiona, I'd be delighted." This "promenade" might also serve his purposes quite well, he thought, as he saw Mohamed emerge from the stairs. No time like the present to put his plan into action.

Mohamed still harbored a bitter resentment of Julia's duplicity, and he burned with questions concerning her strange and inexplicable behavior. He'd thought he knew this woman so well. She was a kind, caring, compassionate person who would never intentionally hurt anyone—man or beast. From the day they'd first met, he'd known her to be a staunch pacifist. She loathed politics. Her passions were for nature and beauty, in all its forms.

And for him, of course.

Guilt abruptly suppressed the inapt surge of ego, and the guilt was almost as quickly displaced by despair. This was the cycle—the pattern— that had tormented him for the past few years, from the day he'd set eyes on her—his beautiful, passionate, loving Julia.

The conflict within him at times was unbearable. The attraction had been instantaneous, and irresistible. Over the weeks, months, and years, it had only grown deeper, making it impossible to imagine life without her. But what could that life be? Taking her as a second wife had seemed the only answer. Reality demolished his dreams as he acknowledged the improbability of that ever coming to pass. He could barely support one wife. How could he even think of taking another?

Oh, of course, Julia had her own financial resources. That fact only brought more guilt. She'd always been wonderful and creative in the generous ways she devised to help him. He smiled, remembering her many kindnesses, not only to him but to his family as well: the gifts at every holiday on the calendar, always including something for Shahida. And then there was Shahida. His taking another wife would break her heart. He struggled endlessly to reach a decision about the future, but remained torn. His conscience made the path clear. Each time he beheld Julia, or even heard her voice, his heart veered violently from that path.

And now this. The torment was compounded a thousand-fold by this outrageous stunt. What in the name of Allah was she *doing?* What was she *thinking?* He knew that she knew, and had thought she understood, the very real danger that existed here, ever-present, barely beneath the surface of the superficial tranquility presented to visitors. The threat from the government was bad enough. Stories were commonplace of unwarranted detainment in unspeakable Egyptian prisons and unlawful torture.

The militants presented another worry altogether. They played by no rules whatsoever. Any atrocity was permissible that furthered their cause of establishing Islamic governments ruled by Islamic law. Egypt's proximity to Israel and the long, bloody history between the two countries produced a constant state of turbulence and unrest among the Egyptian fundamentalists. They steadfastly supported the Palestinian cause: a cause which most historians and authorities on Middle Eastern politics credited as the deep-rooted source of the global Jihad.

Julia knew all this. They'd discussed it many times. In spite of all that, here she was, somehow involved in it all. And a man was dead.

He approached the barman to ask for an orange juice as the arms dealer and the English woman crossed his path.

"Good evening," Alexander said pleasantly while Fiona preened at his side. "We were about to have a drink. Won't you join us?"

Mohamed eyed the American with suspicion. A diversion from his dismal thoughts had some appeal. Besides, he wanted to know more about Alexander Bryant—a whole lot more. "Why not?"

Fiona practically swooned at her good fortune in being the only female in the company of the two most attractive men on the boat. In fact, the two most attractive men she'd ever been with in such close proximity. A sigh of transparent satisfaction escaped her bright red lips as they all sat at a table near the bar.

"Quite an unfortunate incident this afternoon," said Alexander.

"Incident. Yes," agreed Mohamed quietly. "We were lucky to have been allowed to leave so quickly."

"Did anyone learn who the victim was? Or why he was killed?"

Mohamed studied the other man closely as he spoke. "He was a vendor in the *suk*. The police believe it concerned a feud over the theft of a donkey."

"Well, I for one am of the opinion that the police had no business detaining us at all," sniffed Fiona. "After all, what in the world could we possibly have to do with such a tawdry affair involving one of the natives?"

The two men exchanged a wordless look.

"Anyway," she went on, oblivious to the fact that one of the "natives" sat beside her, as well as to the clear disapproval of her callous remark, "we're back on schedule now, aren't we, Mr. Zahar? What time will we be passing through the locks tonight?"

Mohamed suppressed the spark of anger at the thoughtless insult and flashed one of his devastating smiles. "The captain says ten o'clock. *Inshallah.*"

He knew, of course, that the schedule might change and wasn't the least surprised when it was, in fact, long past midnight when the *Isis* slipped through the locks that controlled the flow of the river from Aswan.

Julia lingered before the dresser mirror fastening a heavy gold ring in her ear. The unexpected jangle of the telephone next to her bed, louder to her ear than it probably was, made her jump, causing her to drop the earring. It bounced off the dresser onto the carpet and rolled under the bed as the phone continued its strident ring.

"Good evening, Julia," came the dreaded polite voice. "Were you planning on joining me for dinner?"

It was almost eight-thirty. Dinner started at eight. "Yes, Mohamed. I'm coming. I, ah, I'm running late. Sorry." Recovering from the shock from reading those sickening words on the heels of the gruesome murder had taken a considerable amount of time. Neither the herbal tea she'd ordered to her cabin nor the long, hot bath had dispelled the turmoil raging inside. One irrevocable conclusion became unmistakably clear: The situation had changed.

It had changed radically from the simple mission with "practically no danger" to one of imminent peril, for both her and Mohamed. He had the right to know what was going on. She, and the instigators of this ill-fated affair, had no right to jeopardize his safety—innocent husband and father—without his knowledge or consent. What they had done to him was wrong. She determined to tell him everything. Everything. Then she would insist that he return straight away to Cairo, the minute they reached Aswan.

Upon entering the crowded dining room, Julia felt dismay to see the English twit seated between Mohamed and Alex. The presence of the Langleys almost made up for it. Almost. All three men rose as she approached and Ali, her devoted waiter, appeared out of nowhere to pull back the chair on Mohamed's right, who looked askance at her attire with a decidedly disapproving eye. He wasn't the only one who noticed.

A long silk scarf didn't completely camouflage the knit pants and top clinging provocatively to her curves. In the private company of fellow westerners, Julia saw no need to strictly adhere to the more modest form of dress she assumed in public.

"Please accept my apologies for being late," she said, forcing a smile. "I had an ugly headache."

"Apology accepted," pronounced the officious Ms. MacDonald while she looked Julia up and down. Her beady black eyes glittered with envy, and perhaps a touch of malice, as she added, "Small wonder that you should have a headache after all the unpleasantness this afternoon. Fortunately, I have the constitution of a horse—nerves of absolute steel." She flipped a hand, as if swatting at a fly, to prove her point. "No, no. No silly vapors for this girl." She practically preened as she leaned in close to Alexander.

He turned to regard her with utter disbelief. It would seem that her insensitivity knew no bounds. He noted for the first time that her oversized upper teeth presented a subtle equine-like resemblance, to go along with the professed constitution.

At a complete loss for words, Julia stared at the woman as if beholding a kind of rare and unpleasant reptile. Mohamed pressed his leg against hers under the table in camaraderie and smiled at the reptilian rose. "You are most fortunate indeed, Ms. MacDonald. Many people find it difficult and disturbing to witness the death of a fellow human being."

Henry and Henrietta had remained silent throughout the tense exchange. A slight frown tugged at the corners of his mouth while Henrietta reached across the table to pat Julia's hand. "Now, I'm sure we're all sorry for that poor man." Then she made it clear that the subject was closed. "What's on your agenda for tomorrow, dear?"

The meal progressed interminably, thankfully with the men doing most of the talking. Henrietta sat quietly, glancing frequently at Julia with evident concern. Not once did Julia look at the face of Alexander Bryant. She ate sparingly, smiled occasionally, and added little to the conversation, clearly disturbed. Once her decision had been made to confess all, she wanted to get on with it.

Mohamed declined, with perhaps more vehemence than necessary, Alexander's invitation for after-dinner drinks in the lounge. He led Julia determinedly up to the deck. They headed for a secluded corner at the stern where he turned—back to the rail, arms folded across his chest— to face her. She sat on the edge of a lounge chair looking out over the river. An awkward silence hung between them. After several long moments, Julia tore her gaze from the mesmerizing water, looked him squarely in those reproachful eyes and began at the beginning.

"Say something," she said hoarsely. He'd stood motionless throughout the mind-boggling tale. Julia had to admit, as the incredible story unfolded, it sounded—even to her ears—a far-fetched fiction.

"If I didn't know you better, Julia, I would say that you are lying. But I do know you and I know that you never lie. Except," he added in a deceptively soft voice, "you have been lying to me since you first arrived."

Her head hung low, unable to meet the hard, well-deserved look of rebuke. "I know, and I'm sorry, Mohamed. I *honestly* believed that everything would go as planned and no one would get hurt. I know, I know. I was stupid and naïve," she wailed as he snorted derisively. "They insisted on secrecy and I truly thought it was best for you not to know."

"Ah, Julia," he murmured with chilling contempt, "it is reassuring that you *honestly* and *truly* believed you knew what was best for me. And yet, after your many protestations of love and respect, you led me unsuspectingly into a situation that could easily result in my imprisonment. Or my death."

Tears ran freely down her face as the cruel truth of his words bit into her heart. What *had* she been thinking? She'd been used and manipulated. She'd allowed him to be used and manipulated. How could she have done this to him? And what was she to do now? Because it was crystal-clear that she couldn't just send on the message and walk away from the horrifying information she'd learned today. She couldn't send the short, written message over the internet. It wasn't safe. She really had no choice but to make direct contact with Brad. That might blow her cover. And further expose Mohamed.

After Kom Ombo, the terrorists might have her under surveillance anyway, and so might the Egyptian authorities. Well, she'd already made up her mind about his returning to Cairo. That's what she would insist he do. He must be far away from Aswan before she took any further action.

"Mohamed," she said, with as much forcefulness as she could muster, "you may hate me for what I've done, but, please believe me: I never meant to cause you any harm. In fact, when I learned that the governments of both our countries knew of our relationship, I thought my agreeing to the assignment would buy their discretion. It was a kind of blackmail—a bargain with the devil. I have never, ever, done anything willingly to cause you problems or pain. And never anything to knowingly put you in danger."

His resentment evaporated at the sight of her tears. He reached out and grasped both her hands. "I know, Julia, I know. I'm sorry for being so hard on you. Please don't cry."

They struggled for a moment, as always pulsating with frustration that he couldn't take her in his arms. When she managed to stem the flow of tears, she squeezed his hands once before removing hers to wipe her eyes with trembling fingers. After inhaling deeply, she said in what she hoped was a decisive voice, "Tomorrow morning, as soon as possible, you must leave the boat and fly back to Cairo. Act as if you've been called home on an emergency. Then you'll be out of it. Safe."

He looked at her steadily before replying. "That won't work, Julia, for several reasons. First, my leaving so abruptly after the murder would look suspicious to the police. Second, I would have to include Shahida in the fabricated emergency, which would make her suspicious. And last, but far from least, I could not think to leave you, knowing that you may be exposed to danger. And defenseless."

He was right, of course. She hadn't thought that far. Her only thought was to extricate him from this mess.

"What do you plan to do next?" he asked, with narrowed eyes and mouth molded in a frown.

She gave herself a mental shake, shifting gears from the issue of safety. "I'll go as soon as possible tomorrow to send the first coded message. At the same time, I'll send an email with a request to call my contact." Galvanized by the thought of action, she came to her feet and stepped up to the rail. "It's the only way I know to convey the second message. Once I've done that, my job is finished. Then I stick to the ridiculous itinerary and fly back to San Francisco." As she spoke, she cautiously pulled the mutilated flash drive from her satin cocktail bag and let it slip into the murky depths of the river.

She found his wordless, sidelong glance unnerving, for once unable to even guess at his thoughts. Julia knew well that his sympathies lay with the Palestinians, along with those of most Egyptians. It made her uneasy to think there might be the slightest, most remote chance that his personal views on the subject might influence his actions in this appalling situation. Not that his feelings on the matter would alter his position on—or opposition to—violence as the answer to the problem.

She was sure of that. Wasn't she?

"What about Bryant?" he asked, catching her off guard. "From what you have said, he's involved in all this. It sounds as though he may be on the wrong side of it." He looked thoughtful. "And he was at the scene of the murder in Kom Ombo when we arrived."

He gave her a sideways glance and saw that this thought had already occurred to her. "You are not thinking of doing something crazy, Julia. Are you?"

The color drained from her face. He knew her well. Without question, she planned to advise the agency of the arms dealer's presence and possible involvement. The little voice in her head kept whispering *He carries a gun.* Another idea had also occurred to her. She kept seeing the murder scene. Seeing Zed's empty, staring eyes as he lay in his own blood in the dirt. Something else about that image troubled her until she had at length realized what it was. Or wasn't, as the case may be.

The cloth bag he'd carried away from the stall in the *suk* hadn't been anywhere near his slain body. Of this she was certain. Where had it gone? She'd arrived right behind the other bystanders and was positive no one there had picked it up. It must've been removed by the killer.

Alexander had come into the lounge several minutes after the others. What if he'd slipped away to hide the evidence? If she could gain access to his cabin, she could possibly identify him as the murderer. Of course, failure to find the bag there wouldn't absolve him of the crime, she mused.

Mohamed interrupted this bleak train of thought. "Answer me, Julia. What are you planning?"

CHAPTER 23

Alexander glanced down at the heavy gold Rolex watch clamped on his wrist. He'd at first been put off by the pretension of the gift from one of his clients. He could not, however, deny its utilitarianism and had to admit it sent a message of status that proved useful in his line of work. It accurately told him now that his contact was late.

This was the third—and last—designated rendezvous point today. Jalal had failed to show at the first two. The day had dragged on, Alexander's apprehension growing with each no-show. If the regrettable incident in Kom Ombo had unnerved the customers, he was out of luck. At this stage, he had no way to make further contact. His only course of action was to follow the instructions he'd been given and wait. Waiting had never been his strong suit.

The restaurant, several blocks from the corniche, buzzed with conversation. Local businessmen occupied nearly every table. A few foreigners mixed in among them were enjoying a late lunch. Alexander sat, back to the wall, with a clear view of the room.

An impressive Middle Eastern man, probably in his mid-thirties, sat at the table nearest his own. His neighbor's companion appeared considerably older, and his grotesque features contrasted sharply with the other's classic ones. A web of scars ruined his sun-scorched face. One puckered the left side from hairline to chin, drawing his upper lip up into a perpetual sneer. Alexander heard them exchange an occasional low word in Arabic but, although he had a passable understanding of the language, couldn't make out their meaning.

At long last, after ordering a meal he didn't particularly want, he breathed a sigh of relief as the familiar face came through the door. Jalal paused with a fleeting look around the room and his eyes flickered across the men at the next table before he moved to join Alexander. Jalal sat in the chair next to him, allowing for a clear line of sight for the two men seated nearby.

"Marhabba kaif halak."

"Greetings and good health to you as well," replied Jalal smoothly in English. "Please accept my apologies for the delay. Much has happened since our last meeting." He surveyed the room again with a cautious eye before continuing. "The unfortunate events in Kom Ombo have made things considerably more complicated. We must proceed with extreme caution."

Jalal fell silent as the waiter approached bearing several dishes. He laid out the typical regional meal of roast chicken, hummus, salad and black olives; he placed a plate before each of them, and retreated without having said a word. Alexander made note of the waiter's atypical reticence and it added to the tension already tightening his jaw. He suppressed his uneasiness at the reference to Kom Ombo, and waited.

"The police are under the impression it was a simple robbery. Rumor has it that the victim carried a large sum of money in his bag, which seems to have disappeared." What could only be described as a smirk passed across Jalal's face.

"All of the activity surrounding the murder has made everyone understandably nervous. The meeting has been rescheduled for tomorrow." He nodded in acknowledgement of Alexander's barely-concealed impatience.

"We realize this presents a change in plans for you. You must leave the boat in the morning and check into a hotel. Go to the Old Cataract when you leave here and book a room for a few days. There should be no difficulty. We will contact you there tomorrow afternoon with instructions for the meeting later in the evening." His voice remained steady, but Alexander sensed a high level of strain pulsing beneath the surface of his deliberate calm.

They ate in silence for a while, each clearly absorbed in his thoughts, before the Brother spoke again. "There is another small problem. We have reason to believe that an American spy may be on the boat. Our sources in Cairo did not send an alert, but her presence has been detected en route."

Her presence echoed like a drum in Alexander's ears. He didn't like the sound of that.

"What do you know of the woman called Julia Grant? And the man she travels with?"

It was a no-win question. Alexander couldn't admit his own suspicions, as that would further incriminate her. If they knew for certain that she was an agent and he attempted to exonerate her, it would cast doubt on his own credibility, jeopardizing his mission—perhaps even his life. He settled on a diversionary tactic.

"Don't know much about either of them," he said, feigning indifference. "Supposedly, she's touring the country doing research for writing a book and he's her guide." He leaned closer with an insinuating air. "They do appear to be working rather closely, if you take my meaning."

A sly smile stole across Jalal's face, his active libido clearly relishing the idea of the pale American beauty with the Egyptian man. "Well, let us hope for her sake that is her only crime."

Alexander clenched a fist under the table to keep from swiping away the lewd grin. Uttering the suggestive implication had left a dirty taste in his mouth, but it was the best he could do on the spur of the moment.

He noticed the two men at the next table exchange a look. The unsightly face wore a broad, offensive leer. The handsome one did not.

A rich cerulean-blue sky, the kind found only in desert regions, spread wide overhead, almost completely uncluttered by clouds. In the west the great ball of fire had begun its eternal descent, sinking into the other world—according to the ancient Egyptians, the world of the dead.

Raising a hand to shade her eyes, Julia followed the flight of a large bird, probably a hawk. A row of bright white feathers stood out against the dark on the underside of its powerful wings as it soared high into the velvety blue sky.

No, she thought with excitement: It's an eagle—a golden eagle. As always, she felt envy at not being able to spread wings and join it: to ride the breeze over the Valley of the Kings and along the mighty Nile. In the world of centuries past, eagles were thought to be messengers. The sighting of this majestic bird must surely be a good omen.

Absorbing the dramatic atmosphere from the upper deck, Julia once again experienced a surge of fascination for the ancients and their worship of the sun god over thousands of years. *Amun-Re.* He gave life. And he brought death.

As she continued to watch, the sky shifted into a stunning kaleidoscope of color, made possible by the billions of tiny sand particles in the air. The few clouds hanging low on the horizon became shadows of deep blue-gray surrounded by brilliant streaks of orange light. Taking in a deep breath, Julia forced her brain to return to the task that lay ahead.

The decidedly heated debate had continued late into the night. After endless recriminations, tedious declarations of remorse and redundant promises of caution (all on Julia's part) Mohamed eventually—reluctantly—agreed to conspire in her plan.

After a fast breakfast that morning, they'd left the boat, now docked along Corniche el Nile Street in Aswan, and headed for the nearest establishment offering wireless internet access. Even though the shop was meant to open at eight, by almost nine o'clock, it showed no signs of life. Almost choking on her angst, Julia sat down across the street, staring at the untouched minted tea before her while Mohamed made several calls on his mobile phone.

The time crawled by before his phone finally rang. "Come, Julia," he ordered, snapping it closed. "My friend is on his way to open the shop."

Hunched in the furthest corner while Mohamed distracted the proprietor in lively Arabic, Julia opened the laptop, signed on to the internet and sent the email with the coded message attached. She then sent a second email she'd composed and coded through *Vocabulary* in the wee hours of the morning. In it she sketched a brief overview of yesterday's traumatic event, made a caustic reference to one Alexander Bryant, international arms dealer, and requested permission to contact Brad directly by phone as soon as humanly possible.

With this out of the way came considerable relief. It was short-lived. When she clicked onto the publishing house website and checked the *Special Events* page, she discovered a posting from yesterday. The sight of it brought a new wave of anxiety. Copying it and saving it as instructed, she decoded it on the spot—in direct rebellion of her instructions. Desperate times called for desperate measures.

The message came from Brad, letting her know they'd learned of the "incident" in Kom Ombo and cautioned her to stick with the plan.

Easy for him to say. She checked her watch. It read almost ten a.m. San Francisco was ten hours behind, making it only midnight there.

There was no telling when Brad would retrieve her email. At eight a.m. in San Francisco, it would be six in the evening here, she calculated. Well, at least that would allow her time to prepare for her audacious plan.

They spent the day going through the motions of the ridiculous itinerary. By the time they returned to the internet café at six on the dot, apprehension had wound them up and spit them out as a couple of limp rags. The reply to her request to call Brad popped up on the screen, brief and to the point: If absolutely necessary, she should go ashore tomorrow morning and call from a private booth at the Old Cataract Hotel at precisely six a.m.

This was, his message said, the most secure location for placing the call. Further instruction directed her to use his office number, where the call could be scrambled. It would be eight in the evening of the previous day in San Francisco. His reply made no mention at all of the content of her first message—the coded message from Zed. Nor did it refer to Alexander Bryant.

Now, with a last wistful glimpse of the dazzling sunset, she turned away to return to her cabin and dress for dinner.

Julia squared bare shoulders and advanced upon the dining room, elegantly clad in a figure-hugging cocktail dress. The richly colored russet silk perfectly accentuated her shining auburn hair and amber eyes. Only in the relative privacy of the boat or a hotel would she have worn such a thing. Several heads turned in her direction as she made her way across the room. Henrietta Langley smiled approvingly and glanced over at Alex.

Part of the plan was to appear, especially to *Alex*, as innocently feminine as possible. Apparently things were going according to plan. She smiled at Ali, her faithful waiter, and he practically fell over himself to reach the table and pull out her chair. Already seated, besides the Langleys and

Alexander, was a pleasant couple from Belgium—Gregor and Christina Braun—as well as the faded rose, who had evidently abandoned her group to pursue her prey fulltime. Fiona scowled as she took in the sexy dress and its contents.

"Good evening," Julia smiled to the table at large as she slipped into the chair being held by the smitten Ali. She wasn't sure if he anticipated a big tip or dreamed of special favors. Probably both.

One of the aspects of contemporary Egyptian society she found infuriating was the male obsession with sex. Of course, it was common in all societies to a certain degree. Here, it pervaded like an unreachable itch. The issue invariably arose in any dealings between a Western woman and any Egyptian male. *It's because they think we're all promiscuous,* thought Julia, *but it's damned annoying.*

Other societies at least have some kind of legal protection for women, or else the men have just learned how to conceal their foul fantasies. Julia had known women who'd had extremely unpleasant encounters here: one with a driver who made inappropriate references to female underwear, and another with a doctor who'd fondled her breasts during an examination. Disgusting perverts.

Shaking her head to dislodge these unwelcome images, she scanned the room for her accomplice. Half an hour later—with a growing edginess—she was still searching for sight of Mohamed when he at last sauntered in. He spoke affably to the young Italian woman who clung possessively to his arm, virtually glowing with an unmistakable aura of promise. Passing Julia, he flashed her that "what can I do? I'm so irresistible" look and continued on to escort the girl to her group at a nearby table.

The girl's mother thanked him much more warmly than the courtesy warranted, wearing a mischievous smile distinctly suggestive of her desire to make her gratitude more personal. What was it, Julia wondered, that made people (including herself, to be brutally honest) behave like lascivious idiots on these trips? It appeared that the loins somehow short-circuited the brain.

Oh, well, at least he was here now and she could relax and try to swallow a few bites before tackling the nerve-racking job she'd created for herself. Since embarking upon this madness, she'd basically stopped eating, as well as sleeping. In addition to all the stress, Julia remained extremely careful about what she put in her mouth. One near-death experience due to invasive microscopic creatures was more than enough.

The bad news was that this was bound to soon have a serious deleterious impact on her mental capacity—if it hadn't already. The good news was that she could once again easily zip all her pants. *One can never be too rich or too thin,* she thought to herself, giggling out loud. Unfortunately, her inexplicable mirth occurred during a lull in the conversation and Henrietta's head swiveled in her direction with a decided look of concern.

"Sorry to be late," said Mohamed smoothly as he slipped into the chair next to Julia. "Natalia was impressed with the quarry today and had many questions about it."

"I'll bet," muttered Julia. Natalia and her mother were among a cast of hundreds, probably thousands, who threw themselves at the dreamy-eyed men they encountered on their tours. This one happened to be young, rich and particularly well-endowed. Who could blame Mohamed for enjoying the attention? No doubt she had lots more questions for him, which could take all night.

Not tonight, honey. He has other plans.

Turning away from Mohamed, Julia gave Alexander an overly-sweet smile as she inquired, "And how did you enjoy the sights today, Alex?"

Her demeanor towards him had thawed considerably, he observed with skepticism. Their paths had crossed a couple of times, and they'd enjoyed an impromptu afternoon tea in a friendly group at one of the hotels on the corniche. Interesting.

He returned the saccharin smile with a tight one. "Quite fascinating. How the ancients managed to produce those multi-ton obelisks is a real mystery. The logistics of mining granite on such a large scale and transporting it without machinery is a remarkable accomplishment."

The remainder of the meal passed in convivial conversation with those around the table. Even the predatory Fiona somehow managed not to blatantly offend anyone. Mohamed excused himself when the coffee arrived, proclaiming the need to make arrangements for the rest of the evening.

"Don't worry, Julia, everything is under control," he assured her as they passed on the staircase twenty minutes later. He slipped her an envelope. "My friend on the desk came through. Bryant is joining me, along with Gregor and Christina and a couple of the other passengers, at ten o'clock. I'm taking them to a nightclub that features the best belly dancer in Aswan. We will be off the boat late into the night. *Inshallah.*"

"No. No *Inshallah* on this one, Mohamed. You make sure to keep him away. Damn sure." Knowing as she did how much Mohamed loved belly dancing, Julia had no doubt he planned to be off the boat half the night.

She could only hope that *Alex darling* would be equally enthralled.

CHAPTER 24

Julia watched from the rail on the upper deck as the rowdy group, mostly men except for Christina and the insidious Fiona, walked across the gangway onto shore. All Mohamed needed to do now was to keep them away long enough for her to complete her little burgling project. Restlessly, she plopped down in a lounge chair with a book, to wait for the other passengers to retire to their cabins. It wouldn't do to be caught breaking and entering.

By eleven-thirty she was finding it impossible to concentrate, becoming increasingly agitated to get on with the evening's criminal activities. Did these people never sleep? The last surviving trouble-makers were an older married couple from India. After all their years together, what in the world could they possibly have to talk about in such annoying animation?

At last they departed, her glare of disapproval prodding them on from over the top of her book. Slapping it shut, she went to her cabin and quickly changed into jeans and a large, shapeless blouse. A cotton scarf wrapped around her head covered her hair and most of her face. All was quiet in the corridor, so she slipped from her cabin and glided toward Alexander's. Fortunately, it was on the same level as hers, the last one on the other side of the central stairway. After what seemed a century of trying to get the key to work in the lock, she entered and almost fainted with relief to be inside. Not now, she told herself severely, you can faint later. Just get on with it.

The cabin was an exact replica of her own.

Somehow, she'd managed to persuade herself that discovering anything incriminating before the call to Brad might help circumvent the terrorist plot. Mohamed remained unconvinced. She searched the room thoroughly, being careful to leave everything exactly as she found it. Nothing appeared out of the ordinary. No sign of poor Zed's wretched bag—or the alleged gun. Damn.

She withdrew a card from her pocket that Mohamed had managed to procure, along with the cabin key, and entered the numbers scrawled on the face of it onto the keypad of the safe. It clicked open on the first try. Huh. *Nice to know how easily members of the crew could open the cabin safes.* Unfortunately, it contained only cash and a slim, old-fashioned address book. No guns. No bags belonging to murdered secret agents.

Oh, hell, she thought in frustration, I need to get out of here. Pocketing the card, she closed the safe and hurried to the door. As she reached for the knob, she heard a key being inserted in the lock on the other side. She snatched her hand away and watched in horrified fascination as the knob began to turn.

Maybe, she thought frantically, it's the cabin boy.

Maybe not.

Wildly, she looked around for a place to hide, to escape. Not enough time to reach the open window and jump into the river. Turning toward the bathroom, she ducked her head as the door opened and Alexander Bryant entered his cabin.

His movements were ominously swift and chillingly sure. Out of the corner of her eye she stared with pure mortal terror as he deftly closed the door with one hand while pulling a gun from inside his jacket with the other.

Speechless, head still bent, her eyes locked on the sheen of the barrel as he directed, "Don't move a muscle or make the slightest sound."

An expression of pure delight lit Mohamed's features as he watched "Princess Tazzia" ripple the coins encircling her enticingly exposed and well-muscled abdomen.

Gregor grinned as he leaned in. "Wow. And va-va-voom."

Reluctantly turning to the Belgian to reply, Mohamed felt an unpleasant jolt to find an empty chair. "Where's Alex?"

Gregor shrugged. "Went to the men's room."

Mohamed nearly turned over his chair as he got up. The man was nowhere to be found. One of the boys begging from the tourists outside the entrance of the Oasis Club said a man fitting Alex's description left a while ago. He dropped a few coins in the boy's grimy palm and hastily returned to the group.

"Gregor, I must leave. Something has come up. Will you please see that everyone returns to the boat safely?"

"Sure, what's up?" the Belgian called after Mohamed's already retreating back.

He raced along the corniche, dodging tourists, peddlers and scrounging dogs. *I let him get away.* The words rang in his ears, over and over, like a broken record.

He'd known this was a mistake. Mohamed cursed himself for allowing Julia to undertake this foolish scheme. The man was dangerous. He carried a gun. He was a notorious arms dealer. In all that was holy, he wished he'd dissuaded her from this stupid plan.

His pace did not slow as he approached the narrow gangway. The turbaned heads of several boatmen turned as he flew past, startled to see him move in such unusual haste. Going to Julia's cabin was out of the question so he went to his own, grabbing up the phone to dial her number. No answer. He struggled to suppress mounting alarm, left his cabin and tore up the stairs to the upper deck. His eyes raked the area for sight of her. Nothing. What now?

Julia's head wobbled like a hula girl on a dashboard as her frenzied brain sought an excuse to extract herself from the line of fire. That was going to be damned difficult as he stood less than three feet away.

"Step back slowly and sit on the bed with your hands on your knees." The gun didn't waver. "And don't even think of doing anything foolish."

Too late for that acerbic bit of advice. She sank down onto the bed, hands on knees like a good criminal caught in the act, to watch him back guardedly to the couch beneath the open window. Lights on the other side of the river twinkled behind him. He sat warily, lips compressed in a grim line.

"All right, Julia. Tell me exactly what this is all about." His eyes had turned to an opaque gray.

She wanted to wipe away the beads of sweat that had sprung up on her forehead but didn't dare raise a hand. "Oh, Alex," she said with a nervous laugh, "it was meant to be a joke. Like the stuffed T-shirt prank the other night." It sounded lame, even to her ears.

"Don't insult my intelligence. Please. Let me tell you what I already know and then you can take it from there." His cool tone contradicted her awareness of his body, coiled tight as a spring, ready to respond instantly to any misstep on her part.

"You were seen with the man in the market in Kom Ombo just before his murder. You were also observed, prior to that, in conversation with a questionable character in Esna. You and your friend Mohamed have been behaving like a couple of subversives and I want to know now—right this minute—what your connection to the dead man was. Or I'll turn you over to the local police."

Slack-jawed and glassy-eyed at the unexpected threat, fear temporarily forgotten, Julia gasped. *"You'll* turn *me* over to the police? That's a good one. You're the one carrying an illegal weapon. You're the arms dealer who supplies terrorists with the means to kill thousands of innocent people. And...," she choked as she caught herself in the nick of time before accusing him outright of shooting Zed in cold-blood. The man was, after all, pointing a gun in her general direction.

Narrowing those cold, hard eyes, he slowly lowered the gun, resting it on his tensed thigh. He eyed her speculatively before responding in a deceptively reasonable voice. "You're quite well-informed. Tell me more."

Julia bristled with indignation. "I'm not gonna tell you anything, *Mr.* Bryant. I may be guilty of bad judgment for illicitly entering your cabin, but I don't think you'll risk exposure by calling in the police." She folded her arms defiantly. "Or anyone else."

She did have a point.

Silence drifted down between them.

She found his eventual response disconcerting. Sighing wearily, he shook his head and replaced the gun in the holster inside his jacket. He leaned back and spread both arms out across the back of the sofa. "All right. I'll make a few educated guesses. You're probably working for some ill-informed, ill-prepared branch of the secret service. You must've been sent here to make contact with an agent who's been collecting information on militants in the area. How'm I doin' so far?"

Julia glared mutinously as he continued. "The man killed in Kom Ombo was either your contact or a messenger. Now that he's dead, you don't know what to do. Communicating directly with headquarters is not only difficult, it could prove fatal. You've managed to discover a few things about my background that's led you to believe I'm involved with the bad guys. You decided to search my cabin in hopes of finding evidence to that effect."

Julia saw a light flash in his eye as another idea evidently dawned on him. "Or possibly you even suspect that I pulled the trigger."

She frowned down at her hands in confusion. What could she say? It was as if he could read her like a book.

His voice softened as he added, "And I'll bet the farm you're not a professional spook. How in the world did you get involved in this mess, Julia?"

This was, of course, the question Mohamed asked her when she'd initially confessed. And the question she'd kept asking herself, again and again, since seeing Zed's body in the dirt. To her mortification, a big fat tear formed at the corner of her eye and rolled down her cheek. The situation was becoming more complicated and treacherous by the second. But she could not cry in front of this man, this…this *killer*. She simply could not.

Alexander felt a long-dormant stirring deep inside. Here before him sat this beautiful, usually intelligent woman, on the verge of breaking into tears. It took every ounce of self-control he possessed to restrain himself from the impulse that throbbed throughout his body. The desire to take her in his arms and hold her tight almost superseded reason. Almost.

The information he'd learned from Jalal earlier that afternoon had left him feeling distinctly uncomfortable and undecided regarding Julia Grant. The militants—the bad guys—were onto her. He had no idea how far they would go if they learned that she in fact was an agent, albeit an unlikely one. Her life could be on the line here, and he was tempted to tell her just that. First, he urgently needed to convince her that they were on the same side.

Julia struggled for control, saved ironically by the passing of a boisterous party boat on the river, music blaring and blazing with lights.

"Listen to me, Julia. I am *not* an arms dealer, not in the literal sense of the term. My business is strictly confined to that of an advisor on practice and procedure for defense, and recommendations for the appropriate hardware. Those services are *never* offered to militants or terrorists." The gray eyes, bent on persuasion, fixed on hers with a compelling force, as if he could will her to accept his words as truth.

"Then what are you doing here?" she asked in a voice heavy with doubt.

He subjected her to that penetrating stare for a few seconds longer before answering. "Because you seem to be involved in all this, I'll tell you, but only what you need to know—for your own safety. As you're aware, I'm a retired Army officer, and, yes, now a military advisor and consultant. During my service I spent several years in England working with British Intelligence. I live near London now, and have maintained relationships with a few of my former British colleagues."

He paused, considering how much more to divulge. "Occasionally, I'm asked to undertake fact-finding missions for Her Majesty's Secret Service. My position and reputation allow me access to situations that would be difficult for their regular operatives to infiltrate quickly."

He spoke in a low, steady voice. His eyes never left hers for a second. She found his explanation peculiarly unsettling and at the same time reassuring.

"Recent intelligence has led the Brits to believe that a terrorist operation is in planning here in Egypt. MI-6, the British Secret Intelligence Service, has requested that I look into it—unofficially. Fact-finding, that's all. No selling of arms to terrorists. No assassinations. For the record, I did not kill the man in Kom Ombo. Or anyone else, for that matter."

A sharp knock at the door sent Julia's heart to her throat.

"Commander Bryant, are you there? Is everything all right?" Mohamed's muffled voice came from the corridor, heavy with concern.

Julia instinctively knew the concern was for her and not the cabin's regular occupant. Alexander sprang to the door as he cautioned her to keep still. He reached it in three long strides, opening it halfway.

"Come in," he ordered authoritatively, standing aside to give Mohamed clear sight of Julia sitting ramrod straight on the bed.

With no thought whatsoever for his own safety, he brushed past Alexander, grabbed Julia by the shoulders and pulled her to her feet.

"Are you all right?"

"Yes," she breathed, nodding her head.

Alexander watched the interaction between them with interest as he closed the door. "Everyone is fine, Mohamed. Let's all just try to keep our cool." He leaned against the wall and folded his arms across his chest, assessing the situation.

Christ, he thought, what the hell have I gotten myself into here? He scrutinized the pair, oblivious for the moment of anything save one another.

"We need to talk. But not here. It's not safe. Julia, you leave first. Go to your cabin and pull yourself together. We'll meet you up on the deck in ten minutes. Go now," Alex ordered.

And she went. Without another word.

Mohamed regarded the other man while examining his own resentment with interest. What was going on here? Julia rarely took direction this meekly, from anyone. Something must have happened to alleviate her suspicions concerning the arms dealer.

He continued to study him while Alex glanced at his watch then commanded, "Let's go."

When they stepped out into the corridor, they found a cabin boy loitering outside the door with a stack of towels across his arm.

"Sorry to cause concern. Only a touch of 'pharaoh's curse,'" Alex said in a voice convincingly tinged with embarrassment. "Nothing to worry about. Come along, I'll buy you a drink."

The boy smiled and bobbed his head as the two men walked away.

CHAPTER 25

Julia stomped back to her cabin and jerked open the door. "He must think I'm a complete fool," she muttered as she ripped the scarf from her head. Turning on the tap at the bathroom sink, she splashed cold water on her burning face.

"Not that I give a damn." She could care less what he thought of her. Or could she?

Everything had become so damn confusing. There were many layers of truth here, she reminded herself—very little black and white—only layer upon layer of ambiguous shades of gray. Nonetheless, there remained one inescapable truth: The terrorists were plotting their brutal attack, and she would do everything within her power to prevent it, regardless of what Mohamed *or* Alexander Bryant said.

She snatched up a towel and rubbed her cheeks with a vengeance. After an attempt at taming her hair and jabbing on some lipstick, she forced herself to try to calm down. By the time she reached the top of the stairs, her roller-coaster emotions had plummeted to a new low.

She spotted them in a fore corner and paused to catch her breath.

A few short hours ago Alex had been the unequivocal enemy. Now it appeared he'd become an ally. They stood side-by-side, watching her cross the deck, and the differences between the two men couldn't have been more pronounced. Mohamed, the charming scholar, aware of—but choosing not to participate in—the perfidious politics swirling around him; a man of peace, in touch with his emotions and uninhibited in expressing them. Alexander represented the quintessential tightly-controlled, self-disciplined soldier; a warrior accustomed to giving orders. Orders that sometimes cost others their lives.

How could it be that she had simultaneous—and deeply intense—feelings for two such dissimilar men? *Oh, my god!* Her body jerked at the realization. *I really do have feelings for him.*

She didn't mean Mohamed.

Her fingers came up to touch her cheek, irritated from the scratchy towel, as she joined them at the rail.

"Your face is red," Mohamed said needlessly.

"Yes," she replied gloomily, "in more ways than one. But we have more important things to talk about."

Alex coughed, covering his mouth to hide an uncharacteristic grin. "I've brought Mohamed up to date with the same information we shared earlier."

Mohamed nodded with apparent acceptance of the truth of what he'd been told. *Interesting, thought Julia, that he seems this easily convinced. We both appear to be susceptible to "the Commander's" authoritative air. Well, maybe that's a good thing. Without question, he has far greater experience at this sort of thing than we do. If we could establish a basic level of trust, it would only increase the chance of stopping the attacks.*

On the other hand, he may be a double-dealing, lying, snake-in-the-grass.

"All right, Julia," Alex interrupted her troubled thoughts. "It's time you filled me in on what your role is in this maneuver."

Julia glanced at Mohamed and found his reproachful eyes on her. She cleared her throat and chose her words with care. "Your earlier assessment of the situation was mostly correct. Obviously, I'm *not* a professional 'spook,' as you called it. I was approached—recruited, if you will—by U.S. Intelligence to collect a communication on their behalf."

Alex noted her discomfiture as she conspicuously avoided looking back in Mohamed's direction. "They chose me because I've made several recent trips here and Egyptian Intelligence has exempted me from suspicion as an agent. I picked up the message, coded of course, and have already forwarded it on. No idea what it contained. End of story."

She turned to look out over the river while Alex studied her profile. Tight muscles around her mouth and the set line of her jaw aroused a tingling feeling of skepticism.

"But that's not all, is it, Julia? What is it you're not telling me?"

"Alexander, you are a very, very bad boy!" The shrill admonishment came from the lips of an incensed Fiona as she bore down on the triumvirate. "How *could* you leave me alone and unprotected in that *den of iniquity?*"

With ill-concealed aggravation, Alex turned away to face the on-coming assault, but not before saying under his breath, "We'll have to continue this later. Meet me here tomorrow morning at seven."

That would give him time to consider his options.

Fiona seized his arm, ignoring Julia and Mohamed as if they didn't exist, and literally dragged the commanding ex-military officer away as easily as a poodle on a lead. It was all Julia could do not to burst out into loud, hysterical laughter. She covered her mouth with both hands and sputtered as she leaned over the rail, feeling real hysteria begin to build in the pit of her churning stomach.

"Control yourself, Julia. Please." Lines of irritation etched gloomy grooves across Mohamed's brow.

She gulped air. "I don't know how much more of this I can take. Things have become much too complicated. Complicated and scary."

He nodded, leaning with his back and elbows against the rail, watching Alex watch the two of them as the insufferable woman continued to reprimand him. "Do you think he's to be trusted?"

"I have no idea. But, one way or the other, we'll find out in the morning when I call San Francisco. After that, we'll come straight back to the boat, collect our luggage, and get the hell out of here."

"It is a most inconvenient time for this," complained Mohamed. He trailed Julia's stalking figure along the corniche toward the Old Cataract Hotel at half-past five the next morning. Like most of his fellow countrymen, he was a creature of the night. "I hate rising this early, especially when it involves something as distasteful as this. We will probably not be allowed to enter the hotel grounds in any case, much less be able to place the call. Security there is very tight."

The Old Cataract, as he well knew, was considered one of the finest hotels in Egypt, a bastion of elegance situated on well-guarded grounds and surrounded by a high, gated wall.

"Well, we'll have to think of something. There's not a chance in hell I won't be making that call on schedule."

"You have been cursing a great deal lately, Julia. It's most unbecoming."

"Trust me, if I don't get to that phone on time, you'll hear words you never even knew existed. Not to mention everyone else within twenty miles of here." She advanced with determination up to the uniformed man, asleep on a stool in the guardhouse inside a heavy wrought-iron gate.

Startled awake, the guard instinctively reached for a battered rifle propped against the wall. Mohamed spoke to him in soothing Arabic tones. The man shook his head from side-to-side with an unpleasant look on his face. Being awakened at this ungodly hour, even if he was technically on duty, hadn't gone over well.

"Tell him we're checking in," Julia said through a forced smile.

After more head shaking and some arm waving, Mohamed slipped several bills into the man's moist outstretched hand and steered Julia by the elbow through the gate and up the gravel drive. They entered through a large revolving glass door and walked quickly down a grand entrance hall to the reception desk. An immaculately suited desk clerk greeted them as Mohamed inquired in Arabic for directions to the phone booths. A lengthy conversation ensued that did not seem to bode well for their mission.

The clerk turned to address Julia in polite, precise English. "I am sorry, Madame. It is the policy of the hotel that the phone booths are for guests only."

She flashed her best smile. "My name is Julia Grant and I'll be checking into the hotel tomorrow. I have a reservation. I would be most grateful if you would extend me this courtesy. It's urgent that I place a call to the United States. My mother is ill and I must speak with her doctor as soon as possible."

Mohamed's jaw dropped. The clerk, visibly enthralled by the tall, elegant woman and overwhelmed at the thought of her gratitude, bowed his head as if to royalty. "Of course, Madame Grant. Please follow me."

"So much for hotel policy," grumbled Mohamed, following them around a corner and down another long hall. They encountered no one else along the way. Because everyone with any sense is still asleep, he thought moodily. He also made a mental note to speak to Julia at the earliest possible opportunity regarding her shocking proficiency at concocting such a spontaneous, bald-faced lie.

Cursing and now lying. What was happening to his angel?

"Please let me know if you require any further assistance, Madame." The clerk all but clicked his heels as he bowed again before departing back the way they'd come. A mistake must have been made somewhere because he knew for sure he held no reservation in Madame Grant's name.

Alexander returned to the boat following an early morning walk after a restless night. He was making circuits around the upper deck, deep in thought, when he saw Julia and Mohamed emerge from the gangway and turn along the corniche, heading south.

"Oh, Christ," he said under his breath, "what are those two up to now?" Without wasting a second, he sprinted down the stairs to follow the scheming, exasperating pair at a cautious distance.

CHAPTER 26

D ebra Manning sniffed disdainfully as she removed dirty cups from the debris on the coffee table in Brad Caldwell's office. Disapproval radiated from her like a corona.

Well, she's got it right, thought Brad irritably. What a goddamn fiasco. The meeting had been a long and contentious one. The message from Zed caused a predictable uproar. Even their small group couldn't agree on how best to share the information within the dysfunctional U.S. Intelligence agencies, so how the hell were they going to decide how to pass it along to all the other countries involved?

And how were they supposed to verify the mind-boggling plot? Their undercover agent, whose presence had supposedly been unknown to Egyptian Intelligence, was dead. His unconfirmed communiqué had been passed on by a civilian with no credentials whatsoever.

Nevertheless, if the information checked out, it demanded immediate action.

Code Red action.

And what could be urgent enough for Julia Grant to request this break with protocol to call him, jeopardizing her cover? She knew the risk in that. Was she simply overwrought because of the murder? After all, Julia was an untrained civilian, he reminded himself sullenly. She didn't know a damn thing about protocol, and who could blame her for being overwrought? Or could there be something else? Jesus Christ, what more could there be?

The presence of Alexander Bryant on the scene presented an unexpected stroke of good luck. Brad had had him checked out thoroughly and he was solid. At least as far as they could tell, anyway. He rubbed the stubble on his chin as he checked the time. Only an hour to go before her call. Bob Bronson would be back to participate in the conversation. The additional reports should be in by then and Brad had damn well better have a plan of action to suggest by the time his boss returned.

It took several tedious tries before the call went through. When the connection finally came, Brad picked it up on the first ring. "Caldwell," he said brusquely.

"Brad, its Julia Grant."

"Yes, Julia. Bob is here with me. I'm putting you on speaker."

Julia looked nervously over her shoulder at Mohamed, who waited outside the booth. His steady gaze and reassuring presence provided much-needed confidence. She smiled at him through the glass.

"Julia? Are you there? What's going on?"

"Yes, Brad." She drew a deep breath, attempting to focus on keeping her words as concise as possible. "Have you received the first message?"

"Yep. It's in the pipeline. What else?"

She shook her head, not quite believing what she was about to say.

"There is more. It's short but definitely not sweet. Quite the opposite. Is it safe to read it to you?"

The two men exchanged a pained look. "You have it with you, written down?" Brad asked, censure clear in his tone.

Fireworks exploded in Julia's head. "No, damn it, of course not! I have the damn laptop with me, as per my strict instructions, okay? You'll have to run it through Vocabulary." Her knuckles turned white as she clenched the phone.

"Right. No criticism intended. Go ahead."

The laptop lay open on her knees, open to the file with the original, coded message as it had been written on Zed's folded piece of paper. She'd burned the paper—flushing the ashes down the toilet—and deleted the decoded file. She could hear the patter of his fingers on a keyboard and then silence as the message decoded at his end. The silence stretched out between them across six thousand miles.

Julia sat with head bowed, again agonizing over the full impact of what that message conveyed. How was it possible that these fanatics could imagine that God—their revered Allah—would condone this kind of mass destruction of humanity? It was unthinkable. Unimaginable. And yet, it could prove devastatingly real. The ground seemed to fall away beneath her.

Some inner compulsion forced her to break the long silence. "What can we do?"

Bob cleared his throat and responded with unmistakable authority. "You are to do nothing, Julia. Absolutely nothing. Your part is finished and we are forever in your debt. We'll take it from here." After a few seconds he added, "Be careful, finish the trip as planned and return home safely. Do you understand?"

A wave of relief engulfed her, though edged with guilt. How could she walk away now and forget all she'd learned? But, after all, what else could she do? Then she remembered to ask, "What about Alexander Bryant?"

Again the two men exchanged a telling glance and Bob nodded approval before Brad replied. "Bryant is definitely okay. Although retired from a distinguished military career, he still takes on the occasional assignment for us as well as the Brits. You can trust him."

"But, Julia," interrupted Bob, "I repeat: Your work is done. There's no need for any further communication with him or anyone else regarding this matter. Do you understand?"

"Yes, of course. I understand." Her voice grew tenuous as she asked, "Will I hear from you again?"

Brad's response held a comforting ring of familiarity. "Keep sending your daily emails and checking the publisher's website. Stick to the plan. We'll be in touch before the end of the day."

"All right then. Goodbye. And good luck." Those words, while without doubt the most heartfelt ever to pass her lips, seemed hopelessly inadequate.

"Take care, Julia," she heard Bob say before the line went dead.

Her eyes closed for a moment as she took a shaky breath. As she turned on the stool to push back the folding door, she raised a weary head, expecting to find Mohamed's comforting presence. Instead she found herself looking directly into the hard gray stare of Alexander Bryant.

Brad Caldwell pressed the intercom for Ms. Manning. "I want everyone in the conference room in ten minutes. Everyone." He replaced the phone in its cradle and looked at his boss. Bob had walked to the window and stood looking out at the lights glittering on the bridge and all across the bay. The night shone remarkably clear.

Bob Bronson sat mutely near the back of the room. He'd spent his entire career, indeed his entire life it seemed, in U.S. Intelligence. Straight from Annapolis, he'd been swept into military intelligence and from there to the CIA. When things on the international scene shifted several years ago into the current and treacherous minefield of global terrorism, his experience and level head propelled him to new heights of responsibility, focusing now on the organization and distribution of information.

In over forty years of service, he'd seen and heard many mind-boggling and unspeakable things. Nothing in his experience had prepared him for dealing with a situation like this. He'd told Julia Grant they were in the fight of their lives. He inwardly shuddered at the thought of how true his words might prove.

If the Islamic jihadists got their hands on the Israeli nuclear weapons, it could mean the end. The end of everything. Try as he might to maintain a proper perspective, he found it impossible to keep from his minds-eye the image of Armageddon. And of the innocent woman he bore essential responsibility for placing squarely in the middle of it.

Caldwell strode into the room, thumping the door shut behind him. He scowled at a short computer printout before addressing the group assembled there.

"Okay. We suspect they already have a stockpile of perhaps as much as eighty percent of what's needed to accomplish their goals and have laid strategic plans for the invasion from the borders of Egypt, Syria, Lebanon and Jordan. Funding is probably being supplied from numerous sources in several countries. The elimination of any one single cash flow would have no effect on disrupting the plan. Arms must be coming from several different sources as well, so the same principle applies." He turned to face the map of the Middle East projected on the wall.

"We've already informed the State Department. Clearly, all governments concerned must be notified. Security will be strengthened around all Israeli borders as well as the nuclear facility. The governments of the bordering countries will begin exhaustive searches for the stockpiled arms. Unfortunately, we have no idea how many of the weapons have already been smuggled into Israel."

He turned back to face the solemn group. "But here's the hard part."

"*Here's* the hard part?" The flip question came from Linda Boyd, one of the more outspoken members of his team. Incredulity shone plainly across her intelligent face.

Brad frowned, ignoring the outburst. "There was an additional message. Again, we have no way to verify." His lips tightened before opening Pandora's Box. "It appears that their plan includes a 'distraction' to divert attention from the invasion and the take-over of the nuclear facility."

He paused, all eyes riveted on his tense face, and a breathless silence filled the room. "The Mujahideen are planning to use chemical weapons indiscriminately on the entire population of Jerusalem."

Julia's hand shook as she added too much sugar to her brimming cup of café au lait. The table out by the hotel pool overlooked the river and stood far removed from other tables and chairs. Not that anyone was around who might overhear. Sunrise crouched on the edge of the horizon. Desert stars still blazed in the pre-dawn sky while a faint blue line lightened the rim of the distant hills.

The *Fajr*, the morning call to prayer, swelled across the rooftops. Mohamed discreetly excused himself to observe the call and show obedience to Allah.

Alex considered the lovely, distraught woman across from him and once again struggled to suppress an almost overwhelming urge to take her in his arms and hold her close. Her face appeared touchingly thin in the growing light.

"I had to call the office," she said quietly. "That's all."

He continued to study her, noting that her demeanor had altered perceptibly from last night: from suspicion and nervous confusion to profound relief tinged with a resigned, deep sadness. Whatever happened to render this change, it was imperative that he discover the cause, one

184

way or another.

The laptop case she was never without lay on the table next to her cup. He suspected that everything he needed to know resided in that computer. But without her cooperation, it would take time to access the information. Time they might not have.

"Listen to me, Julia. We need to level with one another. Completely. Everything I've told you about my reason for being here is true. But there's something else you should know." He hesitated as she raised troubled eyes. "I'll tell you all I know, in good faith, if you'll do the same."

"I can't promise that."

"Fair enough. But you should know that you and Mohamed may both be in grave danger."

Her body jerked involuntarily. "What do you mean?"

He delivered a brief, edited version of his lunch conversation of the previous day. She sat dumbstruck, incapable of speech. This was the worst possible development. Not only had she put herself in a vulnerable position with these ruthless, murdering men, she had also, definitely and irrevocably, placed Mohamed squarely in their crosshairs.

"Let me give you a piece of advice, from one American who is only trying to prevent more violence, to another: Call your contact back. Tell him what I've just told you and then let me speak with him. We can work together on a plan to get you and Mohamed safely out of this."

The insistent phone was ringing as Brad Caldwell barreled through the door. He snatched it up with a curt, "Caldwell."

Static on the line for a few seconds made conversation impossible before a woman's voice said, "Brad, it's Julia again. I, ah," she paused momentarily at a loss for words. "I have more news."

"Okay, Julia, go ahead." His steady voice belied the roiling of his gut. He listened without interruption, trying to relax his grip on the phone.

"Okay. Let me speak with Bryant. Then I'll speak with you again."

At least this latest bad news came with a silver lining. One of the decisions arrived, at only moments ago, was to bring Alexander Bryant into the loop. He, in turn, could alert the Brits. Unofficially, of course. This would circumvent having to try to verify the information before communicating it through proper channels.

Julia watched Alex's tense face while he spoke with Brad. They stood disconcertingly close, crowded into the tiny phone booth. All of the conflicting emotions she'd felt for him in the past few turbulent days—attraction, disappointment, admiration, aversion, suspicion—flew around in her head, like kites on a windy day.

"Understood. Understood." Alex passed the phone back to her.

"Julia, are you there? Listen to me closely. I want you to share the full content of all you've learned with Commander Bryant. Give him the laptop. Show him the procedure. He needs to know everything you know." Brad paused before adding, "Everything, Julia, do you understand?"

"Is that 'just in case,' Brad?"

He cursed under his breath. "We'll get you out, Julia. You have my word on that."

"And Mohamed?" she asked in a low voice.

"Uh, yeah. Mohamed too."

Julia found the slightly hesitant reply far from reassuring.

"In the meantime, cancel your reservations back to Cairo and both of you check into the Old Cataract. The hotel has wireless internet access. At six p, your time, send your usual transmission. Check *Special Events* on the website for further instructions. Is that clear?"

"Oh, yes, Brad. It's all clear. Perfectly clear."

Acrimony plumped each slowly-delivered word. The thought came too late as she hung up that she'd forgotten to ask about the other agent on the boat who was supposedly assigned to keep an eye on her.

Mohamed removed his shoes and reverently began the ritual of washing of his face, hands and feet before entering the mosque. He had done this thousands of times in his life. A lifetime, he thought with despair, that may very well be nearing its end. Finding a place in the crowded building, he attempted to focus on his prayers. The voice of the *Imam* guided his movements while the voice of his conscience continued its tirade.

This unthinkable situation had become a source of increasing, unbearable conflict for him. He was a man of peace. Peace on Earth was the ideal for the world of Islam. War was abhorred. The Koran made this clear.

But it made equally clear that there were times when there was no alternative but to fight. According to Islamic Law, armed struggle could be initiated to defend one's community or nation from aggressors; to liberate people from living under oppressive regimes; or to remove any government that would not allow the free practice of Islam within its borders.

The Jihadists contended the Israelis were guilty of all three. The Western governments who provided support for Israel shared equally in the blame—America at the top of the list. Although Mohamed disapproved of the violence being enacted around the world in the name of Islam, he—along with an overwhelming majority of his Arab brothers—agreed with the judgment against the state of Israel.

Hamas proclaimed "they felt God's hand guided them" in the violent and bloody response, paraphrasing the Koran—exhorting Allah to deliver the faithful from the Infidels.

Until now, as far as Mohamed was concerned, disapproval had been the extent of his commitment. Now, his *haram* relationship with Julia forced him to the junction of having to act. One way or the other. By helping her in this deplorable assignment—into which he'd been indifferently thrust, without even the courtesy of enlightenment—he would be working against his Islamic brothers. Even by doing nothing, thereby allowing her government to circumvent the attack, his failure to act would result in the probable death of a number of Muslims.

Jerusalem remained the crux of the decades-old conflict. The Palestinians were adamant that East Jerusalem be the capital for their long-promised independent state. Israel continued to make it abundantly clear they would never give it up. The idea of hundreds of thousands of innocent people dying there—Muslims as well as Christians and Jews— was sickening and, of course, unacceptable.

That atrocity must be stopped at all costs.

Conversely, he could alert the Brothers to the discovery of their plot, thereby saving their lives. But by doing this he would certainly be further endangering Julia.

Julia. His angel.

She, more than once, had discussed with him the concept of making the ancient city of Jerusalem—that figured so importantly in three religions— an independent state, like the Vatican, and have it ruled by the United Nations. Her sincere and passionate desire for a peaceful resolution to the conflict made her, in his eyes, a remarkable woman. The woman he loved more than he'd ever loved anyone or anything. The woman he desperately wanted for his wife. She'd believed in him, helped him through a difficult time in his life, giving unselfishly her counsel, comfort, and love.

And money. Don't, he thought with renewed guilt and shame, forget the money.

Was this his punishment for a *haram* love? Was it a test of his faith?

CHAPTER 27

Alexander looked up to see Mohamed come through the arched doorway leading from the hotel. He saw them still seated at the table on the far side of the pool, and approached in his usual lithe, fluid gait. Alexander's eyes narrowed against the morning sun.

Julia had told him the entire story. Without going into intimate details, she'd revealed the closeness she'd shared with the enigmatic Egyptian, as well as the unscrupulous advantage taken by the intelligence boys in using the ill-fated relationship to leverage her cooperation.

The sons-of-bitches, he thought angrily. It was one thing to manipulate government employees or members of the military, who all-knowingly and willingly volunteered for hazardous duty. Blackmailing innocent civilians into taking part in chancy operations for which they had no background or training was untenable. Especially a woman like Julia Grant.

Over the past few days, he'd seen her handing out pens and *baksheesh* to grubby children at every opportunity. Seen how she smiled compassionately as she put bills in the weathered hands of the poverty stricken, toothless old women—some probably no older than she—but aged beyond their years by hardship and deprivation.

On the edge of the granite quarry yesterday, one of the men from the boat had teased a starving dog, making it jump high into the air for crumbs of stale bread. Julia had gently pushed him aside and knelt down in the dirt to give the scrawny beast slices of cheese dug from her bag. One could always judge people by their treatment of animals, thought Alex.

He knew he'd allowed his feelings for her to grow beyond a prudent regard. The story she'd shared only amplified a growing respect for her as a compassionate and caring human being. A large part of her feelings for Mohamed, he told himself, was clearly compassion—and her apparent need to help those less fortunate. Relentless logic instantly ridiculed this judgment for seeing what he wanted to see.

Regardless of what drove her to commit countless acts of kindness, he must—at all costs—protect her and extricate her safely from all this. Anger again flared as he thought of the cold, calculating men who'd put her here. The sons-of-bitches.

"So," inquired Mohamed without enthusiasm, "what's the plan?" He slumped into a chair across from Julia, his dark eyes watching her shut down the laptop.

She shot a look at Alex, with a clear, unspoken message: Didn't I tell you?

For she'd known Mohamed wouldn't miss the significance of the open computer. Alex had wanted to keep his new role in the affair a secret, but she insisted that Mohamed be told of all that transpired in his absence. Mohamed had been used and manipulated, she protested vehemently. It wasn't fair and she would no longer be a part of any deception. She trusted him and whether they liked it or not, they were all in this together. "'All for one and one for all,'" she declared with finality.

Julia pushed the laptop to Alex. "He knows everything. It's his problem now."

Alex nodded reluctantly and turned to Mohamed. "I realize you've been an unknowing and unwilling accomplice in all this, Mohamed. I'll do everything within my power to see that you don't suffer for it."

If Mohamed felt surprise, he failed to show it. "So. What next?"

Both men looked to Julia's gaunt, pensive face. She, in turn, looked out at the river. In the distance she could see a colony of milky-white egrets congregating on one of the many islands in the middle of the swiftly flowing water. The confusion and uncertainty of the past few days weighed heavy on her heart. Inhaling deeply of the fresh morning air, she said, "All right, Mohamed, this is where we are."

He received the news more calmly than she'd expected. This, for some reason, bothered her. Not that his seeming passivity was totally out of character. He often took time to reflect on things before responding.

Nonetheless, his compliance made her faintly uneasy.

After ordering a breakfast of which very little was consumed, they agreed to return separately to the boat. Alexander watched the striking pair cross the terrace, heads on a level plane, her burnished hair shining in the full light of day.

Jalal waited nervously in the back of the cramped coffee shop. He picked a stray thread from his slacks and re-crossed his legs for the umpteenth time. The call came at the last minute, with instructions to meet here. He went back over in his mind, again, their last conversation. Ahmed and his companion, the remarkably repulsive and equally deadly Faoud, had observed and overheard yesterday's meeting with Bryant. Ahmed had not been convinced of the innocence of the woman and her guide, the man Zahar.

He made his contempt for the pair clear as he instructed Jalal to keep them under close surveillance. The leader was correct. Their early morning visit to the hotel was decidedly suspicious.

Not only the lovebirds, but also the fact that Bryant had covertly followed them.

Tight security surrounded the hotel. The Brother assigned to follow failed to get onto the grounds, and their regular contact there was not on duty. As a result, they were not yet able to learn what transpired inside. He did not look forward to bringing Ahmed this news.

When he spotted the striking figure in the doorway, he half rose from his seat then sank back down on the rickety chair. Ahmed, dignified in a plain gray robe with a snowy white turban, looking for all-the-world a prophet, greeted the proprietor in flowery Arabic before joining his Brother. He spoke in English as it was less likely, should they be overheard, that their words would be understood. After a cursory greeting, he came straight to the point.

"What have the Infidels been up to since yesterday?"

Jalal glanced at the outwardly serene face and proceeded with caution. "It may be as you suspected." He related the morning's unusual activities.

Ahmed did not interrupt. He sat motionless, with eyes half-closed looking out the dirty window at people in the street passing by. When Jalal finished, he mused aloud, "The 'Commander' followed them without their knowledge. Perhaps, after your questions yesterday, he attempts to learn if the woman is a spy."

Jalal held his tongue, having learned it best to wait until asked to comment. Ahmed's reputation for a violent temper was well-known, and, though seldom aroused, the frightening consequences, legendary. The shrewd, aristocratic features remained unreadable for a few moments of reflection before finally softening into a benevolent smile.

"We shall proceed as planned. Contact Bryant and set up the meeting for tonight at ten o'clock."

This was the safest time—early enough for people to still be at dinner and not so late as to draw suspicion from the police. "And," he added in a deceptively pleasant tone, "I want Zahar."

Alexander hadn't been entirely candid with Julia—or with Brad Caldwell. He felt distinctly uncomfortable with the way the situation had deteriorated into a tangled web of pretense and half-truths. But there wasn't a damn thing he could do about it until James gave him the go-ahead.

He pushed himself from the chair by the pool, now fully exposed to the relentless sun, and headed for the reception desk to confirm his reservation. After yesterday's meeting he'd stopped by to book a room. As foretold, there was no problem. The deluxe suite, in fact, came at a most reasonable rate. It would be ready and waiting for him anytime after noon. Alexander couldn't decide whether all three of them staying in the same hotel would prove fortuitous, or disastrous.

Reservation confirmed, he headed for the privacy of the phone booth—the same one he'd used to place the call to James in the wee morning hours. Although he lacked Julia's feminine charm, his generous use of cash resulted in the same end. He knew setting up the call on a secure line would take a while—secure at the other end, in any case. This wasn't the kind of news one could just blurt out.

Julia and Mohamed walked in silence along the corniche, oblivious to the activity around them. Neither could think of anything else to say. As they approached the gangway, he stopped.

"Go ahead and prepare for moving to the hotel. I will come for you when it is time."

"Where are you going?"

"I need to think. I am going for a *narghileh*," he answered, defiance ringing in the last few words. A while ago he'd succumbed to what he referred to as Julia's "constant nagging" and quit smoking. It was a source of irritation to her that he didn't consider the water pipe as smoking. This did not seem a good time to debate that issue.

"When will you be back?"

"Soon. Plan to leave for the hotel at noon." Without further comment, he started up the aged stone steps.

She stood still to watch him reach the top and, as he'd done once before, long ago, turn to look down at her for a poignant moment before disappearing into the crowd. She couldn't tell whether the vague prickle of foreboding came from a sense of déjà vu or from her on-edge nerves over the increasingly volatile situation.

Mohamed made a brief stop at a corner shop then continued on to a café a few blocks down the street. He pulled out a chair at a sidewalk table and waved to the waiter to bring him a pipe.

Honestly, things were spiraling out of control. He would have to call Shahida to let her know there would be a delay in his returning home. That was the least of his worries. He had no doubt whatsoever that if the Brothers suspected him of involvement in activities to thwart their plans, his life would be worth less than a scraggly dog on the street.

To add insult to injury, he had a growing uncomfortable feeling that Julia was becoming emotionally attached to the American. It left him with a bitter taste of the anguish she must have felt from the beginning of their relationship—due to his marriage to another woman. He hated this feeling of jealousy and had no legitimate grounds for it. As she'd said many times: The decision was his. That hardly made things easier. He brooded to the sound of the gurgling water as he pulled smoke into his lungs.

"Marhabba kaif halak," murmured the man who took a chair at the next table. Egyptian but, like Mohamed, wearing Western dress, he signaled the waiter for a pipe. "My wife is always after me about smoking the *narghileh,"* said his neighbor sociably.

"A man must take care of his needs," replied Mohamed philosophically.

Once he had unwrapped the new, clean mouthpiece and the coals glowed, the man said, "You are Mohamed Zahar, are you not?" Without waiting for a reply he went on. "We met once at the home of your sister, before her marriage. Her husband, Hedayet, is a good friend. I am Hassan."

They shook hands. Although the man did look vaguely familiar, Mohamed found no recollection of their having met. But then, in his business, he met so many people. It was not unusual to forget a name or a face. They sat companionably for a while, enjoying the pipes and casual conversation. The welcome diversion relieved him from his unsettling thoughts. Eventually, the conversation turned to automobiles, a universal topic of interest to all Egyptian males.

"Hedayet is thinking to buy my car. It is a fine machine, a 1998 Saab," said Hassan proudly. "Would you like to see? I am parked around the corner."

Mohamed agreed willingly, leaving a few notes on the table, and followed his new acquaintance. He led the way around the corner and down a narrow street, keeping up a constant stream of chatter on the wonders of his fine car. The typical backstreet had vehicles lined up on the curb and cats lounging in the dirt.

A dust-covered van parked close to the wall forced them to walk single file in order to pass. The man calling himself Hassan motioned for Mohamed to walk ahead. When a side door of the van sprang open, the man gave him a hard push from behind. Mohamed fell sideways onto a pile of scratchy blankets as a smelly wool sack was thrust over his head.

"Shut up and be still," rasped a second voice of pure menace, "if you wish to live." He jerked Mohamed's hands behind his back and bound them roughly with a worn, dirty piece of rope.

CHAPTER 28

Julia tossed clothes into the open suitcase on the bed while she tried to sort out her muddled feelings. It was almost impossible to separate the many and wildly divergent thoughts that darted through her mind like maniacal sparrows. At least everyone involved in this nightmare agreed on one thing: They would do whatever necessary to stop the terrorists from the unthinkable horrors planned for the people of Jerusalem.

There was ostensibly nothing more she could contribute to prevent the taking of the nuclear facility. Responsibility for that fell to the governments. On the other hand, despite Bob's words of dismissal, she knew—to the core of her being—that she would do anything she could to prevent the chemicals from making it across the Egyptian border.

Alexander wouldn't like it. Mohamed definitely wouldn't like it. Regardless, when Brad made contact later today she resolved to make her determination to help fully understood.

Mohamed's involvement presented another dilemma altogether. He was at much greater risk than the two Americans. He lived in this country; there would be no escape for him if the militants learned of his complicity. The Egyptian government wouldn't much care for it either.

He could so easily simply disappear one day, never to be seen or heard from again. His fate might never be known. Julia shivered at the thought.

She'd touched briefly on this while filling Alex in this morning but, what with all of the information to impart, perhaps she hadn't fully conveyed the strength of her feelings on the subject. She planned to correct that at the first opportunity.

It was imperative that he understand and apply whatever influence he might have to help get Mohamed out of all this safely, without repercussions. Brad said he would take care of it. Common sense told Julia, with more pressing things to think about at the moment, Mohamed's safety might slip his mind. Nor could she trust that he would be in a position to honor his word.

She felt a surprising awareness of a budding feeling of solidarity, and trust, in Alexander. In spite of the fact that he came from a world she'd always regarded as reprehensible, he now represented safety—protection. She found herself yearning to lean on the strength of it.

And there was something else.

Basic, raw, masculine appeal radiated from him like a beacon of light on a stormy night at sea. Each time they met, she felt more drawn to him. A sexual tension crackled between them. Mohamed felt it, too. She could tell. It amazed her that she could be attracted to two such different men. Compounding that anomaly was the fact that neither man would have even come close to passing her famous litmus test for husband material. Sarah would never let her forget this.

If Julia survived to tell her about it.

Berating herself in disgust for indulging these frivolous thoughts while other issues of such paramount importance loomed, she went to the bathroom and began throwing cosmetics into a bag. After scanning the room for anything overlooked, she checked her watch to find the time half past eleven. Her scanty breakfast left her stomach rumbling, so she decided to run down to the lunch buffet.

As she passed the reception area she noticed Peter the Bookworm exiting the boat, shouldering a heavy carry-on bag. One of the stewards followed behind with two oversized suitcases. Well, so much for the idea of him as her guardian agent, she thought despondently—unless he turns up at the hotel.

Ali greeted her as she entered the dining room with his usual cheerful expression and she reminded herself to give him an extra tip. She'd already left generous gratuities for the rest of the crew. The Langleys sat at a table nearby and Henrietta waved her over.

"Well, Julia, you must've been up with the roosters this morning. We rang to see if you wanted to accompany us to visit the gardens on Kitchener's Island, but you'd already flown the coop."

Julia sank into a chair next to the kindly, reassuring presence of the elderly woman. "Yes, I had to make a call to the States." Going on quickly to prevent any questions, she added, "I'm sorry that today will be our last on the boat together. It has *truly* been a pleasure to meet you both and share Egypt with you." She reached over and squeezed the frail hand resting on the table. Henrietta returned the gesture with surprising strength.

"We, too, have enjoyed your company immensely, my dear. It's a shame we can't spend more time together. But I do have some exciting news." She looked affectionately at her devoted spouse of over fifty years. "As I've fallen madly in love with Aswan, Henry presented me with a lovely gift this morning. We'll be extending our trip to stay here for a while."

Pleased for her new friend's obvious delight, Julia smiled and gave her hand another squeeze. "That's wonderful. Where will you stay?"

"Henry pulled out all the stops and booked us into the Old Cataract. It will be like a second honeymoon." She blushed like a young bride.

A faint bell tinkled in Julia's subconscious. "But that's amazing. I've decided to stay here for a few more days as well. Mohamed has agreed to stay on as my guide and we'll also be at the Old Cataract."

"Excellent! He's such a charming young man, and always so interesting to talk to. Perhaps the four of us could have dinner this evening. We'd like that, wouldn't we, Henry?"

Was this too coincidental? Of course not, Julia admonished herself. How could she possibly doubt the genuineness of this gentle pair? She was becoming paranoid.

Alexander left the hotel and returned to the boat to efficiently pack his belongings. His hand hesitated over the phone, uncharacteristically undecided about his next move. Should he check in with Julia to make sure she was all right?

What in the world was the matter with him?

He was behaving like an adolescent. Dialing her cabin, he listened impatiently as the phone continued to ring without answer. Annoyed, he noted the time: twenty past one. They must've already left the boat for the hotel.

The London call had taken an irksomely long time to go through and then he'd grabbed a quick lunch at the Old Cataract. He picked up the phone again and rang for a steward to collect his luggage. He could have easily managed it himself, but passengers were expected to allow the staff to perform every possible service. The obligatory gratuity doubtless represented a large portion of their income. Alex didn't begrudge them an honest living, although he found the custom bothersome at times.

While he waited he looked out at the river through the open window, analyzing the conversation with James. A sharp knock interrupted his dismal thoughts. Assuming it to be the steward, he opened the door with suitcase in hand—only to be confronted by Julia, panic written unmistakably across her pale, expressive face.

"May I come in?" The faint words were almost unintelligible.

He wordlessly reached for her arm and pulled her in before poking his head back out the door. Just coming around the corner, the steward smiled. Alex stepped out into the corridor with his bag and handed it over, ensuring that Julia wasn't seen. With bag dispatched along with instructions to hold it at the reception desk, he closed and locked the door.

She stood looking out the window in the same spot he'd been only a moment before. At the sound of the lock, she whirled around to face him. "Mohamed has disappeared."

He swiftly crossed the cabin to grab her hands and pull her down next to him on the couch. "Tell me exactly what happened—from when you left the hotel."

With a monumental effort to suppress the sick feeling of fear that crawled up her throat, she said, "We came straight back to the boat. He didn't come aboard though, said he was going for a water pipe. He was upset. And understandably angry. He said he'd be back to leave for the hotel by noon." Tears sprang into her eyes as she took a ragged breath.

"Is he usually punctual?

"Yes. Unless he's prevented. And then he calls. Always."

"Stay here." Alex went to the bathroom and returned with tissues for the tears that escaped her brimming eyes and trickled down her cheeks. She accepted them gratefully, blotting her face, then rose to pace the cabin.

"They have him, don't they?"

Their eyes locked across the room. The possibility pulsed between them like a live wire. He didn't need to say anything. She knew the answer. She closed her eyes, reeling from shock and shame. As his arms closed around her, she began to cry.

He felt the inconsolable sorrow that emanated from the woman as he held her tight against the pounding of his heart. Over the top of her head, through the wide window, he watched the perennial, swift flow of the River Nile, remembering James's last question that morning.

What about this guide? This Mohamed? Can he be trusted?

The sack reeked of livestock. Probably made from a camel or donkey blanket, the scratchy fabric had clearly never known contact with soap and water. Mohamed was led through a low doorway, where he bumped his head painfully on the frame. A steely grip guided him to a bench against a rough wall. The raspy voice ordered him to sit.

They'd driven in the van for what seemed like hours before arriving at this destination. He had no idea where they might be. His thoughts gyrated between trying to pick up clues about his captors and prayers to Allah. After a while, he became aware that all movement in the room had ceased. Thinking himself alone, he started to get up.

"Sit," came the harsh command from nearby. He sat.

After an interminable passage of time, he heard the squeak of a door and felt, rather than saw, sunlight shoot into the room. Several pairs of feet shuffled in, but still no one spoke. The sound of a chair being dragged across a dirt floor preceded a pleasant voice with a perfect upper-class English drawl.

"Welcome, Mr. Zahar. We appreciate your taking the time to meet with us."

Another man's snigger ceased as quickly as it began, no doubt silenced by the displeasure of the man-in-charge.

"Please pardon us for not removing the hood. As uncomfortable as it may be, it is much healthier for you in the long run. It would be most unfortunate if you were to see our faces." The cultured voice paused, giving his next words a theatrical effect.

"For we would then be forced to slit your throat."

❖

Despite the gentle breeze sweeping across the water, a merciless sun made the afternoon uncomfortably warm. Julia and Alexander leaned against the rail on the deck in what, under other circumstances, might be called a companionable silence. Following her descent into despair, they calmly discussed their options. Julia, at length, agreed to wait at least another hour before taking any action, and returned to her cabin in a vain attempt to repair the ravages left by her breakdown.

When she emerged on deck, large dark glasses covered her still-puffy red eyes. No one would notice as long as she didn't have to socialize.

"Alex! Oh, Alex, darling!" came the dreaded shrill cry. "The Fiona," as Mohamed dubbed her, approached at an alarming pace. A low growl rumbled in Julia's throat.

"Stay here. I'll get rid of her." *Alex Darling* stepped swiftly away to cut off the assault. With protestations of friendship, affection and the extraction of a pledge to call when he returned to London, he managed to maneuver the supercilious, clinging creature to the top of the stairs.

She had one foot on the top step when she remembered to call out, "So long, Julia. Say goodbye to Mohamed for me."

Julia planned to do that very shortly.

She froze in the blazing sun as she caught sight of Mohamed striding up the gangway. Back at her side, Alexander turned to look in the direction of her fixed stare.

He touched her arm and said with urgency, "Take a taxi to the hotel. Both of you. Call my room in an hour."

His words released her from the trance that locked her clenched hands to the rail. She nodded mutely as she returned the reassuring touch, grateful for his understanding, before rushing to the stairs.

Mohamed stood in the corridor outside his cabin, inserting the key in the lock. She gasped at the sight of a dark, ugly bruise on his cheek. At the sound, he looked up to find her hastening toward him. Wordlessly, he grabbed her arm and shoved her inside ahead of him.

The door banged shut as he jerked her into his arms. His lips came down on hers with such force she hadn't time to protest. Not that she was sure she wanted to. Never before had he exhibited such savage, uncontrolled passion. There would be bruises on her arms where he held her. It was a searing kiss—as if he might find the answers to his dilemmas in its depths. With sudden equal force, he released her. If she hadn't been able to stumble back against the wall, she would've fallen.

"Mohamed?"

At first he didn't answer. His back was to her now as he bent over the open suitcase on the unmade bed. When he turned to face her, she saw again the nasty bruise on his face, his lower lip cut and swollen.

"You must leave. You cannot be here. Have your luggage taken downstairs. I will meet you there in a few minutes."

"What happened?" Her voice was barely a whisper.

"Can you not, *for once,* do as I ask, Julia? Without endless questions and debate?" Despite the carefully controlled words spoken through clenched teeth, she knew by his shaking hands that he was as close to loosing control as she'd ever seen him.

The boy had a hard time keeping up with Alexander's long-legged gait as they walked the short distance from the boat to the hotel. He turned in at the wrought-iron gate, reclaimed his bag and dropped a few bills in the small, outstretched hand.

"Shukran!" called the grinning boy after him as he strode up the gravel drive.

In his room, Alex deftly unpacked the bag. The luxuriously elegant décor escaped him completely as he went about arranging his few articles of clothing and toiletries in a precise and orderly manner. Once the contents had been removed, he pressed a spot in the corner to release the false bottom. These days, it was unadvisable to carry anything through Customs in the concealed space, but it still proved useful at times. When necessary, he had other methods for procuring firearms once reaching his destination.

Secured there were the other two revolvers. With the hand of an expert, he removed the Beretta and loaded it. He snapped the chamber closed, ensuring that the safety catch engaged, and laid it on the dresser. He reassembled the false bottom and put the bag in the closet. With nothing to do now but wait, he went to the picture window and opened the drapes all the way to reveal the scene below.

His third-floor suite provided a sweeping view of the river and the barren desert beyond. He noted several *feluccas* moored at the water's edge, most likely for hire. Alexander checked the time: forty minutes to go before Julia's call, then three hours before her next communication from Brad Caldwell. Several of the graceful sailboats flitted across the sparkling current below. He considered the implications of Mohamed's mysterious disappearance.

This definitely complicated things—even further, if that was possible.

CHAPTER 29

Sarah Littlefield stared down at the sheet of paper in her hand. Unbelievable. The woman was stark raving mad. Well, Sarah had suspected this for some time. But Julia was nobody's fool. At least she'd had the good sense to leave this missive outlining the entire far-fetched story. But this? Too incredible.

The whole "I'm going hiking" thing sounded fishy from the start. As the days passed with no word from Julia, Sarah became increasingly apprehensive. No answer to her emails and ditto on the cell phone. Julia always answered her cell phone. By the morning of the sixth day, her concern drove her to hop into her fuel-efficient hybrid Prius, still in sweaty running clothes, and zip across the Bay Bridge from Berkeley to San Francisco. Sarah had insisted that Julia give her a spare key to her rented studio apartment during her illness.

"So you can discover the body?" Julia asked.

Very funny, ha, ha.

Sarah let herself in and surveyed the room. As she'd suspected, a white envelope lay on the table, her name written across the front in a bold hand. Ripping it open, she scanned the page then sat down and read it again, carefully, from the top. Unbelievable. She bit her lip as she looked out the window into the lifting fog.

Exactly one hour later she sat in a chair across the desk from Special Agent Brad Caldwell.

"I don't give a damn about rules and regulations *or* national security, Mr. Caldwell. You either tell me exactly where Julia is at this precise moment and how to reach her or you can be sure the whole nasty story will headline the evening news."

She sprang to her feet to lean forward on tight fists, livid green eyes shooting sparks across the desk. "My family may not always approve of my activities, but they *will*, with all the might of their *considerable* resources, stand behind me on this, I assure you. And just in case you don't know, they not only own a big chunk of the media in this town, they have some mighty powerful friends."

He did know. And those resources could prove more than considerable.

Sarah left Brad's office and went directly to that of her father, Charles Dormer Littlefield, III. Prudence, his secretary of over thirty years, saw the blonde cyclone exit the elevator and blow down the hall toward her father's penthouse office suite. Even though she knew her boss to be on an important conference call, she buzzed him. "Sarah's on her way in."

All parties involved knew there was no way to stop her when she'd built up this kind of awesome momentum. Outwardly, Prudence felt obligated to disapprove of the way Sarah had her father wrapped around her little finger. Secretly, she admired her and reveled in seeing the titan of industry reduced to putty in his daughter's diminutive hands.

"Damn it all to hell, Sarah! Can't you see I'm busy here?"

She came around the desk and planted a loud smacking kiss on his forehead.

"Sorry, ladies and gentlemen, I'll have to get back to you." He tried to frown as he slammed down the phone but couldn't prevent the corners of his lips from curling up at the sight of his darling, dynamic daughter. "All right, Sarah, what's so all-fired important this time? Someone not treating their pets properly? Draining their pool into the bay?"

The impressive man sat back in his big leather chair and listened with growing interest as she delivered a concise and scathing summary of Julia's predicament. He'd known his daughter's best friend for years. She'd spent numerous holidays with the Littlefield family, and he'd come to think of her as one of his own.

"Well, well," he rumbled ominously. "Those dirty bastards are up to their same old tricks." With steepled fingers before him, he pursed his lips, and his half-closed eyes settled onto the shining green ones.

"What kind of hair-brained scheme are you concocting?"

Brad Caldwell did not look his usual dapper self: jacketless, with expensive silk tie askew and a greasy stain near the breast pocket of his wrinkled shirt, the rolled-up sleeves revealing tense, muscular arms. A five-o-clock shadow, the result of not having shaved for the twenty-four hours he'd been in the office, completed the look of a shady detective in an old B movie.

It had been more than five years since he'd done any real work in the field. He'd thought those days were long gone. The wound in his side still gave him trouble in cold, damp weather—a regular reminder in the San Francisco fog. Nevertheless, he had jumped at Bob's directive that he fly to Egypt. The thought had already occurred to him, and his hesitation in bringing it up was only due to trying to think of a plausible way to suggest it himself.

He snapped his briefcase shut as a rap sounded at the door. Linda Boyd entered and came to sit in one of the chairs facing the desk. How the hell did she manage to look this fresh without sleep? he wondered disagreeably. Her medium-brown hair, cut short, emphasized wide-set hazel eyes, perpetually on the alert, and seldom missing a trick. She would never be called beautiful, but there was something decidedly appealing about her trim, athletic and always energetic persona.

"All set, Boyd?"

It was unanimously agreed that she would accompany him. The pair, traveling together as man and wife, would draw less attention than his going solo. Aliases with passports to match would at least give them time before the Egyptian authorities caught on. If—when—they did, things could become very unpleasant. It couldn't be helped.

He felt personally responsible for the deterioration of Julia Grant's "simple" assignment. Damn it, he *was* responsible. The whole thing was his bright idea. He'd pressured her in. It was up to him to get her out. He felt less than optimistic about the difficulties involved in protecting Mohamed Zahar. That part wasn't going to be easy. But he gave Julia his word. He would do the best he could.

"Yeah, I'm set," Linda said, regarding him with annoyingly clear and appraising eyes. "You look like hell."

"Thanks. The look corresponds directly with my mood, so you might take that into consideration before making any more astute observations."

His partner for this hasty operation shrugged with a grin. He didn't intimidate her. They'd worked together before. Before his near-fatal injury. In fact, they'd briefly been lovers. That was a long time ago, she thought with lingering regret. She still had a soft spot for Brad. But as far as her job was concerned, she was all business.

"The car's waiting downstairs."

He ran a hand through tousled hair as he scanned the unusual litter of papers on his desk. "Okay. The communication's been sent. We have barely enough time for me to run home to change and pack. We'll go straight from there to the base." He'd contrived to hitch a ride on an Air

Force jet leaving for Kuwait in less than two hours. From there, they'd take a commercial flight directly to Aswan.

Without further comment, she followed him down the endless corridor, her long legs easily keeping pace with his. She had her doubts about the advisability of all this. The Egyptians weren't going to like it one iota.

But Linda Boyd was a professional. Her tenacious ambition and unrelenting drive had brought her up the company ladder like a rocket. At the age of thirty-three, she was the highest ranking woman in her division. Despite her stinging wit and acid tongue, she followed orders—no matter how much she might disagree.

Besides, she would have followed Brad Caldwell anywhere.

Sarah Littlefield looked her father straight in the eye, intrepidly implacable, as she calmly announced, "I have to go to Egypt and bring her back."

Brad Caldwell had been unable—or unwilling—to reach Julia by phone and somehow Sarah, "the blonde bundle of highly-explosive antagonism" according to her father, had learned of the imminent departure of the two secret service agents. Once she'd managed to cajole Charles Littlefield into applying some of his considerable family influence, Sarah bulldozed her way onto the plane. She gave no thought whatsoever to the possibility that she might encounter obstacles other than persuading Julia to return home.

So here she was, on the Air Force jet to Kuwait with Brad Caldwell and Linda Boyd, marshalling every molecule of her five-foot-two, anti-war activist frame to retrieve the dove from the clutches of the imperialist hawks. After all, how many times had Julia come to her rescue, bailing her out of jail—more often than not in the middle of the night?

Once on board, Brad promptly retreated under a blanket for some much-needed sleep. This conveniently spared his guilt-ridden conscience from having to fend off Sarah's questions during the long flight. He kept thinking that things couldn't get any worse. And then, of course, they did.

CHAPTER 30

Mohamed could barely see beyond his wrath to pack up the rest of his few meager belongings. At least his enraged state prevented further questions from Julia. But he knew that was only temporary. He must calm down—try to think clearly. The inevitable interrogation might be delayed but not, by any means, avoided.

The taxi driver who took them to the hotel thankfully spoke enough English to make discussion unwise. Two bellmen accompanied them to the elevator. When the door opened on the second floor, one of them stepped out with Mohamed's suitcase.

Mohamed gave Julia a dark look. "Meet me out by the pool in an hour." The doors closed between them.

He sincerely hoped that would allow enough time for him to regain control of his thought processes. A decision must be made about what to tell her. Not only the cause of his injuries—but also what action they must take.

All in all, he knew he was very, very lucky. Lucky his assailants hadn't slit his throat and dumped his body in a ditch. He shuddered, vividly recalling the nerve-wracking scene. The man with the husky voice made it clear that would be his first choice. Mohamed felt the overwhelming contempt and inexplicable hatred emanating from the stranger as if directly from the fires of hell.

The other man, the one who spoke bafflingly in Oxford-perfect English, was more circumspect. After questioning him endlessly about Julia, their relationship and their activities, he remained silent for a long while.

Mohamed stuck doggedly to his story. Julia Grant was writing a book about Egypt. He'd been hired as her guide. He'd worked for her before and did not believe she could be involved in any kind of covert activities. As far as he knew, her brief exchange with the man killed in Kom Ombo was perfectly innocent. She bought a blanket and that was all. He vehemently denied any illicit romance.

It was at this point that someone struck him...slapped him with such force it knocked him to the floor. That blow produced the nasty bruise now morphing into a rainbow of color on his cheek.

His abductors were careful not to divulge anything that might identify them or their purpose. After the interrogation, there had been no discussion among them—the only sound the faint afternoon call to prayer filtering through thick mudbrick walls.

At last, the cultured English voice spoke in Arabic, to deliver a harsh sentence. "You dishonor Islam and your namesake, Mohamed Zahar: by consorting with Western Infidels and failing to answer the call to Jihad. For this, you should be executed."

Sweat trickled down between Mohamed's rigid shoulder blades. He'd never imagined such fear. It was shame for that gut-wrenching, all-consuming fear that ignited the firestorm of fury. He sat up straight as a rod on the hard bench, mustering the shreds of his wounded dignity. "We are all sinners in some way. I am a devout Muslim and strive to live each day by the wisdom of the Prophet. If I am to be punished for my sins, it is for Allah alone to decide."

Silence echoed in the close, stifling room. Ahmed's eventual response came in the placid English persona, as if it could be switched on and off like a light. "Well said, Mohamed Zahar, well said. We will spare your life today. With one condition."

Another long pause sifted through the heavy air as Mohamed forced himself to continue to sit straight and tall, even as relief drenched every fiber of his being.

"You must speak of this to no one. Especially the woman. We have eyes and ears everywhere and will learn if you fail to obey. Should you choose otherwise, it will mean instant and painful death for you."

The words rang in Mohamed's ears as the soft voice added, "And an excruciating one for her."

Faoud spat on the dirt floor as the van drove off. "Why did you let him go? We should have killed him."

"Do not distress yourself," came the unruffled reply. "He is of much more use to us alive at the moment."

"But he will surely tell the whore."

"Of course he will tell her. She will quake with fear for him," Ahmed murmured with satisfaction as he spread a worn prayer rug on the floor, facing in the direction of Mecca. "Perhaps this will make her careless for her own safety."

Wind filled the white sail as the *felucca* slid across the river. The near-toothless *reis*, skin burned to mahogany leather by days of exposure in the extreme elements, sat hunched over at the stern, bare feet protruding from the worn hem of his dirty *galabeeya*. His passengers huddled together in the bow of the boat, apparently enjoying the beauty of the scene.

213

Julia sat between Alex and Mohamed, hair blown back and eyes closed, savoring the feel of the sun and wind on her face. Being out on the water not only rejuvenated her weary spirit but provided the privacy required for the grave conversation that had just taken place.

Mohamed decided, after managing to tame his temper, in favor of telling her everything. Annoyance was his first response at her insistence that Bryant be included. Then he realized it was to their advantage for him to know. It was imperative that they both understood the severity of the situation. Bryant's suggestion for the sail gave him the opportunity to recount his frightening experience, in bone-chilling detail.

The color drained from Julia's face when he repeated the foretold consequence of his seeing the faces of his abductors. Bryant said little but Mohamed saw the disturbed look behind his restraint.

"That's quite a story. Now it's crucial that you stay on the hotel grounds. Both of you." Alex made sure his back was to the *reis* as he reached inside his jacket to pull out the Mauser. "Julia, take this."

She leaned away, shaking her head. "Oh, no. No way."

"Goddamn it, you need protection. And he can't carry it." Alex jerked his head at Mohamed. "If he got caught, he'd go straight to jail."

"Forget it. It's pointless for me to have it." She folded her arms tight over her chest. "Listen, in case you haven't gotten this yet: I'm a pacifist. I would never, ever, intentionally harm another living creature. It's just not in my DNA."

"Even if another creature intended bodily harm to you? Or him?" He jerked his head again at Mohamed, who watched the heated exchange in silence.

Julia and Alex traded glare for glare. With irritation and a frustration heretofore unknown, Alexander replaced the weapon in his jacket pocket. As long as they stayed on the grounds, it probably didn't matter. Probably. He felt confident he'd be able to protect her, should it come to that.

He deliberately withheld the news of his appointment later that night with the militants. Once the next message came from Brad Caldwell, he would reconsider his options. The bottom line was to get these two safely out of the operation and as quickly as possible. Their presence was making his job much more difficult. As the boat turned back toward the other side of the river and the hotel, he felt uncomfortably aware of the proximity of this woman who had become hazardously important to him.

When they reached the shore, Alex jumped out, balancing the laptop case now hanging from his shoulder, and offered Julia a hand. The trio, in a glum truce, filed up the stone steps leading to the pool deck.

"Well, hello! Alex, how delightful to see you here. We thought you'd slipped away without so much as a fond farewell." The familiar chirpy voice came from the shade nearby.

Startled, they all looked over to find Henry and Henrietta Langley sitting on the surrounding wall with legs dangling. A pair of powerful binoculars hung from each of their necks.

Alex bent to brush her thin cheek with a kiss. "Never, my dear. Julia told me you were staying on, so I knew we'd meet again. I'll be here for another day or two."

"How lovely. You must all join us for dinner this evening here at the hotel. No, no. No excuses. We insist, don't we, Henry?"

The faithful Henry as usual beamed and nodded a good-natured assent.

Alexander couldn't have been more pleased. This meant the other two would remain safely on the grounds and he'd be able to keep an eye on them. He always enjoyed keeping an eye on Julia.

Julia felt relief at the prospect of a diverting evening in the company of the amiable couple, although she felt a trifle uneasy about those binoculars. They must have been bird-watching. There were plenty to watch from here. Silly, she chided herself again, to suspect the elderly pair. Her overwrought mind was imagining things.

Mohamed, neither pleased nor relieved, simply glowered. All he wanted was to get the hell out of here. He carefully kept the left side of his face turned away but there would be no way to avoid comment on the ugly bruise when they met for dinner. And the call he'd made earlier to Shahida was difficult. She appreciated the generous amount of money—Julia's money—he'd wired to her that morning, before making that luckless stop at the coffee shop, but she expressed skepticism about the unexpected change of plans.

"Who is this woman?" she asked again. "Is it only the two of you there at the hotel?"

He hated lying to her—hated lying…period. It was not something that came easily and usually came back to bite him.

"No, several people from the boat have decided to stay over," he said in what he thought at the time to be a lie. "We will all be touring together."

She seemed to accept this. But he could tell she wasn't happy about it.

CHAPTER 31

James Marshall removed the stopper from a vintage crystal decanter to pour a hefty snifter of cognac. With glass in hand, he padded across a worn, yet still fine Persian rug and sank heavily into the wingback leather chair facing a flickering fire. The black Labrador retriever sprawled beside the chair lifted his graying head, grunting contentedly as his master leaned down to stroke a silky ear.

"There's a good boy, Tarquin, there's a good boy," crooned James before straightening to glance at the Georgian clock ticking away on the mantel. There was no telling how late the call from No.10 might come. Come though it would. He could be sure of that.

The liquor burned down his throat as he gazed into the hypnotic flames, organizing his thoughts in preparation for speaking with the Prime Minister. Alex's call several hours ago had been an unusual break with security, but James understood the move once he heard the news.

The "show," it seemed, wasn't intended for the U.S. or Europe as he and his colleagues had feared. Several terrorist groups were evidently collaborating in an alarmingly precise plot, in deadly secrecy, and had been for quite some time.

Of course, the Israelis had never officially acknowledged the existence of their nuclear arsenal, but that was beside the point. It was common knowledge they possessed perhaps as many as two-hundred nuclear warheads. If the terrorists gained control of Dimona for their Holy War, it would virtually open the gates of Hell. There seemed no end to the depth of insanity these radicals would plunge, taking themselves along with the rest of humanity.

The disturbing information came from the Yanks through irregular channels—most irregular. And to complicate matters, none of it could be verified. The PM would love that. His government continued to take searing heat for the intelligence failures that led to the invasion of Iraq. The damnable thing about this latest development was, if they waited for verification, it would almost certainly be too late.

Perhaps much too late.

This presented the kind of disaster James had long feared. He was an Englishman, through and through. But he was also a pragmatist—and well-versed in history. The role played by the British government in the Middle East over the past two-hundred years was a murky one, at best. Their meddling in affairs, in the opinion of many learned historians, was the underlying cause of much of the turmoil that existed there today: their "protection" of Egypt, for decades; the poor planning in the creation of the state of Israel, alienating the Palestinians and most of the Arab world; their collaboration with other Western powers in the creation of Iraq and Saudi Arabia; and their continuing support of totalitarian regimes throughout the region. The list went on and on.

No one could argue against the fact that the carving up of the Ottoman Empire following World War I created a situation destined to incite rage, resistance and rebellion. It was futile to attempt to lay all the blame on the governments of the problematic countries. James long ago acknowledged the hard truth: Diplomatic double-dealing and military incompetence resulted in devastating political upheaval, and his country had much to answer for.

Liz Marshall poked her head into the shadowy room. "I'm off to bed, my darling. Don't forget to let the dog out. And do damp down the fire before you come up." She peered at her husband over the top of trendy, red-framed reading glasses. "Last week you nearly burned the house down."

"Humph. No, I shan't," murmured James. "Night, darling." He blew her an absentminded kiss as his thoughts continued to sort through the grains of truth that made up this thorny mess.

It was easy to denounce the Islamic fundamentalists for their despicable actions, but all religions harbored similar violence in their past. People misused religion regularly for their own self-serving purposes, and the misguided Muslims, one must admit, did have some legitimate grievances. This, of course, could never condone what was happening all over the world under the auspices of a religious Jihad—this call for "blood for blood."

Regrettably, the very dictatorial regimes supported by Britain and the United States—not coincidentally, sources of the much-sought-after almighty crude for their energy-driven economies—created perfect environments for the rise of fundamentalism. For the seasoned diplomat, seated in his comfortable chair, this was all too familiar uncomfortable territory. The debate thundered on even among James's closest allies. Thompson, the current Minister of Foreign Affairs, was positively apoplectic when James suggested a drastic alteration in course. But even the most self-satisfied in their presumption of superiority knew bloody damn well it was going to take a new strategy to defuse the kind of hate—the kind of anger and violence that over the years had become so deeply entrenched on both sides of the savage conflict.

While the international community stood together in condemning the Islamic terrorist attacks, many equally condemned what they considered the brutal treatment of the Palestinian people by Israel—an issue they felt to be at the root of the Jihad. The Israeli invasion of Lebanon, Syria, Jordan and Egypt in 1967, when they occupied the Golan Heights, the West Bank and the Sinai Peninsula, resulted in hundreds of thousands of Palestinians having to flee their homes, taking up permanent residence in refugee camps. These camps quickly became festering sores of squalid conditions and degradation. Now, after generations of religious persecution and poverty, they virtually guaranteed unrest and revolt.

From the beginning, often standing alone against the rest of the world, the American government provided Israel with unwavering support, not to mention billions of dollars in aid each year. Along with the Yanks, Great Britain and a host of other nations continued to make sporadic attempts at mediating the Middle East peace process.

The Israelis remained immovable in their refusal to reconsider their controversial annexation of East Jerusalem, or to concede to the Arabs' insistence that it be made the capital of a future Palestinian state. They also continued to encroach and build settlements upon the disputed lands, retaliating with brutal force each time their neighbors struck a blow in opposition.

Popular Palestinian support for the violent acts of *Hamas*—unspeakable suicide bombings and rocket launches from Gaza into Israel—did nothing to further their cause, while a stagnant, corrupt Palestinian government failed repeatedly to agree upon a cohesive, sustainable resolution to bring to the negotiating table.

James drained his glass. *Oh, yes, there was plenty of blame to go around, all right.* The violent conflict would continue to perpetuate instability throughout the region, and indeed the world, as long as peace between the two adversaries remained an ever-elusive dream.

Tarquin lifted his heavy gray head at the sound of his master's weary sigh. And the old clock on the mantel ticked on.

CHAPTER 32

The *Isha* floated through the evening hush, calling the faithful to the final prayer of the day. In the distance, the weary cry of a migrating bird echoed with a melancholy note. Palm trees stood at ease against the blue-black sky, fronds rustling in the dry air, cooling from the heat of the day. Tables draped with alabaster linen cloths, elegantly set for dinner, some already occupied, clustered on the terrace above the pool.

Julia paused in the arched doorway, framed by the glow of lights behind her and the purple bougainvillea cascading over whitewashed stone walls on either side. She wore the same chic dress from the night of burglarizing Alexander's cabin. Could it be possible that was only last night? It seemed a lifetime ago. She spotted Mohamed and Alex at the poolside bar and started down the steps. Every male head in the vicinity turned to watch her descent with appreciation.

Her focus, oblivious to the stares, was on the two men standing side-by-side to greet her. Once again, she felt a pang of guilt at the stark contrast between them: one, twelve years younger than she, and the other at least that many years older. "Her men," she thought morosely. She was ashamed to admit that a part of her wanted them both, but ruthless self-recrimination forced her to do it. Dejection quickly supplanted shame at the realization that she could have neither: Mohamed, because he belonged to another; Alexander because he represented almost everything she'd opposed her entire adult life.

"You look lovely, as always." Alexander wore a deep emerald-green silk tie that lightened his gray eyes to the color of a forest in the spring.

Mohamed looked especially attractive this evening in a black jacket, white shirt open at the collar to reveal the bronzed skin of his throat. The ugly bruise on his cheek, however, amplified his clear disapproval of her attire.

Before she could sit on the stool he pulled out, they heard Henrietta approaching, gently chiding her indulgent spouse. "You see, Henry, I told you they would be early. Now we can all have a nice cocktail together before dinner."

Kisses on the cheek exchanged all around, Henrietta fussed like a mother hen over Mohamed's injury, "from running into a door," and promised to provide a healing cream. They moved to a table away from the bar, chatting like old friends. The hosts ordered champagne cocktails and Alex a beer while Julia and Mohamed had their usual sparkling mineral water with lime.

With drinks in hand, Henry raised his glass. "To long life and happiness," he pronounced. At least three of the cozy group seconded the toast with heart-felt enthusiasm.

"Well, my dears, did you enjoy your nice sail on the river this afternoon? It looked as though you were all much too serious out there."

Julia leveled a speculative look on her frail and unfailingly affable friend. *Yes, there very well might be more here than meets the eye,* said her acerbic inner voice. As they adjourned to the dining area, it didn't escape Julia that both her host and hostess had noted Alex carrying the laptop case. Now that she thought about it, they'd probably observed it earlier as well, down by the river.

Before she could think of a credible explanation, Alex said in a convincingly off-hand way, "I've become Julia's pack mule. Can't imagine how she's managed to lug the heavy thing around all this time."

The Langley's easy company over dinner provided a perfect relaxing end to an exceptionally stressful day. The last message from Brad had been brief: *Stay where you are. Don't leave the hotel under any circumstances. Wait until someone comes to escort you to safety.*

Mohamed's frightening experience that morning gave Julia second thoughts about any further involvement in this nightmare. It forced her to admit she was in way over her head. Her small part was done and it now lay in the hands of the professionals. Staying put suited her just fine.

In fact, as she breathed in the pure, clean air, perfumed with the scent of jasmine, at this juncture an extended stay at the Old Cataract Hotel held tremendous appeal. The setting could hardly be more beautiful—or romantic. It was disappointing that she wouldn't be able to enjoy that aspect of the ambiance. Oh, well, perhaps another time.

After dinner, Mohamed excused himself to make a phone call, politely thanking his hosts for a pleasant evening. Henrietta extracted a promise from him to collect her magic healing cream at the concierge, which she would send down for him shortly. As he retreated, she stifled an affected yawn.

"My goodness, I believe I'm all but done in. Would you two excuse the old folks if we retire?" She failed, almost comically, to hide her kindhearted expression of conspiracy.

Alex rose to kiss her cheek and shake Henry's hand. "Not too obvious, is she?" he said, resuming his seat with a sheepish grin.

Their eyes met across the candlelit table. A thrill of pleasure ran through Julia's veins and she quickly lowered her lashes to look down at a bowl of exquisite magenta orchids. Even though it was hidden beneath the thin fabric of her dress, she felt the weight of Mohamed's golden angel charm, on a chain around her neck. She self-consciously adjusted the silk scarf draped over her shoulders, but it failed to completely cover the bruises on her upper arms left from that violent embrace in his cabin earlier in the day.

Silence hummed along until Alex asked in a quiet voice, "So. Are you still in love with him?"

A melancholy smile lifted the corners of her lips. The question came as no surprise. "It's complicated." She shrugged, still looking down at the flowers. "We've been important to one another. He…he needed me." She frowned then, adding, "Of course, he's married. As he's also a devout Muslim, we could never be together unless we're married." Her eyes came up to meet his with a challenge. "We both know that we can never be more than friends. Just good friends."

The low voices of other diners in the background surrounded them as the implication of her words registered fully. *Could never be together unless they were married. Just good friends.*

Did that mean they weren't—that they'd never been—lovers? Was this possible? Hope rushed into his heart. Once they were safely delivered from this mess, he promised himself, he would court Julia Grant. With all the energy and means he possessed.

A solicitous waiter jarred him from his revelation. Regretfully, Alexander looked down at his watch, sorry to see it was later than he thought. He came to his feet and reached for the laptop case. "It's late. I'll walk you to the elevator."

Julia felt surprise at the abrupt end to a promising evening, along with a crushing disappointment. After winding their way through the tables on the terrace, they passed through the dimly lit lounge and turned a corner. Ahead lay a dazzling arched hallway, typical of Islamic architecture. Exquisite perforated brass lamps inset with multi-colored stones hung from the high ceiling, sprinkling the walls with diffused, jewel-toned light.

Julia stopped to admire the enchanting effect and, as she did, the scarf on her shoulders slid down onto the marble floor. They both stooped to pick it up, and their fingers met on the silky cloth.

Alexander placed his hands on her arms and raised her slowly to her feet. When he pulled her to him, she didn't resist. They looked searchingly into each other's eyes before their lips came together. At first unexpectedly tender, the long, lingering kiss intensified until both their bodies grew warm with a rising urgency.

The elevator bell rang, breaking the spell. Alex moved reluctantly away, his hand slipping down her arm to take her elbow and guide her to the elevator door. When it opened, several people got out, chattering away in Spanish, and went into the lounge. He reached in, pushed the button for her floor, and stepped back into the hall.

"Bolt your door. I'll call you in the morning." His eyes held hers until the metal doors closed between them.

Julia moaned as she collapsed against the wall. This was terrible! But at the same time it was wondrous. After so many lonely years, she now found herself being pulled apart with desire for not one but two men. In addition to the internal conflict over this, they were all at risk here. Any one of them could lose their life if they weren't careful.

A lightning bolt of alarm flashed in her brain as the elevator door opened on her floor. *Why hadn't he come up with her?* Their rooms were on the same floor. Where was he going?

With fear tempered by a healthy dose of irritation, she jabbed the lobby button. The descent was thankfully swift. She stepped out and looked up and down the hall. No Alexander. She dashed through the lounge into the lobby. Squinting toward the main entrance, she caught sight of his back in the revolving glass door.

What was he up to? Then she remembered. He hadn't said anything tonight about making contact with his "customer." But that didn't mean a damn thing. And he had the laptop. What the hell was going on?

She realized that she'd stopped moving while her mind whirled and barged down the hall. Emerging on the other side of the revolving door, she caught a glimpse of him exiting the gate and turning left on the corniche. Without a moment's hesitation or a second thought, she hastened down the gravel drive, determined to follow—wherever he went.

Mohamed hung his head in frustration and despair. Witnessing the kiss had brought a sorrow that robbed him of reason. Coming upon the unsuspecting pair, he backed into the dim lounge. There he remained in concealment while Bryant walked briskly past. He stood there still, agonizing over the scene, when Julia unexpectedly reemerged from the elevator and flashed by.

Sorrow shifted to suspicion. What was all this? He followed Julia warily down the main hall, up to the revolving door. As his hand fell on the metal bar to push it around, a firm, kindly voice stopped him in his tracks.

"Wait, Mohamed. Don't go."

He turned to find Henry, Henrietta one step behind. "It's not safe for you to leave the grounds. I'll go."

Henrietta placed a thin hand gently on Mohamed's arm as Henry slipped into the opaque night.

"It will be all right. Let's go sit for a moment, shall we? I'd like to tell you a few things. Things you may find most interesting."

She led him unwillingly to a plush sofa in a deserted corner of the lobby. They were an incongruous pair, sitting close, her white head bent next to his dark one. She spoke in a steady murmur for quite a while.

❖

Julia zigzagged through the crowd along the corniche, thankful she'd worn low heels. She was torn between calling out to Alex to confront him about leaving without telling her, or continuing to follow surreptitiously behind. *What if he wasn't as "okay" as Brad Caldwell thought?*

Before she could reach a decision, he nimbly crossed the congested street, turned a corner and disappeared. Cursing under her breath, she clutched the scarf closer over her bare arms and increased her gait, mindless of her surroundings.

Faoud, lurking in the shadows across the street from the hotel entrance, saw the arms dealer come through the gate. As he stepped from concealment to follow, the woman came hurrying out. A sinister smile marred his ugly face as he stole along on the opposite side of the street, keeping slightly behind.

Henry emerged from the gate and paused, searching for Julia. With her long legs trying to keep pace with Alex's even longer ones, she was already a considerable distance from the hotel.

"Julia! Wait!" The old man moved much more quickly than one might expect, but he was too far behind for her to hear. The clamor of the heavy evening traffic drowned out his call.

Still on the river side of the thoroughfare, Julia darted through the throng of pedestrians. Henry pressed on in pursuit. He didn't notice the man on the other side until it was too late.

When Alex disappeared, Julia plunged into the street, to find herself perilously caught between honking cars, horse-drawn carriages and motorcycles whipping in and out everywhere. As she crossed, Henry bounded into the traffic, still some distance behind. His eyes swung back and forth between Julia and the vehicles speeding past. He managed to reach the other side slightly before she did, and closed some of the distance between them.

He cupped his hands around his mouth and called out. "Julia!"

Again, she failed to hear, but Faoud—directly behind her now—turned at the call. A cold, hard fear gripped Henry at the shocking expression of pure evil on the unsightly face. He broke into a run—faster than most men half his age could muster.

Julia reached the other side. Her attention having been focused on imminent survival, she was completely unaware of the threatening figure close behind as she turned the corner.

A sinewy brown hand shot out and grabbed her arm in a painful grip, spinning her around. She gasped, momentarily paralyzed by the gruesome face—only inches away—amplified a thousand-fold by the expression of hatred in the glowering, murderous eyes. Her delayed struggle failed to prevent the wet rag from being pressed over her nose and mouth. Within seconds, the world spun into oblivion as she lost consciousness and slid to the dirty street.

Henry reached the corner, panting, expecting the worst. The worst was nothing.

Both Julia and the man with the fearsome face had vanished.

CHAPTER 33

A heavy gloom now obscured the night, the moon hidden by clouds, and street lamps restricted to main thoroughfares. Alexander turned off the Corniche el Nile onto a side street. He could just make out that it was joined by several even darker alleys. Without slowing his pace, he turned down one of them in the middle of the block. At this point, he stopped to allow his vision to adjust to the near-total darkness.

The directions he'd been given were clear enough, but the claustrophobic closeness of the narrow passageway quickened his senses. Near the other end, the door of a parked van opened and a man stepped from the driver's side. Even in the dark, he recognized the figure of Jalal.

"Come," called the familiar voice, barely loud enough for Alex to hear.

As he neared the van, Jalal spoke quietly. "Please excuse us for the necessary precautions. It is for your safety as well as our own. Bend your head and close your eyes."

Alex did as he was told, only stiffening slightly as the scratchy sack settled over his head. The clamor of the city faded as the van left the congested turns behind and headed in a straight line. Soon, all Alex could hear was the rattle of metal as they continued along a bumpy road. When they eventually came to a stop, Jalal guided him into a small building, warning him to duck his head. Once inside, the Egyptian lifted the sack.

"He will be here soon. Do you have the merchandise?"

Alexander moved with slow, deliberate caution. Any sudden or unexpected action on his part might cause undue alarm. He shrugged the laptop case from his shoulder to place it on a rickety wooden table. An oil lamp burned beside it as he pulled back the zippers. When he raised the top, the case revealed—not the computer for which it was intended—but the Magnum and the Beretta. Before dinner, he'd exchanged the weapons for the computer, leaving it safely hidden in the false bottom of his suitcase.

He glanced at Jalal, whose ebony eyes sparkled with reverence in the lamplight as they caressed the gleaming metal. It was always the same. Men were invariably drawn, like magnets, to weapons. And to the power they represented. Alexander allowed no sign of his weary condescension to show as he peeled off his jacket and unbuckled the holster under his arm.

"You must face the wall during the meeting. Do not, under any circumstances, turn around."

It didn't need to be spelled out. Alex understood the consequences for failing to comply with this "request." No sooner than he'd balanced on a low stool facing a white-washed mudbrick wall, he heard someone come through the doorway.

"Good evening, Commander. So we meet at last. I am Sharif." Ahmed wasted no time on pleasantries. "Jalal has apprised you, I believe, of my needs?"

Jalal backed away from the guns.

Ever so slightly, Alex cocked an ear. That voice rang a bell. "Yes. These models should meet your requirements."

Ahmed picked up the Magnum. "Why these?"

Alex succinctly recited the features for each. Jalal shifted nervously in the background as "Sharif" examined each weapon.

"There is," Ahmed drawled, "some sense of urgency in completing the transaction. A long-standing tribal feud in my native Saudi Arabia threatens to interfere with a cousin's wedding. We must take all precautions." He paused before the next lie. "Receiving the merchandise there could prove problematic. We would prefer to take delivery in Sinai. Within the week."

Even as Alexander felt his chest clench, he kept his tone matter-of-fact. "It's a tight timeframe. That'll inflate the price. I'll make inquiries and let you know." He waited for a response. When one failed to come, he ventured to add, "An order for handguns only is kind of unusual. Have you no need for heavier artillery? Automatic rifles, or missiles?"

Ahmed made a sound that was more like a purr than a laugh. "No, Commander. This will do for now." He snapped a barrel shut. "I will keep these samples, with your permission, of course."

The thinly veiled demand kicked Alexander's adrenaline up another notch. He'd already considered the possibility of this unfortunate development. His tone remained strictly casual. "That might not be such a good idea. These pieces could be traced back to me. Besides, if they should be found in your possession here in Egypt, it could land you in some serious trouble."

Behind his back, Alex could feel the violence that flared in the terrorist's eyes.

Ahmed did not care for being denied. A threatening silence permeated the stuffy room before he sighed, his passion passing like a summer storm. "As you wish."

The final negotiations took a while, with Alexander attempting to discover as much as possible without appearing overly inquisitive. The most important thing he learned was the point of delivery: a village along the east coast of the Sinai Peninsula, on the Gulf of Aqaba. He promised to let them know by six the following evening if delivery could be made within their timeframe.

After "Sharif" departed, Alex—head once again covered by the sack—was driven a short distance in the van. When it stopped, the sack came off and he was transferred to a horse-drawn carriage that plodded along interminably before at last reaching the waterfront. The clip-clop of the horse's feet and the clicking of the carriage wheels created a kind of mantra that induced the composure he needed to analyze every nuance of the past few hours.

It still struck him as odd, the request for handguns only. Surely these maniacs would need heavier artillery for their ambitious plan. One thing was certain, even though he'd heard only a few words from the neighboring table at lunch the previous day: He unequivocally recognized the voice of "Sharif" as that of the striking Arab.

Still deep in troubled thought as the carriage finally drew near the hotel, he looked up to find Mohamed storming out the front gate with the Langleys close on his tail. It was then he learned of Julia's abduction. A raw, gnawing fear gripped him as Henry's description of the scar-faced man left no doubt as to the identity of her captors.

A tense silence lay over the room like a heavy blanket as those present listened to Alexander Bryant's side of the phone conversation. Following his concise report, there was not much to overhear, apart from the occasional single-word response.

"Understood," he said brusquely for the fifth time. Replacing the receiver, he remained for a moment with his back to the others gathered in the sitting room of his suite.

Henry and Henrietta sat on the sofa, legs touching, hands folded in their laps. Brad Caldwell sprawled in one of the big chairs next to them, with Linda Boyd perched on the arm. Mohamed stood in the corner looking out the window, his rigid back to the room. Sarah Littlefield sat up straight on the other end of the sofa, sharp green eyes alert for the unspoken accusations bouncing off the walls.

None of them had slept during the endless night. The group from San Francisco had arrived an hour before, travel-weary and staggered to learn of Julia's abduction.

Brad asked the obvious question. "So?"

Alex turned, clearing his throat. "As expected, the same response as yours: The Brits regret the unfortunate turn of events but there's little they can do. Even if contact is made for a ransom, their government doesn't negotiate with terrorists. Officially, their hands are tied."

"And unofficially?" The quiet question came from the corner. While the calls were made, Mohamed had remained ominously silent. His internal conflict about the situation had evaporated, like smoke in the wind. These bastards kidnapped Julia. They took his angel—with god only knew what evil intentions. Unfortunately, he knew all too well their probable intentions, as did everyone involved. Not a shred of doubt clouded his conscience that he would do anything and everything he could to save her. Anything to save the woman he loved.

Again, Alex cleared his throat. "Unofficially, they'll make whatever resources they can available to us, should we choose to pursue the matter."

He and Caldwell exchanged a steady, significant look.

"Should we choose to pursue the matter," repeated Mohamed in the same deceptively soft voice. "So, as far as the British and U.S. governments are concerned, she's to be regarded as 'collateral damage,' is that it?" He turned to face the ex-military officer, his mouth twisted with savage contempt, dark eyes pools of anger and pain.

"That's what you call it, isn't it, 'collateral damage'? Such a bland expression to define the death, destruction and maiming of innocent people caught in the midst of your crusade to bring what you call 'democracy' to the 'developing' world?"

The harsh words shot out like bullets, piercing every heart in the room.

Henrietta broke the uncomfortable silence. "We know you're upset, my dear. We all are. But let us please try to focus here. We will all, *and I do mean all,*" she added sternly, directing a sharp look at Brad Caldwell, "do everything within our power to bring her back safely."

Mohamed looked from face to tense face. His burning eyes lingered on Alexander's studiously expressionless ones before settling on a troubled Henry Langley. "I should have gone after her," he said, heavy accusation plain behind the words.

Henrietta put a protective hand on that of her husband. "No, dear, then you would have been taken as well. Or worse."

The debate stormed for over an hour before they agreed upon a plan. Most of those present were professionals. They possessed the training and instincts to deal with the difficult circumstances. All except Mohamed and Sarah. She chafed at having to remain at the hotel—and dug in her heels for a fight.

Brad stepped up to take her on. "Look. Someone has to stay to field communications if anything turns up. Or if the kidnappers should call."

As an Egyptian citizen, Mohamed knew he was particularly vulnerable. If the Jihadists didn't punish him for his involvement, his government would. Nonetheless, rock-solid determination steeled his nerves and cleared his brain. "There's not a chance in hell you will leave me out of it. Besides," he pointed out with cool calculation, "I'm the only one who knows the territory and can speak to the 'natives.' They will remove their hostage from the vicinity as quickly as possible. If they haven't already."

"Assuming they're holding her hostage." Linda Boyd's words, quietly spoken, fell into the momentary hush.

Henrietta's clear gaze watched both of Mohamed's hands clench.

"We'll fan out in pairs." Alex was already grabbing up his jacket.

Naturally, the Langleys would work together, as would Caldwell and Boyd. That left Alex and Mohamed. They eyed one another warily. Even though Mohamed now knew and accepted that the arms dealer had no intention of arranging to sell weapons to the terrorists, each still felt the other had contributed to Julia's abduction. Each felt burning guilt for failing her. They formed an uneasy alliance.

Immediately upon the arrival of the other Americans, Commander Alexander Bryant had insisted on having a private conversation with Special Agent Brad Caldwell. The two squared off, assessing one another guardedly. Brad could feel the other's palpable resentment, and contempt, even before he spoke.

"It is absolutely inconceivable to me that you would actually involve a civilian in this kind of operation." Guilt then ambushed Alex's indignation, as he remembered his insistence that Julia carry a gun. Thank god she'd refused. If she'd had it on her, it would have most certainly made things worse. A whole lot worse.

In the end, the two men came to a truce, of sorts. Alex filled in the blanks of his involvement and purpose, which was to flush out and identify the militants for British Intelligence—nothing more, nothing less.

Once they'd taken each other into complete confidence, they argued briefly over whether to bring the rest of the group fully into the loop or provide information only on a "needs-to-know" basis. Everyone except Mohamed. He already knew most of what was happening anyway. It was therefore agreed advisable to keep him apprised—especially as far as Alexander's involvement. The conspicuous tension between the two could cause problems, and anything they could do to alleviate it would be in the best interest of achieving their objectives.

Alex swore under his breath as he sat at a sticky table in the café near the corner where Julia had disappeared. Although working as a team, he and Mohamed affected indifference to one another in case they were being watched. He pretended to read the newspaper spread before him as he kept the Egyptian in his peripheral vision.

Mohamed spoke heatedly with one of the waiters. He's too damn intense, thought Alex. He needs to relax if we're going to find out anything useful. Alex was convinced this was a waste of time anyway. There might be a better way to discover what happened to Julia.

CHAPTER 34

Mohamed had reacted slowly to the revelation of the true identities of Henry and Henrietta Langley. Concern for Julia hindered his ability to think of little else. Henrietta, seated beside him on the lobby sofa, told him the entire story of how the elderly couple came to be in Egypt. It was the best way she could think of to keep him from rushing out after Julia into the treacherous night.

They had met during World War II, when they were both impossibly young and blissfully innocent. Each brought up on a farm in the great Midwestern United States, they shared many values. He was a fresh-faced pilot in the Air Force, recently graduated from flight school, she, an administrator at the Air Force hospital in Langley, Virginia. The spirited pair, introduced at a U.S.O. dance one fine spring evening, laughed at the double coincidence of their names and of Henry Langley being stationed in Langley. It was love at first sight.

They spent every possible moment together, even celebrating their twenty-first birthdays, less than a week apart. The inevitable marriage took place shortly thereafter in a civil ceremony, with one of the doctors giving Henrietta away and Henry's commanding officer as best man. Due to war shortages, no one from either of their families had been able to attend the nuptials. Their union marked the beginning of a lifetime of love, devotion and mutual respect.

Two weeks later, orders sent Henry to London. Henrietta determinedly pursued a reassignment and soon wangled her way across the "big pond." There, they weathered the nightly bombings, shared an admiration for the stoicism of the British people, and experienced the horror as the truth began to emerge about Adolph Hitler's concentration camps.

It was during this time that Military Intelligence recruited Henry. He worked closely with the British and did his part to bring the war to a successful conclusion.

At the outset, Henrietta insisted on being included in his secret work. "We're a team," she said adamantly, "partners." If he was to risk his life, she would be right by his side. The recognition of her natural talent for languages and skill at deciphering codes quickly induced the British to gratefully accept her contribution to the war effort. They needed all the help they could get.

After the war, the inseparable couple returned home, settling in Indianapolis. Henry became a flight instructor for a private company. Henrietta taught French and Spanish at a local high school and became involved in community affairs. Not being blessed with children only brought them closer. And all the while, they continued to serve their country.

On a fairly regular basis, they took nice, long vacations to foreign lands. Friends and relations envied their travels, never suspecting the trips invariably involved an undercover assignment, some quite daring and dangerous. They worked together like a well-oiled machine, protecting each other with skill and courage. Over time, their minds became so in-sync, words were almost unnecessary. This proved to be extremely useful in espionage.

Throughout the Korean War, the Cold War, Vietnam and now the War on Terror, they remained equally devoted to each other and to their country. The older they grew, the more valuable they became as agents. Who, after all, in their right mind would suspect the mild-mannered, white-haired septuagenarians as master spies?

When Brad Caldwell had called at the last minute, they welcomed the opportunity with enthusiasm. They'd always wanted to visit Egypt. The assignment seemed straightforward enough: join a tour, keep an eye out for the newly recruited agent and report back should anything go amiss.

Once they learned more regarding the "recruitment" of the "new agent," they shared a strong disapproval. Henrietta made her feelings known, in no uncertain terms, to Brad as well as his boss, Bob Bronson. They had worked with Bob for years and had never heard of anything this scandalous: sending an untrained, unprepared civilian out on what was clearly potentially hazardous duty.

Meeting Julia amplified their disapproval into condemnation. Her sensitivity and gentle, caring nature made her incredibly vulnerable in the volatile situation. The whole thing was just wrong.

"Team L," as Henry and Henrietta jokingly referred to themselves, made the decision to check into the Old Cataract even before contacting Brad. Fairly fluent in Arabic, Henrietta had overheard Mohamed mention his plans of staying at the hotel to one of the boat crew. They'd both already spotted the telling bruise spreading across his cheek, and it confirmed their qualms that the situation might be starting to deteriorate.

Henry prudently got in touch with the office, resulting in Brad Caldwell and Linda Boyd hot-footing it to Aswan.

At first incredulous, Alexander quickly appreciated the value of the Langleys' involvement. No one would ever suspect them as agents, and their presence could be useful in providing a cover. A thin cover, to be sure, but every little bit helped. When the unexpected faction arrived from San Francisco a few hours later, he abandoned all hope of taking a routine approach to the increasingly convoluted operation.

There was nothing routine about any of this.

Five o'clock found a hot, tired and frustrated group gathered back in Alex's suite. After they'd all spent endless, fruitless hours of asking around town for any hint of the kidnapper's trail, the only information gleaned was that the cousin of a brother of one of the waiters might have seen the woman described. A van similar to the one used in transporting both Alex and Mohamed may have been seen driving out of a shed on a side street late last night, heading north.

Sarah, somehow managing to suppress her frustration at her assignment as their room-bound contact liaison, had received no calls— for a ransom or anything else.

Alex surveyed the unlikely group. His incontrovertible air of authority gave him a slight advantage in attempting to direct their efforts. The more manpower he had, the better the chance for success—as long as everyone followed orders. He frowned at the notion. Mohamed and Sarah were the wild cards. There was a slim-to-none chance they might be persuaded to leave this to the professionals; but he simply would not risk the possibility of their haring off on their own and getting themselves—and possibly Julia—killed.

So, for the time being, he determined that keeping everyone together appeared the most viable plan. "As little as that tells us, it fits in with my theory, based on what I learned last night." He reached for a map on the dresser and flipped it open on the coffee table. The others drew near to look down at a map of Egypt, including the Sinai and its bordering neighbors.

"They want the weapons delivered a few miles south of here." He pointed with a pen to the town of Nuweiba. "Mohamed, what do you know about this area?"

Mohamed surfaced from the depth of his gloom. "It's a seaside resort, known as the 'pearl of the Gulf of Aqaba,' with tourists traveling all around the area. It also has a large commercial port, with boats providing regular service to the town of Aqaba in Jordan."

Alex nodded, the words feeding the seed of an idea. "What about the boat service?"

"Ships carry various cargos. There is also a fast boat, a hydrofoil, mostly for passengers. Tourists take that route to visit Petra, the legendary capital of the ancient Natabaean Kingdom."

Henrietta smiled approvingly. Taking on the familiar role of lecturer seemed to have a soothing effect on the distraught Egyptologist.

This information further supported Alex's idea. "Here's what we can surmise." He made brief eye contact with each of the up-turned faces before going on. "It looks like they may be taking Julia with them to the rendezvous. We can only hope that's the case." His forehead wrinkled as he added, "No mention was made of her at last night's meeting. Hopefully, they've concluded there's no connection between us."

Henrietta's shrewd eyes searched his guarded ones at the flat statement. His voice betrayed no emotion—but at what cost?

"If the van went north, they might be headed to one of the villages along the coast of the Gulf of Suez. Somewhere they could take a boat to Sinai," said Alex.

Mohamed interrupted eagerly. "It would either be Al Qusayr or Hurghada. Hurghada is nearest. The roads are not good but from here they are the closest towns along the coast." His new-found enthusiasm waned. "This region," he pointed to a large area on the map between the Gulf of Suez and the River Nile, "is not safe. Militants are known to operate there."

Brad and Linda exchanged a guarded look. This was near where Abeer

241

Rashad's body was found.

Mohamed added, shaking his head, "Anyone driving in this area is required to obtain special permission from the police."

"Where would they most likely go to reach Sinai? And where would they land when they got there?" asked Brad in a steady voice.

"Ferries run regularly from Hurghada to Sharm el Sheik, and there may be ferry service from Hurghada to El Tor, on the southwestern coast. The service can be irregular and unpredictable. Hurghada is a popular center for water sports, with many boats for hire. If they have a private boat they could go anywhere." Mohamed's voice again showed signs of desperation.

Linda shook her head. "No, Mohamed, not anywhere. U.S. war ships regularly patrol the entrance to the Gulf of Aqaba these days. They wouldn't risk being stopped there. The most likely scenario would be to take a boat to the west coast and drive from there."

Alex nodded in agreement. "Right. Where else might they land?"

All eyes turned back to Mohamed. "The southern tip of Sinai is Ras Mohammed National Park. It is a very large and famous nature site, attracting many tourists for scuba diving and snorkeling. Security is tight there," he said, regaining a modicum of confidence and a glimmer of hope. "It would have to be north of there." He again pointed to the map.

"Once they make landfall, what next?" prompted Linda.

"There are two possibilities: The only road goes north or south. South leads past the entrance to Ras Mohammed, then to Sharm el-Sheikh and up the east coast through Dahab to Nuweiba."

"Wasn't there another terrorist attack in Sharm el-Sheik recently?" asked Henry gravely.

"There was," confirmed Linda. "A bomb exploded in the lobby of a glitzy resort hotel. Several people died. Most of the casualties, as usual, were locals working at the hotel and a nearby café, rather than the intended victims. Security will surely have been stepped up all along that corridor."

Mohamed's finger traced a route on the map as he continued. "The road north meets another to cross the mountains, past St. Catherine's Monastery and Mt. Sinai. It is a difficult drive so not well traveled. Once through the mountains, it connects with the east coast road, between Dahab and Nuweiba."

Silence descended for a moment before Alex spoke. "Then that's our best supposition. If they're taking a hostage with them, it's the most likely route."

That's a big-ass "if," thought Linda Boyd, but kept it to herself.

"That's it then," pronounced Sarah. These were the first words she'd spoken since the others returned. All heads swiveled in her direction. Potent, unrelenting determination radiated from her clear green eyes.

"We go after her."

They unanimously agreed, after extensive deliberation, to proceed with the weapons transaction. This would make them all prosecutable criminals in any court of law but possibly buy them precious time. They couldn't risk faking it. Alex would give the go-ahead to his client at six o'clock and insist on personally overseeing delivery in Nuweiba.

Meanwhile, the rest of the team would make preparations for the trip. Mohamed and Brad were to hire a van to accommodate the seven disparate partners. Although it might make things easier, they decided against hiring a driver. Apart from the matter of space, it was impossible to count on the discretion of a stranger. Taking turns with the driving would allow them to speak freely along the way.

Their cover would be that of a tourist group, with Mohamed as their guide.

Brad, alarmed at involving yet another civilian, suggested they split up;

but this raised predictable heated opposition from Mohamed and Sarah. Unexpectedly, Alex and Henrietta agreed. Although Brad and Linda chafed at having to take them along, it appeared—all things considered—the best plan. The unlikely task force pursued an unpredictable enemy and desperately needed a diverse approach.

Ahmed stood looking out over the lush green field sloping down to the river, arms folded across his chest, his thoughts miles away.

The rich continue, as they have done since the beginning of time, to further enrich themselves at the expense of the poor and middle classes. Even in the supposed democratic American utopia there is restlessness and growing discontent. The Infidels never learn the lessons from the past to overcome their base instincts, perpetuating this destructive cycle. Democracy is only a euphemism for capitalism. Everything is about money. Everything.

The Western Infidels remain blinded by their relentless greed.

They refuse to deal with the disease of the conflict in Palestine—a disease of their own making—obsessed with vicious pursuit of revenge for the symptoms of that disease. The symptoms are the brave acts of heroism by the faithful Islamic Jihadists to release their Palestinian Brothers from decades of enforced poverty and humiliation. The Infidels believe they can continue to commit their acts of aggression with impunity. They now begin to learn the error of that belief.

These lessons Ahmed had learned and learned well. He now spread the word with fervent conviction to enlighten his Islamic Brothers. His dedication and commitment to Jihad were absolute.

The removal of the woman called Julia Grant was easily justified. Casualties were a fact of war. Her role, at the least, had been that of an innocent pawn; at most, that of a spy: an enemy combatant.

Either way, her involvement would be made to serve Allah.

CHAPTER 35

"Uncle Benny!" cried the girl, brown curls bouncing as she tore across the yard and threw herself into her uncle's arms. "Where have you been? What did you bring me?"

"Judyth! Mind your manners," scolded the smiling woman that followed close behind to kiss her brother on both cheeks. "Where have you been? We haven't seen you for days."

The compact yet powerfully built man lifted the giggling child high into the air and gave her a hard, affectionate squeeze before setting her down. He held her hand as they all walked into the house. "Work, as always, all work. I will be away for awhile and had to come for a visit with my best girls before I go." He refrained from expressing the thought that he hoped this visit would not be the last.

Benjamin Richter knew that he was regarded, by all accounts, an unusual man. It was unusual for a man such as he to have remained single all these years. But his dedication to his parents, his sisters and his country came first, leaving little time for much else. The family now lived in a suburb north of Tel Aviv, a beautiful place on the Mediterranean Sea.

Out on the terrace, Benjamin absentmindedly listened to Judyth's childish chatter while his sister went to make some tea. The familiar saga of the Richter clan replayed itself in his mind, as it often did when he came here.

During World War II, his parents had fled Germany but not before his grandparents fell victim to the Nazis. Benjamin had heard the story many times. After the war, the family was stunned and profoundly grateful to learn that his father's mother survived the indescribable atrocities of Auschwitz. She came to live with them and, every day, besieged them with tales of the unspeakable horrors of the death camp. Every day, until the day she died.

In his parents' minds, the creation of Israel was fulfillment of the edict, "God having given the Israelites the land in covenant." It was nothing less than the answer to their prayers. Although thankful for the existence of his country and faithful to the teachings of Judaism, Benjamin secretly harbored uncertainty as to the justification of the taking of the Palestinian lands.

He felt that the Israelis continued to pay a heavy price for the establishment of their homeland. Sadly—but predictably—from the beginning, its creation had brought constant strife and violence. Each time another person lost his life—on either side of the conflict—he would ask himself: How could anyone have failed to anticipate this? *When one people's liberation was founded on the dispossession of another?*

Benjamin, born in the late 1950s, remembered spending his early childhood happily unaware of the volatile political situation churning around him. His best friend, Malak Zalouk, lived next door and they, practically from infancy, became inseparable. Innocent of the cruel reality that one being an Arab and the other a Jew made their friendship improbable at best, they played endless games of soccer and soldier, marbles and chess.

Until one day in 1967, when both boys were only ten, armed Israeli soldiers came and forced his friend with his entire family—at gunpoint—from their home, forever. With only the clothes on their backs, they were escorted away. Everyone was crying and wailing. The last memory Benjamin had of Malak was one of tears flowing down his best friend's cheeks, creating rivers of pain on his dusty little face. It was the last time Benjamin ever saw or heard of him. The Zalouk home—along with thousands of others—was appropriated by Israeli forces.

As he grew up, Benjamin attended school at New York University, receiving a degree in European history. When he returned to Israel to complete his mandatory military service, it was with a considerably broadened view of the on-going conflict.

He never regretted his choice to remain in the service of his country, moving up rapidly in the ranks. In time, he transferred to Intelligence in Shin Beth, the Israeli equivalent of America's FBI. Both at work and at home, he kept his political opinions strictly to himself—no small feat. He felt sickened by the Palestinian suicide bombings and other acts of violence. But he never forgot the injustice witnessed as a boy.

"I won't ask where you are going," said his sister quietly as she placed a glass of cold tea in Benjamin's hand. She took a seat beside him in one of the comfortable chairs on the terrace, keeping her voice low. "Or what dark thoughts trouble you today."

They each stole a glance at the old man, their father, seated not far away. A soft sea breeze cooled the heat from the bright morning sun. His tired eyes softened at the sight of his daughter pulling young Judyth onto her lap.

Another memory rudely elbowed the tender scene aside. One day, his mother and youngest sister had gone shopping in downtown Tel Aviv. Recently engaged, his sister went in search of her wedding gown. A suicide bomber walked into the café just as they were leaving. Both women were killed. His father now spent most of his waking hours in a rocking chair, as he did now, prayer shawl draped over shriveling shoulders, praying and rocking. Rocking and praying and grieving.

Benjamin sipped his tea.

After that, his transfer into Mossad, the agency responsible for planning and carrying out covert operations to prevent terrorist acts against Israeli targets abroad, was easy. He dedicated himself to the prevention of the development and procurement of non-conventional weapons by hostile countries that figured prominently in the mission of Mossad.

Some of the organization's activities did trouble him at times. Arguably one of the most successful intelligence services of any country in the world, Mossad was known to have conducted kidnappings, bombings and assassinations in a number of countries. Shortly after Benjamin's transfer, a Mossad team was credited with blowing up nuclear reactor parts in France, destined for Iraq, as well as assassinating a leading nuclear physicist who had agreed to work for Saddam Hussein.

Through all the years and all the pain and suffering inflicted by both sides, Benjamin Richer struggled to be objective. He pondered endlessly about what it would take to defuse the anger. It was the radicals who exploited the situation, continuing the blood-for-blood cycle of violence and murder—not the Palestinian people.

This resolute objectivity made him, without question, an unusual man.

But when Benjamin learned of this latest heinous plot, it was too much, even for him. Israeli forces went into immediate action to deal with the threat of attack on the nuclear facility in Dimona. He was one of the few high-level officers included in the briefing on the second, more lethal, threat: the threat of a chemical attack on Jerusalem.

The cooling sea breeze could not dispel the sweat that leapt to the surface of his entire body at the thought of it now. *The holiest city on earth—for Christians, Muslims and Jews. An indiscriminant massacre of his neighbors—men, women and children. Another holocaust.* No. There could be no justification for this. And he would do everything within his power to prevent it.

Or he would die trying.

"The intelligence is unverified," reiterated the head of Mossad to the three officers facing him. "But we know our enemy well enough to know the probability of its truth." A frown further darkened his hardened features. "The chemicals will almost certainly come through Rafah. Security on all borders is in highest alert. With Gaza under Palestinian control, and the border open to Egypt, it's the most likely point."

"They could have already brought small amounts of chemicals through the tunnels," said one of the men from across the table. Underground tunnels between the two countries had been used for years for arms smuggling and illegal immigration. Every time they discovered one and shut it down, another wormed its way through the earth.

"This information must be held in strictest confidence," commanded the officer at the head of the table. "If word leaks out that we know of the plan, it will only make our job more difficult. And it might lead to a premature strike."

In a short time, they agreed upon a course of action. Tightening security in Jerusalem would be business as usual. It happened on a regular basis and would raise no alarm. Each of the three officers would designate and command a tight, elite force to investigate and attempt to uncover the entry point for the chemical weapons: one in Gaza; one in the West Bank, along the Jordanian border; and one at Israel's most southern tip, on the Gulf of Aqaba.

Benjamin insisted they consider that possibility. He had a gut feeling as he looked down with heavy-lidded eyes at the map spread out before them. The hairs on the back of his neck prickled as he considered the close proximity of the borders of Israel to both Egypt and Jordan.

"Richter, you take the West Bank."

Benjamin looked up. "With all due respect, sir, I'd be better with the Gulf sector." He went on quickly before his superior could object. "I am, I believe, the most knowledgeable about that territory and have the linguistic ability to work most effectively there."

Rays of the setting sun collided with the golden Dome of the Rock, sending shafts of light back onto the surrounding hills of the Holy Land. Benjamin sat on a stone wall at the far side of the large square, watching the constant surge of fellow Jews, praying and studying, as they did every day and every night, year after year.

He faced the Western Wall, commonly known as the Wailing Wall, that represented the most sacred shrine in Jewish and national consciousness. In the midst of the Old City of Jerusalem, it was *the* destination for pilgrims from throughout the world. He never tired of coming here.

He took comfort in the fact that—while Jerusalem was divided into three sections: West Jerusalem mostly inhabited by Jews and East Jerusalem mostly by Arabs—the walled Old City contained Jewish, Christian, Armenian and Muslim quarters, where people of differing faiths managed to live side-by-side. It was here that he had moved after the murder of his mother and sister. It was here, in this convergence of three great religions, that he came to contemplate the incomprehensible complexities of the conflict in which he lived every moment of his life.

Benjamin glanced at his watch and reluctantly rose from his seat on the wall. As he moved toward this latest atrocity—walking the narrow, cobbled streets of the Old City in the Judean hills, with its long and intricate history—rage threatened to overwhelm reason, despair to annihilate hope.

This city—this land he called his homeland—had been contested for thousands of years. He knew the history, all too well. He knew that, in addition to Israel's being a natural land bridge to three continents that made control economically desirable, ancient religious hatreds had caused endless disputes and bloodshed.

But never before, in all those thousands of years, had there been a threat so vile—so profane—as this.

CHAPTER 36

A massive jolt catapulted Julia back to the world of the living. Instant recall of recent events flooded her brain, sending a blast of alarm coursing through her body. Instinctively feigning continued unconsciousness, she struggled to untangle her wildly incoherent thoughts. Another hard jolt almost brought a cry of protest from her parched throat. A cacophony of squeaks and rattles foretold the vehicle's state of disrepair. It appeared to be bouncing over a field of rocks.

She lay on her side on a pile of coarse, smelly blankets that penetrated the thin fabric of her cocktail dress. Another blanket covered her, stifling in the heat. A wave of pure, unadulterated panic swept over her as she discovered her hands securely and painfully tied behind her back, and ankles similarly bound. The revolting rag covering her mouth made it difficult to breathe, much less cry out. Julia's entire body, petrified beyond imagining, stiffened as another fearsome thought struck her.

What had become of Alex?

After endless lurching over the tortuous road, the vehicle rolled to a stop. A door groaned and she heard two men speaking in slow, conversational Arabic. Another door creaked open, closer to where she lay. The voices grew louder. One of them said something that brought raucous laughter before the door slammed shut. The voices drifted away, leaving a void of silence, interrupted only by the sound of a barking dog in the distance.

Tears began to soak the dirty rag and Julia sobbed uncontrollably into the blanket. She didn't know how long she'd been left to her desolation. The sound of opening doors warned her to fight back the tears, and the vehicle began to move once more. The road evened out, and after a while, from exhaustion born of sheer terror, she drifted into a surreal, disturbed stupor.

When she awoke a second time, all was quiet—save the unmistakable cry of birds. They sounded like seagulls. Seagulls? They must be near the sea. Brilliant, she mocked herself, as her brain processed the implication. Without warning, a door only inches from her head screeched open, slicing through her befuddled thoughts. It scared her almost to death. A hand threw back the blanket covering her. Glaring sunlight blinded her completely.

"Close your eyes and sit." The gruff command came in heavily accented English.

Barely able to move after her long, uncomfortable confinement, she struggled to sit up but couldn't do it. Rough hands grabbed her bare shoulders, pulling her up, accompanied by muttering in Arabic. The ropes binding her wrists cut excruciatingly into her skin. As unsympathetic hands removed the gag, she gasped for air.

A hard object was thrust against her mouth. Recognizing it as a plastic bottle, she tried to quench her desperate thirst, but choked and fell back onto the blankets. She heard more angry muttering as the hands groped to raise her again. Before any further ill-treatment could be inflicted, another voice spoke with authority. Released, she fell back and listened to a sharp, unintelligible exchange before hearing heavy footsteps stomp away.

"Our apologies, Ms. Grant, for any discomfort we have caused. Please keep your eyes closed."

Not that it would make any difference if she opened them. The bright light of day still rendered her virtually sightless. The hands that now brought her up to a seated position were strong, and gentle. One arm around her shoulders steadied her against a solid chest while the other carefully pulled a cloth sack over her head. It felt soft and smelled clean and, once it was in place, the man lifted the edge to expose her nose and mouth. His smooth fingers rubbed water soothingly across her dry, cracked lips.

"Lick your lips." Happy to obey, she greedily licked the precious moisture. Two more times he administered the luscious fluid. Nothing had ever felt or tasted so good.

"Now try to swallow." When she managed it without choking, he brought the bottle to her mouth and cautioned, "Drink slowly. Take small sips." The warm, healing liquid brought indescribable relief—even as the thought flitted across her mind that it probably swarmed with parasites.

"We are going to take a voyage, Ms. Grant. Your cooperation will make the journey a much more pleasant one. For you, that is. If you do as you are told, you may sit on deck and enjoy the fresh air. If not, you will be stowed in the cargo hold. There, I can assure you, the trip will not be nearly as enjoyable."

He paused for a moment to allow her time to consider her options. The silky voice of her abductor was cultured and beautiful, delivering the forbidding message in perfect and polite English. He could have been discussing literature or the opera.

"Will you cooperate?" he asked patiently.

Images of a hot, dark hole, smelling of rot and inhabited by rats, flashed in her mind's eye. She would probably be seasick, too. Swallowing, she nodded her head. When she forced out the single word, it was barely a whisper. "Yes."

"Excellent. Now remain silent while we finalize the necessary preparations. I will attempt to make you as comfortable as possible in the meantime. No one will hurt you."

His touch felt paradoxically tender as he untied the ropes around her ankles and turned her to the side. Tightening a muscular arm around her shoulders, he lifted her to the ground. She couldn't stand, so he supported her until the feeling returned to her numb legs. Then he guided her to a shaded area.

Deliverance from the airless vehicle into a fresh breeze brought overwhelming relief. Light filtered through the sack covering her head. The heat of the sun didn't feel overpoweringly strong. It must be morning, she thought. Led to sit on a low bench, a *mastaba*, she heard the refined voice speak in Arabic. A woman's voice answered with a few words.

"Your needs will be taken care of now. Do not speak or attempt to escape. You will regret it, I assure you." Light footsteps retreated following the honeyed threat.

Small, fleshy hands raised her to her feet and helped her cross a threshold into total darkness. The woman led her to a stool where the ropes binding her hands behind her back were untied. Stiffness in her arms made it impossible at first to even move. Thankfully, the sack covering her head was lifted. Dragging her hands around, she found wrists swollen and crusted with blood.

Julia blinked in the dim light as she watched her warden shuffle to a table against a mudbrick wall and hold a match to a kerosene lamp. She adjusted the wick so that the flame revealed the room more clearly. The short but wide nut-brown woman, typically covered in dusty black robes, head wrapped in a black scarf, resembled millions of others across the

Middle East. A low ceiling added to the closeness of the windowless room. The only other light came from the old wooden door, standing slightly ajar. They could be anywhere.

The sound of a bolt shooting into place after the door closed behind the black-clad figure punctuated the hopeless reality of her predicament. Julia's head fell to her chest as she took her first real breath in hours. Raising it, she looked around more closely at her surroundings. A lumpy mattress lay on a primitively constructed wood-frame cot, no doubt inhabited by colonies of vermin. Beneath it stood what must be meant to serve as a chamber pot. Besides that, the table, and the stool on which she sat, the room was bare.

More feeling had returned to her legs so she rose from the stool to approach the table. Lamplight revealed an old-fashioned and cracked water pitcher with matching washbasin and a frayed but relatively clean towel. Next to the lamp lay a tray covered with a linen cloth. She lifted it to find a plate of cheese, bread and dried figs. And two unopened bottles of water. Evian.

She picked up one of the bottles, staring at it dumbly. Then she clutched it to her chest—as if her life depended on it—and sank to the dirt floor, rolled into a tight ball, and cried like a lost child.

Julia lost track of time before she heard the bolt slide back, followed by the door squeaking open. The old woman entered to find her sitting up straight on the stool, hands folded with composure in her lap.

After she had spent the last tear left in her bruised body, she rose to wash her face and the blood from her wrists in the cool, refreshing water and wipe the dust from the rest of herself as best she could. Pulling the stool up to the table, she methodically consumed every bite of food. It would have been easy to drink both bottles of water, but she prudently saved one for later.

For Julia was determined that there would be a "later."

There would be no more hysteria or tears. That was over. From this moment forward, all her energy, senses and resources would be conserved and concentrated on accomplishing one thing: Escape.

She would cooperate, take strength from whatever substances were provided and be ever-vigilant for her chance at freedom.

Ahmed was not, he assured himself, a monster. He had no desire to inflict needless discomfort or pain. His years at Oxford had resulted in an appreciation for many of the customs and finer things of life found in Western cultures. It was unfortunate for Julia Grant that she must become a tool for the successful completion of his operation, possibly a most useful tool. That did not mean, however, she need suffer unnecessarily in the process. He had been duly impressed in Kom Ombo on witnessing her kindness and generosity for those less fortunate.

Coincidentally, she bore a strong resemblance to a young woman he had known in his first year at school in England. This girl, also American, attracted and captivated him with her lively inquisitiveness about life, and with her giving nature. Her effortless natural beauty tempted him beyond endurance and they became lovers. Who knows what might have happened if she had not suddenly been forced to return to her family in New York?

After she left, he turned to his faith for consolation for the emptiness in his heart.

He came to accept that the relationship had been *haram*, and a mistake. He would do penance for his sin and try to be a better Muslim.

At the mosque, he fell in with a group of fundamentalists and began to lean towards their teachings of defiance. This group advocated a radical and violent overthrow of governments across the Muslim world they deemed apostate. Totally opposed to democracy, they advocated the creation of Islamic states around the world. In a short time, he began to gravitate more and more to the extremists and support their cause.

Holding Julia in his arms and touching the water to her lips brought back memories of the delicious and sinful pleasures he shared with his one and only lover. He would do his best to ensure that her death was as painless and honorable as possible.

It would also be widely covered by the international media.

Ahmed turned from these thoughts at the sound of shuffling feet to observe the two women emerging from the hut. One was draped in the universal robes, with a *burqa* concealing her face. The other, the shorter of the two, guided Julia's footsteps across the sandy courtyard.

Beneath the *burqa's* woven grill, the sack blocked her vision. Her hands were firmly tied, in front this time, which was immeasurably more comfortable. Her legs remained thus far free of bonds, and for that she was profoundly grateful.

"Remember—make no sounds," came the quiet command.

He led her to the vehicle and allowed her to sit upright on a back seat. They pulled noisily away and drove a short distance before coming to a stop. Even through the layers of heavy cloth, she could smell the salty sea air and hear the cry of seagulls overhead.

A cool, refreshing breeze swept across the open deck of the boat, penetrating the confining garments, doing wonders to uplift Julia's spirit—and strengthen her resolve. She *would* escape. And in the dark moments of utter despair on the dirt floor of the hut, she made another resolution: She would, without the slightest doubt, do all she could to sabotage whatever these bastards were up to.

After a while, the gentle motion of the waves lulled her into a state of mindlessness, and she drifted into a deep, dreamless sleep. A voice calling her name faintly penetrated the depths of her oblivion, drawing her reluctantly back to the surface. When she opened her eyes, panic seized her to find only darkness. Then everything came rushing back. The black robes kept out the light. But not the fear.

"Madame Grant, you must wake up now. We must talk."

Their talk lasted a long time. He was, at first, patiently inquisitive. With her mounting denials of any wrongdoing, he became edgy and increasingly irritated.

"You expect me to believe that your purchase in Kom Ombo was only that? The simple purchase of a blanket? And that you are not lovers with the man Zahar? I think you are lying, Madame Grant." His contemptuous emphasis on the word "Madame" made his meaning clear. "And you endanger your life with your lies. If I tossed you over the side right now, you would sink like a stone."

The threat closed in and smothered her, making her gag. With her face hidden by the robes, she hoped he would interpret her quavering voice as tearful. "We are not lovers. I wanted to be, but he would not. He is a devout Muslim and would not. I used the excuse of writing a book to come back to Egypt one more time to try to make him mine. Does that make you happy? Happy to know of my humiliation?"

The genuine torment behind this poignant and deeply personal revelation was more convincing than any denial of espionage would have ever been. Ahmed looked up from the huddled black mass, out over the blue-green water sparkling in the sun. She could be telling the truth. He had seen how she looked at Zahar in Kom Ombo. Now that he thought about it, it did not really matter, one way or the other. He would leave her in peace. For now.

CHAPTER 37

Traveling the route along the western bank of the Nile presented a nerve-wracking experience, especially at night. Vehicles just stopped—right in the middle of the road—with their lights off, creating a deadly obstacle course. Top-heavy with luggage piled on the roof, the van careened around one of them to come within inches of an on-coming donkey cart, naturally not even equipped with lights. The overburdened animal, plodding at a snail's pace, didn't flick an ear as the van veered around it.

"I told you the roads were not good," said Mohamed, hunched over the wheel.

"The understatement of the century," murmured Linda in the back seat as she kept a death grip on the armrest.

Miraculously, he hadn't crashed into any of these hazards—yet—while the van tore along the pitted, bumpy road. Well, perhaps "tore" wouldn't be the right word. He went as fast as the treacherous circumstances would allow. With their "guide" at the wheel, no one dared complain about having the fillings jarred from their teeth.

Lights glared in the rearview mirrors as an overloaded truck came bearing down on their rear. The driver leaned maliciously on his horn as he sped maniacally past.

"These truck drivers use stimulants to stay awake," said Mohamed through clenched teeth. "Just like in America."

Alex, in the front passenger seat, gritted his and glared out at the road. Darkness made it difficult, even with his exceptionally good night vision, to see the next obstruction, or the gaping holes, in time to prevent the vehicle from plunging into their depths. He only hoped the damn thing held together and that the luggage, tied haphazardly to the roof, stayed put. He pointed up ahead. "Slow down."

A wall of flashing lights stretched across the highway.

Mohamed had already seen them. "It's the police. There's probably a wreck. Or maybe a road block, checking for travel permits."

No one said a word. There hadn't been time for them to obtain a permit.

As they slowed, drawing near the lights, blinking red and yellow against the black night, Mohamed pulled over, several yards back from the roadblock. "Stay here."

The others watched apprehensively as he got out and walked up to the group of policemen. Dressed in rumpled uniforms, they were having a fine time harassing the driver of the truck that had passed in such a hurry. One of the officers poked the contents loaded on the back with the barrel of a rifle. The driver showed ominous signs of resentment. Eventually, he pulled a wad of bank notes from his pants pocket and shoved it at one of the policemen. A look of smug satisfaction spread across the man's hairy face. The driver turned to stalk back to his truck, waving his arms and shouting as he went. His outrage could still be heard as he drove away.

Now it was Mohamed's turn. He spoke to the three men at length, gesturing back at the van where his "tour group" sat watching nervously. When he turned back towards them, his face was set like stone—with perhaps a hint of fear.

"Give me your passports."

As each member of the group dug for their documents, Alex kept an eye on the policemen. "Are they likely to search us?"

"Thinking of your arsenal, Commander?" Mohamed compressed his lips until they became a thin line. "Hopefully they will not. As you are American tourists, their supposed primary concern is for your safety. They want to send a man with us, for your 'protection.' This may become an expensive negotiation," he said, turning a baleful eye on Brad.

One of the officers kept up a running dialogue with Mohamed as he and two others scrutinized every page of each one of the passports. Mohamed's agitation increased as he gesticulated wildly and raised his voice.

"I think it's time to send in a heavyweight," surmised Brad. All heads swiveled in his direction as he added, "Okay, Henrietta, you're up to bat."

The frail, white-haired agent gave a curt nod and opened the door. She approached the tense group clustered ahead in the glaring lights, clasping her handbag before her and projecting a saintly smile.

With raised eyebrows and a noticeable attempt to keep the censure from his voice, Alex asked, "Was that wise, Caldwell?"

Brad and Linda just grinned. Henry leaned forward to touch Alex reassuringly on the shoulder. "Those fellas don't have a chance."

In less than two minutes, Henrietta opened her purse and removed a small jar.

Mohamed looked down, incredulity plainly written across his face. She reached over and patted the man he'd been speaking with on the arm as she handed him the jar. After another minute, she again reached into the purse and took out her wallet.

Alex kept his focus on the silent tableau. "How much cash is she carrying?"

Henry smiled. "Don't worry. She won't need much."

She didn't.

Mohamed couldn't help but laugh. "After she commiserated with the man in charge about the cold sore on his mouth and gave him the cream, all he asked for was the cost of the permit."

Henrietta triumphantly waved the handwritten note, signed by the commanding officer of the region, giving them unrestricted permission to travel anywhere throughout the district.

"If we're on the right track, they must be almost a day ahead of us," Brad calculated from the back seat. "But they'll have to be careful not to attract attention and that will slow them down." He practically shouted to be heard over the rush of wind that roared through the open windows. "If they make any stops, and we keep going, we might catch up before they reach Nuweiba."

"If we're on the right track," murmured Linda into the wind.

Mohamed tightened his grip on the wheel and pressed down harder on the accelerator. It was a long night.

In the last hour before the dawn, the now-dusty white van approached the equally dusty outskirts of Hurghada. Mohamed pulled over abruptly and spoke to a pile of rags beside the road. The pile stirred and a turbaned head emerged, the heavily lined face of a man beneath it. After a quick exchange, Mohamed dug in his pocket and tossed out a few bills. The van sped off. "We will go directly to where the ferry runs. When it runs."

"What time is the first boat?" asked Linda, yawning. No one had gotten much sleep, only a few minutes now and then before descending violently into the next crater.

"I am an Egyptologist, not a common tour guide. I have not memorized every bus, train and ferry schedule in all of Egypt."

Alex recognized the signs of battle fatigue on Mohamed's taut profile.

"How're we doing on petrol?"

"Near empty. I will look for a station."

"Right. When we stop, I'll take the wheel." Mohamed adamantly refused to relinquish the driving throughout the long night. It was understood without anyone having to express in words that he needed to be occupied to keep panic at bay.

Henrietta kept a watchful eye on Alexander as well, but she was pleased to see that military discipline prevailed, allowing him to keep his emotions firmly in check. The last thing they needed was a blow up between the two men.

Only Mohamed could have recognized the dilapidated building as a gas station, all in darkness and without any visible signage. He pulled up to a metal relic anchored in the cement. "Wait here."

Moving stiffly to the front of the building, he pounded on a closed door until a light came on behind the dirty glass. Loud words flew back and forth at length in Arabic before the door swung open. A barefoot man in a grubby *galabeeya* muttered continuously as he unlocked the age-encrusted pump and filled the tank.

When Alex, standing beside the driver's door, handed over payment, the muttering changed into a broad smile. *"Shukran,"* he said, nodding happily, showing a mouth half-full of brown teeth, *"shukran."*

"You fed his entire family for a month," grumbled Mohamed as he got into the front passenger seat.

At these sour words, "Team L" exchanged an unspoken message. Henrietta bided her time, keeping a close watch on Mohamed as he directed Alex to the ferry terminal, such as it was, only a few miles away. He pulled into the adjacent parking area and switched off the engine. Alex sat for a moment, along with the others, in subdued silence. The long, haunting cry of a seagull prompted him to open his door.

The others followed, piling out of the van to stand on the pavement to stretch, trying to regain feeling in their limbs. Their bodies, stiff from sitting anxiously upright through the harrowing ride, cracked and creaked. All except for Sarah. She'd offered to ride in the baggage space, where she curled up and managed to grab a few hours sleep.

"Let's see if there's a schedule posted," suggested Linda.

They limped over to what amounted to the ferry terminal. Mohamed bent down to squint at a tattered paper taped inside the greasy glass.

"The ferry is canceled. Indefinitely." He spat out the words in the voice of doom.

"Then we'll have to hire a boat." The brisk response came from Brad. He'd suspected that this might be the case so wasn't discouraged at the prospect. "As soon as possible, Mohamed, you and I will make arrangements. The question is: Will we be able to find one to carry the van across?" All eyebrows lifted at that unforeseen complication, but no one ventured to voice doubt. "What time will things start to open up?"

Mohamed sighed. "Probably around six."

Seven wrists came up encircled with watches.

"We should spread out and ask around to find out if anyone remembers seeing them," said Linda, always the practical professional.

"Same teams?" inquired Brad of his subordinate.

"No, I think I'll go along with Mohamed," said Henry, surprising them all. He seldom spoke unless he had something specific on his mind and his infrequent words carried all the more weight as a result. Henrietta nodded approvingly.

"Right," said Alex, once again assuming command. "It's almost five now. Since no one seems to be out and about yet, let's see if we can find a place to get something to eat. Then we'll spread out to learn whatever we can."

It was a motley group that shuffled into the shabby lobby of the Cleopatra Hotel. Mohamed assumed it was used mostly by tour groups, which proved to be the case. "Yes," said the young waiter, "we would be happy to serve an excellent breakfast to your group."

They availed themselves of the facilities, washing dusty faces and gritty hands, before being shown to a large round table near the buffet. Henrietta made a point of sitting next to Mohamed, who ordered coffee before slumping into a chair.

The others went straight to the meager array of peculiar foods that comprised most Egyptian breakfasts. The display consisted of hard-boiled eggs, dry toast and boxes of cereal, along with plates of cheese, olives and unidentifiable local delicacies of strange textures and suspicious colors.

"My dear Mohamed, may I speak with you frankly?" inquired Henrietta in her kindly way.

He sighed, fingering the handle of the coffee cup without looking up.

"You obviously care for Julia a great deal. We've known that from the start."

At this, his liquid dark eyes looked up to meet her steady gaze.

"We will move heaven and earth to get her back. On that, you have my word. If the word of an old woman means anything."

This brought a fleeting smile to his lips.

"Henry and I have found ourselves in many a difficult situation over the years. The most important and constant lesson learned in all that time was to remain calm. Remain calm and take the best possible care of yourself that circumstances will allow. Take advantage of any and all opportunities to keep yourself operating at maximum capacity. That means sleeping when you don't feel like sleeping and eating when it's the last thing in the world you wish to do."

Even the dark smudges under his eyes didn't dim the radiance of his smile as Mohamed leaned over to kiss her cheek. "You are an angel, Henrietta. Truly an angel."

With that he rose, gallantly pulled out her chair and they advanced, arm-in-arm, on the dubious buffet.

❖

Half an hour later they left the hotel, dividing into teams. Mohamed and Henry would work the back streets, as it was less likely English-speaking locals would be found there. Henrietta said she would tag along with Brad and Linda as they made inquiries at the hotels on the main street. This was the first occasion she'd had to speak with him privately, and she had a few choice words for Brad Caldwell.

That left Alex and Sarah to work the waterfront.

Linda looked over her shoulder to watch them walk away. A more mismatched pair would be hard to imagine: the tall ex-commander striding grimly along, trailed by the diminutive blonde, looking at least ten years younger than her actual forty-something years. They could have easily been mistaken for father and daughter.

"Wait just a damn minute!" Sarah shouted at his rigid back as he marched away.

Alex froze in his tracks, incensed at the indiscretion, and whipped around. In spite of the seriousness of their predicament, it was all he could do to keep from bursting out laughing. Her righteous indignation—fists clenched on narrow hips—made her look for all the world like a fiery little dragon. The grin slipped from his face when she spoke again.

"You've made it *quite* clear that you resent my presence here," she fumed. "Well, get over it. Julia is *my* friend and I loved her long before you did."

What did she say? The entirely unexpected accusation struck like an arrow dead-center on target. He recovered quickly to return to tower over her. "Keep your voice down, for Christ's sake," he hissed. "Have you lost your mind? We don't want to draw any more attention than we already have."

"Well, *excuse* me if I don't measure up to your exacting military standards."

His behavior towards her from the first oozed with disapproval and disdain. When he wasn't ignoring her completely, he eyed her with ill-concealed contempt. She wanted to throttle him. But what did that involve? Did it require a weapon of some kind? A throttle, perhaps? And where did one find such a thing? His infuriating behavior did make her wonder if there might not be a place for a little violence now and then after all.

"Look," she informed him with the forced patience of a parent scolding a wayward child, "it's clear as day that you've fallen in love with her. Who could blame you? Men do it all the time. But they mistake her compassion for a more common emotion. She's usually oblivious to it all. Apart from being beautiful, she's kind and caring and always trying to do 'the right thing,' even when it costs her dearly—which it frequently does. What man could resist a woman like that?"

The courageous soldier stood on the sidewalk in the breaking dawn looking down at this pixie-like woman, completely cowed by her words. They stung and soothed with equal force. She knew Julia. She was her best friend. Standing near her, he experienced a peculiar kind of salve to the wound festering inside.

"But Julia is not a helpless victim. She knew what she was getting into when she came back here. She had a purpose—a mission: to make a contribution to a cause she supports from the bottom of her heart: peace."

Breath now came hard to Sarah as tears glistened in her eyes. Her clenched fists hovered between them as if on the verge of striking out any second at his broad, solid, chest.

"War accomplishes nothing. Nothing but death and destruction. History teaches that lesson repeatedly, but those in power refuse to learn it. You *soldiers* follow orders and perpetuate the cycle of violence. *Over* and *over* and *over* again. That's what puts innocent people like Julia in danger. And gets them killed."

With a strangled gasp, her fists suddenly uncurled and fell to her side as she hung her head. "I'm sorry. I shouldn't have said that."

Alex, incapable of a clear-headed response, could only stare.

Seconds ticked by before she looked up and went on, clearly making an effort at self-control. "You may not like the fact that I'm here, but let me tell you something: I know Julia. I know how she thinks and the kinds of things she's likely to do. That knowledge might make the difference in whether she lives or dies. And I'll tell you something else. She's a lot tougher and a lot smarter than you think. Under that soft layer of generosity of spirit lies a solid core of iron will. Once she makes up her mind to do something, she doesn't rest until it's done.

"She will *not* surrender to those murdering bastards. She will *not!*"

CHAPTER 38

The sack still covered Julia's head beneath the *burqa*, but at least she was free of the suffocating gag. For now. As long as she remained silent she might avoid that extra element of torment. When the boat reached shore, after what seemed endless hours on the open water, they herded her along and once again guided her into a back seat.

She wiggled across it in an attempt to untangle the cumbersome robes and, in the process, found herself the sole occupant. Occasionally, she heard low voices exchange a few words up in front. By listening intently, she made out that there were still only two of them. They always spoke in Arabic, so she couldn't guess what was said, able to understand only a few basic words.

But she knew exactly where they were.

On her last trip to Egypt, while Julia waited in vain for Mohamed to make up his mind about their relationship, she ventured out on her own to explore the Sinai Peninsula. Bravely taking on the midnight climb to the top of Mt. Sinai formed one of the highlights of her time spent here.

The climb started at St. Catherine's Monastery, already at four-thousand feet above sea level, with the additional four-thousand foot ascent done at night to avoid the ruthlessness of the sun. A breathtaking meteor shower that night provided spectacular entertainment during the difficult climb.

Breaking dawn on the precipice where Moses was said to have received the Tablets carved with the Ten Commandments was a memory that would remain with her always. Sculptured red mountains spread out into eternity beneath misty shades of blue-gray sky that created stunning, shifting patterns in the growing golden light. A truly mystical experience.

The descent, much easier in the light of day, brought her, along with other newly-inspired travelers, back to tour St. Catherine's, the legendary home of the biblical burning bush. A small enclave of Eastern Orthodox monks still inhabited the remote monastery, with its world-renowned scholars' library and carefully-tended surrounding gardens.

Her captors stopped briefly along the road after leaving the wharf. As her veils were lifted for a drink of water, she glimpsed a sign, in English as well as Arabic, with directions to St. Catherine's.

They'd crossed the gulf to Sinai. She'd suspected as much. After driving for a while, they slowed to a stop. Both front doors opened then slammed shut. The door beside her creaked open. She heard two men speaking in a heated debate nearby as someone led her into a building and up a flight of stairs.

Gentle hands, the same as before, removed the *burqa* and untied her wrists before leading her to a chair. When he lifted the sack from her head, the voluminous black robe remained the only encumbrance. This welcome reprieve lessened her fright, if only a fraction. Fingers of daylight crept around the edges of closed shutters, providing the only illumination in the dim room. He addressed the first words to her since their arrival.

"You have done very well, thus far, Madame Julia. Continue to do so and you will live to see another dawn. We are in the house of a friend where we will take food and rest. Please do not entertain any foolish ideas. A guard will be posted outside your door."

As he spoke, he moved across the room to open the shutters. A heavy wrought-iron screen covered the window. When he turned back to face her, daylight illuminated his knowing smile. A sharp intake of breath betrayed her shock at his handsome, aristocratic face.

This was the face of a hero of legends—not a murdering terrorist.

Fathomless, dark, beautiful eyes, lushly fringed with sable lashes, full of mockery, regarded her with unmistakable understanding of her thoughts.

"You may call me Ahmed. I will bring what you need to refresh yourself."

Disconcerted, Julia continued to sit on the straight-backed chair until he returned a few minutes later. He placed a wicker basket on the neat cotton spread of the bed and a pitcher of water on an antique dresser that had seen finer days.

"Make yourself comfortable. There will be food soon." The lock on the door clicked behind him.

With a sigh, she rose and went to the bed. Her hand was steady enough as she removed items from the basket: a pair of clean khaki pants and shirt, a hairbrush, toothbrush and toothpaste, and a jar of moisturizer. Tears sprang into her tired eyes, red from the blowing sand in the hot air that penetrated everything, even the layers of cloth that covered her. It was the moisturizer that did it. What kind of man was this? A man who could be this gentle, this thoughtful and considerate, while plotting the deaths of thousands—possibly millions—of innocent people?

A new fear seized Julia with sharp, piercing talons. Her fingers sprang apart, dropping the jar like a burning coal.

He had shown his face.

Mohamed's description of his nasty encounter with this man came back to haunt her. *He had shown his face.* What did that mean for her?

When the whirling, sickening panic subsided, a wave of potent determination mercifully followed. She shoved the straight-backed chair under the doorknob and swiftly removed the robe. Her reflection in the cloudy, cracked mirror above the dresser gave her quite a start.

The once elegant cocktail dress, now torn and smudged with dark grease stains, hung like a feed sack. Somehow, the silk scarf still draped around her neck had survived relatively unscathed. She stroked it as if it were an old friend. It was an old friend. Sarah gave it to her for her last "significant" birthday.

This positive psychological connection brought with it a forceful surge of energy. Julia stripped off the dress, gave it a last look of reluctant regret before tossing it aside. She unwound the scarf from her neck, wrapped it around her bare waist, and gave the talisman a final loving stroke before drawing on the clean, crisp pants.

Whatever lay ahead, she would be ready.

CHAPTER 39

Henrietta stood rigidly on the wharf, looking with unadulterated dismay at the boat. Henry tucked her arm firmly in his own and pronounced with a confidence she felt certain he didn't feel, "We'll be all right, dear. The captain says he makes the trip frequently and has yet to capsize."

"Yes," said Mohamed, positioned a few feet away with legs spread apart and arms folded across his chest, reminiscent of a forbidding pharaoh. "This boat has no doubt made the trip many times over the past few thousand years."

It looked as though it had. A peculiar looking craft, kind of a cross between a barge and a *felucca*, its wooden beams moaned as the crew shouted orders at each other while scurrying around the deck in all directions. The other members of the group came together with fascinated apprehension as one of the barefoot youths jumped behind the wheel of the van. He gunned the engine before heading—with alarming speed—toward the skinny planks of wood, apparently meant to serve as a ramp.

"I hope we maxed on the insurance," murmured Linda to no one in particular.

They held their collective breath as the weighty vehicle, with luggage still piled precariously on the roof, rolled down the ramp onto the boat's narrow deck. The scene reminded Henrietta of a caricature of an "exotic" vacation. All the men on deck waved their arms and shouted out instructions at the driver, whose face shone with excitement. He ignored them completely, coming to a squealing stop less than an inch away from mowing down the mast.

Everyone applauded the successful loading, especially the audience on shore. The captain frowned his approval and signaled them to come aboard.

"Well, I've had a long and happy life," sighed Henrietta as she clung to Henry's arm and started resignedly down the ramp. "I suppose it would be wishful thinking to imagine there might be lifejackets. I've never been especially fond of water sports."

Her comrades-in-arms laughed, one or two in a higher than usual pitch. With everyone on board, the ragged ropes flew from their iron railings on the equally decaying wharf, releasing the craft out into the crystal clear, blue-green Gulf. Under any other circumstance, this might be construed as an exciting experience, an adventure.

Wind gusted into the patched rusty-red sail that rushed up the weathered mast, lending a helping hand to the engine laboring beneath the deck. The trip across the Gulf of Suez would take three hours, more or less, Mohamed told them. Depending. No one needed to ask what he meant by that disclaimer.

"I suggest we all try to get some sleep," said Alex. Team L had already gone to a pile of blankets heaped on the deck. Henry bent over to hand a couple of them to Henrietta and she, in turn, passed them to Linda, smiling as she patted her arm. Once everyone was provided with the basic means of comfort, the elderly couple lay down, spooning on a nest of blankets, and closed weary eyes.

Mohamed gravitated to the bow, staring out across the water in the direction of their destination on the eastern horizon. Brad signaled wordlessly to Alex and they moved toward the stern, with Linda close behind.

Sarah leaned against the rail, her unruly blonde curls dancing in the sea breeze. For the first time since arriving in Aswan, she allowed her thoughts to drift from the desperate circumstances she'd stumbled into. She felt sure they were on the right track. And had confidence in the abilities of these new-found friends to accomplish their mission. She simply would not allow herself to think otherwise. Pessimism was not in her nature. What now concerned her was the situation regarding Alexander Bryant and Mohamed.

She now fully understood, after meeting the attractive and enigmatic Egyptian, Julia's obsession with him. He presented an irresistible combination: that of a man-child, sparking a compelling appeal to his undeniable charm with a simultaneous desire to relieve his burdens. This would have been impossible for Julia to resist. Her need to be needed was, undoubtedly, a huge part of the merciless attraction. Julia always picked up strays. Not that he was that—but he was definitely a man in need. Not to mention unavailable, another perverse psychological anomaly.

He'd changed his mind several times over making a real commitment: The man in him postponed their marriage, while the child refused to let her go. Sarah shook her head with compassionate regret as she glanced over at his profile, where he stood motionless and brooding in the dazzling sun.

The military man posed another problem altogether. True, he represented the antithesis of all that she and Julia had fought for all these years; but she had to admit he had undeniable allure. No way could Julia have been completely immune to that. He was a sexy man: intelligent, tough and confident, with an aura of strength that gave the impression one would always be safe in the circle of his care.

Except that Julia was not safe. To be honest, she had only herself to blame for that. Damn her hide! What the hell possessed her to leave the hotel grounds? She planned to have a nice chat with Madame Julia when she saw her next.

Sarah couldn't suppress the grin that sprang to her lips at the thought of that reunion. Julia would be flabbergasted, to say the least, at the unexpected sight of her "comrade-without-arms" in the midst of this fiasco. But Sarah had felt not one second of uncertainty about traipsing thousands of miles after her imprudent friend. Had their positions been reversed, Julia would've done exactly the same.

Sarah's faith in the people responsible for this catastrophe was minimal, at best.

It was a huge relief to find Alex and the Langleys with Mohamed in Aswan. Between the seven of them, surely they would save Julia.

They just had to.

CHAPTER 40

The petite, wiry woman removed a dirty, limp hat from her closely cropped graying hair and wiped sweat from her brow with a shirt sleeve. Reluctantly, she called out to her *reis* in charge of the dig.

"Ragaa! We must stop for the day." She would normally have pushed the workmen and gone on right up until dark. Archeological fever always charged her with an intense energy the minute she returned to the site each year. She had excavated here for the past four years now and felt much more at home on the dig than in her native Paris. A dedicated Egyptologist and leader in the field, Mariette Chatillon had already published one book on her discoveries at the remote site in the mountains of the Sinai. The promising finds would provide material for at least one more.

"Shall we finish sifting the baskets, Madame?" Ragaa, a most reliable and knowledgeable fellow, Bedouin by birth, led the workmen with dependable dedication and skill.

"*Bokra,*" she called back. "It can wait for tomorrow." In spite of his thoroughness, she hated not being around in case anything of interest turned up. Having to drive down to Feiran, the nearby and largest oasis in Sinai, was a bother, but she'd promised to deliver medicines to one of the Bedouin families there. The children were always coming down with something, and medical care in the area was practically nonexistent.

She plodded across the rocky sand to a modest stone-and-mudbrick house. One large room served as living room, dining area and kitchen, with two bedrooms and a utilitarian bath chamber completing the home-away-from-home. An eclectic array of furnishings—comprised of priceless, well-worn rugs from throughout the region, local crafts and French antiques—created layers of interest and a cozy comfort. Two large amphorae—the two-handled, narrow-necked, swollen-bellied vessels used throughout the Mediterranean since the 15th century B.C.E.—stood in far corners of the room. It gave Mariette an inspiring sense of connection with the past to fill the porous ceramic vases with water, as had been done for thousands of years, so that the evaporation served as natural air-conditioning in the oppressive dry heat.

It took a moment for her eyes to adjust to the dim interior after the harsh sunlight, but her movements didn't falter as she went to the kitchen sink. She knew the exact number of steps from one place to another in the compact space.

Before her husband of over twenty years, also an eminent archeologist, died, they'd kept a lovely—much grander—house down near the oasis. Two years before, while visiting relatives in Israel, he was killed by a Palestinian suicide bomber. Now living and working alone, Mariette found this arrangement much easier, to be right on the edge of the dig. And it spared her some of the reminders and haunting memories, at times unbearably sad, of her married life. *C'est la vie;* life goes on.

She vigorously washed her gritty hands under the running faucet then splashed cool water on her face. After several long drinks of bottled water from the refrigerator, she dragged a comb through her hair. *Bon.* The rest could wait until her return.

Her dented wreck of a Jeep started on the first try. Although not much to look at, it was well-matched to the challenging terrain. Most vehicles deteriorated rapidly in this hostile environment. A rasping noise assaulted the air with the shift of gears; a cloud of dust blew up behind as she roared down the hill.

She delivered the medicine and explained patiently how it was to be administered. The mother thanked her profusely and insisted on filling her basket with dates from the oasis as a token of gratitude. Mariette, anxious now for her bath and dinner, placed the basket on the back seat, climbed behind the wheel and bent to the ignition. As she leaned forward, the rear view mirror reflected a common sight: A van, turned off the main road, pulled over to the side. Great clouds of black smoke billowed from the engine.

She watched as a Middle Eastern man, in Western dress, stepped out from the driver's side. His passengers remained where they were. He went to open the engine door and more black smoke poured out, sending him into a coughing fit.

"Mon dieu." Mariette shook her head. Engine trouble in this out-of-the-way place could be a serious problem. There were no services for miles. It had happened to her many a time. She got out of the Jeep and walked toward the van, calling out good-naturedly, *"Bon jour, monsieur.* May I be of assistance to you?"

Inside the van, Faoud turned in his seat. "One word from you and the woman dies."

Julia had no doubt he meant what he said. The sack no longer covered her head under the *burqa.* But, even with her vision still impaired by the woven grill, she read the unmistakable menace on his repugnant face.

"Bon jour," replied Ahmed. He glanced back at the defunct vehicle. "It appears we do have a problem." He bestowed one of his devastating smiles.

They agreed that Faoud would remain with the van. Ahmed used his mobile phone to call for help, but who knew when it might arrive? Mariette generously offered the comfort of her humble home to the driver and the woman accompanying him while they awaited assistance, which would most probably not be until tomorrow. If they were lucky.

"I am Sharif," said Ahmed smoothly, "and this my wife, Omayma." He helped Julia from the backseat, exerting a cruel grip on her arm. The warning was unnecessary. She had no intention of being the cause of harm to this stranger and kept her eyes, behind the woven grill, lowered to the ground as "Sharif" led her to the Jeep.

Mariette, alert with a growing curiosity, regarded the heavily veiled woman as they entered the house. Ahmed spoke to her in fluent French.

"My wife comes from an isolated region of Saudi Arabia and speaks an obscure dialect." He shrugged as he added, "As she speaks no other language, this makes it impossible for her to join in our conversation."

An indefinable note of discord surrounding the shrouded figure piqued the French woman's interest. For one thing, she was too tall. For another, a glimpse of her ankles when she got out of the Jeep revealed skin much paler than one would expect.

No, there was definitely something not quite right about this.

Having spent many years traveling and working throughout the Middle East, Mariette knew better than to question or challenge the authority of the male figure. Subtlety would be required here if she was to learn anything about this peculiar situation. She offered refreshments, for which Ahmed expressed courteous thanks.

"Would it be possible for my wife to rest in one of the bedrooms? She's finding the long and difficult journey rather exhausting." His dark, hypnotic eyes settled on Mariette's. "She is accustomed to the harem, in any case, and would prefer to take her meal in solitude."

Bedazzled, as intended, Mariette showed them to the guest room and discreetly returned to the kitchen to begin preparing the evening meal.

"Very good, Madame Julia," Ahmed whispered, his warm breath penetrating the fabric covering her ear. "Remain silent and no harm will come to our amiable hostess." Her eyes followed his movements as he made a quick search of the room, removing a pen and notepad from the nightstand drawer.

When he returned to the main room, Mariette gestured for him to be seated at the table. Her frank stare of admiration for his manly virtues prompted the corners of his lips to lift, further enhancing his chiseled features. Ahmed knew how to use his assets to best advantage. He'd had plenty of practice. They came in handy in circumstances such as this, and he exhibited them with a practiced ease.

They chatted while she worked. When the dinner was ready, Mariette picked up a neatly laid tray and turned toward the door leading to the back of the house. "I will take your bride her dinner, *oui?*"

Ahmed's chair, tilted back on two legs, rocked forward as he sprang from it like a panther to block her way. *"Merci, madame."* He reached for the tray. "Allow me."

Mariette froze, startled by the unspoken threat.

He found Julia exactly as he'd left her, sitting on the edge of the bed. Placing the tray on a table next to it, he raised her to her feet to lift the *burqa* before whispering, "You must eat with your wrists bound, I am afraid. Not that that will stop you from doing anything foolish." He smiled sweetly. "The only thing that will prevent that is the knowledge that I will not hesitate to kill you both."

All in all, it was a most enjoyable evening. Mariette served a simple and delicious meal of lamb stewed with vegetables and couscous. Ahmed entertained her with tales of his years at school in England and his mythical life in Saudi Arabia. She'd received her doctorate at Oxford and they reminisced of happy years spent at the venerable institution.

"Ah, yes," nodded Ahmed, "most of the valuable lessons I learned there also came from outside the classroom."

Mariette, feeling the comfort of camaraderie, ventured to ask, "You have recently been married, Monsieur Sharif?"

"Yes, at her family's home. We were betrothed many years ago." He shrugged with brilliantly feigned indifference. "An arranged marriage, of course."

Try as she might, Mariette failed to coerce further information about the shy bride. Midnight approached as the two sat on divans, sipping a final cup of excellently-brewed Turkish coffee and nibbling dates from the oasis when a musical tone jingled in his shirt pocket. Ahmed removed his mobile phone.

"Ah, *Shukran*," he murmured, *"shukran."* He snapped the instrument closed and switched on the smile. "The vehicle is repaired. I must reluctantly bid you *adieu.*"

Mariette raised a skeptical brow. "You must have excellent connections, Monsieur."

Ahmed opened the door of the back room to find his "bride" curled up on the bed, feet bare and eyes closed. Even with her hands securely bound, she'd somehow managed to remove the black robe. The open neck of the drab khaki shirt exposed several inches of smooth, creamy skin. Her shiny auburn hair fanned out across a snowy white pillowcase. She was, he thought with a twinge of regret, such a lovely woman.

Crossing noiselessly to the bed, he sat close, took her hands in one of his and simultaneously placed a finger to her lips. Startled eyes flew open, clouded with bewilderment and alarm, evidently not at first remembering. He leaned down and sent a chill along her spine as his lips brushed her ear. "Do not speak," he whispered, "I will help you into the robes. Keep your eyes down."

She obeyed without a sound. Once again certain she would be anonymous beneath the robes, he led her to the door. Sorrow tangled with hope as Julia looked back at the bed—at the message she'd left there. He guided her outside to the waiting Jeep and helped her into the back seat.

Mariette fired up the beast and rolled off to return her unexpected guests to their fortuitously repaired vehicle. At the bottom of the hill, she slowed for the turn. Lights from an oncoming truck on the main road illuminated the Jeep and she hit the brakes, automatically glancing in the rearview mirror.

Flashing eyes met hers—so startling, she almost gasped out loud. The message there was not that of a blushing Saudi Arabian bride. A fierce intensity burned from these pools of amber fire. And sent a clear, desperate signal. A signal of heart-stopping anguish.

A frantic cry for help.

Mariette dropped off her intriguing guests and returned to the house. A powerful sense of urgency drew her to the room where the mysterious woman had spent the evening in seclusion. Her dinner tray sat on the table, without a crumb left on the plate. The coverlet on the bed was rumpled but had not been pulled back. As she bent to straighten it, her hand came in contact with a metal object. She lifted the pillow to find a broken gold chain.

Next to the chain lay a beautiful gold charm, in the shape of an angel.

CHAPTER 41

James Marshall was exasperated. Exasperated in the extreme. With the intelligence report passed along through proper channels, there remained nothing left for him to do—as far as his government was concerned, in any case. He'd been personally congratulated by the PM for his foresight in sending Commander Bryant to Egypt.

Nonetheless, Alexander walked a fine line here. To actually arrange for the delivery of arms to known terrorists constituted a capital crime. At the very least, Alex could end up in a prison cell, taking James along with him. The idea held very little appeal for Sir James. He was too damn old to be expected to give up the creature comforts of which he had become inordinately fond. Hardship was considered part of the territory during his active days with MI-6, and he, along with his compatriots, wore the inconveniences and injuries like badges of honor. But that time had long since passed.

He emitted one of his mighty sighs as he reached for the phone.

"Good afternoon. Greystone Manor," said the meticulously pretentious voice at the other end of the line.

"Is that Willoughby?" inquired James, pressing on without waiting for a reply. "Master James here. Is the Mrs. about?"

"Good afternoon, sir. No. I'm sorry, sir. Madam has gone down to the village. It's her afternoon for tea at the vicarage. After which she planned to attend her yoga class."

The disparaging inflection placed upon the word "yoga" made clear Willoughby's aversion for something he found questionable, if not downright reprehensible. He perpetually projected a hint of recrimination, as if Lord and Lady Marshall were always committing obscure but unpardonable social *faux pas*.

With no small amount of relief at not having to make excuses directly to his wife, James instructed his officious butler. "Well, let her know the moment she returns that I shan't be home this evening." He could feel disapproval flowing down the wire. "I'll be stopping overnight at the flat in town."

"Yes, sir. Very good, sir. Shall I inform Madam that you will ring her later?" he suggested inappropriately.

"No. Just give her the message. That's all." He slammed down the phone. Damned insolent man. Should've fired him years ago. Thinks he runs the place. Rubbing a bristly chin, James dismissed that irritation and forced his attention back to the other. Once again picking up the phone, he punched in the number scribbled on a pad before him.

William Hirschfield represented all that James found unattractive. Never had he met a man so totally devoid of all charm. "Slippery Billy's" flashy, tasteless clothes emphasized the artificial darkness of his overly-suntanned skin, suggestive of unnatural and repulsive habits. One couldn't have a conversation of the shortest duration without his dropping at least half a dozen names of his supposed jet-set social circle.

To have to actually sit down across the table from the man pushed things to the out-and-out limit. He would, of course, do it for Alex. Especially since James had been the instigator of this sortie. According to Alex, Hirschfield was the only man who could guarantee delivery of the required weapons in such a ridiculously short timeframe.

It had been a long time since James had heard the sense of urgency—almost desperation—in his old friend's usually dispassionate voice. This business of the kidnapping aside, their last conversation was most troubling.

What the devil was going on down there?

Henrietta expressed her sincere gratitude to the captain. The decrepit craft had proved as reliable as his claim. Although the journey across the Gulf turned out to be near five hours instead of the estimated three, they reached El Tor safely and without incident. He and his entire crew worked like animals to make the crossing, the captain wheedled, and their efforts should be fairly rewarded. The already exorbitant fee, interpreted Mohamed with tightly compressed lips, had almost doubled from the original amount.

There was no escape for Brad Caldwell from Henrietta's reproachful stare. He took out his wallet and shelled out the king's ransom to free the vehicle.

Mohamed went to speak with several men lounging around the El Tor dock area and learned that two men, with a heavily veiled woman and another van, came across the day before, in the late afternoon. This meant they were less than twenty-four hours behind. If the others stopped for any reason, they might be able to close the gap.

If they were on the right track.

After another hair-raising episode of ejecting the van over the shaky ramp to land safely ashore, they all piled in. Brad took his turn at the wheel, with Linda up front. Everyone managed to get a few hours sleep on the boat, and Linda had the foresight to purchase enough food items to provide a basic but adequate lunch. It wasn't exactly what she would call a festive group, but the mood improved immeasurably from only a few hours before.

Brad drove like a demon. The others clenched their teeth and held on to anything they could grab to keep from bouncing off the walls.

❖

Mariette Chatillon spent a restless night. Misgivings about events of the previous evening nibbled away at her. She'd prudently taken note of the van's description and license number. Now she must decide what to do with that information.

Rising at dawn as usual, she downed a cup of coffee and a boiled egg before climbing up to the dig. The early hour made it impossible to place phone calls, in any case. Ragaa, already on the site, gave orders to the men. She conferred with him over the work for the day and attempted to focus on the excavation.

When they stopped for a mid-morning break, she walked back to the house. After rinsing the sand from her hands and arms, she went to the elegant French desk. Her sun-browned fingers dug through the top drawer until they located a worn leather book. She leafed through the pages, found the name and number she sought and placed a call. With a slight feeling of accomplishment, she proceeded to polish off the leftovers from last night's dinner then returned to the site.

By four o'clock, Mariette abandoned any further attempt at work. Those amber eyes haunted her, making it impossible to concentrate. The very least she could do, she admonished herself, was to ask around down at the oasis to see what the locals may have observed. The languid pace of life in these remote villages guaranteed that any out-of-the-ordinary activity generated much interest, to be noted and discussed—usually at great and elaborate length. She called a halt to the day's work, made a quick stab at achieving a presentable appearance, and grabbed up her keys.

The Jeep pulled up in a great cloud of sand and dust outside the open-air café in Feiran. Another van, with a mountain of luggage piled on the roof, was parked in front. A man stood in conversation with the bent old proprietor in the shade of the palm frond roof. A group of tourists sat around a table under a nearby gazebo. Numerous bottles of water cluttered the table, where a serious debate appeared to be in progress.

❖

The old man pointed at the woman getting out of the Jeep and Mohamed turned to look in her direction. *"Shukran,"* he mumbled, tossing coins in the outstretched hand. *"Bonjour, Madame,"* he called out as he closed the distance between them. After a few brief words, spoken in French, Mariette dug in her pocket and produced the charm. She was taken aback at the quick descent on Mohamed's face from anxiousness to angst.

In this stranger's palm lay the golden angel he'd given Julia as a token of his love. He snatched it up and rushed to the others.

"She was here." He held out the charm. "She left this."

The pronouncement landed like a heavy, dead weight. Mariette noticed with interest how his hand closed tightly around the charm. "She wore it on a chain around her neck. Never took it off. It was either left as a clue—or lost in a struggle. She would never have been careless with it. Never."

Sarah nodded grim affirmation as she glanced at Alex. His face was a blank.

Everyone at the table snapped to attention and listened raptly as the French woman repeated the events of the previous evening.

Alexander looked down at his watch, exerting strict control over the pounding in his ears. Julia lived. And she'd had the presence of mind to leave this clue. "If they left around one this morning, they're fourteen hours ahead. We're closing the gap."

"And if they had engine trouble," said Sarah in a voice filled with contagious hope, "maybe they'll break down again."

The rescue party scrambled to collect their belongings and sprinted for the van.

Mariette grabbed Alex's arm. "I will go with you."

He forced himself to stop. "I don't think that's a good idea."

"*Monsieur,* vicious bastards like these killed my husband. I will come. Besides, I know the road. And I am a friendly face to this 'Sharif.'" She'd been powerless to prevent the death of her husband. The idea of helping to save another victim offered a form of retribution—a respite from her feelings of grief and despair.

The soldier's strategically-trained mind clicked on. Her encounter with "Sharif" might provide a crucial diversion when—if—the time came.

The van followed the Jeep up the hill and Mariette went to a stone hut where she found Ragaa with some of the other men. She told him she would be leaving unexpectedly, possibly for several days. After instructing him on how to proceed in her absence, she sprinted back to the house, where she quickly packed a small valise. Throwing whatever food supplies came to hand into a wicker basket and grabbing up a first-aid kit, she locked the door and joined the group waiting impatiently in the shade of the veranda.

"I will lead the way," she announced. "One of you should ride with me."

Mohamed stepped up, but Henrietta mused out loud, "Perhaps it would be best if it was someone they wouldn't recognize." Everyone understood what she meant. If they suddenly came upon the kidnappers, a familiar face would give them away in an instant.

And that instant could prove fatal for Julia. It came down to Brad, Linda and Sarah, all of whom eagerly volunteered. Linda broke the stalemate. "It should be a professional and it should be a woman. We're less likely to be considered a threat." She grinned. "Especially here in macho-land."

They clambered into the two vehicles and tore down the hill. Mariette needed no prodding to set a rapid pace. The memory of those haunted eyes still burned in her brain. In the van, Alex and Brad shouted to be heard over the roar of the engine and the wind. The good news was that they were on the right track and narrowing the gap.

The bad news was the call Mariette had made earlier that day.

CHAPTER 42

Abdel Handoussa exited glass doors at the front of the enormous brown building on Tahrir Square in the heart of Cairo. The complex, with manic traffic swirling around it, housed thousands of the bureaucrats that clog the Egyptian government. People swarmed through the series of metal detectors, mostly failing to remove anything from their pockets, which constantly set off the alarms. The security guards, whose job it was to see that they did, took no notice. Boys bearing trays of drinks and snacks wove their way through the throngs pouring in and out in various stages of agitation and aggravation, adding to the general turmoil. It could take a novice days to even discover where he needed to go within the labyrinth, much less to resolve the problem that drove him there.

Handoussa chewed thoughtfully on the toothpick protruding from his thick lips as he crossed the chaotic street. It had been a while since he'd come across any information that might be of interest to the Brothers. Information they might be willing to pay for, in any case. He was not what one might call "dedicated to the cause." After all, he rationalized, he had a family to support. If he could help the Brothers and earn a little extra on the side, that was all to the good.

His government-provided university education led to a position with the police force where his climb to the middle of the vague lines of hierarchy was tiresome—and slow. Not that he was particularly ambitious. His current position in Intelligence provided excellent opportunities to supplement his income. The captain to whom he reported was either unaware of his entrepreneurial activities, or he turned a blind eye to them. Handoussa didn't know which and didn't much care.

The call came in that morning. He informed the French archeologist that, unfortunately, his superior was out of the office for a few days. Could he do anything to help? Mariette hesitated briefly but decided it best to leave a message. Perhaps Monsieur Handoussa could reach the captain and relay it? Certainly, he said, he would do his best. Most fortuitous, he thought once again.

Mariette and Captain (then Lieutenant) Rashwan had met several years before during an investigation of antiquities smuggling. She'd provided valuable information that led to the successful break-up of the illicit operation, which resulted in a promotion for Rashwan. A mutual regard sustained their relationship and they stayed in occasional touch. She felt confident in expressing her qualms about the "newlyweds" and relaying the vehicle's description and license plate number to him.

It was simply serendipitous for Handoussa to have taken the call in his superior's absence. It was nothing short of uncanny that the vehicle in question had been part of a shipment of merchandise he'd overseen through Customs last year.

A container full of stolen cars, vans, motorcycles and various miscellaneous electronics had come from Japan. Such deliveries arrived a couple of times a year, and the Brothers were often interested in purchasing the vehicles, since they were difficult to trace. Handoussa happened to remember that particular vehicle because he'd been the one to arrange for the new license plate—stolen, of course.

He swaggered into the coffee shop, removing aviator sunglasses with mirrored lenses. Groppi's was one of his favorite haunts. Once the most famous café, tearoom and patisserie in Egypt, it had been "the place" to be seen by Cairene society in the 1920s all the way through the early 1950s. Today it was a mediocre shadow of its former glory but continued to serve delicious pastries.

Handoussa ordered a coffee with cream and an assortment of cookies and sprawled back in a chair to wait. Powdered sugar drifted down onto his protruding belly as he greedily contemplated how much this tidbit of information might be worth.

Ahmed stood by the side of the road in the pre-dawn light, cursing silently. Smoke billowed from the engine. His dark eyes clouded, foretelling the imminence of a great storm. "Can it be fixed?"

Faoud's mouth twisted into the usual scar. "It must cool. Then I add more oil. But it will happen again."

Ahmed turned away sharply, flipping open his mobile phone. He offered no word of greeting as a voice answered. "Get another vehicle. One that runs. Meet us in Wadi Ghazala."

Without further comment, he disconnected and stalked back to the van. It was his own fault. They could have easily hired a newer, more reliable vehicle. His innate sense of prudence had led him to use this piece of crap. Anything too new might attract undue attention. Now, stranded here beside the road, they might not only attract attention but could delay the operation. He cursed under his breath as he yanked open the back door.

Julia flinched at the sudden noise. She'd been lost in thought at the possible ramifications of another delay. It could only be good news for her, she thought—until she caught sight of her abductor's face. Instinctively, she shrank back with dread. Up until now, his treatment of her had been respectful, above reproach. This new ferocity sent a spasm of alarm vibrating to her toes.

"Get out."

A sense of self-preservation told her to do as ordered—without comment or delay. He addressed a few curt words to his accomplice before slinging a rucksack over his shoulder and taking a firm grip on her arm. He led her away from the road out into the rocky desert. Jagged red mountains surrounded them on all sides. The going was tough, especially in the thin-soled ballet slipper-style shoes Julia wore to that memorable dinner by the pool in Aswan, a lifetime ago.

They'd covered a considerable distance across the difficult terrain before his pace slowed and he released the grip on her arm.

"Forgive me, Julia. These delays are rather inconvenient." His taut features relaxed as he slipped back into the role of bafflingly urbane host. Pointing to an outcrop of rocks at the base of the mountains he said, "See the acacia trees there by the entrance to the wadi? We will go there and take refreshment in the shade while we wait for the engine to cool." He wanted to be as far away from the vehicle as possible should trouble arise.

It always seemed strange to Julia to find plants growing in this desolate landscape. She'd learned that the extreme conditions of the ecosystem, over thousands of years, had triggered transformations in the structural organisms, enabling them to adapt to the harsh environment. The *wadis*, fossil beds of age-old rivers when there was much more rainfall, cut a maze of valleys across the vast region of the Sinai. They could be miles long and hundreds of meters wide, or merely crevices in the rock.

The area was sparsely populated. Apart from the occasional oasis and Bedouin camp, it was inhabited mostly by rodents, reptiles and the odd stray camel. It could be an excellent place to hide—if one could manage to maneuver without a compass, avoid the landmines buried from innumerable wars, and steer clear of snakes and other poisonous reptiles.

If one had water to survive the brutal temperatures of the long, hot days and blankets to shelter from the raw cold of the night.

Julia recalled vividly the bone-chilling cold at the top of Mt. Sinai, shivering beneath smelly camel blankets rented from the enterprising Bedouins at its peak. She also remembered the sanctuary of St. Catherine's Monastery.

Ahmed had long since abandoned any attempt at anonymity, along with the fearsome Faoud. Julia knew this did not bode well for her future. If she could get away, with even a small head-start, she could easily disappear. Whatever her chances might be in the inhospitable mountains, they would be better than what faced her now. If she could make it to St. Catherine's, the monks would protect her.

Julia trudged along the barren ground, her frenzied mind searching for a plan. She started when he came to a stop. They'd reached the grove of spindly trees and it was now fully light. The sun had risen quickly in the sky, causing the temperature to jump at least twenty degrees.

Ahmed removed a wool blanket from the rucksack, a worn version of the one Julia purchased from Zed that terrible day in Kom Ombo, and spread it out in the filtered shade of the largest tree. She sank gratefully down and kicked off the flimsy shoes, full of sand and sharp pebbles that cut unmercifully into her feet. As she did, she noticed a rock beside the blanket, about the right size to fit into the palm of her hand. If she could only free her arms, and distract him long enough to pick it up.

"Not exactly the appropriate footwear for such an expedition," he commented dryly.

Hot, exhausted and beyond caution, with feet bloody and sore, she shot back without thinking, "Well, perhaps in the future you'll let me know the agenda ahead of time so I can dress properly."

At this, the terrorist threw back his head and laughed out loud. "Ah, Julia, you are an interesting woman."

Encouraged by this unexpected display of familiarity, she pressed the advantage. "Listen, since we're out here in the middle of nowhere, could you remove this awful thing?" She flapped her arms inside the dusty, stifling *burqa*. "Wearing black in this sun is like roasting in an oven."

He looked down at her for a thoughtful moment. "Yes, I don't see why not."

Free from the constricting garment, she felt a surge of emboldening hope. With as pathetic a look as she could muster, she held out her securely bound wrists. Again, that unnerving look before he shrugged and untied them.

When he offered a bottle of water, she drank deeply and then splashed her face. Unencumbered and thirst quenched, she looked around at the stark landscape. Many thought it depressing. Julia found it hauntingly beautiful.

The unmistakable appreciation on her flushed face so clearly revealed her thoughts, even in her dire situation, Ahmed was moved to say, "I'm sorry you have become involved in this, Julia."

She turned to look up at him and was astounded by the sympathetic expression on his beautiful face. Here they sat, she thought in wonder, in the middle of the Sinai desert: two strangers brought together by unimaginable circumstance, on opposite sides of a conflict not of their own making.

"Why, Ahmed? Why are you doing it?"

He seemed far away for a time as he gazed out across the sand. The words came softly, like a prayer. "It is for Allah. And it is right. The Islamic world has tasted the humiliation and degradation in Palestine for more than eighty years. Why do you suppose men and women around the world line up to plead for permission to become martyrs? The Western governments are corrupt and must be stopped."

He tilted his head back to take in the infinity of sky and spoke as if a script were written there. "In the rest of the world, Western political assumptions are so taken for granted that no one thinks about them anymore. But at least one of these assumptions—the modern belief in secular civil government—is, for us, an alien creed. For more than a thousand years, we have avowed faith in a Holy Law that governs all of life." That sweet, sweet smile caressed the corners of his lips. "The Jihad is to eradicate the cancer of your 'democracy' and prevent it from spreading."

The absurdity of this discussion—in this place, under these circumstances—escaped Julia for the moment. "I agree that many mistakes have been made. But why does it have to be this way? With violence and pain and death for innocent people? You're an intelligent, educated man. There are many like you who believe in your cause.

"Why can't you, together, find a better way? A peaceful way?"

Even as she spoke spontaneously from the heart, Julia reminded herself of the risk in saying these things. If he were to discover that she knew of his real purpose, things would be much worse for her. Much worse.

"Ah, so now you will try to reform me?" Mischief danced in his eyes. Beneath them, she noticed sunlight glinting off a silver charm that hung from a chain around his neck. It represented, she knew, the five pillars of Islam: Faith in God and Muhammad as His messenger; the ritual of prayers five times each day; Charity to the needy; the annual fast of Ramadan; and the Hajj, the pilgrimage to Mecca all Muslims hoped to make at least once in their lifetime.

His lips lifted at her stare. He was, undeniably, the most amazingly beautiful man.

Julia tore her eyes away. This classic face masked an underlying, unwavering intent to commit appalling acts of destruction. To look at him, to hear him, made it near impossible to believe that he, along with his fellow terrorists, was planning the unthinkable, unimaginable horror of genocide. It would be conceit of the highest order to think for one second that she could reform him.

But she had to try.

"It's not for me to say who's right or wrong. The only thing I know for sure is that violence is wrong. It only begets more violence. The lesson is there throughout history. I agree that there needs to be a revolution of sorts: to redistribute global wealth more equally and reform the corruption and immorality that's tearing the world apart. But peaceful revolutions can work. Look at Mahatma Gandhi and all he accomplished. Without violence. It can be done!"

The words erupted from the depths of her soul with such potent conviction it made her eyes bright with unshed tears. Her upturned palms reached out to him, fingers spread wide, in a gesture of desperate appeal.

The sight of her, kneeling on the blanket in the filtered rays of the sun, looking up at him in her passionate plea, touched a place deep within Ahmed. An infinitesimal spark of doubt stirred, like a shooting star.

A shrill sound startled them both from the riveting exchange. The flicker of doubt died away. He reached in a pocket to retrieve his phone, turning his back as he moved away.

Julia drooped down, worn out by effort and emotion. Her eye fell to the rucksack, less than a yard away. Her heart stopped at the sight of the handle of a gun peeking out from its depths. But before she could scoop it up, Ahmed turned back. With nerves still aquiver, she leaned back on the corner of the blanket. Her hand brushed against something hard and warm. The rock. Cautiously, keeping watch from the corner of her eye, she picked it up and slid it into the folds of her robe.

Ahmed returned to find her lying on her side, eyes closed, with the loathsome *burqa* rolled into a ball beneath her head. The sweet smile softened his features as he sat on the edge of the blanket to watch her as she slept. There was another reason for his smile: Arrangements for the last delivery of weapons was confirmed. Everything was going according to plan.

Feigning sleep, Julia watched him through lowered lashes as he watched her. Her mind kept pace with her thundering heart. If she could get him to bend down, perhaps to examine her damaged feet, she might have a chance. Hit him on the back of the head as hard as she could, grab the sack with the water and the gun and run like hell. It wasn't far to the wadi. She could make it. As long as she hit him hard enough to knock him out or at least stun him for a few precious minutes. And as long as he wasn't carrying another gun.

While her head swirled with the possibilities, not once did her deeply-rooted pacifism interfere. At last, summoning every shred of courage in her soul, she gripped the rock, opened her eyes, took a deep breath, and stretched her legs. The movement caused her to wince in real pain. He tilted his head in question before his eyes followed hers down to her feet.

She sat up slowly. "My feet are destroyed. I don't know if I'll be able to walk." In a small, hesitant voice she asked, "I don't suppose there's water to spare for rinsing them off?" The rock burned in her hand, concealed beneath the crumbled robe beside her.

He showed no expression as he knelt at her bruised, bloody feet. She stared in bewilderment as he gently lifted one, cradling it in his hands. The tingling sensation that reverberated up her leg at his touch shocked her into immobility. Their breath simultaneously quickened as their eyes locked in mute comprehension of the arousing connection.

"Ahmed!"

The cry came from the distance. "Ahmed!" Faoud stood, waving his arms, halfway between the road and the acacia trees. Shimmering on the golden sand in the blinding sun, he could have been a mirage. He was not.

Eyes still holding hers, Ahmed slowly lowered the battered foot, to place it just as gently back on the blanket. In a single fluid movement, he came to his feet, raising a hand to acknowledge the signal. He tossed her a bottle of water and removed a cloth from the rucksack. Tearing it into strips, he dropped them in her lap. "Wrap your feet before replacing the shoes. And put those back on," he added, pointing to the wadded up robe and *burqa*.

His eyes never left her as she followed the terse command.

Her feet attended to and shrouded once more, Julia rose, keeping the rock hidden in the folds of her robes. Had she not, he would have seen it when he picked up the blanket. They started back, walking abreast, back to the road and the defective van, now ready to carry them closer to whatever destiny awaited. When his long stride put him slightly ahead, and he couldn't see, she let the rock sink back into the scorching desert sand.

CHAPTER 43

Five athletic-looking men followed Benjamin Richter into the terminal at Eilat airport. Not wanting to draw attention to their presence, the Mossad officers traveled in pairs and took a commercial flight. The first one of the day put them on the coast just before seven in the morning.

Benjamin chose the best men available. Security forces were stretched critically thin, as usual, but he'd worked previously with each one of the members on this hastily-assembled team and had total confidence in their abilities. They would, without fail, follow orders to the letter, even without having been fully informed of the grave nature of their mission. As far as they knew, it was a matter of routine intelligence work to flush out deadly Muslim terrorists, ever-present in their midst.

Christ, he thought bitterly. *Routine intelligence to flush out deadly terrorists*. What had the world come to when you could say—even think—something like that?

The men moved efficiently through the airport and took two separate taxis to their initial destination. Benjamin decided to maintain secrecy of their presence in the area. The local authorities would not be brought in unless something concrete was discovered—and only then at the last moment. The risk of exposure was too great in this morass of treachery.

Benjamin, once more, reviewed the facts that led him here. Eilat lay at the southern tip of Israel, on the Gulf of Aqaba where it funneled down to a narrow strip along the coast. The Egyptian border town of Taba was only a few kilometers to the west, with the Jordanian border town of Aqaba equally close to the east. All three had active ports. Due to the proximity of the three countries at this point, loyalties often became blurred.

Both Jordan and Egypt were now recognized supporters of Israel, but Jordan remained her strongest ally in the entire Middle East. The late King Hussein established peaceful relations with the Jewish state and this relationship continued with his successor and son, King Abdullah. Benjamin respected him for this. In the face of severe criticism from most of his neighboring Arab countries, King Abdullah stood as a buffer for Israel on its western border, and continued to work on the Israeli-Palestinian peace process.

Security would be on full alert at the border of Taba. The nagging worry buzzing around in Benjamin's head concerned security along the Israeli-Jordanian border. Jordan was known to have the tightest, most excellent intelligence service in the region. In spite of this, not long ago, terrorists had managed to accomplish three simultaneous bombings at top hotels in the Jordanian capital of Amman. Thousands of Jordanians protested against the Mujahideen for the indiscriminate murder of innocent—and mostly Muslim—citizens.

What worried Benjamin was the possibility of the chemical weapons being smuggled from Egypt into Jordan. From there it would be much easier to cross the border into Israel, into the vastness of the Negev Desert. It might be a longshot, but it was the kind of audacious plan that would appeal to these bastards. Not only would they accomplish their loathsome objective, they would also implicate Jordan in the act, thereby placing the Jordanian King in an impossibly compromising position.

Benjamin never underestimated this enemy.

Oh, no. The men who devised these heinous attacks displayed intelligence, meticulousness and—above all—patience. A plot of this magnitude must have been in the planning for years. They would have been careful to have men ensconced in strategic positions all along the way, establishing a network of formidable proportions and means.

His mission was to discover and infiltrate that network. He and his carefully chosen team had only a few days—at best—to accomplish this daunting task.

One of the taxis, carrying Benjamin and two of his men, pulled up in front of a second-class hotel on a back street near the port. He paid the driver, took rooms, and waited for the others to arrive.

"We will spread out in teams of two. First, check out the usual channels. Use extreme caution in this. We must not raise any speculation. Look for anything out of the ordinary. It is doubtful that this route will turn up a lead of significance, but we must first make the effort. After that, we go undercover."

Each man knew what that meant.

Twelve hours later, the news was disheartening but pretty much what they'd expected. Now they would have to go underground, again in teams of two. Benjamin surveyed the five attentive faces crowded into the shoddy room.

"Ibrahim, you go with David, Ezer with Aharon. Joshoa, you will come with me." The youngest and least experienced of them all, Joshoa tried not to show the pride he felt at being chosen to accompany his commander. His minimal experience in the field was exactly why Benjamin chose him. Joshoa was a good man but perhaps a bit brash. Should there be any action, the leader felt compelled to have him under his close supervision.

Over the next arduous twenty-four hours, what little they turned up brought only discouragement, although a tense air seemed to permeate the usual deviant haunts. But Benjamin knew, from past experience, that could be their imagination. The one solid piece of information unearthed was particularly disturbing.

A well-known Jordanian terrorist had recently resurfaced. Faoud Arabiyat had been a leader in Hamas and active in the Palestinian conflict. The last Israeli Intelligence knew of him, he was arrested and jailed in Egypt for attempting to smuggle guns into Gaza. That was over seven years ago. Those years spent in the unmitigated hell of an Egyptian prison appeared to have done little to curtail his appetite for violence. After his release, rumor had it, he hooked up with the Mujahideen in Jordan and was, several times since, seen in Aqaba.

The hair on the back of Benjamin's neck again prickled as he stared down at his square, sun-browned hands. He looked at the watch on his wrist. His parents had given it to him on his twenty-first birthday. To Benjamin, it was a symbol of love and honor. It represented all that he strove to defend and protect—and it gave him strength. The glowing dial now read six minutes past midnight.

"All right. We will take four hours' sleep. Ibrahim and David, you will stay here and see what else you can turn up. The rest of us will rent a car and drive to Aqaba.

The ill-fated childhood friendship that ended so painfully left Benjamin with a valuable legacy: He spoke fluent Arabic with a convincing Palestinian dialect. The other three men in the car spoke Arabic as well, in varying degrees of proficiency.

Due to the relatively friendly relations between the two countries, the Israelis had no difficulty crossing the border. Once in Jordan, they stopped to make slight alterations to their appearances. Although the changes were subtle, the four Israelis could easily have been completely different men.

As dawn broke over the mosaic of rooftops, they split up to spend the day scouring cafés, coffee shops and mosques in search of anything that might bring them closer to the men they sought. As nightfall drew near, Benjamin met with success.

His Palestinian accent enabled him to get friendly with a couple of fiery youths with ties to Gaza, both seething for retribution. In the course of a long, tedious tirade on the evils of the Western Infidels and the need to eliminate their Israeli enemies, the fervent young men could not contain their excitement for the "next big plan." They knew of Arabiyat: that he had met here with others. Though no specific details were revealed—Benjamin seriously doubted that any of them, in truth, knew any details—not-so-well-veiled hints were scattered like crumbs of bread.

The breadcrumb trail led to Nuweiba.

CHAPTER 44

"Slow down!" shouted Linda over the Jeep's roaring engine. She pointed up ahead to a darkened vehicle parked by the side of the road. Mariette nodded and pulled over, still a considerable distance away.

She reached for a pair of binoculars. *"Oui, it is the same."*

The others came up behind as Linda jumped out. Mariette followed her to the passenger front seat window of the van. Those inside leaned forward towards Linda as she said, "It's them. What's the plan?"

The archeologist took the lead. "Linda, we will drive ahead and ask if they need assistance. Everyone else should remain here. I am a friendly face and yours they will not know." She turned to Alex in the back seat. *"Monsieur,* you must give me a gun."

He found the request unexpected—but not all that surprising. Clearly Linda would have told their new French confederate something of what was going on. And he'd already handed over the Beretta to the female agent. Brad Caldwell had managed to smuggle his own weapon through security in Aswan. That feat of secret service professionalism impressed Alex more than anything about the man he'd learned thus far.

He glanced at Brad, who shook his head in disapproval while throwing up his hands in consent. Alex pulled the Mauser from inside his jacket and passed it through the window.

"Don't show it unless you have to. Wait for Linda's lead," ordered Brad. "If you're still there in five minutes, we're coming in."

"Je comprends." Mariette shoved the gun in her jacket pocket and without further discussion headed back to the Jeep.

Linda stood speechless, with raised eyebrows directed at her boss. Brad shook his head again and rolled his eyes then gestured her on. "Play it by ear."

He ran a hand over his disheveled hair. Great. A shoot-out in the Sinai involving terrorists and civilians. Bob Bronson'll love it.

The sound of the Jeep grinding into gear set everyone's teeth on edge. A full moon allowed them a good view of what went on up ahead.

As Mariette approached the immobile van, both women tensed. She drove slowly past and pulled up in front. "I didn't see anyone, did you?" asked Linda in a low voice, looking back in the side mirror.

"Non, but we will see." With a last glance in the rearview mirror, she stepped down as she called out, "Hallo? Sharif, is that you? Do you need assistance?"

No answer. Only silence in the desert wind.

Linda kept her eyes anxiously fixed on the side mirror and removed the safety on the Beretta as Mariette approached the van. After circling it and peering in all the windows, she turned to survey the surrounding landscape. Nothing. In all directions—nothing but mountains, shadows and sand. She raised a hand to wave for Linda to join her and reached with the other for her phone.

"They can't have just disappeared," groused Mohamed.

Henry saw Alex's eyes narrow and answered Mohamed's unhelpful comment quickly before the other man could say something they all might regret. "No, of course not. There are several possibilities. A passing driver might have picked them up. They could have been met by a confederate with another car. Or..."

"Or," interrupted Sarah in a voice filled with wonder, "they could've been carried away by the Bedouin."

"Oh, for Christ's sake," began Brad irritably. Then his tone changed to one of incredulity as he repeated with far less vehemence, "Oh. For Christ's sake."

They all turned to look in the direction of his stupefied gaze. A caravan of camels approached beneath the blue moon. The band of Bedouin, only a few hundred yards away, seemed to have magically appeared from the desert sands.

"This thing just keeps getting better and better," murmured Linda, shaking her head.

Mohamed and Mariette strode toward the caravan and approached the lead beast. Its rider, a man of indeterminate age, bared blackened teeth as he inquired in broken English, "You want camels? We have good camels. Good price."

Mariette held her tongue as the camel-seller answered Mohamed's sharp inquiries about who might have occupied the abandoned van.

None of the others spoke as they watched Mohamed stomp back across the rocky sand, trailed closely by the pensive French archeologist.

"Their van broke down," Mariette said unnecessarily. "There are still only three of them. One of the Bedouin took them by camel to an oasis not too far from here, called Wadi Ghazala. We can reach it much faster by automobile."

Alex looked down at the scuffed toes of his shoes without comment. She was still alive. And they were closing in.

A brief exchange resulted in unanimous agreement of the foregone conclusion: Accomplices must be meeting the kidnappers at the oasis with another vehicle. Catching up with them on the camel track was out of the question; but beating them to the oasis presented a distinct possibility. Naturally, the Bedouin didn't know the exact time the others had set out through the mountains, but it couldn't have been too long ago.

They might be able to get to the oasis first, if they drove like hell.

No one articulated the depressing thought that occurred to them all: If someone was bringing Julia's captors another vehicle, it no doubt meant reinforcements as well.

The chilling fury on Ahmed's face when the engine started to choke again shocked Julia, filling her with dread. When his phone rang she thought at first the call might assuage his anger; but then his voice rose and he shouted profanity in several languages. She shrank back into the seat, trying to disappear.

Ahmed slammed the phone down on the dashboard, visibly shaking in an attempt to control his wrath. "That French bitch! She called the police. Praise Allah that the message was intercepted before any harm was done."

Even so, they needed to lose this piece of crap and get the other vehicle as soon as possible. Who knew what the Infidel whore might do next? Faoud was right—they should have killed her.

Faoud always wanted to kill people. Ahmed had gotten into the habit of automatically saying no. Next time, he would give the suggestion more consideration.

Had it not been for the almost miraculous appearance of the Bedouin, offering their camels for hire, things might have turned very ugly. The one thing the helpful purveyor of transport failed to mention to either the kidnap party *or* the rescue party was how ill-advised it would be to attempt the trek in the dark. Even with the light of the moon, it was treacherous terrain.

Julia spent several long, frigid hours huddled in one of the Bedouin tents alongside the three men. She shivered as the icy air seeped into every crevice of her aching body, alongside the fear. Ahmed sat upright, with eyes closed and ears alert. Faoud slept the deep sleep of a man without a conscience.

Mariette and Linda at the same time saw headlights appear over a distant hill, coming from the opposite direction. The Jeep slowed and they watched as another car followed the first down the hill.

"The turn off to the oasis is not far ahead," shouted Mariette. She stopped by the side of the road and kept the engine running.

It was a good thing they drove without headlights and even better that they waited, because the two cars ahead slowed and made the turn onto the road to Wadi Ghazala. By this time, the van had pulled up behind the Jeep. Both front doors swung open and Brad and Alex jumped out. The others followed suit as Linda and Mariette joined them.

"Did you see the headlights?" asked Linda. Seven heads nodded yes.

"This oasis is not large. The arrival of these cars at this time of night is, ah, a bit unusual." The French woman pursed her lips before adding, "Nothing happens in a place like this without being observed. It would, I think, be a mistake for any of us to drive in there now."

Dawn was but a few hours away. After their now-routine debate, they agreed that as soon as there was enough light, a scout team including Alex, Mohamed, Brad and Mariette would take the Jeep as far as they could without being seen or heard from the oasis. After parking it well off the road, they would climb the hill on the western side, where, Mariette assured them, they would have a full view of the small community.

Team L offered up their binoculars. Mariette brandished a pair as well. The others would remain with the van. Certain members of the party weren't happy about the arrangements, but Henrietta, in her gentle fashion, smoothed the ruffled feathers. By the time they finished making preparations and consuming what remained of their provisions from the harrowing Gulf crossing, dawn drew near.

Mariette turned off the sand-strewn road into a wadi barely wide enough for the Jeep to pass. Her male passengers lurched to grab whatever they could to try and keep their seats as she shot up a sudden uphill grade. A second sharp turn around an enormous boulder and she switched off the engine.

"Here we are hidden from the road. Now we climb." Mariette took out her mobile phone and switched it off. "These, we do not want to ring, *non?* Besides, in these mountains, they do not work so well."

The short distance turned into a long climb. More than an hour passed before they reached a point with decent visibility and adequate cover. The spectacular sunrise created a curious sense of unreality, with shades of pink and lavender tingeing the sky over the top of the blue-gray mountains.

Crowded together behind a low ridge, the scouts held three pairs of binoculars zeroed in on the oasis below. Smoke curled up in several plumes above the village from fires lit against the last of the cold night air, and to cook the morning meal. They easily spotted the two cars from last night, parked near a cluster of tents on the southwestern edge of the palm grove. No human activity yet stirred.

The entire interminable day passed with little activity other than the workers in the palm groves, who harvested dates. All they could do was wait. They took turns keeping watch and tried to take advantage of the time for getting some badly needed sleep. The sun drove down fiery shafts onto their heads and turned the stones around them into a giant oven.

Finally, as sunset began to lengthen the shadows, two men emerged from the tent beside the parked cars.

A low call from Alex brought the rest of the scout team back to the ridge in a flash. They watched the two men intently until Mariette stiffened and raised a cautionary finger to her lips. They held their collective breath and no one moved.

Two seconds later they all heard it: the sound of steady, heavy footsteps on sandy gravel. The steps came closer—alarmingly close—from an unexpected direction. They hunched down behind the rocks as the camels trudged past on the path directly below, less than twenty feet away.

The lumbering rhythm of her mount's plodding feet on the narrow path produced a strangely hypnotic effect. Julia dozed in a state of semi-consciousness as the caravan made its way through the *wadi* and over the mountain pass. This wasn't the first time she'd ridden a camel. Many found the experience disagreeably uncomfortable but, as an accomplished horsewoman, Julia took it in stride. It seemed to her now, however, that they'd been winding up and down the steep and narrow passes forever.

The sudden descent after cresting a rise brought her back fully awake and she started at the sight of a picturesque oasis in the valley below. Not for the first time, Julia marveled at her ability to appreciate the beauty of the scene under such traumatic circumstances. She'd always thought of herself as a "glass-is-half-full" kind of person but, honestly, this was way over the top.

Still, the grove of date palms, lemon and mango trees amidst the sun-baked rocks presented a magnificent sight to behold. She knew that underground springs provided the water for irrigation as they had done for centuries. The desert dwellers learned long ago to utilize to the fullest the water supplies in these verdant areas.

The green of the grove proved farther away than it appeared and it took quite a while for them to reach its outer fringe. A few words from the

Bedouin brought their mounts to a halt. One of the men waiting there, with the aid of a stick, cajoled the beasts to their knees, not without loud complaints from the disgruntled dromedaries.

No one paid the slightest attention to the stiff, limping, black-clad figure as Julia was led to one of the tents.

As soon as the caravan passed, the scouts cautiously raised their heads. Four camels: two men in the lead, then a black-garbed figure, with another man behind. With their backs to the scouts, identification was impossible. The path wound down the hill, and as the riders turned again towards the west, rays of the setting sun illuminated the profile of the last man—unmistakably that of the fearsome Faoud.

Alex, crouching next to Mohamed, gripped his arm as the Egyptian started to rise.

"Wait."

They watched to see what happened next. The tortuously slow descent of the camels was observed from below; several more figures emerged. Two men approached the caravan to greet the riders as they dismounted. The black-clad figure stumbled down and was led to one of the tents. Several of the male figures remained in conversation outside before eventually disappearing behind the flaps of another tent.

No one on the ridge above said a word. Mohamed broke the tense silence. "What are we *waiting* for?"

The ex-military officer and the secret service agent exchanged a hard look, but it was Mariette who answered.

"*Excusez-moi*, it is a difficult situation, *non?* One thing is certain: It is unlikely that your friend is in imminent danger. If they meant to kill her, they would have done so by now. Let us return to the others and discuss what we do next." Without waiting for an answer, she replaced her binoculars in a worn case and started back down the hill.

Almost complete darkness made the descent difficult, and they were all worn out by the time they reached the Jeep. Night fell quickly after sunset in the mountains. And the temperature dropped dramatically in the last half-hour. The men were grateful Mariette reminded them to bring jackets.

When the headlights of the Jeep shone on the van by the side of the road, the weary scouts could not at first believe their eyes. The vehicle looked like a grotesque monster, with the weird shape of the luggage piled on the roof. Thirty yards back from the road, the others sat around a glowing fire.

"Sarah found the scraps of wood," announced Linda cheerfully, "and camel dung. Wilderness training. Who would've thought there'd be wood out here?"

Sarah ignored the compliment, jumping up to pounce on Alex. "What happened?"

Brad delivered a concise summary of the situation. The silence lasted no more than a second or two before Mohamed spat out, "What are we *waiting* for?"

Henrietta came, once again, to the rescue. "Now listen. Everyone. We mustn't lose sight of the fact that Julia's life is in constant jeopardy. Any risky actions on our part could have devastating consequences." She patted Mohamed's arm as she turned to Alex. "Could you tell how many more of them there are now?"

He shook his head, firelight turning the gray in his hair to polished silver. "No. Not definitively. At least two more, to have driven the cars."

Henry cleared his throat. "We'll have to wait. Wait and continue to follow them. When we have a better idea of what we're up against, then we'll strike."

This time, no one argued. Mariette produced a much appreciated *pique nique* from the basket in her Jeep. The campfire provided a soothing atmosphere as they gratefully consumed the roasted *poulet, aubergine* and *fromage de chevre,* washed down with a more than adequate French *vin rouge.*

Mohamed, as always, and Sarah, with responsible abstention, stuck with *eau minerale,* as they had the first watch. They would all take shifts on lookout at the turn-off to the road leading to the oasis while the others tried to sleep. The sentry would change every two hours.

Mohamed leaned against the fender of the Jeep with arms folded over his chest. Sarah sat on the hood, legs crossed Indian-style. Several minutes of strained silence ticked by.

"She will be all right. We *will* get her back."

He sighed. "I know that you know everything, Sarah. Everything about Julia and me." When she failed to comment, he added, "You must think I am a very bad person."

Sarah tilted her head to look over at his profile, striking in the light of the newly-risen moon. "No, Mohamed. I don't think you're a bad person. Just pretty damn selfish."

Stung, he swung around to face her.

"All she ever wanted, from the beginning, was to be with you and to help you. To help you *and* your family. You were the one who made the first move, making her want more, making her believe there could be more. You were the one who proposed marriage, asking her to be your 'number two' wife, for god's sake. Do you have any idea how hard it was for her to accept that? But she did. Then you changed your mind! When she was ready to make all the sacrifice to come and be here for you, you pushed her away. But you won't let her go, won't let her get on with her life.

"I think it's incredibly selfish of you. Selfish to not be a man and make up your mind, once and for all."

He turned away, in tormented silence, beneath the canopy of stars, staring out into the shadowy night.

Inside the tent, Julia hunched down near a burning brazier, a tray of empty dishes at her feet. The murmur of men's voices rose and fell just outside. She looked up as a young girl ducked in through the flap. She wore the colorful dress of the Bedouin, her ears and arms covered with silver and gold bangles and beads.

Julia gave her a smile and a nod as she bent to pick up the tray. The girl giggled and said something unintelligible before she backed out the way she came. The men's voices began to grow faint. Julia's heart raced as she listened to them, clearly moving away. With one eye on the entrance, she took out a small, empty, wooden bowl from the folds of her robe and crawled to the back of the tent, dragging a blanket in her other hand.

That unbelievable scene in the desert seemed to have established some kind of rapport between her and her captor—some level of trust. Unencumbered by *burqa* or rope, Julia had every intention of taking advantage of that. Barely breathing now, she scraped the edge of the bowl against the sandy soil under the back wall of the tent.

Her head bobbed back and forth between the entrance and what she hoped would be her exit. She'd dug a shallow hole, growing more feverish with each stroke, almost wide enough to crawl beneath the fabric wall, when she heard a man laugh, right outside. In a split second, Julia shoved the bowl up her skirt as she flipped the blanket over the hole. She had just enough time to sit on it before a hand appeared inside the flap and Ahmed stepped into the tent.

Flickering flames from the brazier etched deep, sinister shadows on his striking face. He stood motionless—like a cat in the jungle—all senses on alert, instinctively aware of tension in the air.

Brad and Linda took the second shift. They huddled on the hood of the

Jeep, leaning against the windshield with legs stretched out before them, under a blanket for warmth against the icy night air. The endless sky blazed with stars.

"Look," whispered Linda as she squeezed his arm, "you can see the *entire* Milky Way."

Brad shook his head at her inopportune enthusiasm while undeniably enjoying the closeness of her warm body. "We can't both be stargazing, Boyd. At least one of us has to keep watch, remember?"

She snuggled closer, dropping her head on his shoulder. *"Okay,* Caldwell. You look up and I'll look out. They won't budge before morning."

The words were scarcely out of her mouth before she bolted upright. "There they are. Two cars."

She gave a low whistle to the others as they jumped into the Jeep. In less than a minute, both engines came to life and they were off.

It was slow going on the serpentine road through the mountains at night. They drove without lights, and darkness prevented them from seeing the number of passengers in the vehicles ahead. But there was no doubt that the two cars were the ones they saw at the oasis.

With the enemy in clear sight, the rescue party held cautiously back. The van, with its mound of luggage on top, easily gave the appearance of just another tourist group. Brad and Linda followed in the Jeep.

No one spoke during the tense crawl, but they didn't have far to go. Before long the two cars ahead reached level ground and approached the fork in the north-south road along the east Sinai coast. The first set of headlights turned, as expected, left, heading north toward Nuweiba. Alex, at the van's wheel, slowed even more to keep a safe distance from the second car. A collective gasp exploded when it turned right, headed south toward Dahab.

"Son-of-a-bitch!" snarled Mohamed with a rare expression of profanity. "What do we do now?"

In the Jeep, Brad and Linda saw the split. Even though this possibility wasn't discussed, they were in no doubt as to their course of action. Brad watched Alex turn left while Linda punched Mariette's mobile number.

The only cell phones that functioned in the region were those belonging to Mariette, Mohamed and Alex, who had the foresight to purchase one in Cairo. Mohamed reluctantly had given his to Linda, for the time being. All parties understood that they must be extremely cautious about their communications. One never knew how closely the lines might be monitored and who might be listening. Especially on Mohamed's phone.

"We'll take number two," Linda said shortly, "and be in touch."

"Bon, merci," came the cheery reply.

CHAPTER 45

Moonlight still washed the distant mountains when Brad switched off the Jeep's parking lights and rolled slowly past the road where the car ahead had turned in. It led to a nondescript block of flats on the west side of the town of Dahab, the opposite direction of the touristy area along the waterfront. He turned off the engine and both agents slid from their seats.

A dog began to bark as they crept along a side street leading to a nearly-vacant parking lot. Brad watched with a grin as Linda pulled a scrap of cheese from her pocket and tossed it in the direction of the mangy hound. The barking abruptly ceased.

As the pair approached the poorly lit corner of the first building, they heard the sound of closing car doors. Their heads tilted around the corner, thankful that all of the streetlamps were burned out. Two men went to the rear of the vehicle and opened the trunk. Together, they leaned over and lifted out a heavy sack. Linda's sharp intake of breath prompted Brad to give her arm a painful squeeze. Neither needed to express the thought that struck them both: that the sack might contain Julia Grant's lifeless body.

As they continued to watch, one of the men spoke, causing his companion to grunt. After placing the sack on the pavement, the driver closed the trunk while the other knelt down and untied a rope at one end. He reached in with one hand and tugged at something inside. With his back to them, blocking their view, Brad and Linda were unable to see, at first, the dreaded contents. When he stood up and swung a smaller bag over his shoulder, the faint duet of sighs blended with the soft evening breeze.

"Too small for a body," whispered Brad.

"If it's in one piece."

Brad shot his partner a look that spoke bleak volumes. They watched the driver bend over and hoist the larger sack, stooping slightly under its weight. The men approached one of the flats in the second of a row of two-story buildings. Thankfully, their destination was on the first floor. The door closed behind them and lights went on in windows on either side.

"Stay here and cover me," murmured Brad, close to Linda's ear.

She nodded without comment, removing the Beretta from her coat pocket.

He moved stealthily across the open parking lot and sidled up to the first window. The drawn shade effectively blocked sight of anything inside. Cursing silently, he crept across the doorstep to the other window. A triangular tear near the bottom of the shade provided the needed view. By crouching down, he could see a pair of trouser-clad legs moving about in a kitchen. The smaller of the two bags lay on top of a table, the other on the floor beside it. Low voices hummed in another room.

He waited at the window, counting his heartbeats, until another pair of legs appeared. They went to the table. One hand held a knife with a glittering blade. It slit the string at the top of the bag lying there. The other hand reached in and pulled out a dark brown, sticky mass. He dropped it on the table.

Dates.

When his breath resumed, Special Agent Brad Caldwell slipped away from the window like a phantom. As he crossed the parking lot, he took a handkerchief from his pocket to blot the blood on his bitten lip.

"You're on the right track." Linda spoke into the phone as the Jeep sped north towards Nuweiba. "We're on our way."

Brad gripped the wheel as the raw night air assaulted the drying sweat on his face.

The first call to prayer erupted over loudspeakers as the vehicle ahead turned into an alley off the main road leading into Nuweiba. Alex steered the van to the curb. He'd already switched off the parking lights before they turned onto the main road. Driving without lights was common enough and it made them less conspicuous. Hopefully.

He reached to open his door then flinched involuntarily as a wrinkled hand appeared on his shoulder from the back seat. "Let us go," said Henry with a cool decisiveness. Henrietta was already halfway out the side door.

"Right," came the reluctant reply after a moment's hesitation. Alex had to agree that the elderly couple were not only capable but also the least likely to attract undue attention. The occupants of the van watched Henrietta tuck her arm in that of her husband and cross the deserted street.

"It's a warehouse." Henry stood beside the passenger window and gave a concise report. "Two men and a black-robed figure went inside—at least two other men there already."

Alex swallowed his angst. "All right. It's nearly six. We should get the van out of sight and find a place to use as a base of operations. Someone needs to stay here as lookout. No, Mohamed," he added with sincere empathy, "it has to be someone they won't recognize, which leaves both of us out."

"That's gotta be me," asserted Sarah from the back seat.

Alex turned and gave her a level look "All right, Sarah. Take Mariette's phone. Call me or Linda if there's any activity. Anything at all. Someone will relieve you shortly."

Mohamed located a Bedouin camp-style motel a few blocks away that could accommodate his "tour group." Laid out in typical native fashion, three wings of rooms made a u-shape around a central courtyard, with a fire pit surrounded by low cushions in the middle. The fourth side opened to the Gulf of Aqaba. Across the water, the craggy coast of Saudi Arabia rose up in the morning light.

They unloaded the luggage and Alex pulled the van to the side of the building, out of sight. Brad and Linda drove up in front as he came around the corner from the parking area. He signaled them where to go, following on foot. They all walked back to the courtyard while he brought them up to date. Once everyone was present and accounted for, Alex suggested they meet in one of the rooms.

"I mustn't be seen with any of you here," he reminded them.

They drifted in ones and twos to the Langleys' room, apparently the largest. No one would really call it large. With two twin-sized beds, a desk and one armchair, it provided barely enough space for the anxious group.

"I'm to be contacted at noon to finalize the delivery," Alex reminded them.

"Okay," said Brad, who sat on one of the beds, hands rubbing his spread knees. "It's vital that we do nothing to arouse suspicion until we put the plan in play."

"And what plan might that be?" inquired Mohamed evenly. Henrietta smiled approvingly into his bloodshot eyes. His initial rabid frustration at not having plucked Julia from the oasis had subsided back into a steady doggedness.

Linda, positioned by the window, looking out into the courtyard from behind a thin curtain, responded. "We need food and rest. Let's get cleaned up then meet for breakfast. Everyone except Alex and Mariette. Neither one of you should be seen with us or with one another. Mariette, you should stay out of sight as much as possible or get some kind of disguise. Mohamed, you'll need to at least wear a hat and sunglasses. I'll take a quick shower then relieve Sarah."

"Yes, Ma'am," joked Henry at her cool commands. "Anything else?"

Linda grinned. "Once Alex has made his contact, we'll reconnoiter." She looked at the narrowed eyes of her boss. "Back here at noon?"

"Yes, Ma'am," he mimicked.

"Whoever's on guard should have a vehicle," Alex suggested. "In case they make a move."

"*Oui*," concurred Mariette, "and we must obscure the license plate number. I will make a batch of mud."

After she smeared the mess on the plates and bumpers of both vehicles, Linda drove off in the van.

The French archeologist squatted outside the arched entrance of the camp, rubbing the stomach of a stray dog sprawled on its back. The creature moaned in ecstasy at the uncommon attention. Mariette greeted Sarah as she approached on foot.

"Ah, *Mam'zelle* Sarah, here you are. All is well?"

"Yeah." Sarah returned the smile. "All quiet."

"*C'est bon.* Come with me, we are to share one of the *petite* cabins. I will show you."

Sarah's eyebrows lifted at the Spartan accommodations. This wasn't the first time she'd had to rough it, far from it. She'd lost count of the times she'd been arrested for protesting one cause or another and spent time in jail. She smiled with satisfaction at that thought. Julia always teased her about the time she was thrown into a cell with a bunch of prostitutes. Sarah spent the night talking to them and trying to convince them to try to find a better way of life. She gave them all her phone number and one actually called for her help. Naturally, Sarah did what she could for the young woman, predictably scandalizing the Littlefield clan.

This was different. It was supposedly a hotel room, so she'd expected better. Oh, it appeared relatively clean but so minuscule they could scarcely pass without bumping into one another. And the showerhead mounted on the wall of the bathroom hadn't even a curtain to keep water from spraying all over the room.

"*Pardon,* the Ritz it is not, I am afraid," commiserated Mariette.

Sarah grinned. "Oh, I've seen worse. Never mind." The grin turned grim as she added, "With any luck, we'll have Julia out of there by this time tomorrow."

Her roommate sat down on one of the narrow beds and wrapped her arms around bent knees. "You have known your friend Julia for a long time, *non?*

"Oh, yeah. We've been friends—*sisters*—for many years," came the quiet reply.

Mariette burned with curiosity over these extraordinary circumstances. Linda had shared only the most basic explanations and she'd met with a stone wall in trying to learn more during the long day of watching the oasis with the men. She'd observed the curious dynamic and sensed the tension between two of them. This was a perfect chance for a *tête-à-tête* with the American *mam'zelle.*

"Tell me, Sarah, how did your friend Julia become mixed up in this affair?"

Sarah flopped down on the other bed, her golden curls spreading out around her head on the pillow like a halo. "It's a complicated story, and I have a feeling that I'm not up-to-date on things. One thing you should know about her is that she's a confirmed pacifist, in the strongest sense of the word. She opposes violence in any form: physical, verbal or emotional. That's the bedrock of our friendship."

"But this kidnapping, it is a most terrible thing. The men who have her are unquestionably violent." She shuddered at the remembrance of the driver's face. Though now that she understood the situation a bit better, she realized that the man calling himself Sharif was the real threat. A frightening intensity smoldered disturbingly behind the charismatic façade.

"I think this man, this Sharif, should be handled with great care," she said pensively. "He has a most gorgeous face, the manners of a Frenchman and a cold and calculating charm—a lethal combination."

Sarah shivered. "Julia is a very special person. Although she's one of the smartest people I know, she often finds herself being taken advantage of. She always tries to see the best in people. I wouldn't put it past her to be working on reforming the whole gang by now."

"Mon Dieu," murmured Mariette as she tried to picture the black-robed figure attempting to convince her nefarious captors to repent. She could no longer hold back the question that itched for an answer. *"Pardon,* Sarah, is one of these men here her husband? Her lover?"

Not feeling comfortable about discussing Julia's private affairs with a stranger, Sarah merely shook her head and changed the subject. "Tell me, Mariette, have you lived in Egypt for long?"

Mariette gave a Gallic shrug at having her question brushed aside. "Oh, *oui,* I have come for many years. In the winter, I work here excavating and in the summer, I live in Paris. It is a most suitable arrangement." She still could not speak casually about her husband without a lump in her throat, so whenever possible she refrained from mentioning him.

"Don't you find it difficult living here? I mean, well, the heat, the dirt, the poor, the mistreated animals, the dilapidated buildings? It's all, well, kind of depressing." Sarah had had plenty of time to survey her surroundings during the madcap journey. Truthfully, she couldn't imagine why anyone would choose to live here. Especially when their options were places like Paris and San Francisco.

"It is the work, you see. I am an archeologist, as you know, and to excavate here is a fantasy come true. Even as a girl, I dreamed of the ancient pharaohs. Now I can know, how you say in English, ah, 'up close and personal,' how they lived."

Both women laughed at this. Suddenly Sarah popped up and said, "Didn't you say something earlier about breakfast and going shopping?"

Shopping for disguises. Of course. For Mohamed, they found a baseball cap and a pair of sunglasses. Sarah chuckled because she remembered Julia once telling her how he hated wearing hats.

Mariette, with that innate sense of style that all French women seem to possess, transformed herself from the dusty excavator in wrinkled khakis into a sleek *femme fatale* in the blink of an eye. After changing into a pair of form-fitting jeans and a big white shirt, she purchased only a wide belt, a bright cotton scarf and a straw hat with a wide brim. She cinched the belt tight over the shirt, accentuating a slim waist, rolled up the sleeves and turned the collar up around her neck.

With the scarf wrapped around her head to cover her hair, the hat shading her face and a pair of large dark glasses, she was completely unrecognizable. *Formidable.*

CHAPTER 46

Sigmund Freud had called religion "the universal obsessive neurosis." Julia, although brought up and confirmed as an Episcopalian, no longer thought of herself as a Christian at all. It wasn't that she considered herself an atheist, or even an agnostic. Her belief was simple: that somewhere in the universe there was a power on the side of right.

Organized religion, in her opinion, often fell short of honoring that power. It was inconceivable to her to imagine how God—any God— could condone the acts committed in His name down through the centuries, up to the present day. She believed in the honesty and sincerity of the prophets: Jesus, Mohamed, the Buddha. Their intentions, doubtlessly, were honorable and good; but she feared that, over time, their messages had been grossly distorted by their followers to suit their own purposes.

Islamic Jihadists around the world blew themselves up with increasing regularity, murdering thousands of innocent people, to further their cause of creating Islamic states. Muslims cheered in the streets by the millions when planes were flown into the World Trade Center towers and the Pentagon.

The Jewish people of Israel believed they were justified in forcing the Palestinians from their homes into refugee camps—and killing in retaliation when the Palestinians protested—because "God had given Israel to the Jews."

And then there was Christianity. So many acts of brutality and destruction were committed over the centuries in the name of Jesus Christ—from the Crusades to the Spanish Inquisition to the Salem Witch Hunts—it boggled the mind.

And it saddened the heart.

The "leader of the free world" proclaimed that his direction for military invasions of other countries—resulting in death for tens, maybe hundreds, of thousands— came directly from God. This uncompromising religious righteousness and insistence of entitlement from every corner was surely going to be the death of us all, Julia thought bitterly—and not for the first time.

These dark thoughts rumbled through her mind like a churning locomotive as she watched the young militant set up a video camera. Light from a row of narrow, high windows near the roof illuminated the procedure quite clearly. Through the dirty glass she could see white clouds, tinged with gray, rolling across a robin's-egg blue sky. The distinctive scent of the sea wafted through the air.

Her hands and feet were once again securely bound and a gag, thankfully not too tight, covered her mouth. A worn Turkish rug lay on the floor in a corner, with one straight chair in its center. Several automatic rifles, along with a long, heavy-looking sword, stood propped against the cracked, peeling wall on either side of the chair. The camera, on a tripod, pointed towards it.

Julia had no doubt whatsoever as to the purpose of this set-up. The news these days regularly carried images of kidnap victims—bound and pleading for rescue—while surrounded by men in hoods concealing fanatical features. The captors invariably proclaimed their righteousness and enumerated their demands. More often than not, deliverance failed and the murdered victims were found later, frequently with the head severed from its mutilated body.

A creaking door in the outer room announced a new arrival. The young man gave Julia a menacing look of implicit warning as he grabbed up one of the weapons, poised for fire.

Shortly thereafter, Ahmed floated through a wide-open doorway to pause in a pool of sunlight. Resplendent in a fresh, clean white robe, he presented a spiritual sight. After a cursory glance at the cameraman, he projected a sweet and reassuring smile as he approached the table where Julia sat. He snapped his fingers at another man who followed behind.

A plastic bag thumped onto the table. Ahmed reached in and removed a rectangular object. Julia stared dumbly for a moment before registering what he held in his outstretched hand: her cocktail bag—the one she took to dinner at the hotel in Aswan. With all that had transpired in the hellish hours since, she'd forgotten all about it. Confused, she frowned as she looked up into Ahmed's serene face.

"There has been a change in plan."

A new idea came to him with his prayers. The shame he felt for his fleeting moment of uncertainty—that strange moment in the desert—nagged at his conscience. He also repented for the shameful desire that now welled up inside his rebellious body each time he looked upon this tempting woman.

The startling, crushing need he experienced when her held her foot in his hands had made him as hard as a rock. If Faoud hadn't called out from across the sand, he felt certain he would have taken her right there on the blanket. The uncontrollable urge overshadowed everything else, leaving only the carnal desire to feel her firm breasts beneath him as he plunged himself deep inside her, again and again. Even now, as he looked down at her in this sterile building, he felt his manhood stir.

He entertained the notion that she desired him as well. He could see the yearning in her eyes. If she could be made to believe he'd developed real feelings for her, perhaps she could be of even better use to him, better use to the cause.

Julia stretched out stiff hands to touch the satiny purse lying on the table, as he bent to remove the cord around her ankles. Rising gracefully, he placed a hand under her elbow to help her stand. "Come, Julia, let us go to more comfortable surroundings."

She glanced back over her shoulder while being led, limping, from the cavernous warehouse, to see the young man strip the camera from its tripod and viciously kick the wires aside.

The catamaran's engine pulsed beneath his feet as the boat skimmed across iridescent turquoise-blue water. Benjamin Richter stood as far forward as the crew would allow, the early morning wind blasting his solemn face.

Crossing over might be a mistake. They might be entirely on the wrong track.

It was not difficult to acquire two Jordanian passports. Entering Egypt as Israelis would be like sending up a red flare. The Jordanian authorities were most cooperative, not only by providing the false documents, but also sharing their intelligence file on Faoud Arabiyat. Before he'd joined Hamas, his shady background was that of a typical career criminal. No act of hatred or violence seemed too low. The photograph taken after his arrest in Egypt presented the disturbing image of a ruthless killer.

"Sir? Might I have a word?"

The commander consciously cleared doubt from his features before turning around. Although Joshoa had excelled in his training in espionage, Benjamin found it difficult to picture the limpid brown eyes in the innocent young face as those of the lethal operative he now must be. Benjamin had hesitated before bringing him along. The fact was, he needed to act quickly and could not afford to go into what might become an explosive situation without backup.

In the end, the deciding factor was Joshoa's flawless command of Arabic, spoken with a distinct Jordanian dialect. As a boy, he'd spent several years with relatives in the diplomatic service in Amman. Benjamin now placed both hands on his subordinate's shoulders and spoke close to his ear.

"From now on, speak only in Arabic, even if you think no one else can hear."

With not the slightest hesitation, Joshoa slipped into that language to inform his superior that the captain had approved them to be among the first to disembark. As the boat approached Nuweiba, they returned to the enclosed passenger area. A few minutes later, the cat glided smoothly up to the dock. They passed through Customs without incident. One of the Jordanian Intelligence officers had briefed them on the most likely locations to begin information gathering. Predictably, the first stop was one of the myriad coffee shops that punctuated the center of town.

In this delicate matter, the two Israelis knew they walked a hazardously thin line between immediacy and caution.

Mohamed's phone rang, startling them all as they sat around a table at one of the waterfront restaurants. Sarah twitched at the sound and Henrietta patted her arm.

"They're leaving the warehouse." Linda's low voice came through the instrument. "I'm following right behind."

The connection went dead. Mohamed jumped up as he relayed the brief message.

"Wait," urged Brad. "Linda knows what she's doing. She'll call back."

Several tense moments of silence dragged by. Mohamed answered almost before the phone rang a second time. In a split second, with a look of aggravation, he passed it to Brad.

"Go ahead," Brad said then listened while the others sat rigid in their chairs.

"Understood. On the way." He flipped the phone closed, at the same time placing a firm hand on Mohamed's shoulder as he once again started to rise. "Hold on." He relayed Linda's report that the house where Julia was taken wasn't far away and repeated the directions. "We need to stick to the plan. I'll relieve Linda. All of you go back to the motel."

CHAPTER 47

The disguising and disabling *burqa* was replaced for the short drive. Without the use of her hands, still bound before her, Julia couldn't raise the skirts, which caused her to stumble getting out of the car. She made use of the opportunity to steal a look around. A high wall surrounded several buildings inside a compound. Ahmed led her through a gate, up the path to a two-story mudbrick house.

The routine was the same: He escorted her to a room, the outer garments were removed and amenities provided. But there, the pattern changed. An old-fashioned claw-footed bathtub sat invitingly in a corner, filled with water. A stack of thick, fresh towels stood on a table beside it. And a beautiful, expensive-looking white silk robe hung from a peg on the wall.

"I thought you might enjoy a bath. There is soap and shampoo. If you require anything else, tell me now."

She met his benevolent gaze across the bed and felt a prickle of alarm. As if reading her mind he added, "You may lock the door from inside. I will post a guard in the hall. No one will disturb you."

"Thank you." Under the circumstances, the perfunctory polite response struck her as particularly absurd.

The door shut behind him. Julia crossed the room, rubbing her arms in an attempt to rid herself of the uneasy feeling, and pulled the heavy bolt. She leaned back against the door and struggled for calm.

Something had changed here. It was clear in his eyes. The fervent light behind those dark windows to his soul were replaced with. . .what? Not desire, as she'd first feared. It was something else. It was more like *calculation*. She looked over at the bed, to her satin purse lying there.

It contained little when she left the hotel that night, only her valuables and what she might want during dinner: a lipstick, her wallet with a considerable amount of cash and, of course, her passport. One was advised to always carry one's passport in Egypt. First stroking the soft fabric, she dumped out the contents onto the bed. Everything was still there, including all the cash.

"Incredible," she whispered, thinking of the irony of these men who would not break Allah's law governing theft, while planning to commit genocide.

Still pondering this new puzzle, she wondered why the purse was returned to her now. The question circled in her weary brain as she slowly removed the now dirty, wrinkled khaki clothes. The unwinding of the scarf from her waist—her talisman— brought an illogical, nonetheless welcome, sense of consolation before she eased into the tub.

Bathing felt like being reborn. She ducked her head under the cool, rose-scented water and held her breath as her hair fanned out around her face, like that of a mermaid. The anxiety and terror of the past hours and days drifted away in the water, leaving her in a state of numb relief.

The feel of the robe's soft silk next to her clean skin further induced the curious sense of well-being. After toweling her hair, she sat on the bed, back against the carved wooden headboard, legs stretched out on the pale-yellow cotton spread. Drowsiness descended, rendering her incapable of further comprehensive thought. Her fresh-smelling and still slightly damp hair spread across silk-clad shoulders. Her eyes closed in blissful mindlessness.

A quiet knock at the door nearly stopped her heart. She started violently, instantly hurtled back to bleak reality, and went to tug open the cold metal bolt. Ahmed carried in a tray brimming with food. He placed it on a table by the window, pulled out a chair, and motioned for her to sit.

"Come. Join me."

Delicious aromas rose from a platter of grilled shrimp, surrounded by bowls of hummus, olives, salad and fresh, still-warm flatbread. As he poured a glass of chilled white wine for her, Julia noticed the fluid movements of his long, slender fingers. They were both now garbed in flowing white robes. The scene struck her as incongruously domestic.

"I have been thinking about what you said, Julia. What you said in the desert." He fixed her with seductive eyes. "You may be right about there being another way. But I need you, need your help." He reached across the table to take her hand. "I need you to accompany me out of Egypt. If I remain here, I will surely be arrested. In captivity, there will be nothing I can do to try and moderate my Brothers."

Julia found herself ensnared by his intensity, unable to look away.

"In my native Jordan, I can arrange to meet with them to propose other ways to achieve our goals. All I ask is that you accompany me across the Gulf to Aqaba on the catamaran. No one will question us with you traveling as my American fiancée. After that, you will be free to go.

"If," he added softly as he squeezed her hand, "you want to go."

His new plan was simple. Her passport had germinated the idea. Instead of the risky business of attempting to smuggle the chemical weapons on the freighter to Aqaba, they would pack the containers in trunks. Julia, with her American passport, would take them openly on the catamaran as her "trousseau." Together, with Ahmed's forged British passport, it was highly unlikely her luggage would get more than a cursory search, if that. She would think all she was doing was making an effort to reform him. It was a gamble, but all he had to do was convince her of his sincerity, and of his infatuation. And as soon as they safely reached their destination in Jordan, the lovely Julia Grant would act out her final scene.

"But…the authorities will be looking for me. We'd never make it through Customs." She struggled against her fear. The constant strain of duplicity in weighing her every word—knowing she must keep from letting him know that she knew of his real purpose—caused her voice to waver.

He misinterpreted the cause of her emotion and allowed a look of infinite sadness to cross his finely-cut features, incredibly handsome in the filtered light. "No, Julia, I am afraid not. The Egyptian police have not been notified of your, ah, shall we say, 'disappearance'?" This unexpected fact was confirmed again only a short time ago. He did not understand it but planned to make the most of it.

Events of the past few days collided across Julia's bewildered mind's-eye. Reason momentarily failed her. Then anger supplanted confusion and disbelief to suffuse her face with a fiery red glow.

What the hell was going on?

Why hadn't anyone reported her disappearance to the police? Frown lines creased her brow as she looked down at the plate in front of her, into the glassy eye of a shrimp.

Ahmed watched closely, easily reading these emotions across her face, and pressed her hand once more before releasing it. "Your friend Mohamed has returned to Cairo. He is now back at home with his family—with his wife. Perhaps he thought you left because you have wisely chosen to end the unfortunate relationship."

Julia raised her head to meet his earnest, empathetic, lying eyes.

CHAPTER 48

Faoud came out of the house and passed through the gate. Swaggering away, he thought—not for the first time—that they should kill the woman and be done with her.

Women always made trouble. He didn't like the way Ahmed looked at her. They should have both used her and slit her pale throat. Not that Faoud was not a devout Muslim. He had simply become very adept over the years at interpreting the Koran to suit his own needs— and condone his acts of brutality. The noon call to prayer came as he approached the big mosque. He turned inside to offer his convoluted prayers.

After almost four long, wearisome hours spent in conversation with the locals, the Israelis had learned nothing. When the noon call to prayer blasted from loudspeakers mounted on poles throughout the town, Benjamin motioned for Joshoa to follow. Observing the Islamic rituals presented no problem. They both knew the prayers, and the possibility of making a significant contact far outweighed any aversion they might have to reciting them. They fell in with the steady stream of the pious pouring into the main mosque.

❖

Brad located Linda easily from her precise directions. Loitering outside a café, she waved away the barefoot boy chattering up at her in broken English. They sat at a table outside on the corner of the street that led up to the compound.

"Scarface left the house on foot. The others are still inside. They have to pass this way. We'll be able to see anyone who comes or goes," Linda assured her boss. "Jesus, that 'Sharif' is incredible—a real first-class hunk."

Brad snorted and sipped coffee as she picked at an unappetizing sandwich. Without further discussion, he paid the bill. Arm in arm, they strolled up a side street that led to the dirt road that led to the enclosed compound.

The good news was that it stood apart from any other dwellings, making it easy for surveillance. The bad news was that the isolation made it virtually impossible to approach without being seen from inside.

Brad checked the time. *"Okay,* Boyd. You go back to the motel. Leave me the phone and call as soon as Bryant makes contact with his customer."

Linda grinned as she handed him the phone. "Okay, Caldwell. Try to keep a low profile."

He looked down at himself as she sauntered away. Under the circumstances, that might not be so easy. His over six-foot frame clad in neatly pressed shirt and slacks set him distinctly apart from the crowd in this neighborhood. Several blocks from the waterfront area, he doubted if many tourists ventured back this way.

Brad made a sweep of the area, carefully noting each dusty alley as he looked up at the dilapidated buildings, as if they held some architectural interest. Back at the café, he ordered another coffee and pulled a guidebook from his pocket. The "tourist" studied it while the special agent

339

kept an eye on the street leading up to the house on the low hill.

Benjamin and Joshoa, after simulating the prescribed rituals, rose from the final prostration and joined a group of mostly young men loitering outside the entrance of the mosque. They separated and spoke with several of them before crossing the square to take seats outside yet another coffee shop.

"Something is definitely in the air," murmured Joshoa as he sipped the dark, sweet brew. "Nothing concrete, but one comment alluded to 'an event that will be most pleasing to Allah, and will make him smile.'"

Benjamin did not smile. He shuddered inwardly and his stomach roiled violently, not from the endless cups of coffee, but at the thought of these fanatics committing mass murder thinking such an act would "make Allah smile."

Faoud left the mosque and went directly to the coffee shop across the square. Upon entering the dim interior, he strode straight to the back to a minuscule and indescribably filthy restroom to relieve himself.

The proprietor saw him emerge and greeted him warily. His reputation for violence made Faoud not so much respected as feared. He leaned against the counter, drinking tea flavored with sprigs of mint, and asking questions about anything of interest that might have occurred in the vicinity in the past few days. The proprietor, normally a gregarious fellow, doled out answers with caution.

Faoud noisily slurped his tea down to the dregs, tossed out a few bills and left without a parting word. As he exited through the low doorway, he paused and squinted in the sun's glare to scan the crowd milling in the square.

Benjamin saw Joshoa stiffen and his nostrils flare, like a dog on the hunt. He knew better than to turn around. Instead, he glued his eyes to the young man's face and waited.

"Arabiyat," Joshoa breathed, lips barely moving.

They sat, immobile, until Faoud moved from the doorway out into the square. Words unnecessary, they came nonchalantly to their feet. Benjamin left first, keeping far enough back to avoid detection. Joshoa followed at a discreet distance.

Their quarry stopped at a shop to select a few pieces of fruit from the sidewalk display then went inside. In a few minutes he reemerged, carrying a brown paper sack, and continued up the street. At the end of the block he turned down a narrow lane leading west, away from the main thoroughfare.

The sight of "scarface" coming around the corner rocketed Brad's pulse into high gear. Although he'd seen him for only a few seconds in the setting sun in those rugged mountains, there was no mistaking that ruined face. He reached into his pocket, laid a few bills on the table and was about to step out onto the pavement when another man came around the corner and started up the same street.

Interesting. Definitely Middle Eastern, in western dress. Brad fell in cautiously, ten yards behind.

When Arabiyat turned onto an open dirt road, Benjamin stopped, some twenty yards back, and bent down to feign tying his shoe. His eyes never left the Jordanian as he climbed a slight rise to a high wall secured by a heavy iron gate, enclosing a two-story mudbrick house. As he approached, Arabiyat called out. Another man appeared from inside the courtyard, opened the gate, and the two men disappeared behind the wall.

Brad held back behind the corner of a building, peering around its edge. His professional assessment came swiftly and surely: This man was definitely covertly following the terrorist.

That was Brad Caldwell's last conscious thought before he felt a sharp pain on the side of his neck.

Benjamin crouched beside the still form lying in the scratchy shade of a tree in a low, dry ditch. After Joshoa took him down, he whistled to signal his commander. Together, they quickly lifted the slack body between them, arms spread over their shoulders, and carried it to the relative privacy of the ditch.

"American." Benjamin scowled, flipping through Brad's passport. "Are you positive he came after me?"

"Yes, sir. I observed him at the café on the corner, and he followed you from there."

Brad emitted a low moan. His eyes blinked open to find a gun pointed squarely between them—his gun. They'd searched him thoroughly in the short time he was out cold. Clearly these were professionals. But on whose side? They spoke in Arabic but why were they tailing the terrorist? Brad hadn't heard a sound behind him, and his attacker knew the precise spot to induce instant unconsciousness.

Benjamin wasted no time with small talk. "Who are you and why did you follow me?" The brusque question came in English, with a trace of an accent. Brad instinctively knew not to prevaricate with these two.

"I wasn't following you. I was following the same man you were."

The Israeli scrutinized the man on the ground.

"You are an American agent." It was a statement, not a question. "You were trailing Faoud Arabiyat. Why?"

Something clicked in Brad's head. Not only did his assailants know the terrorist's name, the one in charge didn't hesitate in stating it. He took a calculated risk.

"Possibly for the same reason as you." His distinct physical disadvantage prompted him to add, "If you wouldn't mind, I'd prefer to discuss the matter in a more comfortable position—and without being held at gunpoint."

Benjamin grunted and nodded his head at Joshoa, who lowered the gun he was holding unwaveringly with both hands. Brad sat up slowly and brushed dirt from his shirt.

The rescue team, all except Brad, crowded into the room. Alex had just begun to fill them in on the latest information of the weapons transaction when a rap came at the door. Henry, being closest, asked who was there. A stunned silence followed as the stranger behind Brad closed the door. Tension fueled by alarm reverberated amongst them, packed into the small space like sardines, as their comrade cleared his throat.

"You're not going to believe this."

But they did. During Brad's pithy summary and introduction of the Israeli, Benjamin looked appraisingly around the room at the improbable and apprehensive group, clearly taking their measure.

Alexander, standing to his full height with a distinct air of command, dominated the scene. Henry returned to sit next to his wife on the edge of one of the narrow beds. Mohamed sat in the only chair, arms across his chest, censure clear on his stony face. Linda, Mariette and Sarah sat on the other bed, like birds on a wire.

All eyes riveted on the Israeli Intelligence officer as he told his story. It would be easy enough to verify. No one doubted he spoke the truth.

Commander Bryant nodded at Brad with a sign of approval for having brought Benjamin straight to the group. "How much have you told him?"

"Only the basics on how we arrived at this point. Nothing on the game plan for going forward."

The two men exchanged a steady look. Alex thought it unlikely Brad mentioned the subject of the weapons deal. He hoped not. There was no telling how the Israeli might react to the news that they planned to use the delivery as a diversion for rescuing Julia.

"We left his man to keep an eye on the house."

"Excellent. Perhaps we should all introduce ourselves," Henrietta said in a brisk but kindly way, and proceeded to do so. Alex jumped in next, to ensure that everyone understood that his failure to mention the weapons delivery was intentional—and a warning for them to follow suit.

Benjamin felt like he'd fallen down the rabbit hole as each member of the group gave their name and a brief explanation of their involvement in the operation. What an extraordinarily ludicrous situation—especially with all that lay at stake.

When it came back around to Brad he said, "You're probably thinking what an unlikely task force we are. But let us assure you that, so far, we've performed damned effectively."

Henrietta lanced the newcomer with a direct look. "We do realize the seriousness of the situation, Mr. Richter. You must, however, understand that any overt action now could prove fatal—not only for Julia, but for a great many people."

An unreal stillness filled the air. Her straightforward composure gave powerful emphasis to the conviction of her next words.

"Let us also assure you that we are equally committed to preventing the attack on Jerusalem as we are to the rescue of our friend."

This was the first time anyone verbalized that intention. No one challenged it.

CHAPTER 49

The one thing Julia knew with disheartening certainty was that she had no choice whatsoever. She had to go along with whatever Ahmed, aka Sharif, wanted. At least until she found a way to escape. In spite of being exhausted, traumatized and terrified, she remained in complete control of her faculties.

There wasn't a chance in hell her friends weren't looking for her. Mohamed would never have returned to Cairo, even if his life depended on it, which it very well might. And she felt sure that Alexander Bryant would leave no stone unturned to find her. If he was still alive.

If Ahmed spoke the truth—that they hadn't reported her missing to the police—they had a damn good reason. She thought she knew what it was. The first priority, unquestionably, would be to prevent the atrocities. Yet she did believe—from the bottom of her heart—that rescue would somehow come.

She had to believe it.

The other thing she knew deep in her gut was that these men could not afford to allow her to live. She could identify them and, sooner or later, one way or another, they intended to kill her.

So far, her charismatic captor appeared to be blessedly unaware of her role as a U.S. operative. Nor did he seem to know she'd uncovered the despicable criminal plot that appeared to be, if not of his own design, at least under his direction. Thank god for that. If she could convince him of her willingness to cooperate—of her "feelings" for him—she might have a chance. As long as he didn't expect her to consummate their new-found friendship, it might work.

The rousing sensations his touch evoked out there in the desert had alarmed and confused her. After much guilt-ridden analysis, she recognized—with overwhelming relief—that her response had been a natural, human one. Kidnap victims often became attached to their abductors. And she was fairly sure that most kidnappers did not demonstrate such sophisticated charm, not to mention the physical attributes of a dark Adonis.

Her unintentional response did *not* mean that she was a contemptible, weak, sex-crazed deviant. Once she'd reached that conclusion, she found it much easier to control any further irrational urges.

Nevertheless, it was crucial that he continue to think she desired him, and he obviously did. This was a dangerous and deadly game—like dancing with the devil.

"You will need clothes."

Ahmed smiled as he held out the *burqa*. Julia had done her best to convince him that she reciprocated the attraction, and of her sincerity in wanting to help him cross over into Jordan. The idea of his touching her or, god help her, having to allow him to use her sexually, now made her flesh crawl. Ironically, the same Islamic law that tormented her for years, keeping her and Mohamed apart, now provided her salvation. Ahmed would not sin by having sex with any woman other than his lawful wife. He left the outrageous idea of that possibility dangling between them.

He watched her closely as she gave solemn assurance that she would cooperate in the task of purchasing a wardrobe appropriate for a bride for the trip across the Gulf that would supposedly liberate them both.

Joshoa sat back on his heels on the dusty sidewalk with his back against the wall of a block of run-down flats. Although he'd been there for a considerable time, his eyes never left the house. His pulse quickened at the sight of a man coming out the front. It looked like Arabiyat. He walked around the wall and disappeared. A few minutes later, a car pulled up to the gate.

Rising slowly so as not to draw attention, Joshoa saw another man and a black-shrouded figure emerge from the courtyard and get into the back seat of the car. The route they must take came down the dirt road and onto the side street. He moved quickly to the corner of the main street to be in place to follow, whichever way they turned. Without a vehicle, he prayed they weren't going far.

As expected, and hoped, the car turned left toward the main part of town. It was after mid-day and the traffic dense. He kept up easily, inconspicuously blending into the crowd as the car edged along the busy street. Several blocks later, it pulled into an alley behind a row of upscale shops.

A tall man and the figure in black got out and walked to one of the shops in the middle of the block, a women's boutique. The driver, now clearly identifiable as Arabiyat, locked the car and crossed the street to enter a coffee shop. Joshoa stepped back into a doorway and pulled out his phone.

Julia knew the rules. If she spoke one word or made the slightest attempt to communicate with the salesgirl, it could cost both their lives. She submissively let Ahmed lead her to one of the curtained dressing rooms in the back, where he pulled the velvet drape behind him. His eyes met hers with a steady, clear warning before he removed the burqa and the bindings on her hands.

His lips touched her ear, sending shivers—this time only of fear—down her neck before he whispered, "I will speak to you in Arabic. Do not attempt to answer. Try on the clothes I bring and choose whatever you like."

The salesgirl swooned at the dazzling smile of her gorgeous customer.

His wife needed something chic to wear to a wedding in Jordan. What could she show him? He selected several items at her suggestion and took them to Julia.

It didn't take long. She would basically be traveling as herself and her attire was the least of her concerns. As long as whatever she wore allowed her freedom of movement. For she planned—at the first possible opportunity—to run like hell.

With Julia once again shrouded from head-to-toe, they left the shop. One thing she found puzzling, as she passed the sales counter, was the large stack of garments. Why would Ahmed have purchased them all? What would be the purpose of that?

The gag covered her mouth and her hands were bound in front. At least her vision wasn't totally impaired by the *burqa's* grill. As they paused at the door for Ahmed to shake the smitten girl's outstretched hand, Julia stood stock-still.

Across the street she saw a petite woman crowned with rambunctious blonde curls. No. It simply wasn't possible. She must be hallucinating. The head bent over an unfolded map. Julia fixated on those curls as Ahmed tugged at her arm.

One second before she turned away, the head came up and Julia found herself inexplicably looking directly into the sparkling green eyes of Sarah Littlefield.

The deliverance in those dearly beloved, indomitable eyes rang out like the bells of Westminster Cathedral. Thunderstruck, Julia stumbled over her robes on the crowded sidewalk and was only kept from falling by Ahmed's firm grip on her arm. When she regained her balance and looked back, the vision had disappeared. Was she hallucinating after all?

Her eyes desperately raked the crowd for another glimpse of Sarah, to no avail. But then she almost fainted at the sight of another gloriously familiar face: Leaning against the wall of a building halfway down the block was the unmistakably elegant Brad Caldwell.

Hallelujah and praise the Lord! Rescue was on the way. Julia's veins flooded with the most overwhelming feeling of joy she'd ever known. It was all she could do not to shout out to her friends. Her mind whirled with ecstatic and disjointed images of salvation.

Fortunately, the presence of the gag allowed time for her mind to send up a red flag. Why hadn't they grabbed her from Ahmed's clutches? There must be a logical explanation. She could only rely on Brad's knowledge and professional expertise to save her. And wait for them to make their move.

But, oh god, dear god, they were here! Here to save her!

For once, Julia was glad to be invisible in black, lest her euphoria give her away.

"Did she see you? Are you sure?"

"Oh, yeah," confirmed Sarah in answer to Alexander's terse questions. "Message received, loud and clear: The cavalry is here."

Until the instant when her eyes met those of her dearest friend, Sarah hadn't been completely honest with herself about her feelings. Oh, she'd believed they would find her. The feasibility of a successful rescue was another matter, a scary one at that. Now, after being so close, she knew they would get her back. They just had to.

The car drove straight back to the compound. Joshoa insisted on continuing as sentinel. That left the rest of them to reconnoiter and formulate their plans. Mohamed went ballistic when he learned of their failure to pluck Julia from the villains' grasp.

"It's not that simple." A usually flippant Brad had been replaced by a hardened operative. "We don't know how many others were nearby. We don't know if they were armed. But we do know they wouldn't hesitate one second in killing her on the spot." This blunt statement had the desired—sobering—effect.

Alex, Brad and Linda huddled to discuss the pros and cons of filling in their new partners about the arms transaction. Brad stood firm.

"I know you're against this, Bryant. But we have to bring them into the big picture."

"Why? They might tend to react negatively to learn that we're selling weapons to terrorists planning on invading their country."

"Yeah. But we won't let that happen. We really have no choice. We need their help. The only way to guarantee their cooperation is to make them part of the team."

"Besides," Linda cut in, "we'll ensure the Egyptian police are on the scene to confiscate the weapons before they ever leave the warehouse. Those guns will never make it into terrorist hands."

They all sincerely hoped that was true.

Alex spoke briefly with James a short while later, who assured him that, at that very moment, a private yacht flying the British flag as well as a divers' flag was cruising up the Gulf of Aqaba headed for Nuweiba, loaded with a sizeable shipment of deadly handguns. It would not come into port but weigh anchor out in the Gulf, about a mile south of it, near a well-known dive site.

Tomorrow, Alex related to James, he planned to meet Jalal at the harbor, where they would take one of the ubiquitous and unremarkable dive boats out to the yacht to inspect the weapons. If everything went according to plan, another boat—already at anchor near the rendezvous point—would help ferry the crates to a secluded cove under the cover of darkness. Jalal's men would be waiting on shore with trucks to remove the crates to the warehouse. The local police had been generously compensated for being otherwise engaged that evening.

While the transaction took place, the expanded rescue team would descend on the house—hopefully left sparsely defended—and liberate Julia. They hoped to take her captors alive and into custody to try to learn the location of the chemical weapons. With her freedom secured, the Egyptian military would be brought in to arrest the others and confiscate the guns. And, just in case, a U.S. warship stood ready in the nearby Red Sea.

That was the plan.

The group went over it and over it and over it again. Alexander Bryant believed it to be a viable plan. Yet he couldn't shake an uneasy feeling about the contents of those crates.

CHAPTER 50

Ahmed, following the successful acquisition of the handguns, planned to take Julia across. The chemicals would be cleverly camouflaged in several large trunks, disguised as part of her trousseau. She was, after all, marrying a very wealthy man. He congratulated himself on having devised this latest scheme. If Julia gave the slightest sign of betrayal en route, he could easily render her unconscious. He spent the rest of the day working on the final details, and at his prayers.

Julia spent the rest of her day and night alone, borne up on waves of elation—contemplating impending freedom—to the valleys of despair at the thought of everything that could go wrong.

What if things got ugly and someone got hurt? Or killed? One of the people she loved? She couldn't bear the thought of that. If only she could find a way to escape before her friends were put in further danger. Or at least make it easier for them to locate her. She paced the room endlessly, forcing her mind to focus on trying to think of a way. At last, as she lay on the bed wide awake in the dead of night, an inkling of an idea began to take shape.

Her feet swung to the floor. She removed Sarah's gift, her talisman, now wrapped around her neck, and tiptoed to the window. The shutters had been left open, as the iron bars prevented any possibility of escape. She tied the blue scarf around one of the bars, with the ends hanging down to stand out against the whitewashed wall. Sarah would recognize it and know exactly where to find her.

A long, deep breath escaped her lips as her head once again met the pillow. If help hadn't arrived by morning, she would use her feminine wiles on Ahmed to let her take some exercise in the courtyard. She wanted to learn all she could of her surroundings. Just in case.

The sun began its ascent from the Underworld of the Dead. Ahmed and Faoud, returning from the mosque, trudged up the dusty road in the early morning light. Their steps slowed at sight of the length of bright blue silk dangling from Julia's window, dancing in the sea breeze.

"I...washed it. And hung it out to dry."

Ahmed stood before her in her room, the scarf held loosely between his graceful fingers. His electrifying stare caused a deafening rush to howl through her ears. Without having uttered a single word, he turned away, pulling the door closed behind him.

Faoud looked up as Ahmed reached the bottom of the stairs, the scarf still in his hand.

Ahmed shrugged. "It matters not. Either way, her fate is now to serve Allah."

Julia couldn't be sure he believed her disingenuous pleas. That day was the longest of her life. She hoped it wasn't the last.

The reflection of the setting sun turned the water red—blood red. Alex came striding down the dock to find Jalal standing on the deck of one of several dive boats moored there. Everything was going according to plan. It would take about twenty minutes to reach the yacht, already anchored off the coast. By then it would be almost dark.

As soon as the transaction was completed, the crew would start bringing up the crates, and Jalal would make the call for the second boat to approach. Alex was adamant when he last spoke with James that the speedboat on board the yacht must be made available to return him without delay to Nuweiba.

The smaller, faster boat should get him back there in less than fifteen minutes. He would call and let the others know as soon as he started back. They would wait for him before making their move on the house. He hoped to hell things continued to go according to plan.

Mohamed and Sarah sat at a table near another occupied by Henry and Henrietta. Mariette stood on a nearby corner, keeping an eye on the street. The Jeep sat parked half-way down the block. Benjamin and Joshoa had assumed Arab dress and loitered at the edge of the cluster of buildings closest to the compound. Joshoa crouched on his haunches, scratching patterns in the dirt with a stick.

Brad and Linda had taken the van and driven around on the road leading up the low hill behind the compound. The location provided an excellent view of the house and surrounding buildings. Several cars clustered around the front gate. With the aid of binoculars, they could also see both Israelis, who were now in possession of Alex's two extra revolvers. That rendered all four male professionals armed. Linda chafed at the discrimination but had no choice but to follow orders.

"It's show time," she murmured.

Brad, who was watching the Israelis, swung his binoculars back to the compound. A group of men spilled out the gate, piled into the cars and drove away. One car remained beside the wall.

"No sign of Julia. I didn't see the hunk either, did you?"

"Nope. But at least Arabiyat is out. He led the pack. Let's get going."

Brad opened his door. They stepped to the front and he opened the hood.

"Okay. Strategic review. We walk down and ask to use the phone to call for a tow truck. Once we're inside, the others move in. When we hear the signal, I'll distract your hunk. You find Julia. Got it?"

"Got it." She hesitated. "What about Bryant? We said we'd wait."

Brad shook his head. "Listen, goddamn it, every second counts here. We have to strike now, while we have the advantage. I'll deal with Bryant." He shook his head again.

"Anyway, I don't like it. This fanatic son-of-a-bitch is as unpredictable as he is lethal. There're just too damn many assumptions."

"Shit!"

Brad followed Linda's line of sight back to the compound. Ahmed and a black-clad figure were coming out of the gate. They got into the car. He slammed down the hood and the two agents jumped back into the van.

"Acht," hissed Benjamin, reaching into the folds of his robe for the phone. "He's leaving and taking her with him."

"Come on," Mohamed ordered as he slapped shut his phone, shot up and sprinted toward the Jeep.

Mariette saw him—the others close behind—and followed at a run.

When Ahmed drove past the two Israelis, they embraced in typical Arab fashion, to shield their faces. As soon as the car turned the corner, they rushed after it.

The car from the house stopped at the corner where the archeologist had stood less than a minute before. It turned right, in the direction of the warehouse.

Mariette leaned over the wheel, shading her face with the brim of her hat, and Mohamed ducked his head under his arm as Ahmed drove by within a few feet of the crowded Jeep.

"Only the two of them," said Henry. "She's in back. The doors are locked."

The Jeep's engine roared to life and Mariette pulled out two cars behind.

❖

Ahmed pulled up to the side door of the warehouse and got out. Julia shuddered as the car door next to her opened.

"Come." He took her arm and led her to the cavernous room, back to the same table and chair. The camera equipment was gone. In its place, a number of scratched wooden crates lined the wall next to six large, expensive-looking new trunks. There was also a stack of boxes that appeared to contain a new coffee maker, a digital clock radio and other small household appliances.

"Sit."

She sat. He studied her bowed head for a moment before going back the way they came. Julia tried to see, through the woven grill, anything in the vast, near-empty space that might be of importance, or of help. Holding her breath, she listened intently but heard nothing: no sounds to indicate the presence of anyone else. She was alone. Until Ahmed came back carrying several shopping bags. They bore the name of the boutique where they'd shopped for her clothes. He placed them next to the trunks and turned, regarding her speculatively.

"It saddens me to think that I cannot trust you, Julia."

She again dropped her head. At this point, any response might only make matters worse.

"You must surely realize that your failure to cooperate would inevitably result in harm coming to your beloved Mohamed." He smiled. "As well as his wife and precious son. Come. I will put you where you can do no harm." He steered her to the front room, then through a side door. This space was maybe six-hundred feet square, she guessed, with a towering ceiling, like that of the warehouse.

As he started to leave, she blurted out, "Please, Ahmed, can't you untie my hands? The ropes are too tight. They're cutting my wrists."

CHAPTER 51

They huddled in the entrance to an abandoned building near the warehouse.

"Okay," said Brad. "Plan B. We know there are at least two entrances, one with rolling doors for the trucks and a side door for pedestrian traffic. Richter, you and your man circle the perimeter. Look for other exits. And check out the back alley for more vehicles."

As the two Israelis stole away, he pressed his lips together. "Henry, do either of you feel up to going in for reconnaissance?"

Before the elderly agent could answer, Sarah's fingers closed around his arm. "No. Let me do it." She directed a reassuring smile at Team L's expressions of concern. "You might be recognized. They don't know me."

"I'll go," said Linda decisively.

Sarah's curls bounced with the side-to-side motion of her head. "If Julia sees or hears me, it'll reassure her—and put her on her guard." She turned back to Brad. "I can do a pretty convincing dumb blonde routine."

Henrietta broke the stalemate. "It's a rather good idea, I think." She smiled down at the eager volunteer. "Apart from being an unfamiliar face, she presents no visible threat."

Brad looked over at Linda to find her head cocked to one side. He blew out his cheeks to release the pent up air. Bob Bronson would crucify him for this.

"She could pretend to be lost." Linda's impish eyes assessed the anti-war activist. "Can you cry on cue?"

A nervous grin lifted the corners of Sarah's mouth. "Spent a few summers on the boards with Berkeley Rep."

A hush fell while Brad considered the options.

"Okay. Just get in and ask to use the phone. Pretend to call your hotel for directions. And then get out. Try to get a feel for the layout. And if there's anyone else in the building."

His lips almost disappeared as he scrutinized Sarah's grim determination. "If you see Julia, do *not*—under any circumstances—attempt to communicate. No heroics, Sarah. You can't accomplish anything alone. You'd not only risk your own neck, but Julia's as well. Understood?"

She straightened to her full five-foot-two and ripped off a snappy salute. "Yes, sir. Understood, sir."

The big doors in front were rolled down and securely shut. Inky darkness now cloaked the narrow street leading to the side door of the lofty building, creating a forbidding tunnel. A scuttling noise in a pile of garbage caused Sarah to jerk back.

She shivered, poised on the precipice of peril, and real tears sprang to her eyes, no thespian skill required. The side door was closed, so she knocked and then, without waiting for a response, turned the knob. Unlocked, it creaked when she pushed it open.

"Hello? Is anybody here?"

A dim lamp burned on a desk in a corner of the room. Two other doors led from it: one, of regular size, closed; the other, a high double metal door, rolled halfway up, leaving a gaping opening into a big, open space. Sarah moved toward it, fighting against the fright tingling up her spine. A sinister silence permeated the air. So far, she could see nothing but emptiness on the other side.

As she stepped into the warehouse, she gasped at finding herself face-to-face with the imposing—and beautiful—Ahmed Latif.

The pure white *galabeeya* did nothing to diminish the menace of his expression. "Yes? May I help you?"

Slippery Billy Hirschfield sat at the lapis lazuli-topped table he used for a desk. It was one of the luxurious touches he found irresistible about his new yacht, along with the solid gold bathroom fittings and custom Lalique crystal light fixtures. He reveled in the tasteless ostentation. In spite of the astronomical price demanded by the compulsive-gambling, down-on-his-luck Saudi Arabian prince, it turned out to be a bargain once it led to the biggest arms deal of Billy's shady career.

He scowled down at the computer on the desk. It told him that the funds for this deal hadn't made it yet into his bank account. If Alex Bryant weren't involved, he wouldn't have come this far and the customer would be shit-out-a-luck. Billy always operated on a cash-only basis. For that matter, if it weren't for Bryant and his sterling reputation, he sure as bloody hell wouldn't be using his own personal yacht for the delivery.

He loved saying that: his own personal yacht.

"'Ere they come, sir."

Billy looked over the top of reading glasses at his steward. "Thanks, mate."

He tossed the glasses on the table and rose to straighten the collar of his Italian silk shirt, glistening in an extraordinary shade of incandescent green. As he passed a full length, gilt-edged mirror in the foyer, he paused to admire his reflection, pulling down the sleeves of his white linen jacket and patting gold chains, too numerous to count, that dangled around his bony neck.

On deck, the other boat bumped up against the side and he started to call out for the assholes to be careful. Then he saw Alex stepping up, and he restrained himself as he sauntered over to greet the great commander.

"Alex, you old dog. This is all a bit beneath your usual *modus operandi*, ain't it?"

Alexander kept the contempt from his face at Billy's crass greeting as they shook hands. "Hello, William, good to see you." He made a point of looking around before adding, "Nice boat."

"Yacht, Alex my boy, yacht."

Jalal boarded behind Alexander, who turned to make introductions. The three men moved into the hold where Billy nonchalantly gestured at hundreds of neatly stacked crates. He reached into the open top of one and pulled out a handgun.

The Arab's initial aversion to the man was instantly eclipsed at the sight of it, and the crates—crates filled with weapons that would provide the means for the elimination of hundreds of thousands of the enemy: the enemies of Islam.

A smirk contorted Billy's thin lips as he watched.

Alex read both men like headline news. Christ, he thought, this is like navigating a minefield. What if these guns actually make it into the hands of terrorists? Could he live with himself if they somehow managed to pull off their heinous crime? But what else could he have done? Under the circumstances, it was the only way he could think of to save her, to save Julia.

Billy interrupted Alex's misgivings with a murmur near his ear. "It was bloody damn good luck for you that I'ad everything you needed available nearby." Truth be told, he'd shorted an order for the renegade regime in the Sudan to fill this one. Not to worry, he'd put 'em off. He'd also substantially increased the price.

They returned to the deck. Jalal pulled out his phone. Before he could make the call for the other boat, cruising nearby, to approach for the pickup, Billy held up a hand. "Not so fast there, mate. Our business ain't finished yet."

He twitched his head at Alex and the two men stepped over to the rail. "So, where's me bob, mate?"

Alex placed a reluctant hand on Billy's shoulder. "In escrow. I'll make the transfer as soon as I reach shore."

A second ticked by, then another, before Billy turned to face him. As he did, he brushed back the left side of his jacket to make sure Alex saw the gun holstered underneath. "Ain't nobody—or no thing—going anywhere until I get paid."

The man's eyes glittered in the fading light, like the deadly snake Alex knew him to be. He, in turn, kept his eyes pointedly averted from the gun. All of Billy's men would be armed to the teeth—as would the Jihadists in the boat nearby. The muscles in Alex's jaw began to pulse, the way they always did when he found himself in combat. His mind raced to think of a way to defuse the potentially explosive situation.

He'd strategically planned it this way to provide the additional incentive for ensuring he made a hasty departure. What if the plan backfired?

"You can use my computer to make the transfer." Billy waved a hand towards the stairs that led down to the main salon.

Alexander led the way, but not before issuing a few reassuring words to Jalal. He made note of the careful watch Billy's men kept on the Arab. A startling image of Julia in the hands of that murderous maniac back in Nuweiba sent a ripple of fear up his spine as he descended the stairs. He *had* to make this work.

The opulence at the bottom gave him pause, if only momentarily. Alex marshaled every scrap of authority he'd ever possessed to deliver his next words. "This is a complicated transaction, Billy. As well as an exceptionally lucrative one." He knew goddamn well Billy had jacked up the price. He saw confirmation of that flit across the limey's greedy face.

"The transfer requires two passwords. I have one. It's in my computer in the hotel safe back in town. A representative of the seller has the other, a man I trust. Once they have the arms, they let him know. Then we initiate the transfer simultaneously." Did this pure fabrication sound even remotely plausible? Alexander cleared his throat. "You know I almost never get involved in the actual sales transaction. It seemed the best way to set this one up."

Billy pursed his lips. Alex could tell he wasn't sold.

"What I can do is access the account and show you that the funds are there." As he spoke Alex stepped over to the computer on the jeweled table top.

Once the details of the Swiss bank escrow account were up on the screen, Alex stood to his full height and let his gaze roam the room. "I've steered a lot of business your way, Billy. You're going to have to trust me on this one."

The reptile regarded the many zeroes on the screen with hooded eyes. Suddenly he was all smiles. "All right, Alex my boy, all right." The smile vanished more quickly than it came. "Just remember it's a small world we live in, me and you."

Back on deck, Jalal began to issue orders to his men. Billy followed Alex, now itching with impatience to get underway, to the stern where the launch hovered, engine purring. As it backed away from the showy yacht, he looked up at the ant-like flurry of activity of the crates changing hands. The sight left an unusually sour taste in his mouth.

As the launch raced across the water, Alexander felt the wind on the wet patches in the armpits of his shirt. He hoped to god nothing hung up the weapons delivery now. He hoped to god that the others had things under control at their end. Most of all, he hoped to god and all that was holy that they would be in time to save Julia.

"I didn't see a soul except for him and it was very, very quiet."

"What about Julia?" Mohamed had to ask.

"No sign of her." After describing what she'd managed to observe of the layout, Sarah looked down at her trembling hands. She wondered if anyone else could hear the violent pounding of her heart.

Brad looked up as Benjamin and Joshoa noiselessly appeared in the doorway. "All quiet," the Israeli reported. "Only the one car. There are two other doors at the back."

"We should go now." Agitation amplified Mohamed's words in the cave-like room. "Why wait if it's only the two of them?"

In view of the circumstances, he's held up admirably well, thought Brad. I hope to hell he doesn't blow it now. The startling sound of a phone sliced through the air, pre-empting his reply.

"*Oui?*" said Mariette. "*Non,* they have moved to the warehouse. Come straight here. We will watch for you." She closed the phone. "Alexander is on his way. He should be here in less than fifteen minutes."

Linda emerged from the gloom as the solid frame came around the corner. Although he expected something of the sort, Alex jumped back, instinctively reaching for his gun. She held a finger to her lips and motioned for him to follow. They went through a battered door, half off its hinges, to join the others. The beam from a single flashlight outlined their faces ghoulishly in the dark.

Brad laid out the set up.

"I go in first." Alexander was harsh—uncompromising.

"Okay. Richter, you two cover the back. Boyd and I'll cover Bryant." He was still impressed that Alex had somehow managed to conjure up another gun for Linda.

For the first time since his arrival, Brad addressed the others in an icy, sharp command. "The rest of you stay here. You'll only be in the way. And could cost Julia her life—as well as your own. Do you understand?"

Sarah and Mariette nodded acquiescence while Mohamed emanated rebellion from every pore.

Henrietta, unfailingly, came to the rescue. "It's all right, Mohamed. We've all done our parts brilliantly to get to this crucial point. Now it's up to the heavy guns."

No one smiled at the pun.

Still in the guise of their *galabeeyas*, the Israelis floated like phantoms to the rear of the warehouse. Benjamin backed himself into a shadowy corner to cover one of the doors while signaling Joshoa to the other, around a far corner. It was not possible to see them both from any given point. Joshoa melted away into the night.

Once he ascertained that no one else lurked in the vicinity, he looked up at the warehouse. A single-story roof over the door he was to watch joined another wall that abutted a second, much higher, roof. Light shone from a row of narrow windows beneath the highest roof.

A smelly dumpster partially blocked the door. Joshoa pulled the robe over his head, tossed it aside, and climbed onto the top of the dumpster. From there, he hoisted himself onto the first-floor roof and tip-toed to the corner of the old façade. With the skill of an expert climber, he worked his way up, finding niches in the crumbling brick for his fingers and toes. Once making it to the upper roof, he lay on his belly and peered down through the windows into a square, high-ceilinged room.

Apart from a few empty crates, it was completely bare. Except for the woman who stood like a statue in one corner, back against the wall.

CHAPTER 52

Julia, having shed the loathsome robes after convincing Ahmed to remove the bindings from her hands, had complete freedom of movement. He would've known that she would, but why would it concern him? Where could she go?

A single bare bulb hung on a cord from the ceiling in the locked room, next to the one where they'd entered the building. It provided an austere light. She used the time to explore every inch of her latest cell. Like the warehouse, this room sported a row of high windows lining one wall next to the ceiling. Unfortunately, with nothing to stand on, she had no way to reach them. She tried to scale the crumbling brick wall with her bare hands, the only result being more cuts and scrapes. The lock on the door was a simple one, but she had nothing to use as a tool to pry it open.

Patches of dirt checkered the floor where some of the bricks were cracked or missing. In her frantic search, she tripped over one. Hunched down on her hands and knees, she forced herself to stop, to pull in long, deep breaths in hope of slowing the blood ripping through her veins. That was how she came to find the trap door in the floor that led to the underground room. And the guns.

When she heard a woman's faint voice on the other side of the door, unrecognizable but distinctly speaking English, adrenaline shot back into her bloodstream.

It was time. Somehow, she knew. It was time.

She lowered the heavy lid to the tunnel and backed into the corner nearest the door—with a loaded pistol in her hand. As the endless minutes ticked by, she prepared herself as best she could for whatever would come.

Ahmed smirked at the thought of the foolish woman who had gotten herself lost in such a notoriously bad neighborhood. And at her good fortune in coming across him, instead of one of the less scrupulous local thugs.

He waited complacently while she phoned to arrange for a car to come to a location nearby and pick her up. He felt magnanimous now because Jalal had just called to let him know they had the final delivery of guns.

The last box containing one of the garments from the boutique fit nicely into one of the trunks. He carefully closed the lid and locked it. Beneath the clothes, layers of "wedding gifts" would explain the heavy weight of the trunks. Beneath those, the canisters were concealed—and meticulously secured. The beauty of this particular gas was that it took less than two hundred pounds to incapacitate almost a million people.

They would leave for Jordan first thing tomorrow morning. Ahmed added the trunk's key to the others on a ring and glided across the floor to the big open door. He felt the need for further bonding with his "fiancée."

As he inserted a key into the lock of the side room, a dark shape came through the outside door. Even in the dim light, he instantly recognized Alexander Bryant.

Fireworks exploded in his head. *What was he doing here?*

With the hint of a smile, one hand turned the key while the other deftly turned the knob. He ducked through the door, slamming it behind him. Like a flash of light, he flicked the lock, leapt to the far corner of the room and yanked open the trap door in the floor to grab up an automatic rifle.

Julia stood ramrod straight in the opposite corner with her back pressed to the wall, one arm bent behind.

Alexander barked a low command. Brad and Linda, flanking the outside door behind him, jumped inside, guns held above their heads. Alex, the Magnum in hand, was already at the closed door where Ahmed had disappeared. He struggled to keep a level voice.

"Sharif, we need to talk. No need for alarm but it's important."

Julia's nerves snapped at last—at the sound of Alexander's voice—and she pounced for the door. In a single leap, Ahmed flew across the room and viciously twisted her wrist before she could turn the lock.

He snarled, dragging her back, and leveled his rifle at the door.

"Get down in the tunnel!"

His voice, like that of a beast, caused her to fall back and trip over a hole in the floor. She cried out as she fell. And dropped the pistol.

The cry did it. Alexander Bryant hurled his powerful body at the door with such force the rotten wood splintered into a thousand pieces. On the other side, he nimbly righted himself, gun trained on Ahmed.

Julia crawled toward the pistol on the floor.

In the same instant, glass shattered from above as Joshoa came crashing through the high windows. He hit the ground and rolled, landing in a crouch, weapon fixed on his enemy.

Facing two deadly opponents, the Mujahideen growled like a cornered animal, swinging the rifle wildly between them.

"No!" screamed Julia as she came to her knees on the rough floor. The ragged bricks cut through the cloth into her skin as her hands trained the pistol on Ahmed.

It all happened horrifyingly fast.

She saw Alex from the corner of her eye hesitate for a fraction of a second and at the same time heard the explosion of shots, assaulting her ears with a terrible, echoing roar.

The man who came through the window crumpled to the floor. A bright red patch sprung up on Ahmed's white robe, spreading to blossom like an enormous rose unfurling its petals.

Julia caught him just before he hit the ground. She cradled the beautiful, aristocratic head in her lap, tears coursing down her face, distorted by shock and despair. The rising tide of blood soaked her clothing and stained her shaking hands.

"I'm sorry. So sorry." A heartbreaking sob escaped her dry, cracked lips. "It's all so wrong…so terribly wrong."

The sweetest of smiles transformed the face in her lap, now almost as white as the robe once was. The religious icon he wore around his neck lay awash in blood. His voice barely a whisper, Ahmed said, "You are a good woman, Julia Grant. Do not be sorry. I am happy to die for Islam. Happy to die for Allah."

He took one last breath. And his head fell to the side.

The echo from the gunshots grew fainter and fainter, eventually subsiding into a ghostly, accusing silence, as if final judgment had been passed. The other two men in the room—one standing, one lying on the floor in his own blood—still held their weapons, frozen in time, as they stared at the slain terrorist in the arms of his victim.

Julia looked up to lock eyes with Alexander, incomprehension and unbearable grief in hers, before they shifted back down to her blood-stained hands.

CHAPTER 53

All heads turned as the French woman came from the bedroom and closed the door carefully behind her. "I have given her a sedative," Mariette said. "Sarah will stay with her until she falls asleep."

For a moment no one spoke.

"Is she…" Mohamed swallowed to steady his voice, "…is she all right? Has she been," again he faltered, finding it difficult to even say the word, "hurt?"

Mariette crossed the well-appointed sitting room of the hotel suite to the kitchenette and turned on the faucet to wash her hands.

"Physically, apart from a number of scrapes, bruises and rope burns, *non*." A frown wrinkled her forehead and she pursed her lips as she dried her hands. She sank into one of the plush armchairs, rolling down the sleeves of her no-longer white shirt. Her eyes found those of Henrietta, full of compassionate understanding.

"Emotionally, psychologically, we will see."

Alexander looked down at his hands, braced on the tops of his thighs. Conflict ripped away inside—the final tableau repeating over and over in his head. He knew, with absolute certainty, that when Julia cried that last denial, it was directed as much at herself as anyone. And that when he hesitated, that fraction of a second could've cost both their lives.

Henrietta straightened her weary shoulders. "Now, I'm sure we all understand the complexities of the human mind under such trying circumstances. Kidnap victims often bond with their captors and it may take a while for a complete and healthy recovery. Julia is a strong and independent woman. Nevertheless, she has been through a shocking ordeal. We mustn't expect too much too soon."

Again, no one spoke.

"And now, if I may," continued Henrietta in a firm voice as she pushed herself from her chair, "I suggest we all go to our rooms and try to get some rest. There will be plenty of time for discussion tomorrow."

Midnight had long since passed.

There definitely would be plenty of time, as Brad had arranged for several comfortable rooms to be provided indefinitely at one of the luxury resorts in Nuweiba—courtesy of the U.S. government. Bob Bronson was adamant about their sheltering from the press and taking as much time as necessary to determine what their official statement would eventually be. Circumstances surrounding the violent attack and subsequent death of several of the militants had been, thus far, kept under a gag order.

Egyptian Intelligence was necessarily informed, with as much information as they "needed to know." Their security forces confronted the gun smugglers, killing several in the ensuing battle.

The local authorities were at first irate to learn of the operation in their jurisdiction without their knowledge or consent. The blustering rebuke subsided rather quickly when they became aware that the American agent knew of their financially-induced dereliction of duty, and that it would be in their best interest to go along with his suggestions.

The subversive activities of Egyptian Nationals within their own country would be extremely embarrassing should that information find its way to the international media. Not to mention detrimental to the role the Egyptian government went to such great pains to craft for itself as peacemakers in the Middle East conflict.

Brad Caldwell flinched yet remained immoveable when, as part of the briefing with the Egyptians, he insisted on a complete pardon for Mohamed. He did not, to his credit, waver in his insistence that Mohamed had been—in the beginning an unknowing, and later, an unwilling—participant in the operation. Brad made it crystal clear that any actions against him would be considered as hostile towards the United States.

The thinly-veiled threat was readily understood. Brad didn't like making it, but he found the alternative much more intimidating: He would've had to face Henrietta Langley. And Julia. No, on the whole, taking on the entire Egyptian government was preferable, by far.

Joshoa left by ambulance for the local hospital, such as it was, in serious condition; but the prognosis seemed hopeful. The Jordanian passport he carried should keep him safe from the press, if not the Egyptian authorities.

Full-scale operations were underway within Israel and its surrounding borders to locate and confiscate the remaining weapons. As far as the world would ever know, this most recent blow-up was yet another chapter in the on-going conflict.

Concerned and caring faces greeted Julia as she emerged from the bedroom into the crowded sitting room just before noon the following day. Though pale and drawn, with purple smudges beneath somber eyes, she bore no visible signs of mistreatment.

Mohamed stepped out behind her and went to station himself by the window. They'd been together for the past hour and seemed to reach an understanding. His enigmatic face gave no indication as to what that understanding might be.

A faint smile briefly lifted her chapped lips before Julia said, "Please, don't get up." All the men had risen instantly at the opening of the door.

It took every ounce of self control Alexander Bryant possessed not to take her and crush her in his arms. Staying away from her bedside throughout the long, endless night stretched his willpower to almost unendurable limits. Although the dark, unreadable eyes of the Egyptian told nothing of what transpired behind the closed door, the calm way Mohamed Zahar stood troubled him deeply.

Linda came to her feet and broke the awkward silence by greeting Julia with an outstretched hand. "Good morning, Ms. Grant. I'm Linda Boyd from U.S. Intelligence. Please let me be the first to congratulate you and thank you for your brave service. We're all delighted to have you back, safe and sound."

Bless her levelheaded heart, thought Brad as he followed suit and sheepishly offered his hand with heartfelt words of gratitude.

An almost audible sigh of relief filled the air as everyone joined in with congratulations. Henrietta kissed Julia on the cheek and guided the conversation along. While not yet celebratory, the mood lightened considerably.

Sarah, who retired after sitting by Julia's side for most of the night, resurfaced from the suite's other bedroom. With green eyes aglow, she bestowed a brilliant smile on the group and declared, "I'm starving. Where's lunch?"

Whatever tension remained dissolved in an eruption of laughter. Sarah marched across the room, grabbed her friend's hand and towed her to the sofa. Brad located the room service menu and ordered two of everything on it. They all started to talk at once and the celebration began.

"I know you're all wondering if I'm going to go psycho after this," Julia announced quietly once the group consumed most of the feast. Her tenuous smile came close to breaking Alexander's heart.

"I am sorry for Ahmed's death. The same way I'd be sorry for the death of any rabid creature. Sorry for the waste of it all." She made a valiant effort to control the tremor in her voice. "And it doesn't matter whether the bullet that killed him came from my gun or one of the others." She raised her chin. "The point is that I fired it. And I would do it again if I had to."

Ahmed made his choice. She felt little guilt for his death—mostly remorse for the waste of his life. No doubt, that horrific scene was forever etched in her mind. She would just have to learn to live with it. Julia looked down at her dry hands, the cuts and scrapes now clean of the blood that stained them only hours ago. Aware that her friends, old and new, were trying not to look too obvious as they regarded her with concern, she looked up with a hint of her old pluck.

"There's a beautiful beach down there. Are you guys planning to ever let us out of here for a little fresh air?" With remarkable composure, she rose to face Alexander. "We need to talk." Then her head swiveled to Brad Caldwell. "And you're next."

Julia strolled between Alexander Bryant and Brad Caldwell along the sandy beach. Gentle waves lapped at the shore while Brad delivered a thorough summary of all that transpired after she was taken away from the warehouse.

Besides Ahmed, several of his men also died. The Egyptian military rounded up and arrested a number of the militants involved in the arms deal, along with several others found at the flat in Dahab. They successfully confiscated all the handguns, as well as a cache of automatic rifles hidden in the tunnel. The prisoners would be kept in detention and, hopefully, more information about the operation could be extracted from them.

Julia shuddered at that thought. Much controversy headlined the news of late over illegal detention centers in several countries where the rules governing torture could be circumvented. Egypt featured prominently on the list. Even after all she'd been through, Julia still hated the idea.

"Why did they want the guns delivered in Egypt instead of Jordan?"

"We can only surmise that the efficiency of the Jordanian secret service made it too risky." Brad didn't have to say how easy it was to bribe Egyptian officials. "But don't forget, ninety-five percent of the Jordanian population is Sunni Muslim. It wouldn't be difficult for them to find allies there to bring the weapons across in smaller quantities."

"What about Faoud?"

He shook his head. "Disappeared. But a warrant is out on him. With that ugly mug, we'll get him sooner or later."

"Have you learned who killed Abeer Rashad? Or Zed?"

Again, Brad shook his head. "Unfortunately, we'll probably never know."

"And the chemicals?"

Before Julia had allowed herself to escape the ghastly scene, she'd led her rescuers to those new trunks in the warehouse. It was not difficult for her to deduce what might be in them. Everyone looked stunned. Stunned and relieved.

"*Agent 15.* Exposure in aerosolized form induces symptoms within half an hour." Brad's next words painted a gruesome picture. "It causes dizziness, vomiting and hallucinations that can last for several days. The amount we found would be enough to neutralize all of Jerusalem, as well as the area around the nuclear facility for miles."

Julia's heels dug into the sand as the hideous image spread itself across her mind. "How? Where did it come from?"

"Our best guess is Iraq," said Alex. "When I was deployed there, we heard rumors of it being produced and stockpiled in large quantities. When the invasion became a certainty, Saddam Hussein's government would have been only too willing to sell a portion of it at a reasonable price. This crowd got hold of it and managed to smuggle it into Egypt. It would've been too risky to keep it in Jordan."

Brad grimaced. "They may have stashed it in Mallawi."

"So that's why Abeer Rashad was there when she was killed," Julia whispered.

Brad nodded. "Maybe. The Egyptians are tearing the place apart, even as we speak."

Julia turned to face the two men, hands tightly clasped before her. "But I don't understand. I thought the message meant they were planning to *kill* the people of Jerusalem. It doesn't sound like this *Agent 15* would do that. Would it?"

Alex shook his head with a sigh. "You know that public opinion in the Islamic world has become increasingly negative towards the Jihadists after the terrorist bombings that have killed so many Muslims. We are again surmising, you understand. The plan may have been to take advantage of the debilitating effects of the gas to move in and eliminate only non-Muslims. That's what we think the handguns were for."

He'd suspected something of the sort all along.

Julia thought things couldn't possibly be more horrendous. The image of men moving purposefully through the holy city, working their way through the entire population writhing in agony from the awful gas, killing in cold blood any who they deemed an Infidel, brought with it a feeling of heretofore unimaginable sorrow.

Brad covered her hands with his own. "You should be very proud of your part in all this, Julia. Without your help, we might not have been able to stop them. It was a very clever and devious plot, a long time in the making. They used multiple sources of finance and multiple 'vendors' to amass a substantial arsenal. This would've made it near impossible to stop the attack. Numerous cells must've been involved, most of them knowing only their role in the plan. Only a select few were in on the big picture."

He squeezed her hands before letting go. "We suspect Ahmed as architect of the plan. The critical component of the entire operation was the ability to immobilize 'enemy' forces on the ground. He was evidently responsible for getting the chemicals into Israel."

Brad refrained from saying that her help in smuggling the chemicals from Egypt to Jordan, had it come to that, would have made the plan much easier to accomplish. The trunks containing the *Agent 15* were now on board a U.S. naval ship—unbeknownst to the Egyptian government—on the way to safe destruction.

"The Israelis discovered several planes, used for crop dusting, hidden in three different locations in the Negev Desert," Alex added quietly. "It has yet to be verified, but the planes are thought to have been stolen in Iran, Syria and Jordan over the past several months. By using them to spray the gas, those countries would be implicated in the attack."

The scope of the awesomely evil plot humbled them all.

Julia was apprised of the involvement of the two Mossad officers and, after being introduced to Benjamin, insisted on going to the hospital to personally thank Joshoa. Had he not come crashing through those windows, either she or Alex would surely have been the victim. In a quirk of fate—in addition to a shot from Ahmed's rifle—a bullet from Joshoa's own gun ricocheted off the wall to strike him in the chest, narrowly missing his heart. In his attempt to slay his enemy, he'd almost been killed by his own hand.

A somber nurse led Julia down the hall of the shabby hospital. The level of hygiene—or lack thereof—tempered her already sober thoughts. She carried a bouquet of creamy white peonies, fittingly imported from one of Israel's hugely successful flower farms. *How was it,* her impudent inner voice queried, *that the Israelis had managed to tame the arid land so quickly where the Palestinians had failed for so long?*

With a sidelong glance at Alexander, who—along with Brad—flanked her protectively while Mohamed brought up the rear, she promised herself that this was something she would learn more about.

Benjamin stepped from a room up ahead and greeted Julia warmly before waving her in. Alex and Brad moved off down the corridor, speaking in low tones.

The Muslim and the Jew stood outside the door in a moment of silence.

"Thank you for helping to save her." Mohamed could think of nothing more to say.

Benjamin nodded slowly. Each man considered extending his hand. They waited to see if the other would.

Julia took shameless advantage of her position as heroine of the day, certain that it would be short-lived. First on her agenda, she forced Brad to arrange a position for Mohamed at the American University in Cairo, where he would not only have the security of a steady job but benefits for himself and his family.

She laughed when she learned of Henry and Henrietta's background, not in the least surprised. They remained staunchly by her side until the certainty of Mohamed's position was confirmed. The septuagenarians then kissed everyone a fond farewell and departed for home, hand-in-hand.

When Julia heard that an actual weapons transaction had been completed before the raid and arrests, she insisted on being told the complete financial aspects of the deal. The amount of money involved was staggering. Slippery Billy managed to elude both the Egyptian and U.S. military, ostensibly by changing flags on his multimillion-dollar yacht and cruising full speed ahead into international waters, although without his payment for the guns.

The funds remained in Alexander's Swiss bank account over which he, in contradiction to the tale he'd spun for Billy, had sole authority. It took only the slightest pressure from Julia before he agreed to donate the entire amount to Egyptian charities. Some of the ill-gotten gains would go to serve single mothers and orphans. The bulk of it, however, was to be used to establish non-sectarian recreation programs for under-served youths. If they had an alternative, Julia argued, perhaps they might be less susceptible to the lure of Jihad.

The "confiscation" of Billy's "loot" wouldn't do Alexander's reputation in the arms-dealing world much good, but that was a bridge he didn't plan to cross again in any event. Julia would not be deterred from adding to the contribution the ten thousand dollars she received for her "assignment."

Mariette Chatillon viewed her role in the affair with deep satisfaction. Although it did not provide total retribution for the death of her husband, the adventure was most exhilarating—especially as it ended so well. With profuse thanks from all involved and a promise from Julia to visit her at the excavation in the near future, she climbed into the old wreck of a Jeep and roared away.

EPILOGUE

"Twenty years from now you will be more
disappointed by the things that you didn't
do than by the ones you did do.
So throw off the bowlines.
Sail away from the safe harbor.
Catch the trade winds in your sails.
Explore. Dream. Discover."

~Mark Twain

The sleek, refurbished *dahabeeya* plied a swift current amidst sparse river traffic. Wind gusted into the sail as the boat passed icons of antiquity along the shore. From beneath an awning on the upper deck, Julia shaded her eyes from the dazzling sun as she looked up with wonder into a cloudless, cobalt Egyptian sky to follow the flight of two eagles. They soared higher and higher before swooping to hunt in the fertile marshes of the Nile.

She lowered her left hand to smile at the simple gold band on her finger.

A feeling of deep contentment wrapped itself around her heart. Her future was now forever entwined with this remarkable man. Many differences still lay between them, but her confidence in their ability to resolve them grew with each passing day.

He enthusiastically embraced his new career, without a backward glance at all he left behind. And she had finally come to accept that compromise was sometimes necessary to find common ground, and that it did not require complete surrender of one's convictions. Together, they would explore the vast delta of grays that lay between the blacks and the whites of life.

As far as her mission in life, she looked forward to tackling the work she now knew she was meant to do. She counted among her blessings having the luxury of being able to think more deeply about what her real purpose on earth might be—while so many others simply struggled to survive.

A hand came from behind to circle her waist, and she leaned back into the warmth of Alexander's arms.

CPSIA information can be obtained at www.ICGtesting.com
Printed in the USA
BVOW031303250213

314069BV00002B/6/P